BETTER LEFT BURIED

DIANA SLATER

BETTER LEFT BURIED

Better Left Buried

Published by Tate Publishing & Enterprises, LLC
127 E. Trade Center Terrace | Mustang, Oklahoma 73064 USA
1.888.361.9473 | www.tatepublishing.com

Tate Publishing is committed to excellence in the publishing industry. The company reflects the philosophy established by the founders, based on Psalm 68:11,
"The Lord gave the word and great was the company of those who published it."

Cover design by Joseph Emnace
Interior design by Joana Quilantang

Published in the United States of America

ISBN: 978-1-63268-836-1
Fiction / Crime
14.09.29

Contents

Prologue

Fall of 1996

Her coffee grew cold as she looked unseeing through the window. Her hazel eyes failed to brighten as they usually did when she looked at the sunlit backyard. The dogwood was shedding the last of its white cloak in the gentle breeze, almost as if feeling her pain.

The tree had been a slender three-year-old sapling when Brett died. Over the years the tree had endured the buffeting of wind and storm at the hand of nature. The ability to bend and sway had allowed it to reach maturity.

She and Kevin had nurtured the young tree. They had worked the ground and banded it to protect its tender growth from tree worms. They had watered and kept the deer away with a collar of chicken wire. Perhaps the resilience was possible because the tree had no need to deal with the raw emotions that took such a heavy toll on humans.

Sighing, Linda turned and picked up the coffee cup. Her eyes were clouded by her racing thoughts, at odds with the bright-yellow curtains fluttering at the window.

Dreams and disappointments had been discussed around the wooden table that Kevin's grandfather had built for his bride and still held center court in the kitchen. Confidences were shared and decisions made around the gleaming oak circle. Many a drama had played out and Linda wondered how the present one would unfold.

She gazed around the large room. As it had been for generations, the kitchen remained the hub of family activity. She and

Kevin spent many hours sharing the pleasing atmosphere they had created. Each stone in the fireplace had been handpicked from local streams or fallen stonewalls on idyllic afternoons when they had packed a picnic and set out to find stones that pleased them. The stones held memories of happy, love-filled afternoons and added to the personal touches that made the room their own. Kevin had his gun cabinet, bookshelves, and the computer they shared while Linda had added her knitting basket and herb garden. Some of Brett's favorite books and trophies were still on the shelves.

Normally, standing in the kitchen facing the fireplace gave her a feeling of contentment and security. Today she felt cold and unsettled—those feelings that had become all too familiar recently along with the renewed anguish the trial had stirred. Her sigh was deep as she wondered how the emotional storm on the horizon would affect them. Anguish and anger had left deep, raw if invisible scars. Would they now be reopened if they relived those emotions yet again?

Resentment and bitterness swept through her as she glanced at the magazine on the couch. The twilight years should be peaceful and fulfilling, retirement opening new doors. Why had the fates decided that she and Kevin would be different?

The fact that they were not alone did nothing to reassure her. How many others in the quaint county seat would also be battered as new leaves in the story were turned by the current storm? After the many storms and much turbulence in her life, she questioned whether she was resilient enough to withstand further battering.

Who would withstand the new onslaught? Who would be destroyed? Her movements slowed, more by the burden of her thoughts than by age, Linda lifted up the magazine and reached for the newspaper. The headline that had set her thoughts in motion again screamed out the result of yesterday's long, emotional day in court:

Dr. Karl Gunther Arrested for the Nineteen-Year-Old Murder of Brett Conklin

Spring 1976

His gray-blue eyes were alert and bright. In one fluid movement, Kevin swung his feet over the edge of the bed as he reached to shut off the alarm before it could wake Linda.

It was still dark as he turned and tucked the comforter closer around the form of his sleeping wife. Smiling, he watched her burrow even deeper into the bed. If not for the size of her body, anyone seeing the tousled chestnut hair spread over the pillow would have thought that a child lay asleep in the bed.

The morning was cool and Kevin enjoyed the tingly feeling as his body responded to the change in temperature. He visited the bathroom and changed into a jogging suit. Running quietly down the stairs, he let himself out the front door. Stopping on the sidewalk, he went through his warm-up exercises. Breathing deeply, he turned right and began to jog toward Horseshoe Corners. He coveted this time alone while the rest of the world was still sleeping, using it to mentally organize his day.

Jogging past the church and beginning the descent that would lead him past the Gardner farm, his attention was drawn to two cars stopped at the bottom of the hill with their engines running. What were they doing just after six in the morning parked at Horseshoe Corners? Why weren't they at the Stables seated comfortably with coffee in front of them?

Inside both cars the tension was thick. From the black sports car parked downhill, Austin tried to reason with the dour-faced man in the blue sedan. "I'm telling you that everything's all right. My dad took care of the problem with the chief of police," he repeated. His voice unsteady, he said, "I need the stuff and I gave you the money."

Tony Merino didn't answer, looking at Austin. It didn't take a college degree to realize the kid was too stupid to stay out of the powder. Finally breaking the silence, Merino said, "The boss doesn't like loose ends." Watching Austin pale, he continued, "What about the morons who shot Luce? They weren't too bright. How can you be sure they won't start talking?"

"They wouldn't say anything. They don't know who you are."

"You better hope they don't. There isn't room for mistakes in this business." The hard black eyes locked on those of the younger man. "You may carry some weight here in redneck land but not where we come from." Tossing a small package at the window of the Mercedes, the voice continued, "You'd best be careful if you don't want big Al to pay you a visit."

Running down the hill, Kevin heard the pleading tone at the same moment he saw something being thrown at the Mercedes. Recognizing the car as that of John Greene, a colleague, he decided to check that everything was all right. He reached the Mercedes just as the other vehicle, an older Chevy with plates from South Carolina roared up the hill.

Approaching the car, he asked, "Is everything all right?" as he recognized John's son Austin.

Startled, Austin jumped, his hand moving to cover the package lying on the seat beside him. "You scared the hell out of me, sneaking up on me like that."

Frowning at the younger man's tone, Kevin replied evenly, "You were so preoccupied with your friends that you didn't hear me." Not liking Austin's pallid appearance, he repeated, "Are you sure that everything is okay?"

"Yeah, everything's fine, just fine," answered Austin sullenly, putting the car in gear. "I got to go to school." With a final curt nod in Kevin's direction, he drove back toward town. Jogging again, Kevin couldn't shake the niggling feeling at the back of his mind that something was out of place. Something was wrong with the scenario he had witnessed, but he couldn't put his finger on what.

Mentally tabling the issue until later, he concentrated on regaining his stride. Cresting the hill, he noticed that there were now lights showing in several of the houses that faced Lake Avenue. Kevin felt the rush of pride he always experienced when he remembered that the people of the town had trusted him enough to want him to be their mayor, the one to take care of their needs and represent them. Noticing the dew that still clung to the manicured lawns, he made a mental note to cut his own lawn that week.

Letting himself in, Kevin retraced his steps up the stairs, shedding his clothes as he reached to turn on the water in the bathroom.

Descending the stairs, the inviting smell of coffee and the thought of Linda's unconditional support helped him shake his somber mood. By the time he entered the kitchen, Kevin had forgotten the Greene boy's strange behavior.

"Eggs or cereals, which will it be today, my lord?" teased Linda as he moved to get his already-poured coffee on the counter.

"Just toast. I'm due at the courthouse at nine and need to stop by the office first." Scanning the headlines, Kevin asked, "Will you be in before noon or have you decided to become a woman of leisure?"

Smiling as she buttered his toast, Linda threw her reply over her shoulder. "Not yet. What good would it do me to stay home when you don't even have time to eat?"

"You know this is my favorite time of day. I must have slowed down thinking about Greene's boy." Sipping his coffee, he recounted seeing the cars at Horseshoe Corners and his unsettled feeling.

Becoming serious, Linda said, "That boy has been in trouble more than once. Unfortunately, John unscrambles his messes so he doesn't seem to learn. Is he in trouble again?"

"I don't know." Kevin shook his head. "I hope not, for his mother's sake." Putting his cup in the sink, he asked, "When will you be in?"

"I thought I'd run over to the church and see if they're all set for the dinner this weekend. Can you manage without me until two?"

Putting on his blazer, Kevin replied, "Sure. I want to run over to Brett's and tell him about the fishing reservations after court. He planned to be home this morning so I'll try to catch him before he leaves for the office."

The underlying yearning in her husband's voice made Linda's heart contract. Their son loved them as much as they loved him. Yet, because Brett wanted to prove to himself and everyone else that he was his own man, he had refused to join his father's law practice.

Keeping her voice light, Linda replied, "Sounds good to me. When you see Holly, let her know that we'd love to have the kids this weekend if she and Brett want to spend some time together."

"I'll make sure she knows that the kids aren't a problem. Maybe she feels that now that Janie is going through the "terrible twos," she doesn't want to impose on us."

"I don't know." Smiling, Linda continued, "If we changed Brett's diapers before Pampers, I guess we can handle it now."

Nodding, Kevin said, "On your travels, stop in at the Agway and tell Don we'll need several sections of new mosquito netting. Looks like some nosey little raccoons were trying to get in and pushed in the fencing again. Get five yards of chicken wire too. I want to reinforce the caging around the dogwood too."

"Anything else, sire?" teased Linda.

"As a matter of fact, there is," said Kevin, reaching for his wife and removing the coffee pot from her hand. "But I guess I'll have to settle for this until later."

As she listened to the car pull away, Linda stared out of the kitchen window. Holly had been acting strangely. It was almost as if her always-affectionate daughter-in-law were avoiding having any contact with them. Linda had heard enough from the gossip mill to make her concerned. If only Brett and Holly had not become involved in the key club.

The anticipation of seeing his son and grandchildren stayed with Kevin as he drove toward the center of town. His family was the center of his life and knowing he was going to see them always made him happy. The weather seemed to reflect his good mood. Most of the children waiting for the bus had shed their jackets. Still cool, it promised to be a beautiful spring day.

The town, which meant so much to him, looked clean and fresh. He was proud that the people had thought enough of him to elect him as their mayor. It was a position he took seriously and, since being elected, had made sure that the littering and zoning laws were enforced. He had been instrumental in sponsoring a "Clean Town" project where high school students and members of the Legion and VFW worked with homeowners to help repair fences and paint where needed.

Turning onto Upper Main Street, Kevin waved at Walter Stern who was walking toward the bank. Stern was often a guest at Deer Run where he joined Brett to shoot clay pigeons, and he knew the Conklin family well. He waved back. Pulling into the driveway of the colonial which served as his office, Kevin found himself smiling again.

Kevin felt the peace and security surrounding him as soon as he stepped through the door to his office. It had been like this since he was a child napping on the leather couch that had survived innumerable conferences and meetings.

He crossed to the desk that had been his grandfather's. It occupied the area in front of the large window that looked out over the lawn to the street. Picking up the waiting folders, he saw the notes of the last town meeting, received the day before. Smiling, he promised himself that this year, as mayor, he would make the July 4th celebration extra special. In an age of so much discontent and violence, his world was safe and secure.

Kevin headed down the courthouse steps feeling satisfied. His client could only drive to and from work, but Kevin knew the judge had dealt more than fairly with Bollinger. Next time it would be jail. Hopefully, Bollinger would realize how lucky he had been and stop pushing his luck.

Deciding to grab a sandwich before going to Brett's, he headed for the Stables.

The Stables had been a fixture in Taylorville as long as he could remember. The only restaurant in town for years, it had been the preferred meeting place for both business and social gatherings.

Already smiling in anticipation of some kind of raucous greeting, Kevin opened the door.

"Hey! Kevin! Over here! I'm just leaving," shouted John Topper as he stood up and adjusted his holster. A state trooper, Topper had often worked with Kevin on procuring evidence for one case or another.

As he settled himself on the stool, Betty was already approaching with a cup of coffee. "And what does our illustrious mayor desire on this beautiful spring day?"

Checking the blackboard mounted over the coffee urns, Kevin said, "Let me have the sandwich special."

As Betty moved off to put in the order, Jim Walsh, who occupied the next stool, teased, "Now I understand. You have to be mayor or higher to get that lady's attention, because she sure doesn't treat me like that."

The look that Betty threw over her shoulder said it all, and both men chuckled.

A big raw-boned man who had farmed for years prior to working at the local Agway farm store, Jim knew everyone who had anything to do with farming in the county. At the Agway, he had become privy to much of the news that surrounded the customers. "Did you hear about the Williams boy?"

"Other than he planned to apply to West Point, I can't think of anything. Why?"

Shaking his head, Jim said, "He can forget that now. His father had to pick him up from Sheriff Collins's office. He and the Russell kid were higher than kites. They said that they bought the stuff from someone parked by the school."

The only outward sign of Kevin's anger was the movement of his jaw muscle. "We have to do something. It looks like the grapevine was right that the drug dealing is going on right under our noses." Smiling as Betty placed his sandwich in front of him, he continued, "Early this morning I saw a car with South Carolina plates down by the Gardner Farm having a powwow with a local kid. I wonder if that might be related to what you're telling me. Maybe Brett has some idea since he's been dealing with the other case."

Two stools down from Kevin, another man listened intently to the low conversation, cautious not to show his interest. For the past few months he had been coming into the Stables regularly, and he no longer drew attention as a novelty.

Jim's voice resonated with fury at the thought that a local resident could be part of the drug problem. "Do you know who it was?"

Not ready to mention Austin Greene, Kevin was grateful for the interruption as Betty approached to take their money. Checking his watch, he stood and handed the money for his bill to Betty.

Getting into his car, Kevin forced his attention away from the drug problem that could no longer be ignored. Driving back through town, he focused on the myriad shades of green that were only seen during the spring.

Further down the street, Dr. Karl Gunther's car was parked on the curb in front of the Enrights's house. Kevin hoped that Mr. Enright, who was ill and elderly, hadn't taken a turn for the worse.

Though he found Gunther's manner too cold for his taste, Kevin admired his son's friend. Whatever else he might feel for the man, he had to acknowledge that Karl Gunther took his Hippocratic Oath seriously. Dr. Harrison had been right on target when he added the younger man to his staff five years before. In that time Gunther had worked unstintingly with the rest of the hospital staff to provide the best care possible for Taylorville and the surrounding area.

Turning off Maple onto Oak, Kevin smiled again. His grin grew broader as he realized that the feeling of contentment came from seeing "his" town in order on the beautiful spring afternoon. Holly's car was in the driveway, so he left his own car on the street to leave space for Brett in the driveway when he arrived.

Walking up the path, he entered the house through the kitchen as he always did. Nobody ever locked their doors and once again he felt pride in his town.

"Anybody home?" he called as he walked into the sunlit kitchen. Waiting for a response, he admired the artwork displayed on the refrigerator, thinking how clear his grandson's letters were. His perusal complete, he wondered where Holly was. Though the children obviously weren't home, he had never known his daughter-in-law to leave without closing up the house.

Mentally running through the possibilities of where Holly might be, he started up the stairs to the second floor.

Walking down the hall, he glanced at Janie's room through the open door. Suddenly the quiet was broken by a load moan. Filled with anxiety, Kevin quickened his pace and seconds later was in front of his son's bedroom. Nothing in his life had prepared him for what he saw as he looked through the open door. Sprawled amongst the wrinkled sheets, Holly writhed in passion against the man on top of her.

Frozen, Kevin found he was unable to tear his gaze from the passion-filled tableau in front of him. As the man moved slightly to deepen his penetration, Kevin recognized his son's best friend. Everything about that moment in time would remain etched forever in his mind, but nothing more than the look in Holly's eyes when she saw him.

Brett and Holly

On his way back from Elmira, Brett was preoccupied by what he had learned. Prompted by his suspicions of the former acquaintances and business associations of his clients, he had decided to confirm what he knew before his preparations for the trial went any further. There had to be an underlying factor that would explain how they had been involved with Dan Luce, the man his clients were accused of murdering, and he was determined to find it.

"And the time is 9:15."

Hearing the voice from the radio, Brett sighed. He had planned to stop at the house after he finished at the jail, but now he wouldn't have time. He desperately needed to spend more time with Holly.

The feeling of being pulled in the middle had become almost normal during the past year and he should have become used to it, but he hadn't. In fact, Holly's sunny disposition had made it easy to look forward to going home to her when so many other men looked for excuses to stay away. Holly seemed to be happy. At least that's what he had thought until she told him that she wanted a divorce.

He had been aware of rumors as to something going on between Holly and one person or another throughout their married life. He had discarded them without much thought because Holly was a flirt by nature, and he was secure that he had a good marriage.

So, Holly had been quite unprepared for his reaction when she had finally summoned the courage to tell him that she wanted a divorce. Holly had been dumbfounded! She had expected several different reactions, possibly because she expected Brett to react the way she would have. Had the shoe been on the other foot, she knew that she would have yelled, been abusive, derisive, and anything other than calm. She had no idea of the willpower Brett was exerting not to break down and become emotional.

Holly had no response. In spite of the fact that Brett said he loved her, she did not have the same feelings for him. She only felt alive when she was with Karl, and she knew that Karl felt the same.

Now, two weeks later, his expression was somber as he exited the highway on Front Street. He knew he was to blame for the lack of time spent with Holly over the last year. He had been so involved with his work that the little time he had he tried to spend with the kids. He had truly believed that joining the Friday evening dinner group would ensure their spending more time together, but it appeared to have done more harm than good.

Pulling into the driveway that led to the Broome County Jail, Brett's thoughts automatically switched back to his clients and the upcoming visit. He had wanted to understand the motivation behind the crime thinking that it would help him build a line of defense. He had learned that, besides the drug-induced violence, which led to Luce's death, there was evidence to link his three clients to the sale of illegal substances to high school students in both Vestal and Taylorville.

Identifying himself as counsel for Meeks, Radner, and Coombs, he was shown into a visiting room that held the normal bare furnishings of a jail. Taking out the file folders with the pertinent data, he wondered if they would continue to present a united front. He was doubtful because they were all totally different in character. Tim Meeks was frightened, his nervousness escalating daily during the two weeks he had been in jail. He hadn't been the one to pull the trigger, and as an accessory could possibly find the charges dropped if he testified against the others.

As the three entered the visiting room, their attitudes directly matched their personalities. Radner approached the table with his usual cocky stance. Charlie was quiet, on a down as the drugs drifted further away. Meeks was spooked and jumpy.

Holding out his hand for Brett to shake, Radner voiced the question foremost on the minds of all three. "Did you manage to get the trial switched to Taylorville?"

Taking a deep breath, Brett tried to remain patient. "I explained that to you already. The Broome County DA is insistent that this case be tried here in New York. Unfortunately for you, they want to make this a test case and hopefully slow down the distribution of drugs in the area."

"But my parents have a hard time getting here to see me," whined Tim. Meeks was having the hardest time dealing with the situation he found himself in. Nineteen, timid, and jobless, he had been an easy mark for the other two. He had been the ideal middleman between them and their high-school clientele.

Coombs's slow drawl gave away his southern background as he asked, "Did the money arrive for our defense?"

Shrugging, Brett answered, "I guess so because Greene made your case a priority in the office." Wanting to find out if the trio had involved his partner's son Austin in their dealings, he continued, "Did you think that it wouldn't?"

"It ain't that. I just thought that having the fees upfront would help get us released on bail," Coombs said. "This ain't the Hilton."

Tired of the complaining, Radner told his cohorts to be quiet and let Brett speak.

Ignoring the bully, Brett continued, directing himself to Meeks, the weakest of the three.

"At the moment you have no options. You have to wait for the hearing, which is scheduled for next week before we can do anything to try and get you released. There was sufficient evidence to hold you and have you remanded to custody until the hearing. That's where we're at."

Meeks had become visibly upset during this last exchange, beginning to say something and then changing his mind as the bigger man glared at him. Sensing the man's justifiable fear of Radner, Brett decided that he would have a better chance of finding out about the drugs if he spoke to Meeks by himself. Not wanting to cause dissension amongst the men, Brett sent them back to their cells. Once they had left the area, he spoke to the officer on duty and arranged for him to return Meeks to the visiting area.

Meeks's fear was palpable as he came into the room. Wanting to put him at ease, Brett signaled for him to sit down as he said, "I get the feeling that something is bothering you but that you didn't want to say anything in front of the others."

His turmoil evident in his darting eyes, Meeks took a deep breath, looked Brett in the eyes and said, "I'm scared. I didn't have anything to do with Luce but if I don't go along with what he says, Radner says he'll get me."

"You don't want to serve time for murder if you had nothing to do with it."

"No," whined Meeks. "But he'll kill me if I go against them and turn evidence or witness or something like that."

"Tell me again. What did you do the day Luce was killed?" Twenty-five minutes later, Brett left the jail and headed for Taylorville, battling with what he had learned. Meeks had given his indisputable proof that Austin Greene was involved in the sale of drugs to local high-school students. Now he had to decide how to use the information.

Hanging up the phone after arranging for her mother to watch the children, a flash of color caught her eye. The robin hopping around on the lawn seemed so free. Holly knew that she couldn't take much more of the situation. Normally the happy bird and bright sunshine would have been sufficient to make her smile. But lately, nothing seemed the same. Earlier that morning when she had heard Stella's voice on the phone cautioning her to be careful, she had had a premonition that after today nothing would ever be the same.

Holly had first really met Stella when she had begun dating Brett during her sophomore year. They hadn't become close until Stella began cooking and taking care of the children for the Conklin family when Holly went back to nursing. Perhaps because they were so different, they were curious about and interested in each other's situation. They also found that there was a certain semblance of security in sharing their thoughts with someone who didn't move within the same circle of people.

Stella had been happy for Holly when she and Brett had joined the local group that met for dinner on Friday nights at the Inn. Things had seemed to improve between them, and Holly and Brett spent lots of time discussing the "gossip" they picked up over drinks or later around the dinner table. In fact, Holly had regaled Stella with more than one of the stories. But suddenly, in February, things had visibly changed.

Flirting had always been part of her nature, but Holly hadn't intentionally been looking to get his attention. Even when Karl made his intentions clear in February, Holly hadn't intended for anything to happen. But when he touched her while they were dancing at the Ramada, her skin became alive and tingled, a sensation she had never experienced with Brett. And as Karl had told her how he felt, she realized that on his part the attraction had been building up for a long time.

Prior to this moment, Holly had been able to heed the warnings of her conscience as well as the advice of Stella who had become her unwilling confidante. But as the winter dragged on, Holly found herself becoming more and more dependent on the time she spent with Karl. Unconsciously, she made it a point to be nearby when he was at the hospital. More and more often she found herself taking the seat next to him when the group met at the Inn. Toward the end of March, she realized with a jolt that she had fallen in love with him. With this realization came increased dissatisfaction with her life and with Brett in particular.

If he hadn't been so preoccupied with preparations for the murder trial he was handling, Brett might have become aware of the change in Holly. As it was, he had given up what was their "together time" which involved buying the groceries and ended with a movie for the two of them.

Now, on a beautiful May morning, she realized that she no longer had any desire to keep up the pretense of trying to make things work between them.

Staring out the window at the bleak gray day, Ann Gunther wondered how she was going to get through the summer. She had considered herself part of a couple for so long that she no longer knew what to do on her own. Without Karl, her life lacked definition and he had become so distant of late that she couldn't seem to get herself together at all.

Apathy had become a prevalent part of her state of mind when Karl was away from the house. She knew that she needed to admit that her marriage was over and file for divorce, but the idea had a finality she wasn't ready to accept. To return to Karl after the hell he had let her go through would mean that she cared little for her life, who she was, and that she would undergo whatever indignity and humiliation he wanted to dish out.

Shuddering, she remembered the night that had marked the end of life as she had known it. As she thought, the feelings of fear and disgust were as real and intense as they had been the first time around. Only now, as her mind refused to allow her to escape, there was the additional shame of knowing what had happened.

Originally a way to appease their wives, the dinner dates had been the idea of John Greene, at that time president of the Rotary. After reading about "Key Clubs," which was explained as a form of wife swapping, Greene had presented the idea and the group voted to try it. A stipulation was added that nothing needed to happen unless agreed upon by both parties. So the group had dinner and then picked keys.

On the occasions she had found herself talking through the night with Jack Healy, Brett Conklin, or Walter Stern, she had actually enjoyed the time they had spent talking. But the night she had had to spend with John Greene had not been as pleasant. He had been drunk and unwilling to accept her refusal to go to bed with him. It was only after a hair-raising hour of listening to his alternate cajoling and name calling that he had finally fallen into a drunken sleep.

It wasn't only a possible confrontation with John that caused her fear and anguish. She hated the whole idea of the key club. Finding herself in a hotel room waiting for someone other than her husband, with his knowledge, was irrefutable proof that he did not care.

Leaving her purse on the dresser, Ann went and sat down at the table by the window. Any pleasure she had derived from the evening dissipated as rapidly as fog evaporates in the sunlight. The thought of having to spend what was left of the night with someone, anyone, other than Karl, was almost more than she could bear. Yet admitting that she was in the situation because of Karl's lack of concern and disinterest was something that she wasn't ready to face.

She couldn't help the gasp of dismay as she recognized John Greene. Of all the members of the group, he was the one person she dreaded spending time with and tried to avoid. She had never liked him or considered him worthy of the office of commissioner. "Kind of difficult to use the key and get the door open single-handedly," said John with a laugh in his voice.

Realizing that he was more than slightly drunk, Ann said nothing at all. Concerned only with the possibility of seducing Ann, John concentrated on opening the bottle and filling the flutes. His droning monologue dispelled any thought of possible romantic motivation. "No wonder the term 'highway robbery' came into use while there were still public houses," he laughed. "What they charge for a bottle of champagne here is unarmed robbery! Don't you think that forty dollars is a little steep for a bottle that we pay fifteen for in the liquor store?"

Forced to reply or be considered discourteous, Ann cleared her suddenly constricted throat. "I hadn't really thought about it. We have a charge account at the liquor store, so I never bothered to figure out what each bottle costs as we buy it by the case."

John had become irritated immediately. It had been a great coup for the Greenes to be included in the Friday evening gatherings as one of the leading families, a position he and Sally had long wanted but only recently attained. The last thing he wanted to be reminded of was the vast difference between himself and Karl Gunther. Realistically, he knew that he would come out the worse in the comparison, and this did nothing but make him more determined than ever to have Ann. It was the one way he was sure that he would prove to the confident doctor that his medical degree and acceptance in the community made him no better a man than Greene.

Incited by the alcohol and wanting to prove that he was as good as Gunther, John had forced Ann into his arms. Feeling ill from the unwanted contact as well as the oppressive odor of cigarette smoke and alcohol that clung to him, Ann continued to struggle. Throwing her head from side to side, Ann finally managed to free herself when she unintentionally connected with John's chin. The sharp pain and sudden shock succeeded where all the prior words and entreaties had failed.

As pain shot through him, John shouted, "You b——! You're so full of yourself that you have no idea what's going on right in front of your face. You should be happy to have my attention. Your husband certainly doesn't shower any of his on you. But then, he really doesn't have time, does he? Not when he takes care of Holly as well as business."

Panting as she leaned against the table, John's meaning did not immediately penetrate through the semi-shock that shrouded her. Realizing that he had gone into the bathroom, her breathing became more normal and her fear began to dissipate. Only then did she become aware of what he had said. Coming out of the bathroom, John had caught the look of horror and disbelief that seemed etched on Ann's face and had smiled in satisfaction.

"You've always acted as if you thought you were better than everyone else," he sneered. "How does it feel knowing that your husband thinks so little of you that he's willing to have you spend the night with someone else, whether you want to or not, just so he can spend time with Holly?"

Staring into his glass, John suddenly seemed to run out of steam. Time continued to pass, in spite of Ann's frozen state, though she was never sure whether the time lapse was measured in minutes or hours. Hearing the measured breathing punctuated by an occasional sign, Ann suddenly realized that John had fallen asleep.

Forcing herself to stand, Ann realized that she was totally stiff, moving like a sleepwalker. Picking up her purse and jacket, she crossed the room and left. Rummaging through her handbag she found the extra keys to the Mercedes. The fact that she was in no condition to drive never entered her mind, for she really didn't care.

Shaking her head, she tried to dispel the heavy feelings that had dominated the last hour. Coming back to the present, she thought again of the despair that had led her to take the overdose when she returned to the house. Had it not been for the trooper's coming to look for Karl, she would have died that night. And Karl would never have known.

Taylorville, June 2, 1976

The day the world fell apart dawned fresh and clear. It was the kind of day that made one feel that it was good to be alive. The sun shone brightly and the breeze was caressing, a perfect day in early summer. Or so it appeared.

As he followed his usual morning routine, Kevin couldn't shake the feeling that had become his constant companion since that morning ten days before. He had done some crazy things while in the service and had been extremely happy that Linda remained unaware of them to this day. That had been what led to his decision to talk to Holly rather than say anything to Brett following his finding her with Karl.

None of his many experiences had prepared him for speaking to his daughter-in-law regarding her infidelity. No amount of planning would have made his chore any easier, but he certainly hadn't been ready for Holly's reaction. Expecting a certain amount of remorse and shame, he had found anger and resentment instead.

She had listened quietly as Kevin told her that he was aware of her liaison with Gunther and how he hoped that she would work through this rough spot in her marriage. He had even been supportive of her in recognizing that Brett often spent less time with her than he should.

As she listened to her father-in-law, Holly felt anger heating her insides. Who was he to tell her that what she had done was comprehensible and tell her that she should work things out? "How could you possibly understand what I feel or know how I want my future to be, Mr. Mayor?" Holly had said, fury and sarcasm distorting her voice. "Did it ever occur to you that I wouldn't want to work things out with Brett? I don't want any part of any life that doesn't have Karl in it."

The sun-dappled leaves threw dancing shadows onto the path leading down from the highest part of the falls. He had walked up to try and calm himself because he was afraid. Lately he had begun to wonder how he was ever going to get himself out of the mess he was in. He couldn't make it through the day without the stuff and would do whatever he needed to ensure his supply, and they knew it too.

Since Radner had killed Luce, they didn't trust him to handle things by himself anymore. He needed to convince them that everything was all right and that there was no danger in continuing to receive the shipments. If that happened he would have problems obtaining what he needed. They didn't like screwups and they were laying this one at his feet.

It had been Austin's idea to meet at Salt Springs. Though it was considered a park, the parking area was indistinguishable from the rest of the grassy area that held a few wooden picnic benches. Beer cans and other debris gave testimony that couples wanting privacy often used the area. For the most part, the area beyond was clean and untouched. Salt Springs had always left him with a feeling of peace and calm, but today that feeling eluded him.

A white Chevy was pulling into the parking area as he walked down the slope. "I see you had no problem finding this place," said Austin.

"We're here, aren't we?" said Paul.

Austin waited for the other man to speak. He didn't know why, but he was sure that the younger man who had spoken resented his involvement with the group. There wasn't any time that he missed an opportunity to cut Austin down or make him appear inexperienced.

Taking his time to look out the window at his surroundings, the older man finally spoke. A big, obviously strong man, the Captain had a cultured, modulated voice, which he never raised. He knew that the boy in front of him was inexperienced and unaware of just how deeply he was already involved. One of the reasons they chose kids like Austin was because they had Daddy's support to fall back on. "Pretty place. Makes you think of picnics and lazy summer afternoons," he said, getting out of the car.

Eager to establish rapport, Austin nodded his head. "I thought you might like it. Not many people come here."

"Good thinking. It isn't wise for many people to know what you're involved in. In fact, at this point I would say that too many know already," the Captain replied.

Brought up short by the Captain's words, Austin tried to reaffirm his control of the situation. "I told you, none of the three are going to talk. Radner knows that I'll help him when he gets out, and Meeks and Coombs don't know anything."

Leaning easily against the car, the Captain studied the boy before answering. "It's come to my attention that people are asking questions. I can't afford to have anyone get too close. This county is only a small part of our total operation."

Waiting to see that Austin understood the importance of what he was saying, the big man continued, "Fortunately, we have people in different places who can let us know if anything looks as if it's going to create a problem. It seems that the lawyer who works with your father has been traveling around asking questions." Looking Austin in the eyes, the Captain said, "That's dangerous."

Puzzled, Austin said, "Brett?" Suddenly looking relieved, he continued. "Oh, that's nothing. He's defending Radner, Meeks, and Coombs."

Shrugging his shoulders, the Captain let Austin worry before letting him off the hook. He knew how dangerous these high-strung kids could be if they went off the deep end. The kid might even run for help. And none of them wanted any more trouble. "I guess you could be right, but you have to think about how all this looks to the people sitting behind the desks back home. They don't like any complications and would just as soon close up any questionable part of the operation before risking something leading to their involvement." Taking a breath, the Captain said, "Either that or eliminate any problems. You're going to have to keep your ears open and make sure that you let us know if anything out of the ordinary comes up."

Trying hard to convince the Captain that he had everything under control, Austin explained how he was going to manage distributing the product now that the others were in jail.

Giving Austin the package, Paul and the Captain got into the Chevy and turned left toward Taylorville. As they exited the park, the Captain said, "Head to Silver Lake. I need to talk to Russell. We're going to have to take care of that lawyer."

The feeling that something was wrong persisted as Kevin finished breakfast and was still with him when he arrived at the office shortly before nine o'clock. He knew that if he wanted to get anything done he would have to figure out what was bothering him.

The topic was the July 4th celebration, and knowing that it would probably be long, Kevin thought about running over to Brett's to make sure everything was all right. His face fell as he realized that this was probably not a wise idea considering the outcome of his last talk with Holly. Sighing, Kevin's eye was caught by the colorful flyer lying on top of the desk. Focusing on the plans, he put his concern aside.

Many small towns throughout the rural United States centered local activities on parades, carnivals, and field days. These were generally scheduled for the same time as national holidays. Taylorville was no exception.

Now, at the beginning of June, all decisions had been made and were being carried out. Plans had long been put into execution and miles of crepe paper and bunting were being used to finish the floats. The band had been practicing daily, and the grounds had been prepared to receive the booths that would display the local crafts and items for sale. Storefronts were being readied and the local merchants looked forward to a weekend of brisk sales. The underlying anticipation lent a distinct flavor to the day and was the focus of many conversations. Even the weather seemed to be cooperating. All kinds of activities had been planned for families to partake of, from rafting to pony rides.

Gathering his papers, Kevin tried to shake the feeling that washed over him once more. He needed to talk to Brett about what was happening before someone else said anything to complicate things anymore. Not knowing exactly what he was going to say, he picked up the phone and dialed his son's number. Listening to the ringing on the other end, he decided to use his concern over Austin Greene as justification for the call.

"Good morning. Office of John Greene," Sally answered.

"Good morning, Sally. This is Kevin Conklin. Is Brett available?"

"I think so, Mr. Mayor. Just let me ring his office to make sure. Are you going to be giving the opening address on the green next month?"

"That's one of the details we're going to work out this morning at the council meeting, though I'm sure you'll hear before tomorrow," replied Kevin, his humor evident in his voice. Nothing happened without Sally knowing.

Somewhat affronted, Sally said, "Well, you know we need the information this week in order to do a good job with the flyers. I'll call Brett."

"What's up?" said Brett as he picked up the phone.

"The usual," said Kevin. "It's a busy day with lots for me to do, including a council meeting starting in ten minutes." Taking a breath, Kevin said, "I wanted to run something by you and see what you thought. Are Holly and the kids okay?

"Everyone's fine, though I'm wondering how the kids are going to do without their play groups next week. They'll have energy to burn."

"You know that your mom and I are always happy to take them if Holly has things to do." Pausing, Kevin decided to go straight to the problem. "I'm concerned about Austin Greene. I saw him meeting with someone in a car with South Carolina plates around 6:00 a.m. about ten days ago. He acted jumpy when I walked up to the car to see if something was wrong. Then Jim Walsh mentioned the problems they were having with drug sales to the school kids. Do you know anything about that? Given Austin's background it just seems like too much of a coincidence."

Brett was silent as he listened to what his father had to say, his thoughts rushing to link the information he was now hearing to that which he had gotten on his trip to Elmira and his stop at the Broome County jail. From what he knew, all signs indicated that Austin Greene was tied up with the people who had supplied his clients with drugs.

Undisturbed by his son's lack of comment, Kevin continued. "I would have broached the matter with John Greene myself, but you know how he has a tendency to sidestep any issue I try to discuss with him."

Deciding that he would not breach client confidentiality by telling his father what he had learned on his trip, Brett told Kevin about the evidence that was being gathered by the district attorney's office. This evidence linked the sale and distribution of drugs within Broome and Tioga counties in New York to a source in South Carolina. Brett also told Kevin what he had found out from Meeks. Wanting to reassure his father that he would take care of the situation, he said, "I'll try to sound out John and see if he has any idea of what Austin's involved in. Meanwhile, keep what I told you in confidence." Brett continued with a frown, "We don't want to scare them off and we may, if they think we have any idea of who they or their contacts are. I'll talk to you later."

His blue eyes reflected Karl's concern. He knew people would be hurt, it was inevitable. Picking up his rifles and hunting clothes from the garage, he wasn't conscious of doing so. He crossed town rapidly and saw Brett checking the shrubs along the house, his big yellow lab close at his heels. Unwilling to risk an encounter with Holly, Karl Gunther leaned out of the window and called to his friend, "All set to go out and clean up all the squirrels and rabbits?"

"You bet! Just let me tell Holly that I'm leaving," answered Brett, moving to the kitchen door. Entering, he walked over to where his wife was putting dishes into the dishwasher and said, "Everything will be all right, hon. Somehow I'll find the way to make things better." Oblivious to the fact that the person responsible for his current problems was his best friend, Brett walked out and got into the car with him.

Driving out of town, Karl was compelled to tell Brett what he felt. "I probably deal with the town people even more than you do because I see them when they or their families are sick or need medical attention. But I can't seem to get past being an outsider, someone who wasn't born here, so I'll never fit in."

"Small towns are like that, especially rural ones. I wouldn't let it bother you. You're accepted where it counts, so I wouldn't worry. I suppose it's hard to ignore when you're on the receiving end of the cold shoulder treatment, but why worry about it? It doesn't help pay your bills."

Listening to his friend, Karl suddenly found himself laughing. "It's a good thing that I'm not a person who is self-conscious or unsure of himself or I'd be in trouble."

The sun shone warmly and the new green leaves danced in the gentle breeze as Karl turned onto the road that would lead them to Silver Lake. Both men were quiet, each absorbed with his thoughts, not unusual in the two friends for they had learned over the years to share their silences as well as their conversations.

Deer Run

Taking a deep breath, Brett found himself enjoying the vibrant colors of the day, as well as the warm sun coming through the window. If it had not been for the problem with Holly, all would have been well with his world. A fair, just man, Brett reflected that he was not without blame in the situation. He was hurt at the thought that his wife had turned to another man but knew that he still loved her and did not want to live without her. Once he analyzed the situation and sat down with Holly, they would be able to get their lives back on track.

While Brett's thoughts allowed him the leeway to notice the splendor of the day, Karl was completely oblivious to his surroundings. All his thoughts centered on how he was going to tell Brett that he was in love with his wife. Unaware that he did so, Karl sighed and furrowed his brow. Having perfected the ability to read body language and facial expressions as a tool for trials, Brett was aware of his friend's unease. Finally, as the silence continued, Brett asked, "What's bothering you? You've been involved in a mental debate of some kind since we left the Stables. Are things really so complicated at the clinic?"

Surprised but relieved at having been given an out, Karl composed his features and answered honestly, "Things are still complicated. I wish I could say that we've been able to reach an agreement, but that's not the case. I hate having my time taken up with endless discussions on petty matters, and I have to admit that things have been strained since I lost my pharmacy privileges. People are all too willing to think that I was abusing my access to drug supplies."

Brett looked at his friend without answering as he weighed his answer. Recalling a conversation with Ann Gunther, he realized that much as he wanted to believe his friend, there was doubt as to where Ann had been getting the drugs that she was obviously using. "You know I'm here for you should you need a sounding board or want to blow off steam." Brett continued, "In fact I'd hope you take me up on my offer before taking problems home with you. We all have a tendency to overlook how much we expect our wives to put up with. Ann has put up with quite a bit with you so preoccupied with the hospital project."

Unable to speak due to the wave of emotion that washed over him, Karl nodded. The bitter, acrid bile that rose to his throat threatened to choke him. He suddenly realized that this would be the last time he talked to Brett in this manner.

By community standards, Tony and Jan Russell were still newcomers. They had moved to Taylorville when Tony had been laid off from the Ford plant in Mahwah, New Jersey, fifteen years before. Though she had met Tony's cousins, Jan remained unaware of the connection to the Rossi family, and Tony wanted to keep it that way. His father had changed his name legally prior to marrying Tony's mother because he feared that having "mob" relations would only stigmatize his family. But blood was thicker than water. Due to his involvement with the automotive union, the UAW, the Rossi clan had made it a point to maintain contact with Tony while he worked at Ford.

Tony had managed to maintain his distance and stayed on the outer fringes of the "family." He had found himself thankful for the support he received when he was left jobless after sixteen years with Ford. The "family" had called in a marker owed them by a bigwig at the Bendix plant in Taylorville, and Tony and Jan found themselves living in a rural community. The lifestyle change was so far different from the one they had been part of in New Jersey that Jan had suffered a major depression.

"Captain" Joseph Rossi had been present the day that Tony and his father had attended a meeting in New Jersey several years before. As customary, the homage paid Rossi had been obvious, and Tony had later learned that this was the man responsible for the family's operations in North Carolina. He had listened to the discussion and politely answered questions, but had never thought that he would have direct dealings with the Captain or any other member of the family.

Tony tried not to think that he owed his present economic stability to the Rossi family. He had worked hard at his job and earned the promotions and benefits on his own merit. His efforts had provided his wife and children with a good life, not extravagant, but solid. They weren't wealthy, but they were economically secure. After so long, it was easy to forget that his initial "placement" had been through the Rossis.

Rossi's interest in Taylor County had developed when Austin Greene and his cousin had approached one of Rossi's minor dealers with the proposition of opening up a new, untouched market. Not wanting to risk his neck, the dealer had gone to the Captain to explain. Interested with the possibility of a new area of distribution, Rossi had listened and proceeded to evaluate the potential after he researched the area. It was then that he had contacted Tony for the first time.

Up until now, Tony hadn't been asked to do anything other than provide answers to some questions posed. Even more fortunate from Tony's point of view was that he hadn't been included in whatever the Captain had in mind, and he definitely didn't want to be included now. Since his last contact some three years before, Rossi had occasionally stopped in for a cup of coffee and some information, but Tony had always felt uneasy when he saw the broad-shouldered man get out of his car. He had never been asked to do anything specific, so it was easy for him to relegate the "family" interest in the area to the back of his mind.

He had wondered if the increase in drug use around the area was in any way connected to the family interest in the town, but had been able to convince himself that the infrequent visits by the Captain had no connection. Until today.

Rossi had arrived by himself on his prior visits. Now he was accompanied by another hard-faced man, obviously a colleague. The questions were now specific, dealing with the movements of Brett Conklin and, more specifically, his routine in regard to Deer Run—the Conklin camp. He told them that Conklin came up with friends regularly on Wednesdays to shoot clay pigeons. A long look had passed between the Captain and the man he called Paul, and they had left shortly after telling Tony that they were going to look around the area and then head back to town. Anxious to be rid of them, Tony had nodded. He was happy that they would be gone before Jan arrived home and hoped that this would be the last visit for a long time.

As they drove away, Paul said, "He doesn't appear to be interested in the family business, does he?"

"He's never been involved at all, other than answering questions when I come up to see him. He has no idea, and that's fine with me. Let's take a look," said Rossi.

"You do want this to look like and accident, right?" asked Paul.

Nodding, Rossi said, "He's getting way too close and has to be stopped. But there has to be no question of it being an accident or his death is going to bring even more attention on the cases he's been working on. And that's the last thing I want. Make sure it looks like an accident."

On Wednesday, having parked out of sight from the cabin at Deer Run, Paul opened the trunk of the Chevy. At first glance, the trunk of the car was rather dirty and messy with chains and wrenches lying around. Only after he lifted the rug did a divided housing appear in the wheel well, each section holding a specific piece of a gun or rifle. Fitted against the back of the housing was a shelf holding ammunition.

Nodding his understanding, Paul lifted out a shotgun of the type normally used for shooting clay pigeons. His love of the weapon was obvious in the sensual, caressing manner in which he ran his hand up and down the stock. "You want me to use regular pigeon load or something larger for insurance?"

Shrugging, the Captain said, "You decide. We'll get whatever you need to get the job done." Reaching into the well-organized space, he took out two radios and after checking that they were on the same frequency, handed one to Paul. "I'll be waiting over at the Stables. As soon as you finish, call me, get over to the road, and I'll pick you up."

"You got it. See you later." With that, Paul turned around and began walking toward the Conklin campsite. As he walked he hummed to himself thinking that this job was going to be a piece of cake. Used to hunting in the swamps and marshes of the Carolinas, the dry, mostly clear ground presented little challenge. But then again, neither did his unwitting prey.

By two o'clock, Holly's nerves were frazzled. She was glad that Karl had agreed to tell Brett that he was the one that she was seeing and explain to him that they wanted to be together. It would be hard because the two were such close friends. She knew that Brett and Karl had shared much and it was not going to be easy for Gunther to give up his best friend, no matter how much he loved her.

Suddenly, she felt impelled to know how Karl was handling the talk with Brett. Perhaps if she were there too, it would bolster his confidence and make the difficult task easier. Leaving everything as it was, she walked out the kitchen door, got into the car, and began the drive to Deer Run.

Breaking the silence, Karl asked, "Should we drive up into the field with the trap equipment, or park by the cottage and walk?"

"Let's take advantage of the weather and walk. It will feel good to stretch my legs. I haven't had much of a chance to exercise these last couple of weeks because of the defense for the Luce murder," said Brett.

The quiet was absolute as the two men finished loading their guns and placed the miscellaneous items they wanted into the pockets and pouches of the bright-orange vests they wore. The only sound was the faint rustling of the leaves in the soft breeze as if the trees where murmuring amongst themselves as they watched the men. Neither man was worried about time. It was just after two when they started into the woods.

Karl's preoccupation with the upcoming confrontation with Brett had effectively eliminated all other thoughts from his mind. He was unable to focus on anything else.

Forcing conversation, he asked, "How's your leg holding up?"

"Pretty well. I don't think I'll be running any races, but right now it's all right." Unlike Karl, Brett had taken his own advice and was fully enjoying the peace, the quiet and the satisfaction of walking through the woods. He had hunted these woods as a child with both his father and grandfather and was totally comfortable.

Neither man was aware that they were being watched. Having seen them arrive and bypass the clearing, Paul had decided to see where they were going and was following them on a path parallel to their own. As the men continued to walk they opened their vests to avoid becoming overheated. Forced to walk single file along the path, the necessity to make conversation was avoided.

After half an hour of silence, Karl said, "What do you say we go back and set up the birds? I have a funny feeling we're not going to see anything else and I could do with sitting down for a while."

"Sounds good to me," Brett said. Moving into the clearing, he leaned his gun against a tree and stretched his back. "It's incredible how the gun seems to gain weight as the day wears on. When we started out, I wasn't even aware of carrying it, but now it feels as if it weighed fifty pounds," he said, sitting down on a nearby stump.

Reaching his friend, Karl got out a thermos of coffee after leaning his gun against the knot of the tree nearest his end of a fallen log. Trying to smile but finding himself unable, he poured coffee for each of them. Sitting down, he handed one of the thermos cups to Brett who was perched across from him.

Accepting the cup, Brett said, "Hey, do us both a favor and tell me what it is that's bothering you so I can help you find a way to deal with it and you can get back to normal."

Paul had positioned himself strategically to be able to observe and hear the men. Now, hearing Conklin's words and knowing that Gunther had been fingered as being involved with possible drug abuse at the hospital, he decided that it would be beneficial to listen and find out whether the problem bothering Gunther involved drugs. There was always a chance that Conklin would say something that would give him a better idea of how much he knew.

The weight of the entire planet was on his shoulders as Karl looked at his friend. Preparing to speak, he squeezed his eyes shut and tried to control his voice. His throat constricted as he fought to broach the subject of Holly with his friend.

His sigh was audible as he looked at his friend and said, "I'm afraid that from here on nothing will ever be normal again, Brett. I wish I could pretend and say that the reason I'm so preoccupied is because of the problems at the hospital. But, though the fight for control and the cloud hanging over me because of the pharmacy worry me, they're not the main problem."

"Great! You've taken a big step forward if you've managed to disassociate yourself from all the negative talk that was going on over the last few months. Everything should fall into place if you can just hold on."

"Damn it, Brett, can't you listen to me?" cried Karl. "For God's sake, don't continue to shower me with you optimism and good will! Holly asked you for a divorce because she and I are in love and want to be together. There is no way that our lives can go back to what they were!"

As the impact of what his friend had said struck home, the color visibly drained from Brett's face and his body began to tremble. Watching his eyes, Karl saw them darken as he went from disbelief to hurt, to anger, and lastly to sorrow. Karl felt ill too, as if the wind had been knocked out of him.

A slow grin began to form on Paul's face as he realized the importance of what he had just heard. Wouldn't the Captain be pleased! They had been handed a scapegoat on a silver platter. With a patience born of many hours spent waiting for his prey to fall into his hands, Paul settled back to watch as the drama unfolded.

Utilizing every ounce of willpower he possessed, Brett cleared his throat to open it and said, "Can you explain how this happened?"

Karl, having braced himself for recriminations and outrage, found Brett's calm totally unnerving. "How can you be so calm? I've just told you that I'm to blame for Holly asking you for a divorce. Don't you care?" he shouted.

Smiling sadly, Brett answered, "Of course I care. And now I want to know how and why this happened." He continued, "I'm hurt and surprised, but you're my friend and I don't believe that you would intentionally do anything to hurt me or my family."

Karl looked at Brett and for the first time that day smiled in earnest, if ruefully, as he said, "It's small wonder that I admire you. You're the damnedest person I've ever seen. I know how much you feel things. Yet you can manage to keep your cool even after I tell you I'm a Judas."

"You're human, Karl," replied Brett. "Now tell me how this happened."

Drawing a deep breath, calmer now that he had managed to tell his friend about his relationship with Holly, Karl recounted the involvement that had inadvertently begun with the key club.

Though he had to work hard not to wince several times during Karl's narrative, Brett was able to keep his distress under control.

Karl finished saying, "Holly and I feel that the only answer is to be together. You don't often find the one person who makes you come totally alive and now that I have, I don't want to live without her."

Knowing that the entire future of not only his own but also Karl's family lay in his hands at that moment, Brett fought to put his hurt and anger aside and think. He did not want to divorce Holly nor lose the friendship of this man who was suffering as much as he was in his own way. Taking time to space his words concisely and clearly, Brett, responded. "You've told me what you want, now I'm going to tell you what I want and how it is going to be. I do not want a divorce. I also love Holly and I want the opportunity to make her love me again. I have two small children who need me as well as their mother. I plan on being an active part of their lives because I have every intention of continuing to live with their mother, as I already told Holly."

Listening to Karl's confession and watching Brett's reaction, Paul realized that there was little chance of either man becoming violent. He changed his position slightly to be better able to have a clear shot at the lawyer. Though nothing had been said in regard to the Captain's concerns, he still had a job to do.

Sighing audibly, Brett continued speaking, "I am not going to give Holly a divorce and you are going to give up on the idea of continuing whatever relationship the two of you have. Things may be strained for a while, but I think we are all mature enough to handle the situation. And we will never talk about it again."

All three men were so intent on the tableau that was unfolding that none of them had heard Holly approach. She had been standing listening to Karl explain their situation to Brett. She had also listened as Brett logically and calmly told Karl that he would not give her a divorce and allow them to be together. Suddenly the anguish and stress overcame her. Racing forward into the clearing, she grabbed the shotgun leaning against the tree. Her voice almost unrecognizable. She shrieked, "You can't keep us from being together. I won't let you!"

His emotions raw and exposed from the strain of his talk with Brett, Karl was slow to react.

Paul wasn't sure if Holly had seen him or not. Nonetheless, he decided to take advantage of the situation. His instinct told him that the anger of the moment dominated the woman's actions and that she was more than capable of using the gun.

Looking at his wife sadly, Brett said calmly, "I think it's time to go back. We'll work this out. Let's go home."

Finally able to react, Karl stepped closer to Holly, reaching out his hand to cover hers. "Give me the gun."

Hidden at the edge of the clearing, Paul lifted his gun and began to squeeze the trigger.

Beyond reason, Holly howled as she screamed, "No!"

Suddenly the air was split by the blast from two guns.

For Karl, what followed would be a nightmare he would live with for the rest of his life. His reflexes, honed so closely as a physician, carried him to Brett's side where he immediately began the emergency procedures utilized in these cases. But there was nothing he could do.

Brett's pain at being betrayed had passed without comment as he stopped breathing, his heart still.

Who?

The satisfaction he felt on seeing Brett fall was reflected in Paul's eyes. He gave no thought to the fact that a person's life had been ended unnaturally, nor that he had deprived a human being of his God-given right to live. For him, the body lying on the ground with the spreading red stain represented the successful completion of the first part of a direct order. He was one step closer to reporting that everything had been taken care of. In fact, he was looking forward to the next step. Fate had played into his hands. Now it was up to him to make the most of the opportunity.

As the reality of what had happened sunk in, shock overcame Karl, the horror of the situation overpowering him. His normally clear thinking, usually clinical in its analytical approach, suddenly failed him. For the moment the person who kneeled next to his best friend was no longer a doctor but a mere human being whose emotions were running rampant and in all directions at once.

This can't have happened. It can't be true. These were the thoughts, which played over and over like a broken record, in Karl's mind. It might have been a moment or minutes. Suddenly he was brought back to reality as shaken Holly said, "Is he dead?"

Going to her, he removed the gun from her hand, leaning it against the stump. Karl took her in his arms and held her, unable to speak. Time stood still as the birds once again began their chirping and the wind rustled the branches in the sun-spotted woods. But Brett's breathing did not resume nor did he suddenly stand and make some funny comment as to wasting the day. Never again would he comment on anything to anyone.

Paul watched as Karl knelt by his friend and then went to Holly. Each passing moment made him more certain of how he would handle the situation. It was really child's play. Neither Gunther nor the new widow was in any position to argue.

Moving quietly, he picked up the spent cartridge from the ground and checked to make sure that there were no other signs that anyone had been standing thirty feet from where the lawyer had been shot. His task completed, Paul quietly moved into the clearing and waited for Karl to notice him.

Karl was unaware of how long he stood holding Holly. The contact was necessary on his part to ease his own desperation as much as to comfort her. As his senses responded, he began to feel uneasy, assailed by the sensation that someone was watching them. Moving his head slightly to the right, he was startled to see Paul leaning against a tree. Holly, feeling the stiffening of his body and the dropping of his arms, stepped back to look into Karl's face. Seeing his fixed stare, she turned. Seeing Paul, she shrank against Karl.

Holly's reaction led Paul to believe that she had thought she and Karl were the only ones in the woods. But he didn't know if Holly had actually seen him holding the gun.

Turning and looking at Holly and Karl, who were watching him in horrified fascination, he crossed his arms over his chest and adopted a relaxed stance. His expression was quizzical and his tone measured and sarcastic as he said, "This wasn't what I expected to see when I decided to go for a walk in the woods today. Kind of an extreme way to get what you want, don't you think?"

Anger beginning to surpass his feeling of despair, Karl answered curtly as he placed his arm more securely around Holly's shoulders. "I don't know who the hell you are, or where you came from. If you saw what happened, you know that it was an accident."

Continuing to play with the obviously irritated man in front of him, Paul pursed his lips and lifted his eyebrows in an expression of doubt. "Could be, but then again, could be you planned to do the man in. Happens sometimes when you've been fooling aroun' and passion overtakes ya," he drawled insolently.

Realizing that the man in front of them had seen Brett die, and beginning to see just what a difficult situation they were in, Holly spoke. "But he was the father of my children. Why would I want to kill him?"

"I don't know. Guess 'cause he wasn't willing to let you go?" shrugged Paul. "Or maybe you hated him. Don't really matter. Whatever, he's dead."

"I don't know who you are, but this is obviously a tragedy and nothing to laugh at. Why don't you go notify the authorities and let us deal with our grief?" yelled Karl, totally shaken by the other man's disregard for his dead friend.

Tired of playing cat and mouse, Paul decided that it was time to lay his cards on the table. Speaking in a serious tone, he answered, "It didn't look much like grief to me and I don't think the troopers would think so either. Whether you meant to do it or not, there's a dead man over there and you're responsible." Nodding at Holly, he continued, "It would be terrible for the kids to lose both parents in the same day, but that's what will happen if I go call the sheriff. You're holding the gun that shot your husband."

Almost beside herself with fear at Paul's words, Holly calmed herself and then spoke. "Who are you? Are you looking for money? How can you possibly take advantage of a situation this way?"

Paul's eyes met Holly's briefly and then he looked at Karl, trapping his eyes in a hard stare. "Let's just say that I have my reasons. There is a way out if you want to listen."

Holly's blood turned to ice with Paul's words and the sudden image of a jail cell. She turned to look at Karl, imploring him to make things right.

Seeing that he had them where he wanted, Paul outlined his plan. "First of all, you, missy, need to hightail it back to wherever you were and wait for the call that your husband's been killed. Most women are actresses anyway. Just think about this as a life-or-death role. You need to be convincing or nothing we do is going to do any good." Pausing to measure her reaction, he nodded and continued. "The good doctor here, well, he and I will stay here and prepare the scene for when the authorities come."

Looking at Holly and seeing her nerves at the surface, Karl spoke resignedly, "Maybe he's right. Go home and regardless what happens, you don't know anything until they tell you that there was an accident. Be strong, love. We'll get through this."

Glancing at Paul over her shoulder, Holly began walking back toward the camp. Both men followed her progress. When she was out of sight, Paul spoke, saying, "First thing we're going to do is decide on your story." Looking at Karl, Paul said, "As long as it sounds logical and you stick to it, you should be okay."

Pausing, Paul thought for a moment and then laid out the story that Karl would tell the authorities, as well as what he had to do to make the story credible. He also made sure that Karl was aware of the alternatives to doing exactly as he said. Finished, he turned and walked out of sight, turning once to see the doctor slump to his knees. Like it or not, Karl Gunther would do as he had been told.

Subduing the pain that racked his body as he looked at his friend, Karl began to mentally check the list of things that Paul had told him he needed to do and in what order. It was imperative he remove Holly's prints from the gun, thereby making sure that she was not connected with the shooting. Placing Brett's hand around the stock in several places as well as around the trigger produced a feeling of despair and anguish that threatened to overpower him.

Making a visible effort to keep himself under control and stay calm, Karl went through the steps that Paul had insisted be done, never stopping to wonder what had brought the hard-eyed, antagonistic man to the woods to begin with. He double checked to make sure that there was nothing in the clearing or on the path leading to it that could connect Holly to the site. The next step would be to notify the authorities and call an ambulance to take Brett's body to the hospital.

Though he didn't want to leave his friend's corpse, Karl knew that he had no choice but to go and call the police. It was doubtful that anyone would be looking for them yet, but he could not take the chance of another person stumbling into the clearing.

Sighing, he covered Brett's blood drenched chest with his hunting vest, picked up his gun, and began walking in the direction they had originally come from.

The Next Step

Her movements were as those of a zombie as she traversed the wooded area to where she had left her car. She shuddered as the face of Paul appeared in her mind's eye. When he had appeared in the woods and spoken to them, she knew that her life would be tainted from then on. He had made what had happened sound planned and calculated. He made her love for Karl seem dirty and sordid. Anger shaking her out of her state of shock, Holly drove home. She felt like an observer rather than a participant in the usual summer day activities she saw taking place as she reached town.

Pulling into the driveway, she sat in the car looking at the house where she and Brett had built their lives. Tears began streaming down her face as she realized that he would never again enter the door and swing Tommy or Janie into the air. Nothing would ever be the same again.

The competent, decisive doctor seemed to have disappeared. His step dragged and his posture indicated the weight that he carried. Reaching the jeep, Karl unlocked the door and climbed in. He turned the vehicle around and headed for the home of the Conklin's closest neighbor, Tony Russell. Zombie-like, he walked to the door, knocking out of habit as he reached it.

Tony was reading the paper in the kitchen as Jan put the finishing touches on their dinner when the knock came. Getting out of the chair, he said. "I'll get it, hon. I'm hungry and if you stop cooking and start chatting, who knows when we'll eat?"

Opening the front door, his smile faded rapidly as he realized something was wrong with Karl Gunther. "There's been an accident. I need to use your phone," Karl said, already heading toward the phone on the console.

Karl waited. Connected, his voice quavered, "Bob, this is Karl Gunther. There's been a hunting accident at the Conklin cottage on Silver Lake and I need assistance immediately. I'll be waiting for you in the clearing where we shoot pigeons."

Hanging up, Karl noticed the number of the Silver Lake Ambulance on the pad to the left of the phone. He dialed again, aware that as soon as the news went out speculation would be rife as to what had happened.

Wiping her hands on a dishcloth as she picked up, Betty Strope cheerily said, "Hello." Listening to Karl, her face fell as he explained what had happened. She answered, "Right away, Doc," picking up the radio dispatch transmitter that sat next to the phone. She knew the Silver Lake ambulance was out, so her first call was to the state troopers. From force of habit, she automatically jotted down the time of the call. It was 5:30 p.m. Even as she hung up, she was depressing the button that would allow her to transmit the emergency to the other volunteers. Within minutes anyone who heard the call would be on their way to the Conklin camp. Grabbing her jacket, she turned the stove off and raced out the door to pick up Donald, her husband.

Kevin had almost been able to dismiss the feeling that something was wrong. During the town council meeting, he had managed to push the feeling to the back of his mind until the meeting ended. He had stopped at the Stables for a quick lunch and had been distracted talking to Jim Walsh about the sale of drugs at the high school. The situation struck him as more serious, now that he knew what Brett had found out. How to stop the spread in the area was the question. He knew that the sale of drugs was a problem in other areas, but hadn't really thought that rural Ohio would be lucrative enough to attract the big players.

Back at the courthouse, Kevin presented two briefs and accepted a plea bargain on the part of another client. It was after three when he got back to the office on Lake Avenue. Normally, just entering the office and seeing Linda's smile was enough to make any day brighter for him. But today there seemed to be nothing that could rid Kevin of the feeling that something was wrong.

Sitting down behind his desk, Kevin tried to pinpoint just what was bothering him. Deciding that it was probably a mixture of wanting to take care of the town drug problem and needing to resolve the situation with Holly, he pulled the folders on his desk toward him and opened the first file. As he did so, the sun shone on the squadron ring that never left his finger. Deciding that talking to his friend might be just what he needed, Kevin closed the file and picked up the phone.

Coming in with his coffee, Linda heard the lilt in Kevin's voice as he greeted his friend. Smiling, she put the cup on the desk and closed the door as she left. Tim and Kevin had become close while in the army. The friendship had continued, becoming even stronger over the years. Tim would help Kevin work out his problem if anyone could.

A few blocks away another person was also thinking about Kevin. Jim Walsh had known Kevin and his family for years. The family farms had abutted one another and there had been a social as well as a business connection between the families. Kevin's father had handled all the Walsh legal matters until he retired and Kevin had been the one to manage Jim's legal needs later on.

Jim knew his concern about the drug situation had not fallen on deaf ears. Kevin's concern for the children would have made him determined to investigate the situation in any event, but as mayor, he took the problems affecting Taylorville personally. A threat to the town would be considered personal. Checking the outside fence of the Agway before locking up for the day, Jim was overcome by a sense of frustration.

Walking out of office, Jim's attention was caught by a transmission coming over the emergency band that ran all day at the store; several who worked there belonged to the volunteer fire department. He would have listened in any case, but when he heard Betty's voice asking for help at the campsite known as Deer Run, his attention was riveted.

Should he try to find Kevin? He had no idea of what had happened or who had been hurt. He didn't want to be an alarmist but wanted to be there for Kevin. He decided to drive directly to the Conklin home, hoping that nothing serious had occurred.

Hearing the car, Linda glanced out the kitchen window. She had replaced her skirt with a well-worn pair of jeans and was gathering the ingredients to begin making dinner. Recognizing Jim, she smiled, wiping her hands as she went toward the kitchen door. "This is starting to be a habit," she said, holding the door open for him. "I don't see much of you at all, and then I see you twice in one day." Turning, she pointed to where Kevin was working on the wire cage for the dogwood. "He's making good use of the wire you sold me today. Go on out if you want to talk to him."

Nodding, Jim walked into the backyard.

Looking up, Kevin said, "Thought I just saw you at lunch. What's up?" As he became aware of Jim's serious expression he straightened up, his smile replaced by a questioning look.

"I don't really know what happened or who might have been hurt, but I just heard Betty Strope on the radio asking for help at Deer Run," said Jim.

His project forgotten, the tools slipped from his hands at Jim's words. Kevin suddenly felt as if he had been dealt a blow to the midsection. His unease had now been given meaning and he hoped that the accident wasn't life threatening.

Not wanting to worry Linda needlessly, he decided not to tell her that there had been an accident. Turning to Jim he explained. "I don't want to alarm Linda. I'll just tell her that you wanted to take a ride out to the camp and that we'll be right back." Taking Jim's consent for granted, he entered the house. A moment later he was back and they began the drive that would forever change his life.

Responding to the Call

The state police were not the only ones to hear Betty's call for help over the Plektron system. Listening to CB radios was a popular hobby and news of the accident spread rapidly. Game wardens Bob Elliott and Jerry Thorne were going to Taylorville and immediately headed for the campsite.

At the state police barracks, the duty officer quickly contacted Officers Yaskowski and Harrison who were conducting traffic checks on Route 29 in Lawsville. New to the area, they got lost and did not reach Deer Run until just after 7:00 p.m.

The dispatcher at the Taylorville Clinic also monitored the call. Given her penchant for gossip, Jane Swayne knew most of the families as well as the area. That made her an asset when giving directions needed during an emergency. The only drawback was Jane's obsession for sharing any and all news, both good and bad. Finished transmitting the necessary information, she grabbed the telephone and began spreading the news to all who would listen.

As he hung up the phone, Karl turned to find Tony standing near the doorway. "I guess I'd better go back over to the camp and wait for the ambulance."

"I'll go with you. If the injuries are serious, maybe I can do something to help you. I'll just tell Jan, grab a jacket, and we're gone."

Waiting, Gunther looked around. The word that came to mind was "normal." A sense of calm pervaded the room and he wondered if his life would ever be normal again. Sighing, he followed Tony out to the car.

"Do you want to tell me what happened?" asked Tony.

"I really don't know," said Karl, remembering Paul's warning to stick to the story he had been given. "One moment Brett was going after either a coon or a porcupine and the next the gun went off and he was lying on his back with a hole in his chest."

Tony took a deep breath as he realized that he had just been told that Brett Conklin, a man he liked and admired, was dead. His blood chilled as he realized that Brett was the lawyer that the Captain had been talking about. Knowing that the man walking next to him was a respected physician who would have been sure that Brett was dead, he asked, "You couldn't do anything?"

"Death was almost instantaneous. He was already dead when I checked for vital signs."

As they reached the clearing, Karl tensed. He looked at the body of his friend and then at the gun propped nearby. He would never be able to explain what happened. Suddenly he ran to the gun, grabbed it, and started beating it against the closest tree crying over and over, "This gun will never kill anyone else."

As rapidly as the tension had entered Karl's body, it left. Moments before he had been bashing the tree, now he went limp and slumped against it. Tony tried to comfort him by patting his back. "Why don't you go over to that log and sit down. Someone should be here soon to take over."

Hearing footsteps coming from the direction of Deer Run, both men looked down the path to see the game commissioners coming toward them. Donald and Betty Strope appeared moments later.

Checking his watch from force of habit as he walked, Strope saw that the time was just 6:30. Nearing the clearing, he recognized Thorne and Elliott standing with Dr. Gunther and Tony

Russell. A quick survey of the scene told Donald that the man on the ground was beyond help as no one was near him. Russell stood with Gunther to the left of an enormous stump, and several yards from where the two men stood lay a gun with a damaged barrel. A second gun leaned against a tree. As the game commission officers moved toward the body they were careful not to disturb any relevant markings by walking a parallel route.

Nearing Gunther, Betty noticed how pale he was. He appeared to be holding himself together by a thread. As the others came closer, he began to explain what had happened.

"We'd decided to walk into the woods and look for small game before shooting pigeons. Brett took the lead heading back toward the camp and was into the clearing when I saw him begin to run up the path. He seemed to trip and the gun went off. I saw him fall and ran to help him. It was awful. I've never felt so helpless. When I got to him, he was already dead. I couldn't help my friend. I can't believe this happened," said Karl.

Listening, all could see how overwrought the doctor was. Trained in emergency procedures themselves, Elliott, looking at the broken stock of the gun leaning against the tree, had the feeling that something was wrong with Gunther's tale. The doubt growing in his mind, he asked, "How did the gun get beat up?"

Tony Russell answered. "Dr. Gunther came to my house for help and I came back with him. We got back and he lost control when he saw Brett lying there on the ground; he grabbed the gun and started smashing it against the tree."

Gunther's groan refocused the attention of the group on him. "I don't feel well. I don't know whether it's just the stress or my heart is really in distress, but I think I'd better get to the hospital."

Deciding to take charge, Donald did just that. "Betty, you take Dr. Gunther over to the clinic." He continued, "I'll wait with Tony and the officers. Someone can drop me off later. I'll walk over to the car with you."

Walking toward the parking area between them, Gunther said, "I guess I'm more susceptible to shock than I thought."

Watching the group walk back toward the cottage, Thorne stood shaking his head. "Poor guy, it's a small wonder he's taking things hard. Brett was his best friend."

Bob Elliott wasn't as ready to show compassion. He had heard the rumors about Gunther and Holly, and was also a friend of Brett's. "I can't believe that Brett could be so careless. He's hunted since he was eleven."

Thorne nodded. "Yeah, I know it just doesn't seem right. I can't believe he's dead." Pausing, "I'll get the camera; we still have enough light to see."

"Anything we can do?" asked Strope arriving back.

"Just stay out of the way and try not to walk in any of the areas that might have been involved," said Elliott, turning and moving toward the body. Examining the immediate area where the body lay, he looked to find the direction in which Brett had been moving prior to being shot. An avid tracker, he knew that the proximity of the footprints one to another indicated that Brett had been walking, but the importance of this information did not occur to him. Throughout his search of the area, he took extreme care not to disturb anything that might be considered evidence. "Be careful you don't step on anything that looks unusual. I want to see if we can find the root that he tripped over. Something doesn't seem right to me."

Thorne walked over to the body and began taking pictures from various different angles. Later these pictures would later prove to be the only ones taken at the scene.

Elliott noted that the shotgun was lying about six feet away from the body. Gunther's action of beating the gun and throwing it had effectively destroyed any possibility of finding out where the gun had landed after Conklin dropped it. The body was turned in the opposite direction from which Conklin had to have been running, if Gunther's story was correct. This inconsistency prompted Elliott to ask Thorne to take additional shots of the area surrounding the death scene, as well as the body itself.

Looking at the body of the man he had liked and admired, Bob noted that the obvious cause of death was the wound to the chest. He also noted that Brett's shoelace was untied. Yet neither he nor Thorne found any protruding roots or branches Brett could have tripped over within a twenty foot circumference of where Conklin lay on his back.

Continuing to search the area, Elliott found another piece of evidence that did not seem to fit with what Gunther had told them. Twenty feet from the body, the "stump" where Gunther said they had stopped to have coffee, had signs of blood on it. In Elliott's mind, this fact was totally outside the realm of possibility, defying all laws of physics, for in order to have blood on it, Brett would have had to have been much closer when he was shot.

Keeping his voice low so that only his partner could hear him, Elliott voiced his thoughts to Thorne. "I don't like how this feels. The stump has blood on it but look at the distance from the body."

Edging closer, Jerry examined the area on the stump that Bob had pointed out and nodded his agreement. Since Gunther had already left, they decided not to share what they had found until they could verify it with him.

Russell and Strope talked quietly, watching the game wardens search the area and take pictures of the body. The situation seemed surreal and neither man would forget the moment. Conklin would be missed not only by his family but by the community and his many friends, like Strope. Russell prayed that nothing would be found to tie the Captain to Conklin's death.

Kevin let the door of the truck click shut instead of slamming it and Jim did the same. Noticing Elliott's truck, Kevin allowed himself to hope that they would find that the accident was nothing more than the out-of-season shooting of a buck by Brett or his friends. Elliott and Thorpe turned at Donald's shout and saw when Kevin realized that it was his son on the ground. Karl had placed his vest over Brett's chest so the extent of the damage wasn't visible. Yet, Kevin's reaction would never be forgotten by any of the men present. The blood draining from his face, he knelt beside his son, "How bad is it?"

Simultaneously, he realized no one had answered and that his son did not seem to be breathing. His breath became labored as he reached out to find a pulse, all the while calling Brett's name. Not finding a pulse, he lifted the vest. He began to shake and a mournful keening rent the air as he realized that his son was dead.

He wasn't aware he had thrown himself over the body of his son until Jim and Donald tried to pry him away. He refused to let go, the muscles in his arms becoming bands of steel as he tried to will life back into Brett's still body.

Jim had trouble moving toward his friend. Speaking in a controlled voice, Jim said, "Kevin, there's nothing you can do to help Brett now. You have to let go and find out what happened." Trying to reach through the other man's grief, he continued, "Besides, both Holly and Linda are going to need you to be in control. Neither one of them will be in any condition to handle the situation once they find out what happened."

At the mention of his wife, Kevin turned his grief stricken face toward Jim, grabbing his forearms as if they offered a lifeline. Holding his friend in this strange embrace, he verbalized the thoughts running through his mind. "He was so young. How could this have happened? How can he be dead?" Blinking, Kevin suddenly realized that he hadn't seen Gunther and wondered if he was all right. "Where's Karl?"

Donald looked down at Kevin and spoke almost apologetically. "He started complaining of chest pain shortly after I arrived. Betty took him over to the hospital."

As his friends formed a protective circle around him, Kevin demanded to know how his son had died. He became increasingly uneasy as each man added his part to the narration. Before Kevin could voice his thoughts, the attention of the men was arrested by the sound of a car. Turning, they watched as two young state troopers approached.

Corporal Robert Yorken and Rookie William Harrison had been told to go to Deer Run as they had been closest to the scene. Neither one had previous experience with this kind of situation. Both officers assumed that the person was dead. Neither made any effort to examine the body. To his credit, Corporal Yorken took control of the investigation.

Walking over to where the men now stood surrounding Kevin, he nodded in greeting.

"Were all of you here when the accident happened?" Russell answered that none of them had been present. Speaking to all of the men, Yorken said, "Step over here so that we can get statements as to what happened."

As Harrison wrote down names and addresses, Yorken noticed Kevin's distress and asked if there was anything he could do.

Shaking his head as his tears started flowing again, Kevin was unable to answer. Placing his arm around Kevin's shoulders to support his friend, Jim replied for him. "His son is the man lying over there. I picked Mayor Conklin up when I heard the emergency call over the radio and we came over together to see what had happened." Pausing, he said, "I really think that I should take Mr. Conklin home as his wife is alone and doesn't know yet."

"I don't want to leave Brett," Kevin groaned. "I don't want Linda to be alone when she finds out."

Nodding his agreement, Yorken watched along with the others as Kevin and Jim walked down the path. Turning, he addressed the remaining group. "Can someone tell me what happened?"

Strope spoke up. "Brett accidentally shot himself while chasing a small animal."

"Did you see this happen?"

When all present answered negatively, Yorken asked, "How do you know that is what happened?"

Donald Strope continued, "I arrived here in response to a call for the Silver Lake ambulance. When Betty, my wife, and I got here, Dr. Gunther was here with Mr. Russell. Russell told me that he came back with the doctor after Gunther went to their house to use their phone to call for help."

As Harrison continued to record the answers, Yorken asked, "And where is Dr. Gunther now?"

"He was having chest pains and I asked my wife to drive him over to the Taylorville Hospital. They only left a few minutes ago so I don't imagine they've arrived yet. You can check that out by radio," replied Strope.

Yorken next turned to Elliot and Thorne. "And how do you and Thorne happen to be here?"

Irritated by the young trooper's condescending tone, Thorne answered, "The game commission has jurisdiction over any accident which takes place in the woods or at a lake involving hunting. As such, when we heard the call come in reporting a "hunting accident" at the Conklin camp, we immediately responded. Prior to your arriving on the scene, we took pictures of the body and the surrounding area. We also searched the immediate area."

Cowed by the more experienced man's knowledge of the situation, Yorken hesitated. Deciding that he should examine the body, he walked toward it. Following his partner, Harrison visibly paled as he confronted his first dead body. Yorken tried to sound as professional as possible while describing what he saw as the other trooper took notes.

"The body is lying face up on the ground, approximately twenty-five feet from a large stump, in the clearing generally used for trap shooting by the deceased. The deceased is holding two clay pigeons in his left hand, which is extended downward along his body. The right hand is partially clutched and empty.

The legs are out straight. The deceased appears to have been shot in the chest."

"Slow it down, will you?" complained Harrison, "I don't know shorthand."

Looking at his partner to make sure he was ready, the corporal continued, "The weapon responsible for firing the shot is about six feet off to the left of the body. The sixteen-gauge shotgun is lying with the muzzle pointed at the base of a tree on the edge of the clearing, and the butt is broken." Yorken suddenly fell silent as he realized what he had said. Turning toward Elliott, who had moved closer to the body, he asked, "Do you know what happened to the gun? How the stock got broken?"

"Russell told us that Gunther was so overcome when he returned and saw Conklin on the ground, he grabbed the gun and started beating it against the tree," answered Elliott.

Turning toward Russell who still stood with Strope, Yorken said, "Did you see how the gun happened to get broken up, Mr. Russell?"

Russell repeated what he had told the others prior to the troopers' arrival. The game wardens once again exchanged a knowing look as Russell repeated Gunther's statement to the effect that the gun would never kill again. As Tony spoke, all the men had been moving closer to the gun.

Looking around the base of the tree, the young corporal noticed that there were several slivers of the gunstock within a few feet of the tree, where they had apparently landed following the splintering of the stock. "Has anyone touched this weapon since you saw Dr. Gunther hit it against the tree?" asked the trooper.

"No, no one touched it, but I think that the game commissioners took pictures of it," replied Russell.

"I did take pictures of the accident scene including the gun," affirmed Thorne.

What happened next was one of the many incidents which would later be looked at as a mishandling of the evidence. It was one of the many reasons that the Conklin family felt that they did not receive adequate follow-up in the investigation of their son's death.

Yorken was obviously thinking about what would be the next step in a logical investigation when he approached the gun, picked it up, and began to examine it. However, he had not put gloves on and had total disregard for any possible fingerprints. Whether it was his inexperience with shotguns or his desire to retain the goodwill of the game commission officers, Yorken said, turning to Elliott, "Can you see if the cartridges are both spent? I think the chamber is jammed."

Nodding, Elliott took the gun from the trooper. He worked the loading mechanism back and forth and finally managed to remove a green magnum, #4, spent cartridge from the barrel. Continuing to work the mechanism, he also extracted three live #7 purple shells from the magazine.

Thorne was standing close enough to see the shells as they fell to the ground. His look of surprise quickly turned to one of speculation as he glanced at Elliott to see if his partner had realized the importance of the colored shells.

Meeting Thorne's look, Elliott silently indicated his desire to remain quiet. As Yorken continued to dictate to Harrison, walking away from them, the game commissioners turned to each other. "Why would you have magnum loads in your gun if you were trap shooting or going for small game?" queried Thorne. "It doesn't make any sense."

Dismissed by the troopers, Russell and Strope left shortly thereafter, just before eight o'clock. By that time, the light had begun to fade and there did not seem to be much sense in continuing to search the area. The troopers had been in touch with their barracks by radio yet nothing seemed to be happening. "Does it always take this long for the ambulance?" asked Harrison. "If you were hurt, you could be dead before they got around to helping you," he continued with a feeble attempt at humor.

At the non-response of the others, he quickly fell quiet. The silence continued until just before 8:30 when the sounds of a vehicle arriving once again broke the evening stillness.

"I was beginning to think that you weren't ever going to show up," said Elliott to the approaching man, making his way along the path.

Cummings, the local coroner, replied, "I wish I were anywhere but here under these circumstances."

Repercussions

"Thank you, Jane. Let me know when the ambulance arrives."
As the door shut, Dr. Darnell Harrison inhaled as if preparing for something that would take a great deal of energy. An emergency call wasn't anything out of the ordinary, but the fact that there had been an accident at Deer Run wasn't good. Who had been hurt? Once again, he wondered if he had made a grave mistake asking Karl Gunther to join the hospital.

Having Kevin Conklin's unconditional support in the upcoming months wasn't crucial, but it would certainly make things easier. If Gunther were in fact involved in some way with the accident they were talking about, Darnell was afraid he might find himself on opposite sides of the street from Kevin Conklin.

Laying his head back against the chair, his attention was drawn to the framed photographs on the top shelf of his bookcase. How young and idealistic the men in those pictures had been when that picture was taken!

The rural life of his background had not prepared Darnell Harrison for the horrors of the Korean War. Nothing he had lived through had readied him for the feelings of impotence he experienced on seeing life drain away so rapidly without being able to do anything about it. Each body passing through his hands in the MASH unit made him more adamant in his decision to do what he could to save every life possible when he returned home. He had taken the Hippocratic Oath to ease pain and prolong life in all ways possible. He was angered by the blatant disregard for the suffering troops on both sides as the commanders who sat comfortably in their tents directed the slaughter. This blasé attitude toward human pain and the right to life led directly to his decision to open a clinic in Taylorville.

His decision to specialize in OB-GYN came as no surprise to those who knew him. Following graduation from medical school, he returned home and opened an office dedicated to family practice and OB-GYN. Ever an idealist, with the outbreak of the Korean War, he was drawn to enlist knowing his services would be of use. Little did he know just how necessary his presence would be to thousands of young troops who ended up owing their lives to his skill and quick thinking. But it wasn't the memory of the lives he had helped save which stayed with him, it was the useless loss of life that he remembered.

The night the picture had been taken he had been on R and R. As so often happened during the war, he had run into Kevin and one of his friends at one of the more popular watering holes. Fiercely competitive at other times, all branches of the service stuck together when overseas, and Korea was no exception. Darnell had been with several others from his unit and when Kevin and his friends joined them, the group had become pleasantly boisterous. Having pushed several tables together, they had just begun to think about getting food when several officers from an aircraft carrier had joined them. That had been his introduction to the man they called "the Captain."

The deferential attitude of the men with him made it obvious that the tall, broad-shouldered, handsome man with the hard eyes was the one in control. Among many striking, imposing men, there was something about his body language that set Joseph Rossi apart from others of the same height and stature. This impression was heightened by the fact that, though the streets surrounding Perky's Pub were muddy and rank with debris, his dress uniform was pristine down to his shoes.

Joseph Rossi could have had his uncle buy his way out of the war. In fact, his decision to go in spite of the fact that his uncle preferred he didn't, was questioned loudly by other members of the "family." From prohibition when alcohol was the vice of choice, the family had made its fortune providing the weak with their unhealthy "hobbies." The other lieutenants didn't realize that by placing himself in a situation that removed him from the daily working of the family operations, Joseph was making a statement. Not born a Rossi, Joseph didn't have any chance of ever becoming the head of the family. Early on he had spent many hours pondering just how this would affect him. Now he worked to utilize his "distance" to the best advantage. Having decided that the most advantageous position would be that of "consigliere," he had begun to work toward that end.

Thus when he was told he would be shipping out to Korea, he had no doubt that on his return he would be elevated into a position of greater trust and power. If there was one thing that old man Rossi could relate to, it was standing up for your beliefs. Joseph had every intention of making his war years profitable, knowing that this would further raise the older Rossi's esteem.

To Carlo Rossi's credit, he had begun dealing with the Asian connections as soon as he saw the handwriting on the wall. Personally, he detested the drug culture and everything that it stood for, but Carlo Rossi was no fool. This was where the future lay, and if the Rossi empire were to continue, he had to make sure that they were involved from the beginning. That was where Joseph would come in.

For Joseph Rossi, basic training presented no problem. His experience with a rifle caught the eye of the training sergeant who recognized his leadership abilities as well. That led to his being placed into the officer's program. His ability to complete a mission without losing any troops helped his rapid promotion. When he began his second tour of duty in Korea, Rossi was already a captain.

The war had turned the world upside down for the weary Koreans. Anything that came from the west was given special value and dollars were the preferred currency. With life holding so little value, it was not unusual to be able to buy the services of streetwise young women for a pair of stockings and children for a candy bar. From the vantage point behind his desk, Rossi soon had an extended black market network organized which was capable of obtaining anything one could ask for, including any and all kinds of drugs. His presence in Korea had worked to the benefit of the family, as now the drug lords were able to put a face and body to the name Rossi.

Walking into Perky's Pub with his usual group, Joseph had rapidly summed up the action. Glancing across the smoke-blued room he focused on the group in the center with the tables pushed together. Nodding in response to the various greetings, he slowly made his way to the edge of the gathering. Listening for a moment, he decided that Harrison, one of the more solemn officers, was the one to address. He spoke softly, "Mind if I join you?"

Darnell was telling Kevin about how difficult it was to function with the primitive conditions of the MASH unit when he heard the soft-spoken request. Looking up through the haze, Darnell's first impression was of strength. As his gaze traveled upward, the smile he saw reinforced the feeling that the man in front of him was neither friendly nor aloof. It was only when he reached Rossi's eyes with their hard knowing look that he revised his initial impression. Here was a man who could be dangerous. "Why not?" said Darnell. "We're all on the same side."

Sitting down, Rossi extended his hand to Darnell. "Captain Joseph Rossi, 32nd Battalion. I hope we're not breaking up a private party, but this seemed the calmest group in here."

Glancing around at the other tables whose occupants were much more rowdy, Darnell took the proffered hand saying, "I can see what you mean. At least here you can eat and possibly get a word in. Dr. Darnell Harrison, 401 MASH." As Rossi glanced at Kevin, Darnell spoke once more, "That's Kevin Conklin and Tim Reeves of the 152nd."

Leaning slightly forward, Kevin took Rossi's hand, noticing the pressure the other man exerted. There was no doubt that here was a man who would always want to be in control of the situation. Leaning back in his chair to give Tim the opportunity to shake hands with Rossi, Kevin was surprised. Usually the first to try to make anyone feel comfortable, Tim held back and merely nodded when introduced to Rossi.

In the short time occupied by the introductions, no waitress had approached the table. Normally getting service wasn't an easy task as all wanted to be the first serviced. The noise levels drowned out any request made in a normal tone. When not one but two girls approached the table loaded down with fresh drinks as well as a bottle of champagne and glasses that were placed in front of Rossi, Tim voiced the comment which all had been thinking, "Either you own the place or you have a great deal of clout." Tempering what might be taken as an aggressive statement, Tim continued speaking as he raised his glass, "Here's to you and may we all continue to receive the benefits."

As the other men lifted their glasses, Rossi nodded in acknowledgement and then spoke to Darnell. "How long have you been over here?"

"Long enough to have learned that in spite of putting into practice all that I learned in med school and then some, conditions at the 401 and probably every other unit make it difficult to even the odds with the grim reaper."(Grim Reaper)

His glass remaining untouched in front of him, Rossi nodded. "I see that there is a backup in the delivery of sulfa drugs and penicillin." Noticing the surprise and interest of his audience, he continued, "It seems like I'm responsible for ordering most of the supplies for half the units here at the moment. We're buried under a sea of paperwork." Pausing, Rossi asked, "How about blood supplies?"

Listening to the conversation between Rossi and Harrison, Kevin wondered if Rossi's ending up at their table had been accidental. From what he could make out, Rossi was obtaining information, which would only be known to the MASH commanders, and he wondered if Rossi's questions were only idle curiosity. As they were leaving a short while later, Tim gave him the answer.

"Do you know who that was?" Tim asked as they reached the street, assailed by the odors of frying foods and debris.

Shaking his head, Kevin sidestepped a young girl no more than thirteen who sidled up asking if he was looking for a good time. "No, I don't know. And I think I would have remembered if I'd met him before. He's that type."

"He's that all right. Captain Joseph Rossi is said to run the largest black market network in this part of the world. It's also rumored that he has connections with the mob back home. From the way his war is going compared to other people's, I think that in this case the rumors might be true."

"With what you say, I hope Darnell can see past his own idealism and doesn't get involved with him." Already dismissing the information as not pertinent to him, Kevin shrugged. "But that's his problem. We ship out early tomorrow so let's head back. I want to write a letter before I sack out."

Darnell considered himself to be more discerning and worldly than the majority of his companions, and found talking to Rossi, a good listener, a welcome change. The Captain, on his part, decided that it would be beneficial to cultivate the idealistic young doctor.

After he met the man known as the "Captain," Darnell's war became better. Though Darnell did not know it, Rossi made sure that necessary supplies found their way to the 401. He also made it a point to know when Darnell would be visiting on R and R, making sure that he made contact with the doctor. During his infrequent absences from the battlefield, Rossi made sure that

Harrison's every comfort and desire were taken care of. And so Rossi gained the confidence of the doctor.

Leery about joining him when the Captain first suggested a massage parlor, Darnell soon justified the hours spent under the soft warm hand of the masseuse—provided by Rossi—as well-earned relaxation. Though Rossi liked Harrison, he utilized their meetings to obtain information about the area of southeastern Ohio and the western tier of Pennsylvania, knowing that all information was potentially useful.

Once or twice Darnell had bumped into Kevin Conklin on his forays and had included him in the pleasures provided by Rossi. But, alerted by Tim, Kevin was leery of accepting anything from Rossi and soon made excuses to avoid spending time with him. Perhaps because he was not surrounded by the daily carnage which translated itself into the nightmares of inadequacy that often plagued Darnell, Kevin had been better able to distance himself from Rossi's offerings.

With a sigh, Harrison came back to the reality of his office and, rubbing his neck, thought how beneficial one of those expert massages would be at the moment. His thoughts continuing along the same vein, he realized that he was tired and worried. He'd fought so hard and done so much to bring the clinic to where it was. His glance fell again on the photograph and he thought about how much he had managed to accomplish since his return from Korea.

For the sleepy rural county of Taylorville, it was fortunate that (Fairfield County), Ohio. Pennsylvania, met its northern border. The increase of interest in technology had forced the expansion of IBM in Endicott. This created more jobs as well as a need for additional businesses and housing. In effect, the area had both benefited and been cursed with all that normally went with the growth of industry. The outlying Ohio towns began to expand to accommodate the people drawn to the quiet green countryside as they sought housing close to work.

Darnell had been aware long before he left for Korea that the medical services available to the rural community were not sufficient to meet the needs of the rapidly expanding population. With the advent of medical specialization following World War II, many doctors who would have pursued family practice and accepted working in a rural community were now embedded in the cities and suburbs which provided them with a constant stream of patients and a lucrative lifestyle.

After he returned to the area from medical school in the summer of 1950, a developmental study, focusing on northeastern Ohio and the western tier of Pennsylvania, found that the area was considered to be medically impoverished. There was definitely a lack of medical facilities to fulfill the needs of the local population. In response to this, the Hill-Burton Foundation had made available funds in the amount of $70,000 to encourage the local community to develop a facility to meet its needs.

By means of a bequest from one of the four brothers of the original founders of the town of Taylorville, the Landowners, land had been provided for a hospital facility in the middle of town. Added to Darnell's desire to help the community, the moment was at hand to promote a fund-raising event to obtain the funds lacking to begin construction. Funding alone stood in the way of the town and its medical center. The town council enthusiastically asked Harrison to oversee the project. Who would know better the needs of the local community than the favorite son who was now back from the war? As a result, Darnell became a member of the board as well as chairman of the hospital committee.

Others on the board were Sam Stern from the bank, Lyle Greene, the head of the Greene legal office, and Gerald Mines of Mines Oil. The only other younger man in the group had been Kevin Conklin, replacing his father at the other's insistence.

Flattered and enthusiastic at first, Harrison was quick to see that the conservative posture of the majority would only complicate matters. The old school faction was decidedly conservative and was leery of bringing any outside influence into the community. They took immediate offense when presented with the idea that a consulting firm be hired to handle the fundraising. Only Kevin had sided with Darnell in trying to convince them that money spent on the expertise of an outside firm would be recuperated two fold with the successful fund-raising. No matter how many different ways Kevin tried to present the positive aspects, both legally and in terms of the time schedule, the diehard board refused to listen.

Convinced that the fee of five percent asked for by the consultants was excessive, the board refused to move forward with the project, arguing that there had to be someone within the local community capable of organizing and executing a fund-raising project. Thus the board was unable to reach a decision as to how to raise the money.

It was at that point Darnell Harrison had decided to distance himself from the board and continue the project on his own. In spite of Kevin's fervent arguments that they would all be better off if a solution could be found retaining the board's input, Darnell had had enough. He was more than willing to help his community develop the medical facility. In fact, he already considered the facility his, which only increased his frustration.

Prior to leaving for college, Darnell had purchased two acres of prime land situated close to center of Taylorville. This was done with the intention of eventually opening an office as well as making his home there, in the county seat. Knowing that this land was available and confident that he could obtain the necessary funding from the Hill-Burton Foundation, Darnell rapidly reached a point of saturation in dealing with the board members. This led to his meeting with Kevin alone late one day that fall in order to use him as a sounding board.

Arriving before Kevin did, Darnell entered the bar of the Inn and stopped to speak to the proprietor, John Woods. Carrying his scotch and water with him, he sat down at one of the few tables placed by the windows. Sighing deeply, Harrison realized that it had been too long since he had taken time to notice even the simple beauty of the natural country surroundings. Frowning, he thought once again that he was tired of the antics of the board. Had it been up to him, ground would already have been broken.

Approaching the table, Kevin extended his hand and spoke quietly. "You look pretty intense, scowling like that."

Looking up with a smile as he shook the young lawyer's hand, Darnell nodded. "I can't begin to tell you how tired I am of our nearsighted board. But then, you know what they're like because you've been there too." Signaling for another drink, he continued, "I don't think I can stand much more of their nonsense."

"You know it's never easy to get a group to reach a consensus."

"I no longer give a damn about trying to avoid offending anyone. The point is obtaining the funding and building the hospital. The lack of medical assistance in this area is appalling. Anytime any kind of emergency comes up, the nearest hospital is Mercy in Brunswick, and they're overtaxed to begin with. We're fortunate that the triple cities area seems to be improving economically, but it isn't going to do anything for us if we can't provide the necessary services for people coming into the community." Taking a sip of his drink, Harrison looked at Kevin waiting for the other man to reply to his tirade.

"I agree with you, Darnell, but if you're looking to get support from those on the committee, then you're going to have to tone down and compromise. Frankly, I don't see how you can do anything else. You need their help to get the funding and the Hill-Burton support."

"What if I didn't? What if it were possible to obtain the Hill-Burton monies and fund the hospital without the committee being involved? In fact, I even have an alternative location picked out if it isn't possible to have the Landowner property." Pausing for emphasis, Harrison continued slowly, "The only obstacle to having the building physically under construction is my ignorance of the legal ramifications of what I want to do."

"Legally, there is no reason why you couldn't build a hospital on your own, as long as you did not appropriate town funds without the express consent of the council. But what you're saying sounds more like a move toward making the facility a privately run entity." As Harrison nodded again, Kevin said, "If that's the way you want to go, then you wouldn't even need a hospital board because as a privately owned and operated center, while you would be directed by state laws, you would be solely responsible for policy."

"So you don't see a problem?"

"Not really, unless you want to consider offending some of the town fathers, and you obviously don't care about that," said Kevin. "Why didn't you go this route to begin with?"

"I hadn't even thought about making it a privately owned hospital until we started getting nowhere fast with the committee," explained Darnell. "It was only after we had the fourth of the most frustrating meetings I'd ever been involved in that I realized that I wouldn't be able to work with these people. Moreover, I don't want to answer to them. I didn't know if it was legally feasible or not, but now you've answered my question. I think that's the way I'll go."

"You know you'll be criticized."

Shrugging his shoulder, Harrison answered strongly, "Frankly, I don't care. It's sure to upset my family, but even if I am criticized, once the facility is open and operational, everyone will see how much it adds to the community."

That conversation had taken place twenty years before, and with Conklin acting as his legal counsel, Harrison had established the charter for the hospital and obtained the monies from the Hill-Burton society. Within the year, the new hospital had been built and was functioning.

Now, once again needing counsel, Darnell had recently been talking to Kevin to gain his support for the renovation program that was so sorely needed to keep the hospital in good shape. Again Harrison had obstacles to overcome, though this time, due to the people involved, they might prove even more difficult to resolve.

Getting into the car with Karl, Betty was quiet as she drove toward Taylorville. Concerned about Karl's possible symptoms, she kept looking over toward him. She knew that he and Brett Conklin had been friends and automatically assumed that he must be suffering terribly over the loss of his friend. Yet something about his attitude bothered her. Knowing that Gunther should be kept calm, she said, "I can't even begin to know how you feel, but getting more upset isn't going to help you."

"I couldn't have done anything, but it shouldn't have happened. We should have done something. The gun was so loud when it went off," Gunther replied.

Arriving at the place where he spent most of his days seemed to reassure him. "Thanks for bringing me over. I think I'll be fine, though I'll have them check my blood pressure," he said.

As he entered the familiar surroundings of the clinic, Karl felt a little better. Deciding to avoid the scrutiny he would be subjected to in the emergency room, he walked up the hallway to go directly to his office. Nearing his door he noticed that it was ajar. Thus warned, he was not surprised to find that both Darnell Harrison and James Grace, the two doctors who worked with him, were waiting in his office. Whatever they had been discussing was put on hold as they turned to watch him enter the room.

Getting up from where he had been perched on the edge of the desk, Harrison motioned Gunther to a chair, saying, "When they called to tell us you were experiencing difficulty, we were prepared for the worst. Since you're under your own steam and not in major distress, I'd venture a guess that it was stress related, but let's play it safe. I want to take your blood pressure."

A loner, Karl had never gotten close to any of the people he spent his days with other than Holly Conklin. The obvious concern surprised him, but grateful for the respite from the aftershock which was finally setting in, he settled into the chair and let Harrison take care of him.

Patting Karl's shoulder, Harrison returned to his perch on the desk. The silence continued as they waited for Karl to speak. With a sigh, Gunther said, "It was late when we got to camp and all the others had left or maybe they hadn't gone up to the cabin today. I really don't know. Brett was in a great mood and feeling fine because he wanted to walk through the woods before we started shooting."

The mental vision of his friend's wellbeing was reflected on Karl's face as his features softened. "We were on our way back when all of a sudden he saw something move, a porcupine I think, and started running down the path after it. I yelled at him about not being able to hit it as he passed out of my line of vision. The next thing I knew, the gun went off."

Having dealt with people for almost half a century, James Grace listened to this recital with reservations. He was surprised by the seeming lack of emotion that accompanied the telling. Even with all his years serving the medical community, his own reaction would have been stronger.

Harrison nodded his understanding. "Did you turn him over to check for vital signs?"

"Of course I checked," Gunther answered angrily, fixing his gaze on the older man. "When I realized that there was no heartbeat and saw the nature of the wound, I knew he was dead. It was a senseless, inexplicable, tragic accident."

"Stay calm," Harrison remonstrated. "There are normal questions that need answering anytime there is an accident. All I'm trying to do is to garner the necessary information to make this as quick and painless as possible for you. You may be a doctor, but you're also a human. What you need is to get the formalities out of the way and go rest."

"I appreciate your being here for me. This hasn't been an easy day." Looking at Harrison, he continued sadly, "Much as I'd like to take your advice and go home, I still have to go see Holly and Brett's parents. It's the least I can do under the circumstances."

"Do you know where they took the body?" asked Harrison. "Cummings should have been there. Did you speak to him?"

"When I got to Russell's house to report the accident, I tried to call Bob Wood. I couldn't reach him so I guess that the Silver Lake Ambulance finally did the transport. Betty was the one who drove me here after I started having chest pains. I left before Cummings got there."

"I would think that they probably took the body over to Burton's," interjected Grace. "There will probably have to be an autopsy considering the nature of death."

Harrison spoke decisively. "We'll arrange to cover for you at the clinic the next few days. You need to get back to yourself and take care of anything you need to do."

At his partner's words, Gunther's head came up rapidly. With the recent situation with the hospital pharmacy, the last thing he wanted to do was give Harrison a motive to find fault with his procedures or undermine him. "Knowing myself, the worst thing I could possibly do would be to sit around and think. After I talk to the Conklins and Holly, I should be able to be here as usual. If they need me for any routine questioning, it will be brief. I think we should count on business as usual."

Glancing at his watch, Darnell said, "It's almost 8:30. You appear all right at the moment, but if you have a reoccurrence of the chest pain, call me."

As Grace drove Gunther home, the men were silent, each occupied with his own thoughts. Grace was thinking that Brett Conklin had been cut down in his prime. It hurt to think someone as good and with so much to offer would no longer be there.

When Grace stopped the car, Karl got out and walked up the driveway, noticing a reading light on in the living room. Not wanting to waste any more time before he saw Holly, he grabbed the keys to his car off the hook by the door and left, never stopping to speak to Ann.

Reaction

The harsh ring of the phone in her self-imposed silence triggered a reaction in spite of her thoughts being blurred by fear. Holly had thought about the children and how they would react at learning that they would never see their father again. Nor did she know how she and Karl would make it through this situation. Thinking about the problems that faced her, the need to hear and feel her children became too strong to ignore. In the kitchen, she reached for the phone and dialed her mother's number. She cleared her throat to keep her voice normal as she waited for her mother to answer.

"Hello?"

"Have my monsters given you a moment's peace this afternoon?"

"Sweetheart! You know they're always good for me. It's you they drive crazy."

Feeling better at hearing her mother's voice, Holly smiled. "That's because you can give them back any time you want to."

"I never get tired of them before you're ready to have them back. Have you had a good afternoon without them?"

Brought back to the nightmare by her mother's words, Holly was silent as she thought about what to say.

"Holly? Are you still there?"

Clearing her throat, Holly answered, "Sorry. I was just thinking about how I could run over to get the kids without leaving dinner in the middle."

"Don't worry. I have a casserole in the oven so I can bring them home. See you in a few minutes."

As she worked on making dinner, Holly's fear was replaced by anger and frustration. Why had that man appeared at just that moment? And why was he so ready to tell them what to do? Her thoughts continued to whirl without finding any plausible answers. Totally preoccupied with trying to understand the situation, Holly never heard her mother pull up and jumped nervously as Janie grabbed her around the legs.

"Penny for your thoughts," said Ellen as she noticed Holly's reaction. "Deep, dark, and secret, I'll bet."

Smiling at her mother, Holly tried to shake off the gloom that seemed to have hold of her. Finding an answer that would placate her mother, Holly answered, "I was just wondering about which seasonings to use. I only wish I had your sense when it came to using herbs and spices."

Successfully entertained by her daughter's explanation, Ellen proceeded to make suggestions and helped prepare a meatloaf and salad.

"I'd better run and get your father's supper on the table. He coached this afternoon so he'll be hungry when he walks through the door."

"Okay, Mom. I'm going to stick this in the oven and bathe the kids," replied Holly, careful not to mention Brett. "I'll talk to you later. Say hi to Daddy for me." Hoping that the normal, mundane chores would keep her mind occupied, she went to fill the tub.

As they reached the pickup, Kevin braced his forearm against the door and lowered his forehead. Every nerve in his body screamed for the release of tears and anger. Yet, knowing what lay ahead, he didn't dare let go. Kevin finally straightened up and spoke softly, "Thanks, Jim. I don't know what I would have done without you."

Jim merely shook his head and squeezed Kevin's shoulder.

Kevin's eyes appeared dark and murky with his anguish. Looking at the man who had shared most of his joys as well as sorrow, he shook his head as if confused. "How do I go home now and tell Linda that our life is over, that all our plans have no meaning? What do I say?"

Jim shook his head. Words seemed inadequate. Clearing his throat, he tried. "I guess you just take it one step at a time. Right now you have to be strong to help Linda and Holly. Remember, I'm here for you."

As Jim pulled into his driveway, Kevin could see the warm light from the family room spilling across the windowsill and onto the lawn. He sat still not wanting to face Linda. He wondered if there was any place where he would be able to feel warm again.

Jim asked hesitantly, "Do you want me to go in with you?"

Kevin found that he was unable to speak as he got out of the truck. "If you want. I don't even know what to say. How do I tell her our only child is dead?"

As the door opened, Linda's ready smile disappeared as she saw Kevin's pallor and red-rimmed eyes. Concerned, she moved quickly to meet him, only to have her questions stilled as Kevin took her in his arms and held her as if he were drowning. Worried, Linda looked over Kevin's shoulder at Jim, her eyes asking what was wrong.

Straightening, Kevin led Linda to the couch and took her hand, pulling her down. His eyes bespoke both his love as well as his suffering as he very quietly told her what had happened. The high keening of Linda's response was the catalyst for Kevin's tears. As his wife sobbed heartbroken, he cried with her.

Jim's eyes filled too as, leaving the oblivious couple to their sorrow, he let himself out the kitchen door.

Driving Snake Creek Road toward the Pennsylvania border, Paul drummed his fingers on the steering wheel, keeping time to the rhythm of the hit on the radio. He had good news for Rossi. Being able to implicate two of the locals had made his job that much easier. Humming, he let himself into the shabby room of the motel in Kirkwood. "You don't have to worry about the lawyer anymore."

Looking up from where he sat reading, the captain noted Paul's satisfied attitude. "You look happy. I take it things went well?"

"Mission accomplished."

"You don't think we'll have any problem with the three sitting in jail?"

"Nothing that can't be handled. No lawyer, no trial." Smiling, he continued, "What do you say we go grab something to eat? All that work made me hungry. I can fill you in while we eat."

Nodding his consent, Rossi replied, "We're leaving, so get your things. I checked out. We'll stop once we get on the road."

Rossi sat thoughtfully after Paul left the room. Normally he would not have worried, but in this case he wondered. His intention had been to stop the investigation. Now he would have to wait and hope that no one else had been privy to Conklin's records.

Looking at her husband's face as he walked into the kitchen, the question on Susan Walsh's lips was forgotten. She paled at seeing the pain Jim was suffering. Whatever it was, she had no doubt that it had to be monumental to have created this kind of effect on him. Knowing he would tell her what was wrong when he was ready, she moved to the stove and turned the flame on under the teakettle.

Reaching to squeeze Susan's hand, he smiled wearily and began to speak. "I wish there was some way to make this easier on you than it was for me. Seeing his wife's brow furrow in concern, he spoke quickly, once more holding her hand as if to prevent her pain. "Brett Conklin was killed in a hunting accident this afternoon."

"Oh, God, no! Poor Linda and Kevin! How? He's been hunting since he was eleven!"

"I know. It doesn't feel right to me either. He was supposedly running after a porcupine with a loaded gun in his hand and tripped." Sighing, he shook his head. "I guess the best thing we could do to help at this point is try to contact the family and be there if they need us. They shouldn't be alone."

Shaking her head as if unable to assimilate what Jim had told her, Susan cried softly, the tears leaving trails on her cheeks. "We saw him the day he was born and were part of his life almost as if he was one of ours." Nodding his agreement Jim moved closer, and holding his wife, consoled her as she cried.

Slightly more in control, Susan stood and picked up a pencil and pad. "I think one of the first people we need to call is Tim Reeves. He's Kevin's best friend and if anyone can help him get through this, Tim can. We also have to call his brother in Colorado. I'll speak with the church auxiliary and you get in touch with the town council and the Rotary."

Neither Jim nor Susan would recover from the loss of the young man they considered as their own, but focusing on immediate tasks helped them shake off the numbing sadness.

Ben Granger was driving toward the golf course when he picked up the call on his CB radio. One of the three Taylor County commissioners, he had lived in Taylorville all his life and knew Kevin and his family well. Though he dealt with John Greene on legal matters, he was well aware of all that Kevin had done for the town as the mayor.

In fact, he knew that often kudos given to the commissioners were really the result of Kevin's unstinting effort to better the conditions in Taylorville. Any project undertaken by Conklin became part of the county record and reflected well on him.

Pulling into the golf club, he was pleased to see Walter Stern's car in the lot. Leaving his truck, he entered the clubhouse and made his way to the bar where he could see Stern hanging out with a group of friends.

Spotting Granger, Stern waved and yelled, "It's about time you showed up to help put a smooth finish on this beautiful summer day!" Shaking their heads, the others waited for him to continue. Knowing Granger's penchant for exaggeration, no one became concerned. None could have anticipated how the news would affect each of them.

Relishing his role as messenger, Ben said, "Brett Conklin was killed in an accident this afternoon."

Walter Stern, shaken, asked, "How? How could he be killed shooting pigeons?"

"I guess that he and Gunther were up there this afternoon and Brett tripped while running after a porcupine."

Incredulous, the group discussed the news, unwilling to accept what had happened. As they all got up to leave, Granger signaled Stern to stay. Alone, he said, "I didn't want to say anything in front of the others but I wonder whether anything will come out about the key club."

Stern replied tersely, "What do you mean?"

"From what I've heard, it seems that Gunther was with him when he died. So if there is any question, they're certainly going to look into Gunther's activities. If they do, chances are that the key club will become common knowledge. If that happens, the next step would be to ask about the involvement of the members. When that happens, we're all going to come under the microscope."

Taken aback, Stern signaled for another drink. Ben was a man with few sensibilities who had bullied his way through life with little concern for what others thought, so his concern puzzled Stern. He wondered how news of the key club would affect Kevin and Linda Conklin. Did they know that Holly was as interested in Karl Gunther as he was in her?

Startling Stern out of his reverie, Ben said, "There are others who will be affected by this. Has Harrison resolved funding issue?"

"I don't think so. But why should this affect him?"

Shrugging his shoulders, Ben told Stern what he was thinking. "You know how people reacted when Gunther was banned from the hospital pharmacy for suspected abuse of privileges. I just wonder how the 'righteous' members of the congregation are going to feel if it gets out that he was involved with Conklin's wife." Pausing to make sure that Stern was following his line of thinking, he continued, "But then again, I guess Mike Harrison will find another rabbit to pull out of the hat like he did when the committee wouldn't work fast enough to suit him on the hospital financing."

The thin line of his lips was testimony to Stern's concern. He wasn't worried personally, but he agreed that the town would not react lightly should news of the key club become common knowledge. Feeling as if he had been punched in the gut, Stern nodded as Granger turned to leave.

The idea of a club in itself wasn't the problem. No one found it unusual when six couples of this particular group began to get together on a weekly basis for drinks and dinner at the Inn. All belonged to the upper echelon of the town. It was a forgone conclusion that the weekly outing might run as high as $100 or more per couple. For Bob and Cathy Dwyer, the owners of the Inn, this weekly reunion was alike to winning the lottery each week. They happily set aside one of the smaller meeting rooms as a private dining room for the party. In fact, after the first month, when it became obvious that this was to be a weekly event, Cathy graciously offered to prepare a special menu. She also found out the birth dates of all the group members and served a cake and champagne, courtesy of the Inn.

The couples that made up the group represented the power of the town. Stern, along with his wife, June, represented the banking interests. Both were lifelong residents of the town. June's family was able to trace their ancestors to the American Revolution. Jack Healy represented "newer" money. He owned the local car dealership and had moved to Taylorville with his wife, Diane, twenty years earlier. Ken and Sally Loomis ran the local lumberyard, a family business of over eighty years. Karl Gunther was the only "outsider." He had come to the town and joined the group when he became a partner of Darnell Harrison. His wife, Ann, was county born, a member of the church council and Daughters of the American Revolution, which led to group acceptance. Brett and Holly were born and bred in Taylorville. Tolerated as a necessity, to stay on top of what was being planned for the sleepy county, Ben Granger, the county commissioner and his wife, Lena, rounded out those who met weekly at the Inn.

On the surface, these dinner parties seemed harmless, but as with many things over time, negative aspects began to surface. A certain undertone appeared during the weekly get-togethers. Someone had suggested that the couples no longer sit together. Eventually it became an unwritten law that for the evening you did not sit with your spouse. Mutual attractions were thereby unwittingly encouraged. The flavor of the forbidden being within reach became stronger with each successive Friday night.

Walter Stern sighed. The town seemed to thrive on gossip and the dinner group was not immune. It had all started so innocently. Except for Ben and Lena Granger, in their fifties, all members were around thirty. This proximity in age and musical predilection added flavor to the group. Many times after they finished at the Inn, two or more of the couples would go to one of the local night spots in Binghamton to dance.

This seemingly innocent behavior ultimately led to the formation of the "key club." One evening toward the end of February, the Gunthers, the Conklins, and the Healys had decided to continue the evening in Binghamton, driving the twenty miles to go to the nightclub of the Ramada Inn. Shortly after they arrived, it began to snow. As the whiskey and liquor continued to flow, the group decided that they were safer spending the night where they were than driving home. After checking in, the men had met by chance at the ice machine and decided to play a joke on their wives by exchanging the keys to their respective rooms.

When at the next dinner Brett had jokingly told the anecdote, Stern voiced his wish to have participated. Granger said it was never too late, and so it had started.

"Must be your drink doesn't suit you," joked the bartender as he wiped the bar in front of Stern. "You've got a very serious expression frozen on your face."

Brought back, Walter smiled ruefully as he answered the man. "I guess you haven't heard yet." At the guy's questioning look, Stern told him that Brett Conklin had been killed.

"Christ! I can't believe it! He was just in here Monday afternoon to meet Holly after her shift!"

Sisters Laurel Pease and Linda Conklin had been close as children and still were as adults. After receiving the news, she went numb. Shaking as she hung up the phone, she went to find her husband, repeating his name as she called, "Don? Don? Where are you?"

Hearing his wife, Don Pease hurried in from the garage only to stop in shock as he registered his wife's haggard appearance. Normally calm and cheerful, Laurel wasn't easily shaken. "Honey? What's wrong? Is it the kids? Are they all right? Shh, now. It can't be all that bad. Tell me what's wrong."

Her words broken by sobs and hiccups, Laurel recounted the news of Brett's death. As he listened, Don's mind raced ahead as he began to calm his wife. "We need to be there for Linda and Kevin right now." As he lifted Laurel's chin, he continued, "Go wash your face and grab a sweater while I lock up and get the car."

Lost in thought, both remembered happier times as they drove across town. Laurel thought of how Brett was more like another son than a nephew. Don found himself uneasy, feeling that something that Laurel had said wasn't right. Mulling over his wife's words, he couldn't understand how there had been an accident.

Feeling somewhat ashamed, Don was relieved to see Jim's truck in Kevin's driveway. He had no idea how he and Laurel would be able to help Linda and Kevin through what lay ahead, and reinforcements were welcome.

They entered the kitchen to find Jim on the phone and Susan making coffee, while Kevin and Linda sat together on the loveseat in front of the fireplace. The red eyes and pallor attested to their pain and added credence to the unbelievable accident. Rushing over to her sister, Laurel sat down on her other side and hugged her tightly.

After embracing his sister-in-law and Kevin, Don walked over to where Jim had just replaced the receiver. "What happened? Laurel was muttering something about a hunting accident while running after a porcupine, but I know that can't be. Brett would never do such a stupid thing."

Shaking his head to express his incomprehension, Jim agreed. "I know. But Karl Gunther was there and that's what he said happened."v

Still not convinced, Don insisted. "And that's all you know?"

"Right now."

"I just can't digest this." Staring at the sad trio across the room, he continued. "What can I do to help? Christ, Brett was like a son to us."

Nodding, Jim walked over to the sofa and squatted down next to Kevin, speaking softly. "I'm going to go over to Holly's and see if everything is all right."

As his friend began to uncurl his large frame, Kevin grasped his arm. "I'll go with you. Someone has to help her when it comes to making the arrangements." Turning to hug his wife and touch his forehead to hers, Kevin stood up with a heavy sigh. "We'll call you and let you know what's happening."

The look in his caramel-colored eyes matched the ominous frown on Tim Reeve's face as he hung up the phone, staring unseeing at the view of the mountains beyond Boulder that had come with his promotion to District Attorney. Shaking himself out of his pensive state, Tim checked his watch and buzzed for his secretary. With any luck she would be able to book them on an evening flight. Instructions given, he called Darlene at her flower shop and gave her the news, telling her to prepare their bags for the trip to Taylorville.

Next came a list of follow-ups needing attention during his absence. Returning to his desk and turning to the window, he began to analyze once more what Kevin had told him just that afternoon.

Unlike many of the men who lost touch with each other after they left the service, the men of the 152nd squadron made a pact to meet once a year and had done so faithfully. The bond that had been established in Korea strengthened over time. Several of the men made it a point to visit each other or take vacations together each year. The annual reunion gave each of them contacts in many different cities. With this came access to a variety of different sources of information as varied as the men who made up the squadron.

A fleeting smile briefly chased the fierce scowl from Tim's face as he thought about his friend. He truly loved Kevin Conklin. The bond of friendship and trust they had established in a foreign land made them closer to each other than many were to their own family, each unconditional where the other was concerned. Though they did not dwell on the fact that one or another of their comrades was no longer there, neither of them ever forgot that it could have been them instead.

Though they didn't often see each other, they wrote at least once a month and kept in touch by phone. Both being lawyers made their friendship even more special though Kevin had opted to follow in his father's non-criminal law practice and Tim had joined the prosecutor's office in Boulder as an assistant DA after the service. They were always able to discuss their work knowing the other would understand. They were even godparents to each other's children so only a phone call was needed for one of them to board a plane to be there for the other.

Kevin had called that afternoon because he was uneasy about the drug situation and knew that Tim had ample experience in that area. But something else was bothering his friend, even though Kevin had said that everyone was fine.

Now Brett was dead. According to Jim Walsh, who had called to let him know and asked him to come, Brett had died from a fluke accident that just didn't make sense. His eyes narrowing with concentration, Tim reviewed his conversation with Kevin. He had a feeling that the drug problem was the key. He would have to wait until he reached Taylorville to find out why.

Will Billings realized that more than tired, he was disgusted. He had spent all afternoon tying up loose ends connected with the break-in at the Forest City pharmacy, and it was already after six o'clock. When would the idiot parents learn that it was not a "prank" when their kids broke in to steal diet pills, glue, or cough syrup? He had been sheriff of the county for over eighteen years, yet it still amazed him that people could continue to be so blind. Now, he had to deal with the unexpected death of Brett Conklin.

His impression of Conklin had been of a man who knew what he was doing—neither a braggart nor a fool. Only a fool ran with a gun in his hand. Something was not right. He had never gone hunting with Conklin, but he couldn't imagine the man he knew being careless while carrying a rifle. And then there was the rumor of the romance he had recently heard. Was it an accident?

The Next Act

Kevin appeared to sink even deeper into sorrow as they walked the short distance to the truck, and Jim could think of nothing that would ease his suffering, so he remained silent.

Kevin debated silently whether he should bring this strong, gentle man into his confidence. Though he needed to vent about Holly and Gunther, he hesitated. He didn't want to worsen the already-tenuous situation with Holly.

Kevin opened his eyes to see that they had turned the corner and Brett's house was in sight. The windows were illuminated with a warm welcoming light, and his eyes filled. Every part of him hoped that he would feel welcome when he saw his daughter-in-law.

Holly was both mentally and physically exhausted by her efforts to appear normal while she waited to hear of Brett's death. The incessant pacing, coupled with the emotional strain of appearing normal for her mother and her children had drained her. Now after a relaxing bath, she was wrapping herself in a towel when she heard the knocking at the door.

She had spent hours waiting for the news of Brett's death. Now that the moment was at hand, she wondered if she could possibly act as the unknown man had instructed her when given the news. Approaching the stairs, she saw Jim's truck in the driveway and knew that he had to be with Kevin. Knowing that she only had the time it took her to dress to compose herself, she yelled, "Come on in. I'll be right down."

Seeing Kevin blanch, Jim worried whether his friend could stand up to the strain. "Don't you think you need something to drink? You're getting paler by the minute and you need to be strong."

Smiling wanly, Kevin reached across his chest and squeezed his friend's arm in a gesture of thanks. "I don't understand how it can possibly hurt any worse than it did at the time I saw his body in the clearing, but it does." As he heard Holly's footsteps on the stairs, Kevin stiffened, bracing himself for the inevitable confrontation.

Holly, fighting for composure, intentionally kept her voice light as she entered the kitchen, saying, "You could have come in and sat down. I saw the truck..." Any worry she might have felt about acting convincingly evaporated as soon as she saw Kevin. Shocked at his appearance, she asked, "What's the matter?"

Unable to find words to lessen the blow, Kevin walked over to hold her as he said, "There's been an accident. Brett's been killed."

Finally able to release the emotional maelstrom she had been fighting all afternoon, Holly shook herself free of Kevin's arms as her denial reverberated throughout the room. "No! You're wrong. It can't be!" As she spoke, the finality of what had taken place hit her again. She became hysterical and shook her head back and forth negating what had happened. "It can't be. He went shooting pigeons this afternoon just like any other Wednesday. How can he be dead?"

Fearing that one or both would lose control if the conversation continued, Jim dealt with the situation in the only way he knew, literally pushing them into chairs at the kitchen table. Stunned by his unexpected action, both quieted and watched Jim go to the living room. He returned with a bottle of bourbon and three glasses and poured shots for all of them. He said, "Drink this. We all need it."

Downing his own whiskey, Jim took the situation in hand. "You're both going to feel disoriented and confused for a while. Losing your balance isn't going to help either one of you. Right now, like it or not, you'd better concentrate on the arrangements that have to be made."

Focused on the task given them, Kevin quietly began reviewing the list of questions he would normally ask at any family gathering where they were trying to make similar arrangements. He was not surprised to learn that neither Brett nor Holly had ever really gone beyond having funeral costs included in their insurance. Agreeing to use Burton's, Holly called her mother to come stay with the children while she and Kevin went to the funeral home.

❋

After the arrival of the coroner, Trooper Yorken had checked in at the barracks and received instructions to go to the hospital to question Dr. Gunther. Returning to the cruiser, he said to Harrison, "We need to go to the hospital to get Gunther's statement soonest." Pulling into the clinic driveway, Yorken walked in and said to the nurse on duty, "I'd like to speak with Dr. Gunther."

"I'm sorry. Dr. Gunther left a few minutes ago with Dr. Grace."

"Thanks. I'll see if I find him at home."

After the short drive, as they reached the front door, Harrison depressed the doorbell and listened expectantly for footsteps. After several minutes, Harrison said, "You'd think someone would be here. After what happened, I'd think that the doctor would be more than ready to come home. Where do you think he is?"

Going up to the door, Yorken tried the knob. When it turned easily, he turned and said to Harrison, "I don't like this. The people at the scene felt that Dr. Gunther was having a shock reaction. I think we'd better go in and make sure that everything is all right."

The troopers made their way into the house calling out as they entered. Failing to get a response, Yorken switched on the light in the dark kitchen. Everything looked normal. Again calling out for Mrs. Gunther, the troopers moved toward a lighted area, assuming it was the living room. Nothing appeared amiss at first glance. Only after entering the room did they see that it was occupied. Ann Gunther appeared to be asleep on the couch.

Yorken called out once more. “Mrs. Gunther?” Approaching the sofa, he gently shook the woman lying there by the shoulder. “Mrs. Gunther?”

Feeling a weak pulse and noticing the slightest rise of her chest with her breathing, Yorken called out, “Call for emergency medical help. Stat! She’s barely breathing!”

Having transmitted the situation to the barracks, Harrison returned to join Yorken who was removing the pillows from behind Ann Gunther’s head in preparation of CPR. “You press on her chest and I’ll do the breathing and counting. At least we can keep oxygen flowing through her until help arrives.”

Falling into the rhythm of the CPR maneuver, the two men worked on Ann Gunther until the medical technicians arrived several minutes later. Once they had placed her on oxygen, she was transported to the hospital.

In the subsequent rush to ensure Ann Gunther’s welfare, finding Karl was put on hold. Later it would become part of an ironic anecdote that Brett’s death had triggered the events that led to saving Ann’s life.

Disturbed at the thought of having to face Holly, Karl drove rapidly toward the Conklin home. She loved him as he loved her, but he was realistic enough to know that Brett’s death would definitely create problems. How could it not? They had often discussed how much simpler their future would be if their respective spouses agreed to divorce, yet neither would ever have looked at the death of either Ann or Brett as a solution.

As he pulled into the driveway everything looked the same yet life would never be the same again. Brett would never come out the door. And now he and Holly were irrevocably tied by shared knowledge as well as love.

Stopping his car behind Holly's, Karl braced himself to face Kevin. Recognizing Jim's truck in the drive effectively dissolved any thoughts of being with Holly. His close friendship with Brett over the last seven years had made him privy to all the Conklin friends and family. He knew firsthand that Kevin and Jim were extremely close. As soon as his relationship with Holly became common knowledge he would be the epitome of a Judas.

Shutting off the engine, he walked around to the back door and after calling Holly's name walked in. He moved toward the living room to find Holly and Kevin seated with Jim, all looking as if they had received a physical beating. Brett's dog, lying at Holly's feet, was the first to acknowledge Karl's presence by lifting its golden head. The normally happy animal appeared to have internalized the grief that he felt around him and did not wag his tail.

Karl heard himself say, "Are you all right?"

The older Conklin's pallor was obvious as he raised his red-rimmed, grief-filled eyes. He said, "Nothing will ever be all right again. How can it be?"

Karl once again related the events that led to Brett's death. As he nodded his understanding, Kevin simultaneously shook his head as if to deny that it was possible. Slow hot tears began to trickle from Holly's tightly closed eyes. Finally, rising slowly as if not trusting her legs to hold her, she faced Karl. "I'll make some coffee. Kevin is taking me over to the funeral home to take care of the arrangements. We're waiting until my mother gets here to stay with the children."

Still worried about Kevin being in danger of falling apart, Jim refilled the glasses on the coffee table in front of him. "I know I need something stronger than coffee if I'm going to get through these next few hours. Bring some ice with you when you come back."

Nodding agreement, Karl stood, saying, "I'll get the ice." Following Holly into the kitchen, out of sight of the others, he stepped up behind her. Placing his hand on Holly's shaking shoulders, he murmured, "It's all right. Hush now. You need to pull yourself together. You have to be able to think."

Taking a moment to consider his words, she accused, "How can you be so calm?" Sobbing as she turned to face him. "Nothing will ever be right again. I can't take it. I keep seeing Brett fall and hearing that awful man ordering us around like puppets! I can't take it!"

Turning her toward the door, Karl supported Holly whose normally pliant body seemed boneless, incapable of any directed movement. Leading her back to the others, he raised his head to meet Kevin's questioning stare. "The shock has been too much. I'll make the coffee and get the ice," he mumbled as he walked back to the kitchen.

Holding the sobbing mother of his grandchildren against him on the couch, Kevin murmured soft reassurances as his tears trickled down to join hers. "It's all right to cry, sweetheart. It's all right."

Returning to the living room with the promised items, Karl paused to watch Kevin comforting Holly. Every fiber in his body ached with wanting to change places with the older Conklin, but he knew he couldn't. Putting the sugar bowl on the table and filling the cups with coffee, he sat down opposite Kevin and Holly.

"Do you want me to give you a tranquilizer?" asked Karl, his brow furrowed with concern. As Holly shook her head no, his eyes met Kevin's and he saw that tears were once again coursing down the older man's cheeks. "Kevin?"

Conklin took a deep breath before answering, "No, I don't think anything can help." Further talk was curtailed as Ellen Carvella burst through the door. "Oh, my poor sweetheart! My baby!" she cried as she hugged her daughter.

Returning her mother's hug, Holly said softly, "I'm all right. The kids are in bed. Thanks for coming."

Ellen said, "That's okay, love. Both Daddy and I are right here for you. Hopefully the kids will sleep right through. I won't tell them anything. I'm not sure I understand how this happened."

"None of us do," Kevin said, getting up from the couch. "Do you feel up to going with me? If not, I can go by myself," he stated.

Holly answered quickly, seeing the trip as a way to find out if they had accepted Karl's version of the accident. "No, no. I have to go. I can't sit here any longer. I feel as if I'm in the middle of a bad dream and can't wake up. If I go, maybe I can understand what's happening and begin to believe it." As she spoke, she moved off the couch. "Just wait until I wash my face and check on the kids. I won't be a minute."

As Holly left the room, Ellen turned to Karl and said, "How could this happen? I've never known anyone as careful as Brett around guns. How was he running with his back problem? It doesn't make sense."

Holly quickly returned to the room and said, "I guess it would be better if the kids spent the night with you and Dad. I need to decide what to say to them. They're just babies. How do I explain that Daddy won't be back?" Though the words where directed to her mother, her eyes met Karl's; their mute plea was obvious.

Standing as if fighting heavy weights, Kevin answered her question. "One thing at a time. Right now we need to get over to Burton's. There will be time to deal with what to tell the kids once we get back."

Ellen said, "I'll close up the house before I leave. Call me if you need us."

Nodding, Jim moved to the door with Kevin and Holly, not saying a word to Karl.

As the others left, Ellen picked up the phone to call her husband. The absence of dial tone made her wonder if Holly had taken it off the receiver. Hanging up the phone, she was startled when it immediately rang. No amount of preparation would have been sufficient for the information she received.

"Karl!" Trying to catch her breath, Ellen shook her head. "They just called from the hospital. They didn't tell me why, but the emergency crew just took Ann over there."

Racing to his car, Karl had the motor running as he shut the door. In an emergency, his movements were once again sure and controlled. Shaking off the lethargy that had threatened to swallow him, he drove to the hospital.

Just Bad Luck

As the ambulance pulled away from the Gunther's house, the tech checked Ann's pulse. Finding it weak but steady, he covered Ann with a blanket, shaking his head in frustration. "What the hell is going on? Conklin is shot and killed and now the doctor's wife has apparently overdosed. It doesn't make sense. I just hope they located Dr. Harrison and he's waiting for us. She doesn't look too good."

Further conversation was cut off as the ambulance pulled into the parking lot of the hospital. The tech opened the door and released the cot from its moorings, moving it to the room indicated by the orderly. Dr. Harrison appeared and began asking for information. "Where was she when you found her? Was there evidence of distress? Convulsions?"

"The troopers were giving CPR when we arrived. They said that they were there looking for Dr. Gunther. When they found the back door open and no one answered, they went in and found Mrs. Gunther on the sofa in the living room."

As he began to examine Ann, Dr. Harrison asked, "Did you happen to see the prescription she was taking?"

"No, but we didn't stop to look because her pulse was so weak. Do you want us to go back and check?"

Harrison did not need the situation complicated by conjecture as to why Gunther's wife would attempt to take her life. "That won't be necessary. I'll get a hold of Dr. Gunther. I'm sure he'll know. I'm sure this overdose was accidental."

Turning to his nurse, Harrison said, "Bring me the stomach pump stat. As soon as you do that, find someone to call the Gunther house and let the doctor know that he's needed here."

Harrison had almost finished the procedure when the orderly came in and said, "There is no answer at the Gunther house, Dr. Harrison. Do you want me to try somewhere else?"

Finishing up, Darnell realized that the most logical place to look for Karl would be at the Conklin's. What didn't make sense to him was that Karl hadn't been the one to find his wife. She had obviously taken whatever drug long enough before so that she would have been under its effects by the time Jim Grace had dropped Gunther off. Had he intentionally neglected her?

Coughing and fighting the pump, Ann Gunther began to come around. Hearing Harrison's reassuring voice, she stopped fighting and tried to relax as he continued speaking. The return of consciousness brought with it the avalanche of the anguish that had triggered her action to begin with. Why was she still alive? Who had found her and brought her to the hospital? Where was Karl?

Anger coursed through Harrison on seeing the pain in Ann's eyes. He had known her all her life and knew she deserved more than she received from her husband. Stroking her shoulder in an attempt to calm her, he murmured, "Shh. Everything's all right, Ann. You throat is going to be sore so don't try to talk. Karl will be here in a few minutes to take you home."

Ann nodded as tears continued to fall. The pain she felt did not come from her throat or even the stomach pump. It was a deep, throbbing, ever-growing ache which threatened to choke her with its violence. Karl would know that she had tried to take her life and failed. Whether pity or scorn, she did not want to face Karl's reaction. It was then that Ann Gunther realized that she didn't want to die. What she wanted was relief from the mentally abusive situation she was in. Seeking love and attention, she had made herself a victim.

Forcing himself to sit back and relax, as his tension eased, Harrison reviewed the events of his day and the effect that they would have on his plans for the clinic. Placing a piece of paper on the desk in front of him he began a chronological list. The first meeting had been with Kerr and Gunther at 12:15 to discuss the pharmacy situation and the additional capital needed to continue the expansion and remodeling. Both of the others had agreed to his suggestions as usual.

A more sensitive topic was that of the continuing complaints of pharmacist Gerald Weir. According to Weir, large quantities of narcotics were being withdrawn and he pointed to Gunther as the culprit. The discussion had become heated when John Kerr, meaning well, had suggested that the doctors sign for withdrawals of drugs from the house stock.

The tightening of his mouth reflecting his annoyance. Gunther had said forcefully, "What is it with you, John? Don't you think it's enough to have insisted that I surrender my key? There is a log of what we take out kept by the nurse on duty. So far as I'm concerned, that's more than sufficient. I had no problem giving Ben my key when you requested it because it saves me time. It's actually easier for me to let the staff hunt for the medication."

Harrison had been able to diffuse the hostility that threatened to undermine the meeting by changing the subject to the new operating materials, which they would be incorporating in the future.

Now in light of Ann's overdose, Karl's reaction to Kerr's suggestion seemed more important. How long had Ann been taking tranquilizers and why? Darnell wondered if Gunther's involvement in Brett's death would have any repercussions to his fund-raising plans for the hospital.

Gunther was known to socialize with Walter Stern and had been elected to represent the hospital interests in that arena, doing a good job. So now what? The mere fact that Karl had been present at the time of Brett's death might taint public opinion against him and by default, against the clinic. Then there was Ann.

What would people say if it got out that she had intentionally taken an overdose? If that happened, there was no way that the clinic could avoid repercussions. The town's small population was close-knit and the hospital and its staff would be smeared with the same brush: guilt by association.

Being a man who had been married twice, he understood how an attraction could have developed between Karl and Holly. When he had first become involved with his second wife, she had still been "happily" married to her husband.

A firsthand participant in death's frequent triumph over life, Harrison would be the last to criticize the pursuit of fulfillment. Life was much too short and tenuous to waste time in relationships which no longer gave satisfaction. Anyone who became a doctor understood the fragile nature of life. Fighting death was a duty, and since his arrival in Taylorville, Gunther had proved himself a dependable physician with good instincts. Darnell's opinion about Gunther had not changed.

Checking his watch, he saw it was twenty after nine and dialed the Gunther home. When the ringing went unanswered, he dialed that of Brett Conklin. Giving Ellen the message that Gunther was needed at the hospital, he put down the receiver.

Descending in front of the funeral parlor, John Cummings looked up to see Rob Burton standing on the steps. "Hello, Rob. I never like coming here, but this time it's particularly painful."

Nodding, Burton shoved his hands further into his pockets. Speaking softly, he told them where to take the body. He didn't want to believe that this was his friend Brett, and shook his head.

When the others left, Cummings looked at the lifeless face in front of him and sighed. The corpse had taken on a waxy aspect as the blood settled. No expert on gunshot wounds, what he was seeing wasn't what he had expected. A large entry wound would have coincided with Gunther's story, but the diameter of the wound appeared to be no more than an inch and a half at most. These findings were not consistent with the findings he had made in other accidental deaths involving a shotgun. He would have expected the circumference of the wound to be greater even if the muzzle had been flush with the body. The longer he stood there, the more obvious it became that the "accident" was not as clear-cut as Dr. Gunther wanted others to believe. Why would Gunther lie?

Having dispatched the men from the ambulance, Rob Burton rejoined Cummings. "Not implying anything, but this 'accident' doesn't make sense to me. I doubt that you'll be able to find anything when you do the autopsy. The cause of death is obviously the bullet wound to the chest."

Burton's words making him even more concerned, Cummings paused and replied, "I'm not going to do the autopsy. As county coroner I'm responsible for determining whether there has been a death, which obviously there has been. If they want one done, which they probably will, they can ask Dr. Grace." Taking a deep breath, Cummings continued, "I'm going to wait until the autopsy is completed to issue the death certificate. When the cause of death is established, I'll reiterate exactly what the information shows on the certificate."

Surprised, Burton was unable to question the other man's decision. Brett Conklin had been too much a part of the local justice system for Cummings to risk making any mistakes. Nodding, he lifted his head at the sound of the doorbell.

Disturbed by the death of Brett Conklin, Cummings thought that he might be able to make sense of what had happened by writing it down. As was his habit, he dated the top of the paper: June 2, 1976. He wrote, seeing himself speaking to Karl, interjecting questions as he listened to the doctor's version of what happened. The notes became a sort of interview. He had no inkling at the time that he would later be questioned about the veracity of his report. Cummings and Gunther never came in contact either the evening of Brett's death or the next day.

For Kevin the short ride over to the funeral parlor was unreal. He couldn't believe he was actually on his way to arrange for his son's burial. Brett was only thirty, with his whole life ahead of him. How could it have ended when they had spoken only that morning? Sitting silent next to Jim, his thoughts churned relentlessly through his mind.

Upon their arrival, Rob ushered them into the office area. He decided that they would all be better off being as expeditious as possible in making the funeral arrangements and neither Holly nor Kevin seemed to be capable of absorbing any of the details. Quickly Rob organized a viewing and ceremony according to what he thought they would prefer.

Suddenly Kevin spoke brusquely. Both Rob and Holly were startled as he said, "I need to see Brett once more."

Seeing Holly pale at Kevin's words, Rob was quick to try and calm his friend. "Of course you can see Brett." Noticing how she had shrunk deeper into the chair as if trying to escape from what was happening, he said, "Holly, why don't you wait here for us?"

At her nod, Rob got up and guided his friend to the stairs leading to the workshop. At the sound of approaching footsteps, Cummings frowned, bracing himself to face his friend. More times than he would have liked, he had been present when someone he knew found themselves faced with the death of a loved one. Many were accidental, yet this time he felt strange with the circumstances involved.

Kevin managed to look both hopeful and fearful as he greeted his friend. His steps slowed as he crossed the room, as if by delaying the moment he looked at Brett he could avoid accepting his death.

Sighing audibly, Kevin laid his hand alongside Brett's cheek in a tender gesture of farewell as the tears rolled down his face and off his chin. "I suppose I'd better get back to Holly. She keeps repeating 'No, no, no' over and over. I'll have to see about getting her sedated. I have to take care of her and the kids for Brett."

The funeral arrangements were made quickly. When they returned to the office they found Holly speaking about the personal details. Rob made sure that Jim Walsh was going to drive the broken pair home because neither Kevin nor Holly was in any condition. Watching them drive away, Rob returned downstairs to find Cummings still working on his notes.

Both men shook their heads in mute agreement over the sad situation. With a final look toward the table, the funeral director said, "I'll leave you to your work. This is not going to be a pleasant weekend."

Cummings answered, "I'll lock up on my way out." Returning to the notes, put aside when Kevin arrived, John tried to find the brooded as to the most logical way to write the report. He had not spoken with Gunther that night nor the following day, yet he referred to Gunther as if he had.

Later there would be questions as to how professional the investigation had been. Both Cummings and Burton were pathologists yet neither did the logical forensic examination when the body was accessible. Dr. Grace performed the autopsy on the next day, eighteen hours after the shooting. Why had the body been embalmed prior to Dr. Grace performing the autopsy?

Cummings issued the death certificate the afternoon of June 3rd using the information given to him by Dr. Grace, information that was based on the assumption that Gunther's account was true.

Karl had no idea of what had happened to send Ann to the hospital. His concern was allayed by knowing Dr. Harrison was there to handle yet another upset in a long, trying day. Entering the lot, he pulled into his reserved space.

The nurse on duty said, "Your wife is in room 6. Dr. Harrison saw her and she's resting comfortably now. I'll let him know you've arrived."

Nodding his thanks, Gunther continued down the hall, stopping in front of the door to six. The room was dark except for a night-light so he quietly opened the door and walked over to the foot of the bed, reaching for the chart. Glancing at Ann, he noticed the even rise and fall of her chest which meant she was sleeping.

His brow furrowed as he read that they had used a stomach pump to rid Ann of whatever she had ingested. Though he had recommended the prescribed dosage for his wife, the fact that the drug she was taking was the same one he had been questioned about did not help matters. Knowing that Harrison was waiting for him, Karl sighed and replaced the chart. Seeing no point in postponing the inevitable, he left without a backward glance at his wife.

Harrison was waiting for him in his office but said nothing as Karl entered and sat down. Gunther's fatigue and the strain of the day were immediately obvious to Darnell, much different from the semblance Gunther had displayed when he had seen Grace and Harrison earlier. Deciding that he was more apt to obtain a true reading of the scope of the problem if Gunther were at ease, Darnell said, "Ann was resting comfortably when I left her. She should sleep for a while and then you can take her home." Looking into Karl's eyes, he continued, "This has been one hell of a day for you so I'll keep it short. Just a few questions. Have you seen Kevin and Linda Conklin? How is Holly holding up?"

Taken by surprise at Harrison's question, Karl answered, "As well as can be expected under the circumstances."

Seeking a reaction that would shed light on Gunther's intentions, Darnell said, "I imagine this will mean placing your plans on hold for the moment. I can't afford to play games. Nor can I afford to have you make further mistakes." He paused for emphasis, looking to see Gunther's reaction, "So you might as well resign yourself to the fact that I know about you and Holly. Now I need to know your intentions and whatever else is necessary to help us weather the storm, which is going to break out as a result of Brett's death. Not to mention your wife's attempted suicide."

Karl's expression remained grim as he listened quietly. Dealing from a position of weakness, he was wary. He refused to grovel or show his exasperation. Darnell's respect was only gained through calm, calculated actions. Karl knew that for the moment, his best move was to say nothing.

Admiring the younger man's aplomb, especially in light of what he had experienced throughout the day, Harrison continued, "Do you know what might have caused Ann to intentionally overdose? Did anything special act as the trigger?"

The cause came to Karl even as he was shaking his head no. Stopping, he thought about the conversation he had had with his wife that morning. He looked at Harrison with a calculating gaze as he thought about the wisdom of telling the truth. "What difference would it make? She obviously feels pressured and confused, or she wouldn't have done it."

Harrison's annoyance at Karl's words was obvious. "It makes a difference. Depending on what caused her actions, we may be able to come up with a plan which might take the attention of the public off you and, by association, the clinic."

Gunther replied quickly if defiantly, "I seem to recall Ann being distressed this morning after I told her that I planned to divorce her and marry Holly." Rubbing his hand over his brow, he continued, "I really didn't and don't want to hurt Ann. She deserves better, but I refuse to give up the chance at a life with Holly. What I feel for her is totally different from anything I ever felt. I don't want to lose it." Looking Darnell in the eye, he said, "Ann didn't want a divorce. I guess I've known for a long time that Ann was unhappy. I mentioned her insomnia to you."

Harrison nodded. He made no comment, feeling that Karl needed to deal with the issue on his own.

Karl resumed, "I suppose you think I'm very selfish, but I was involved with the plans for the clinic and trying to come to grips with the new feelings I was experiencing at the same time." Sitting down again, he said, "You know Ann. She never complains. I guess she found it easy to think that I was always busy with the hospital."

Harrison said, "I can understand and even empathize with you. What I don't understand is you're not seeing the warning signs prior to Ann's suicide attempt."

"I didn't see any signs because there were none. I also had no inkling this morning that this evening my best friend would be dead. I certainly didn't plan either of the two incidents which you feel might be a point of public censure."

"Don't be ridiculous," snapped Harrison, annoyed. "I'm well aware that you didn't plan for any of this to happen, but it has! So we need to deal with it in a way that won't bring unfavorable publicity to the hospital."

Fatigue obvious in his posture, Karl rubbed his neck, saying, "I'm sure you've got a plan to handle this."

"I do. I've had time to think before I found you. Knowing how the people react, I decided that the best way to handle this would be to keep everything as close to normal as possible. No one will question your needing a few days off to cope with Brett's funeral and to try and help the family. Everyone knows that you and Brett were close."

Nodding, Karl remained silent.

"But I don't think that you should make it a practice of being seen with Holly outside of work." He paused to let his words sink in. "So far as Ann goes, I want this whole episode handled so that people believe what happened was accidental. Whatever plans you were going to initiate in the next few months are going to have to be put on hold, difficult as that may be. What needs to be done is to make sure the clinic doesn't suffer as a result of what happened today. That is your first priority."

Harrison walked over to Gunther's chair and placed his hand on his shoulder, saying, "You're going to take Ann home and make sure that she sees what happened tonight as an accident. Until things die down, you are not to mention divorce again."

Not waiting for Gunther to answer, Darnell left the office. Karl was stunned. The emotional turmoil he had been feeling changed to a deep resentment. He didn't like what he had been told but knew instinctively that Darnell was correct in his assessment of the situation. Gathering his strength, he got up. Once Ann heard of Brett's death she would be more concerned about him than anything else, so getting her mind off divorce would not be hard. Getting his mind off Holly and acting how Harrison expected him to was something else.

Leaving Burton's, Kevin's exhaustion was evident. He was glad that Jim was with him. The pain jolted him once more, approaching the house where his son would never again greet him. He made a visible effort to concentrate on Holly. "Are you sure you'll be okay alone?"

Wanting to be left alone to sort out her feelings, Holly answered quickly, "I'll be all right. I'll take something to sleep and call you in the morning."

As they watched her enter the house, Jim reached over and squeezed Kevin's shoulder. "Everyone handles grief in their own way. Her life has been turned upside down."

Nodding, Kevin closed his eyes and tried to marshal his strength. He hadn't really talked to Linda since they had gotten the news. Pulling into the driveway, Kevin was thankful there were no other cars. "Much as I appreciate the concern and help, I need to be alone with Linda right now."

Jim replied, "I can imagine. I'll grab Susan and we'll be on our way. If you need us for anything, just call."

❋

As the door closed, Kevin felt a shiver work its way down Linda's body. Leaning closer to her, he asked, "Do you want me to get you a sweater?"

Her sigh was audible as she shook her head. "No, having you next to me is what I need. I feel as if I'm in the middle of a nightmare and can't seem to wake up."

"I know. I don't want to believe that Brett's dead. Worse, I can't believe that his death was the result of an accident with a gun. It just doesn't make any sense."

Linda was quiet as she thought about what Kevin had said and compared it to what she had learned from those who had stopped by to see if they could offer assistance. "How's Holly holding up?"

"She seems to be doing as well as can be expected under the circumstances. Ellen took the kids to her house so they don't know anything." Remembering the scene with Karl, Kevin frowned. "I finally spoke to Karl when he came to see Holly. He told me the same thing that I'd heard, how Brett started running after a porcupine. But I still can't believe it."

Alarmed at the news that Gunther had been so quick to be there for her daughter-in-law in light of what she knew about the "key club," Linda decided that if she were ever to get it off her chest, this would be the time. "I wish that they had never gotten involved with the dinner group. It seemed positive then, but lately rumors are going around about Karl and Holly. What are they going to say in light of how Brett died with only Karl there?"

Shaking his head, Kevin sighed, "I know. I love this town, but I'm not blind. People love to gossip and will make an issue of the rumors about Holly and Karl."

Turning to look at her husband, Linda said, "You sound as if there was truth in the rumors."

Reluctant to cause her more pain, Kevin knew that he needed to tell Linda about Holly. "Unfortunately, in this case the rumors you were hearing were based on fact. Remember the fishing trip we took last month?"

At Linda's nod, Kevin took a deep breath. "At noon the day our reservations were confirmed, I went to Brett's, hoping to share the news with him." Unaware of the harshness of his tone, Kevin continued, "No one seemed to be around. Hearing noises, I went upstairs to see if everything was all right and found Holly in bed with Karl."

Linda's eyes filled with pain as if she had been dealt a blow. Now that he had started, he needed to finish. "Holly saw me and if looks could kill, I would have been dead. Afterward I tried to talk to her. She told me that she wanted a divorce. She wouldn't even listen when I tried to tell her that all marriages go through rocky spots at one time or other and that she should try to work things out."

Her mind immediately making connections, Linda's shock was evident in her voice. "You don't think that Karl had anything to do with Brett's death, do you?"

Kevin replied, "I don't think so, but I just don't buy the idea of an accident. Brett was much too careful."

"There will be an investigation, won't there?"

"To some degree. All accidents are examined, but unless there is reason to doubt Karl's story, that will be the end of it." He hugged Linda tighter. "I promise you, I will not let this drop until we're satisfied with the results."

A silence fell over them as each processed the information. Stricken by the thought of losing contact with her grandchildren, Linda suddenly turned toward Kevin. "We can't do anything that will alienate Holly. Even though she told you she wanted a divorce, she is still the mother of Brett's children. If we drive her away, we also lose contact with the kids."

"Easy, honey, calm down. I won't do anything to jeopardize our relationship with the kids."

Appeased, Linda relaxed against his arm again, grateful for the warmth and support. She knew that her world would never be the same again, but how her life would continue was an enigma.

Concern Grows

Leaving the motel, the Captain decided they would eat at the Summit Inn before getting on Interstate 81. They had been surprised to learn how quickly the news of Conklin's death had traveled. Seated with the daily special, Rossi's attention had been drawn to where two troopers sat at the counter. Motioning to Paul, Rossi focused on the discussion taking place.

"I can't believe this. I talked to Conklin this afternoon about his defense for the sorry three sitting in Broome County Jail. The department in Elmira made itself accessible and he managed to connect a whole section of unknown factors to the murder case. He'd finally gotten enough information to try the case. Conklin was so conscientious. I'd bet he really didn't even like any of his clients, but he was really happy he had something to work with." The trooper shook his head. "I've known him for years and I can't believe he would be so careless."

The Captain processed the information he was hearing and came to a decision. Returning to South Carolina would have to wait until he was sure that Conklin hadn't shared his information with anyone else. He needed to be sure that the network he had established would be safe. "We can't head back yet. From what I hear"—he motioned toward the troopers with his head—"we can't be sure that Conklin didn't say anything. In fact you're going to pay the boys in the jail a visit to find out how much of a liability we may have. We can make sure that whoever replaces Conklin is ours, but I want to know how each of them reacts under pressure."

Eyes narrowing, Paul nodded. "I can go up tomorrow and check it out while you make calls."

Agreeing, Rossi returned his attention to his food. As far as he was concerned, the problem was momentarily resolved.

⁂

In his years as a doctor in Taylorville, he had never refused to help someone when they sought him out, so to hear the doorbell ring after hours wasn't unusual. Checking his watch, Jim Grace got up and walked to the door. It was almost ten o'clock, so he was surprised to find Darnell Harrison on his doorstep. It had to be important to bring him here at this time. In all the time both had practiced in Taylorville, this was the first time Jim could remember Harrison coming to his house. "Come on in, Darnell. There may be some coffee and if not, there's ice if you'd like something stronger."

"Thanks, Jim. I hope I won't have any other calls tonight, so a drink would be appropriate. It's been a long day."

Entering the Graces's living room, Darnell sat down to chat with Lila while Jim went to get ice. The basic chitchat was out of the way, so Lila left the men to talk. Smiling at Harrison and patting her husband's shoulder, she spoke in the tone of a conspirator, "I'm going to leave you two men to your devices and go get my beauty rest."

"All right, sweetheart." A smile adorned the older man's face as he got up. He kissed his wife on the cheek saying, "I shouldn't be too long."

"Goodnight, Darnell. I hope you get some rest tonight. I know it's been a hard day."

"Good night and thank you. I just need to take care of a few details with Jim." As he watched the old doctor accompany his wife to the foot of the stairs, Darnell wondered what it was that enabled some men to find happiness in a home situation and a life of sharing.

He had been married twice but his marriages had never given him the satisfaction that he had hoped to find. Was something lacking in him, or had he been attracted to the wrong type? Many nights he would have been happy to go home to the same kind of love and affection that he saw in the Grace household. Yet he had never had that feeling entering his own home.

"Well, now that my honey is off to bed, I guess we can sit down and talk. I assume that's what you're here for. Let me refresh your drink."

Darnell used the pause to collect his thoughts. "You were with me this afternoon when Gunther came in and told us about the accident." Darnell continued, "You know the situation we're going through at the clinic right now. New funding is essential to keep our standards up to par in renovating our equipment. Things are changing so rapidly with the world of computers that if we don't keep up, we're going to fail. That wouldn't be good for anyone. We can't afford to lose the funding or delay the new equipment and renovations to the building."

Darnell's demeanor was not one normally seen by those who surrounded him. He made no attempt to hide his distress and exhaustion from the other doctor. He knew Jim would understand.

"You were with me when Karl came in this afternoon. I'd like your honest opinion of what you felt."

Pursing his lips, Jim answered Harrison. "Knowing that Karl and Brett had a close friendship, I was rather surprised that he wasn't more upset. Even taking into consideration that he is a professional, something seemed off kilter. The victim wasn't a stranger, it was his best friend. Yet, other than the dizziness, there was no sign of grief or self-recrimination. Call it an old man's fancy, but I had a feeling that something was troubling him apart from Brett's death."

Nodding wearily, Darnell agreed. "I felt something was out of whack there too. It didn't seem normal to be so calm and cool. There was nothing wrong when I examined him. Truthfully, I didn't see the need for him to come to the hospital." At Grace's affirmative nod, he sighed. "I don't have to tell you, Jim, that I need what I say to you now to be held in strictest confidence."

Jim sat quietly, listening to Darnell and letting him continue to speak his thoughts out loud.

"About an hour after you left with Karl," continued Darnell, "we got a call from the EMTs that they were bringing in Ann Gunther."

Jim's eyebrows furrowed. "Why?"

"That was my reaction too. She had overdosed. She was taking Valium and sleeping pills, not sleeping well, sad and listless. Both were prescribed by Karl. Even if I hadn't known, I would have found out because Gerald Weir, the pharmacist, came to me accusing Darnell of abusing his pharmacy privileges."

Noting the other man's surprise, he looked directly into Jim's eyes. "We both know that in most doctors' families, medication is obviously very accessible whether through samples or prescriptions, so her having the pills isn't the issue. I don't think she had any inkling of Brett's death. What I am concerned about is with Karl involved in Conklin's death, the mere mention of the fact that his wife attempted to take her life will not help matters at all in the clinic negotiations."

"Knowing this town as well if not better than you do, Darnell, how do you plan to accomplish doing that?"

Darnell had been leaning forward with his drink held loosely between his hands. Now he gave the older man a shrewd glance. "Hopefully I can depend on your help, Jim. We have to establish that Brett Conklin's death was an accident, beyond any reasonable doubt." Pausing to emphasize his concern, Darnell continued, "Due to my involvement with Karl, it would be prudent if I did not sign the official autopsy report. Therefore, I'd like you to do the autopsy."

Jim now knew why Harrison had sought him out. Sipping on his drink, he looked closely at the younger man. Underlying the general fatigue was a tension that seemed excessive. Why was Darnell so stressed if everything seemed to be under control? Brett Conklin's death was sure to be the main topic of conversation long after the funeral. He had been an important piece in the intricate design of the town. His involvement had been extensive in the community and his presence would be missed. But that didn't explain Darnell Harrison's concern. Speculation would be rampant should it become known that Ann Gunther had tried to commit suicide on the day of Brett's death. Ann's overdose in itself would have been sufficient to set the local jaws flapping.

Jim realized that he hadn't heard the last of what Darnell had said. "What did you say? I guess I was trying to absorb all that you were throwing at me and kind of lost track."

Hiding his annoyance with the older man, Harrison summarized. "I was saying that there had been rumors as to a liaison between Holly and Karl a few months ago. Most may have forgotten all about it. But all it takes is one person. If anyone connects the dots, the whole situation will be front page news if the slightest hint about Ann gets out."

"I can see your point," said Jim, leaning back. "But I wonder why you think everything is going to get blown so far out of proportion."

"We're in the midst of trying to get the financing from the bank. Karl is the one who has been handling the bankers and was doing a good job at it. But an ounce of precaution is worth a pound of cure. I don't want to leave the clinic or its principles open to any unnecessary speculation."

"You know I wasn't Brett's doctor," said Grace, his voice reflecting his hesitation. "Kerr was. Accidents do happen but it's unlikely that Brett would run because of his back problems. Linda mentioned more than once how much trouble it gave him. You do know about that?"

"Yes," answered Darnell. "He came to see me last fall when Kerr was on vacation. But as I said, I want to try to disassociate myself from the situation because of the bank negotiations." Shrugging, he went on, "I know you agree that keeping the clinic up-to-date is important for the community. You've devoted your whole life to being here and taking care of the local population. I can't imagine you would leave their wellbeing up in the air if it were at all possible not to."

Jim was uneasy when he realized that Darnell had presented his argument in such a manner as to leave him with no option but to agree to examine the body. Sighing, he put down his glass, stood, and looked at Harrison. "Is there anything else that you want while we're at it?" Though said in a humorous tone, his comment failed to relieve the tension.

"No, I just want to know that I can count on you. The more rapidly all of this is over with, the happier I'll be. I'd appreciate you're taking care of this as soon as possible. Should you happen to find anything, don't hesitate to call me."

His mission completed, Harrison got up and the two men walked to the door, Darnell preceding Jim. As he crossed the threshold and stood on the front stoop, he turned to the older man and extended his hand. "Thanks, Jim. I wouldn't ask if it weren't necessary. But you also have the community's best interest at heart. I'll see you tomorrow."

As he closed the door behind Harrison, Grace thought that there was more behind Darnell's request than he knew. With a shrug, he filed the thought for later and proceeded to bed. Even though he understood why Harrison wanted him to perform the autopsy, Grace was not happy with it. Something about the situation didn't feel right and Jim Grace knew that his instincts were generally correct. Sighing as he shed his clothes, he got into bed and moved close to his soul mate of over thirty years, needing the soothing warmth of her body.

John Cummings agreed that the weekend would be rough. Would Kevin ever recover from this blow? He stretched to work out the kinks and returned to his notes. He brooded as to the most logical and concise way to describe the condition of the body. It normally wasn't hard for him to be objective. This time, he was having trouble distancing himself from the situation.

He wondered if he could find a way to word his report that would not cause more pain. Kevin wouldn't appreciate his using the word "careless" in the accident report. Suddenly it occurred to him that the best way to resolve his dilemma was to write the report as if he were interviewing Gunther.

Imagining that he was talking to Karl, John began to write. "These notes as to how the accident occurred are written based on an interview with Dr. Karl Gunther. They will appear in a question/answer format in order to make review easier." Satisfied that he had solved his problem, Cummings continued to write. It never occurred to him that what he was doing was totally unprofessional as he had neither seen nor spoken to Gunther.

After working for another forty minutes, John was finished. As he had decided not to sign the death certificate until after the autopsy, he packed up the papers, running through a mental checklist as he did so. He wouldn't have any problem if he needed an extra form. He would only have to go out to his garage, which was where he had been filing and storing the county pathology reports for years.

A beautiful day that Thursday dawned fresh and clear. Nature may have been oblivious to the dramatic changes that had occurred in the last twenty-four hours, but none of the people in Taylorville were that lucky.

Since six o'clock Sheriff Will Billings had been trying to find out as much as he could about Brett's death. He had spoken to the troopers, going so far as to visit the barracks to read the report Yorken had filed. He was bothered that everyone, including the troopers, were all accepting Gunther's version of what had happened.

Arriving at his own office just before eight, Will decided to talk to Gunther but was unable to reach him. To avoid wasting time, he tracked down the game wardens and drove over to Laurel Lake where they were stocking trout. Walking to their truck, he grinned. "This is a switch! Usually people get up early to fish. You guys get up to let the fish go."

Jerry Thorne was quick to cut to the chase. "But you're not here for the trout, are you, Will? I'd guess you'd be happier landing some information."

Billings nodded. "I couldn't believe it when I heard the news about Brett yesterday. From what I've heard, something just doesn't seem right."

"That's what I said," replied Thorne. "Nothing about Gunther's story makes sense."

At his partner's statement, Bob Elliott was quick to intercede. "Hang on a minute! You'd better be careful with what you're saying. What we think and the truth might be two different things."

"I know you two well enough to respect what you think, so let me have it. Why don't you think that Doctor Gunther's story is right?" asked Will.

Concerned that what they might say would alienate some of the political higher-ups that they were responsible to in the county, Elliott hesitated. "This is off the record, right?"

Sighing, as this wasn't the first time that political patronage had complicated his job, Will nodded.

Satisfied that Billings would not place him in an uncomfortable position with any of the local leaders, Elliott relaxed. "Jerry and I talked about it after we left Deer Run. Both of us knew Brett well. There are too many inconsistencies to convince me that it happened the way Gunther said it did." Elliott paused to let his partner take up the story.

"Two main points caught my attention," said Jerry picking up the thread. "First, Conklin had clay birds clutched in his hand. How could he have picked up the birds to throw if he entered the clearing on the run, as Gunther says? Also, unless death was instantaneous, wouldn't he have dropped the pigeons as he fell?"

Will fought to remain impartial as he processed what he had heard. Bob felt no need to sugarcoat what he was saying, and continued, "The stump that Conklin used for a seat while shooting appeared to have blood on it, yet the body was a good ten feet away when we saw it. The rifle wasn't even anywhere near Conklin's body! According to Russell, Gunther picked it up and smashed it against the tree when they got back to the clearing."

His attention riveted on Elliott, Will asked, "Gunther actually handled the gun after Conklin dropped it? He admits to holding it?"

"Yes. Stanger yet was what I found when the troopers asked me to unload the gun. The expended cartridge in the chamber was a number four load, while all the others were purple sevens. Why would Conklin have used a number four deer load with his experience?"

"I don't know." Will's consternation was obvious. "Didn't anyone ask Gunther about this? What were the troopers doing?"

His tone reflecting his scorn, Jerry answered, "Gunther went to the hospital because 'he didn't feel good' and the troopers were so green they manhandled all the evidence before I shot it on film. I took the pictures while Bob searched the area, but nothing seems to make sense. There's more going on than we're aware of." Frowning, Jerry asked, "What did Gunther tell you?"

"Nothing. I haven't been able to reach him. Between his rounds and caring for Ann, he's rather busy."

"What happened to Ann?"

"I guess it was a case of food poisoning. Anyway, she was rushed to the hospital last night." Checking his watch, he looked out over the placid lake. Things like violent death and food poisoning had no place in the serene outdoors picture. "Anything else you can tell me?"

At the negative nods from Elliott and Thorne, Will lifted his hand in farewell and got into his truck. As he drove back to town, he mulled over what he had learned. How had Conklin died?

Rossi had wanted to be as close as possible without entering Taylorville. Looking out the window of the shabby motel in New Milford, he was once again reminded of how little the area had to offer. But that's what made it so profitable for him. People were generally lazy. When they found that their lives seemed to be moving toward a dead end, they tried to change it in the easiest way possible. The rural low-income area had been perfect for their operation when the Greene kid had come up with the idea, but the simple logistical plan had become complicated.

The Captain had trained himself to carry all the material he needed in his mind. Anything written left tracks and he didn't want that. Moving to the door of the shoddy room, he breathed deeply. The clean air was probably the only thing of value in this place. While the Bendix plant was still operating at a profit, many of the other local businesses, including the iron foundry in Hallstead, had been shut down. Whether the people realized it or not, the area was slowly dying.

The railroad commuter service was a thing of the past and with its demise, the town lost its economic base, and with it anything not connected to agriculture. How Tony Russell had adapted after living in Jersey, he would never figure out. Maybe he considered himself a big important fish in a miniscule pond. But Tony had been able to convince himself that he was happy. It didn't really matter; as long as there was a market for his product, Rossi didn't care what the locals did.

Stepping back, Rossi again checked that he had left nothing to connect him to having been there. Convinced the room was clean, he walked out to the car as Paul approached from the office.

"I paid cash and asked if they'd be available tonight if we were back this way. You want to go to the next exit for breakfast, or can we go back to the Summit?"

"I think we can risk the Summit Inn as long as we stick to the story that we were only here for the night. Let's drive over."

Speaking only after the bright-eyed waitress had taken their order, Rossi was explicit about what he wanted to accomplish. "Drive me to Taylorville and leave me at the Stables. I'll be meeting with Craig Benjamin from Bendix to see what he knows about Conklin." As Paul nodded, the Captain continued, "You'll drive to the jail in Binghamton and see if you can get in to see those three idiots. What I'm looking for is danger signals, and they might be willing to talk."

"You really think they'd be so stupid?"

"Anything is possible and at this point quite probable. I'm beginning to think that Louie wasn't mistaken when he described the locals as ridge runners." Leaning back, he signaled for more coffee. "I don't want to leave any loose ends." He waited for the waitress to leave. "So, first stop is the Stables. I'll also call Tony, he should know something." Writing down a number on the napkin in front of him, he gave the paper to Paul. "If I'm not at the Stables when you go through town, call me at Tony's."

On Thursday morning, Grace called Burton's and arranged to examine the body after morning office hours. Going through the hallway to his office, he continued to replay the meeting with Harrison. He could understand Darnell's need to distance himself from the situation but he did not get why neither Cummings nor Burton was doing the autopsy. He put the problem aside as he checked his appointments. For the moment he wouldn't have time to think about what lay ahead.

Later, satisfied with a good morning's work, Jim walked back to the house.Hearing the door open, Lila excused herself from

Will Billings and went into the kitchen. Intending to grab a sandwich before going over to Burton's, Jim found his wife waiting for him.

Her tone was apologetic as she said, "Sheriff Billings is waiting to talk to you."

Jim seemed to tire visibly as the smile disappeared from his face and he sat down. "Even though I agreed to perform the autopsy, it's difficult to believe that Brett is dead. I'm sorry now that I said I'd do it. I had forgotten how many details are involved when there is an accident."

Lila smoothed her hand over his hair as if to ease his distress. "I know. I can't believe it either. But the world goes on." Squeezing his shoulder, she said, "I'll fix you a sandwich and you can eat while you talk to Will. I'll go get him."

Nodding, Jim went to clean up. He decided that if he answered Will's questions quickly, he would still be able to get to Burton's on time and only be fifteen minutes late for afternoon hours. More in control, he walked back to the kitchen.

Seated with a cup of coffee, Will was apologetic. "Sorry to interrupt your lunch, Doc, but I want to get everything wrapped up as soon as possible."

"I understand. It's better to get things out of the way. How can I help you?"

"Can you tell me what happened from your examination of the body?"

"No, I can't, because I haven't done the autopsy yet."

Taken aback by the doctor's answer, Will just stared at him, momentarily speechless.

Nodding, Will was quick to turn the situation to his advantage. "Would you mind if I went over with you while you do it? The sooner I have the report the better."

"I guess it can't hurt. Just let me finish my sandwich."

Jim Walsh drove toward the Conklin house, needing to know that Kevin and Linda were all right, if you could put it that way. As if losing Brett wasn't bad enough, rumors were spreading like shock waves, reaching out to encompass more people with each passing hour. The sleepy county seat had never been in such an uproar and suddenly everyone had to give opinions on something or someone.

That's why he had decided to use Tim Reeves as a sounding board. The district attorney from Colorado had enough experience to be able to distance himself from what was happening to be objective. Jim hoped that maybe Tim would be able to make sense out of the situation. He saw Tim's wife, Darlene, wave through the window. "Good morning. You're just in time for coffee."

Smiling back, Jim took the cup. "I never seem to get going until after the second cup. Even when I milked cows, I took a thermos to the barn." Surprised that no one else was in the room, Jim asked, "Kevin not up yet?"

"Oh, he's up. Tim decided that Kevin would be better off with business as usual. They left for the office a while ago."

"Linda any better?"

"She'll never get over losing Brett, but she's more concerned about Holly's being so distant. She'd like to see the children but doesn't want to ask. Give it time and she'll snap out of it."

Nodding, Jim stood, setting his cup on the table. "Well, I guess I'd better go to work. Time may have stopped for us, but the rest of the world is rolling along."

No Simple Answer

Leaving the Captain at the Stables, Paul drove toward the Broome County Jail. He was surprised by the Captain's continued concern for he knew that he had covered his tracks. Double checking on the status of the trio in lockup was understandable. Even pros sometimes got nervous and said more than they should, and these three were no pros.

Watching the coeds walk up the grassy knoll of the community college campus, Paul thought it ironic that more than one of the county's guests was forced to look out at the "jail bait" while already locked up for some related crime.

Approaching the information desk, Paul was hard pressed to keep a low profile. If there was any group he detested more than the city cops, it was the county cowboys.

Looking up from the log he was completing, the corporal on duty asked, "Can I help you?"

"I've come to see my cousin, Charlie Coombs. I drove from South Carolina 'cuz his mama asked me to find out how he is.

"I need some form of identification."

"My license okay?"

"That'll do."

As he handed over the license, Paul wondered if this was a mere formality or whether the police had mounted surveillance on the trio, expecting trouble. Though he had various licenses he could hand over, he would not necessarily know which cop would be behind the desk should he need to come back.

Not looking up from where he was copying the information off the license, the deputy motioned with his pen toward a bank of lockers as he spoke. "Leave all your personal belongings in one of those and come back here."

As Paul stepped toward the desk, the trooper motioned him to the side and directed him to lift his arms, patting him down gently. Satisfied, he spoke into the intercom. "Bring Coombs up to the visiting room. His cousin is here to see him."

Entering the drab room, Charlie was careful not to let his surprise show. He had no idea who the man was, but he wasn't one of his cousins. Taking the hand Paul extended, he sat down and waited for the other man to take the lead.

When the guard had retreated to the corner, Paul wasted no time. "You're smart enough to know who I represent. Just keep nodding every now and then. That cowboy won't pay us any attention." Paul looked to make sure that the guard wasn't listening, and his tone became assured and commanding.

"You boys are in deep shit." The statement was obvious in Coombs eyes, as he nodded as instructed. "The lawyer who was defending you had an accident. It's going to take a little longer to work things out."

"Ya'll ain't plannin' on hangin' us out to dry, are ya?"

Eyes narrowing at Coombs unexpected initiative, Paul shook his head. "No, but we've got to know what we can count on, what kind of damage there may be. With the Ponte family moving into the area and setting up operations at the college, the heat keeps getting worse. My people don't like foul-ups. They won't tolerate any more. It was really stupid to ice that dude." Pausing, he waited for a comment from Coombs.

"Yeah, it was. But there's no holding JR when he gets wired. I couldn't stop him."

"What about Meeks?"

"He didn't have anything to do with it. Fact is, he kept begging off and didn't want to go, but JR insisted." Looking at Paul to make sure that the other understood his meaning, Charlie continued, "He's a wreck, throwing up and crying all the time. He won't last if he's sentenced to the pen."

"Does he know anything?"

Nodding, Charlie clarified. "I don't know how much, but he knows all the local players. He was the main contact for the high school."

"Will he keep quiet?"

Shrugging, Charlie looked Paul in the eyes. "I wouldn't bet my life on it."

❋

The Captain trusted Paul but still played things close to his chest. Walking toward the door, he waited until the car was headed down the road, then crossing the parking lot, opened the door and got into the late-model Cadillac parked at the far end.

As he put the car in gear and began speaking, Darnell Harrison's tone did little to disguise the annoyance he felt. "You couldn't have waited until I was finished with the rounds at the clinic, could you?"

His lip curling in a derisive smile at the other man's obvious pique, Rossi answered, "Seems to me that when you wanted the money to finance your hospital you couldn't wait to see me. Must be you don't need anything now or you'd be friendlier."

Suddenly aware that the answer to his current dilemma might have unwittingly presented itself, Harrison was quick to make amends. Knowing that Rossi generally had someone meet him when he was done, he said, "Anywhere in particular you'd like to go?"

"Actually there is. Let's drive over toward Silver Lake. I want to take a look at an Inn I heard about."

Eager to ensure the other man's future support, Darnell spoke sincerely. "These last forty-eight hours have been hell."

Surprised at the relief he felt at having someone he could talk to, Darnell proceeded to tell Rossi about Brett's death, Gunther's involvement, and Ann Gunther's suicide attempt, including what he assumed had driven her to it.

Keeping his expression neutral, Rossi commented wryly, "I can see why you might be a little edgy, but it doesn't seem that drastic. Is this Gunther man enough to make it through this?"

"I certainly hope so. He's already had problems since I brought him here from New Mexico." At the other man's raised eyebrows, Darnell went on. "A few months ago, the man who's run the pharmacy for us for years insisted that Gunther was abusing his privileges. When you add to that the rumor about his having an affair with Conklin's wife, and that he was with Conklin when he died, it doesn't look pretty. To make matters worse, he's the one who's been handling the negotiations with the banks."

Filing the information away for future reference, Rossi nodded. "I guess I can understand why you're irritable."

Nodding, Darnell asked, "So what was so important that it couldn't wait?"

"You know the organization I represent?"

A feeling of dread washing over him, Darnell nodded. Though they hadn't approached him recently, at one time he had been asked to give them checks in exchange for cash with which he paid the payroll. At the time it had caused raised eyebrows when he didn't make his usual withdrawals from the bank.

"Their interests have been expanding and they wanted to know if you'd heard anything regarding the case that Brett Conklin was working on in New York State."

Relieved, Darnell answered quickly, "No. I really had no personal dealings with Conklin. Gunther is the one he was friendly with."

Nodding, Rossi pursed his lips as he spoke. "I see. And Gunther is the doctor who works with you?"

"Yes."

"Well, I'd appreciate anything you can find out for me." Noticing that they were approaching the lake, fairly close to

Russell's house, Rossi checked his watch. "Pull over. It's nice out and I think I'll walk the rest of the way."

Stopping the car, Darnell said, "You sure you don't want me to drop you off?"

Rossi smiled, sure that the other man wouldn't understand. "No, I won't hold you up anymore."

Dr. Grace arrived at the funeral home at about 12:45 with Will Billings. Burton was surprised to see the sheriff but shook hands and led the way to the workroom downstairs. As they reached the door to the preparation room, his eyes reflected the sadness that he felt. "Brett was so involved in everything related to the town that I don't think that there is anyone who isn't going to miss him."

"I know what you mean." Standing and looking at the corpse sadly, Jim Grace was once again struck by the oddity of the situation. "I didn't know Brett himself all that well, but I do know the family. His passing is going to take a long time for people to adjust to. It always seems more difficult when death takes either a child or a person in their prime."

Looking around, Will decided to place himself on the other side of the table so that he would be able to see what the doctor was doing. "I guess I'll stay over here so that I'm not in your way."

As he had to meet a client, Burton spoke hurriedly. "John and I went ahead and embalmed this morning, so you won't have any problem with bleeding."

Taken aback at the funeral director's comment, Will queried, "Isn't the embalming usually done after the autopsy?"

"In most cases we don't have to worry about any autopsy. Besides, we have Dr. Gunther's explanation as to what happened." At the sound of the doorbell, Burton excused himself. "I had scheduled a slot to discuss burial arrangements with Jim

Brown's son and couldn't catch him to change the time. I know you'll be all right, but if you need anything, holler."

Nodding, Grace removed his jacket and placed it over the chair arm. *How odd,* he thought. *They must be pretty sure that the cause of death was the bullet wound. If not, embalming could considerably alter the findings.* Shrugging, he turned to the table to make sure that he had all the tools he needed. In preparation for the autopsy, Burton had removed the clothing. His first sight of the body made it even more difficult for Grace to believe that the man before him was dead. The only violation of the body was the entry wound, a contained hole about an inch in diameter almost not worthy of consideration as the cause of death.

Knowing the kind of havoc that bullet wounds caused, Grace observed that where the bullet had entered the body made it impossible to have missed the heart. He concluded that the major damage would have to have been to that organ.

The doctor's reluctance was obvious to Will, who asked, "Are you all right, Doc?"

Turning to the sheriff, Jim said, "As well as I can be, knowing that this boy is dead." As soon as he began the well-known but seldom-practiced procedure, his professionalism took over and he was able to view his work objectively. To help order his thoughts, as well as to inform Billings of what he was seeing, he kept up a running commentary of his findings.

He was surprised at the absence of powder burns, pointing out that it was unusual. In all the cases he had dealt with involving a contact gun wound, powder burns were always in evidence. Billings concurred from his own experience.

Corroborating his assumption of death caused by the gunshot, Grace noted that the close charge had removed half of the heart. He also made note of the various pellets that had penetrated the chest cavity and removed a plastic shotgun wad from the posterior portion of the left chest wall.

From what he knew about the accident and the request from Darnell Harrison, Grace decided that the most expedient way to handle the report would be to expand on what he already knew. Thus he listed that the shot entered to the left of Conklin's sternum with a subsequent trajectory to the left and downward through the heart and the left lung. He concluded that his findings concurred with the accidental death reported by Karl Gunther.

As he explained his findings, Will listened without saying anything. After Grace finished, he asked two questions. "Doc, are you sure that Gunther knows what he's talking about? That the death couldn't have been intentional?

"Of course I'm sure. He's a doctor."

Satisfied that he had done his best for Harrison and his town, Grace left the funeral home shortly after 1:30. He was back in his office for afternoon hours.

Kevin waited for the calm to descend as he stood outside his back door late Thursday night. His gaze roaming around the familiar scene, he noticed that the wire cage was now complete around the base of the dogwood tree. Had it been only yesterday that Jim had come to take him to Deer Run? Had it really been little more than a day since his life had changed forever?

He felt as if he were spinning at high speed only to come to a screeching halt as he and Linda dealt with the unwanted details and mindless chores thrust so mercilessly upon them by fate. As busy as they were, constantly surrounded by friends and neighbors, the surreal feeling of preparing to bury their only child was ever present, bringing them up short without warning time and time again.

Linda had suggested that they take on the brunt of the funeral preparations in hopes of opening the door to a better future relationship with Holly. They consulted Holly about everything, but they were the ones who moved forward, giving her time to acclimate to dealing with the children without Brett. While he had to admire his wife's sound thinking, Kevin truly doubted that it would be that easy to smooth over the animosity which Holly had made so obvious. She had accepted his comfort and help but still maintained a wary distance. He didn't know if time would change this.

Turning, Kevin moved toward the kitchen and unconsciously smiled as he saw yet another plate of saran-wrapped cookies on the counter. Kevin and Linda found their wonderful friends and family a blessing. The support made getting through each day possible. Both of them were grateful that Tim and Darlene were staying at the house. Having them there made it easier simply by focusing their attention on something other than the absurdity of Brett's death. Tim and Dar had cried unashamed with them when they had arrived, and since then they had been willing sounding boards as well as doing anything and everything that needed attention, from taking Brett's clothes to Burton's to vacuuming the house. Cooking wasn't necessary for a steady stream of casseroles had filled the refrigerator. They had enough baked goods to feed an army as well-meaning neighbors and friends had inundated their house, as well as Holly's, with food.

The viewing was scheduled for Saturday in order to give the relatives who wanted to attend a chance to be there. He had no idea of how he was supposed to cope with their grief, as he had not yet found a way to deal with his own. There would also be a private viewing for the immediate family on Friday. Fortunately, Linda would be spared of seeing Brett as he had, but her pain was already acute and he hoped he would be strong enough to help her through the ordeal. The funeral itself would be on Sunday after church, followed by a luncheon for family and friends at the Legion. As he unconsciously ran down his mental list, he only hoped he would make it through the next few days without falling apart.

Linda knew Kevin had gotten up and gone downstairs in an effort not to wake her. As she lay there breathing evenly, her body was so pain-racked that she felt as if each nerve ending were screaming to have the contact it would never have again. Never again would Brett's lips affectionately brush her cheek as he came smiling through the kitchen door. Nor would she feel the warmth of his body hugging her at the holidays or birthdays or for no reason other than she was his mother. Her hands seemed to tingle with the need to brush errant hair out of his eyes and feel the solid muscle as she laid her hand on his shoulder. But none of this would ever happen again.

The pills Dr. Grace had given her had helped to numb the sensations but she hadn't been able to escape into the oblivion of sleep. Now alone, Linda gave herself up to feeling the pain wash over her in relentless waves. She stared unseeing as her thoughts kept her from sleep. She had been shocked when Kevin told her about finding Holly in bed with Karl. Being pragmatic, she realized that if they were to continue to have any future relationship with their daughter-in-law and the children, she would have to accept it and let it rest.

How could this have happened? Kevin had just been talking about how when he reached the right age he would teach his grandson how to manage himself in the woods and around firearms, just as he had taught his son. He had taught Brett well and he never went into the woods unprepared. Since his back had been bothering him, he had turned to shooting pigeons instead of the more strenuous hunting that required being in the woods walking. Why had he chased a porcupine? They never hunted those!

Her thoughts chasing each other, Linda knew that they would never have the answers to these questions. Regardless of what he told them, they would not be able to believe Karl Gunther. Though she hadn't seen him since well before Brett's death, she sensed that Karl was covering up something from what Kevin had told her. But what? She had no idea. She was just as sure that he would never have killed Brett intentionally, so what had really happened? It was at that moment that she reaffirmed that they would not let the investigation be closed without an in-depth analysis of all the evidence.

Looking in the mirror, Holly had trouble recognizing herself. What had happened to the happy-go-lucky smile? Had it been replaced forever by the worried wrinkles which she now saw? Her mood seemed to swing as often as the pendulum on the grandfather clock that had belonged to Brett's grandmother. In spite of taking the tranquilizers that Dr. Harrison had prescribed, she knew that feeling as she did, without them she couldn't function.

One moment she was frightened. What was going to happen if anyone thought to investigate Brett's death more thoroughly? The next instant she was furious with everyone, especially Karl. What if they found her prints on the gun? How was she to explain being in the woods? Would they accept that she really hadn't meant to kill Brett and that his death had been accidental?

How typical, she thought. One of her major complaints with Brett was that she felt neglected. Now, because he had been issued an ultimatum from Harrison, Karl had limited their contact to several hurried phone calls and she had not seen him yesterday or today.

When it wasn't fear or anger, guilt seemed to surround her as she suddenly thought of how her children would never see their father again and how she would probably end up separating them from their grandparents as well. It wasn't fair! Instead of things having been simplified by Karl and Brett talking as she had planned, Brett now lay dead and she was no closer to being with Karl than before.

Sighing, her attention was drawn to the ringing of the phone. Crossing the room, she grabbed the receiver, counting mentally to six to compose herself and find the right tone as she said, "Hello?"

Lying in bed with his wife in his arms, Tim still found it hard to believe that they were here, a place they loved, under these circumstances. He had known that it wasn't going to be easy when he got the phone call from Jim Walsh on Wednesday evening, but something other than the grieving of his friends was complicating the situation for him. His sixth sense was telling him that there were underlying factors that he didn't understand. That worried him, for all too often his intuition proved to be correct. It was one of the reasons he was successful as district attorney.

His brow furrowed unconsciously as he mentally ran down the information he had been given concerning Brett's death. As he reviewed it once again, it still didn't make sense. But why would Gunther lie? He and Brett had been friends for years. While he didn't believe that they were as close as he was with Kevin, there was no doubt that they truly cared about and respected each other. Moreover, given the friendship, why hadn't Gunther been more visible around Kevin's house that day? He had heard something about Ann Gunther being rushed to the hospital, but that really wasn't a sufficient explanation for his absence. Ann and Karl had even traveled out west on a vacation with Brett and Holly, visiting Tim's family in Boulder. So why hadn't Karl at least called to tell Linda and Kevin how Ann was doing?

None of this made any sense. As he lay there, Tim's organized mind began to balk at the facts strung out as if they were unconnected rays in space. Somewhere there had to be a center where they would all connect.

"Are you still awake?"

Brushing his lips across his wife's forehead, Tim nodded. "I just can't make sense of anything that I've been told, especially not how Brett died. You know how careful that boy always was. Since he was little you would have thought that it was hereditarily ingrained, the way he respected firearms. Besides, you remember the last time I talked to Brett, about ten days ago? I must have told you he was having trouble with his back again and hoped he wouldn't need another operation. Does that sound like someone who would be running through the woods?"

Sighing, Darlene said, "I really wish I had the answer. It might make it easier to help Linda and Kevin through this. But we're not going to be much use to them at all if we don't get some rest."

Spooning Tim's back, she effectively ended the conversation.

Regardless of where he turned, it seemed Will Billings met with opposition. No one seemed willing to question that something was wrong with the scenario of Conklin's death as scripted by Gunther. But he just wasn't about to accept the smooth explanation as readily as everyone else.

Even the district attorney was placing stones in his path. What Will didn't know was that DA Smalls was complying with a request from his friend Darnell Harrison. When Billings had gone to him complaining that he had not been able to interview Gunther, Ed Smalls had insisted that he hold off. Didn't anyone else see that the story just didn't make sense? Left with no alternative but to follow Smalls's orders, Billings had waited until Thursday to contact Gunther, only to have the doctor put him off.

Deciding that he might be able to shed more light on what had happened through the police, Friday morning Will went back to the state police barracks to take a look at Gunther's clothing.

"Morning, Sheriff. What can I do for you?"

"Good morning, Corporal. I need to take a look at the clothing that was brought in and tagged from the Conklin death."

"I'll be right back. Just let me see where they stored it in the evidence room."

Waiting for the trooper to return, Will thought that maybe he was going to be able to accomplish something. Forcing himself to relax, he again wondered why they had embalmed the body so quickly.

Returning to the front office, the trooper's brow was furrowed. "Sheriff, the only items marked as evidence are the rifle, the shotgun shells, and some casings. There doesn't seem to be anything else."

Frustrated beyond belief at the lack of proper procedure, Will was careful not to criticize his fellow law officers. "If the sergeant's here, maybe he can send someone out to pick up both Gunther's and Conklin's clothing. The clothes might be needed later."

Unappreciative of having anyone else treading on his turf or questioning how the barracks was conducting the investigation, the sergeant wasn't pleased at being called out to see the sheriff, and his attitude was reflected in the curt greeting he gave.

Nodding as he approached, he said, "Sheriff. What seems to be the problem?"

Inwardly groaning as he realized that he did not know the man in front of him, Billings tried to control his frustration. "Sergeant, I was asking whether anyone had been sent to collect the clothing in this case. In the event any question arises due to the nature of the death, it would be better if the clothing were in custody."

"Are you insinuating that we're not doing our job correctly?"

"No. I just want to make sure that all the evidence is available because there is some question as to exactly what happened."

Staring at Billings, the sergeant was silent, not wanting to relinquish authority. Finally, he said, "I'll have the matter looked into."

Not able to do any more, Will thanked him and left his frustration no less than it had been on his arrival. Later, when he entered his office, he found the first good piece of news since Conklin's death waiting for him. DA Smalls had called to tell him that Gunther would be available for an interview in the DA's office that afternoon. Not happy with the favoritism being shown Gunther at having the deposition taken in the DA's office rather than his own, Billings was nonetheless relieved that he would be able to speak to Gunther.

Driving up to the Stables to meet Gary Passmore on Saturday morning, Karl couldn't help but feel the need to have his friend accompany him to the meeting with Billings.

Not wanting to be overheard, Karl finally voiced his concern after they had ordered their food. "It seems as if Sheriff Billings doesn't believe me about what happened the day Brett died, or at least that's how it appears."

Passmore was shocked. "How's that possible? If you already told him that it was an accident, then he knows it was an accident."

Karl smiled at his friend's unconditional loyalty. "I guess that Billings doesn't 'feel right' about what happened. He asked District Attorney Smalls if he could question me, and I guess that Smalls decided it was better to cooperate, as there was nothing to hide." Waiting until their coffee had been served, he continued to speak. "Anyway, Ed Smalls called me yesterday and asked that I go over to his office so that Billings could question me. When I asked what for, he mentioned that it would appear more acceptable if I volunteered to answer the sheriff's questions than be subpoenaed to do so. I could really use some moral support."

"I wouldn't worry about it. I can't believe Billings really thinks that there is cause for an investigation. He's probably trying to cover his ass and needs to conduct the interview as part of the protocol. No one in his right mind would think that what happened was anything other than a tragic accident. If you'd like, I'll go over to Smalls's office with you."

Paying their bill, they got into Passmore's car and drove to the courthouse. As they entered and walked toward the DA's office, Gary said, "I guess I should wait for you out here."

Karl nodded. "This shouldn't take too long."

Seated behind Smalls's desk, Billings was more than a little annoyed at the favoritism shown to Gunther because he was one of the principals at Taylorville Hospital. Anyone else involved in a death case would have had to go to the police station. As he heard Gunther knock, Will looked over at Ellen Mann, the secretary/stenographer. "Are you ready? It looks as if he's here."

Gunther entered the office, nodding toward Ellen and then toward Billings. With only the three of them, the office seemed overcrowded. Sitting down, Gunther asked, "Is Smalls going to be here?"

"No. Should he be?" asked Billings brusquely, his irritation immediately obvious to Gunther. Turning to Ellen and receiving her nod, he began to speak. "You have the right to have an attorney present during the following interview. If you do not opt to have an attorney, I need you to sign this waiver of rights. Miss Mann will be a witness."

"I don't need an attorney, do I?" asked Karl. As Billings shook his head, Gunther pulled the waiver toward him and signed.

Billings consulted a note pad and then began to ask the normal questions relevant to a disposition as Ellen recorded the interview in shorthand.

"Is this necessary? You know where I live," Gunther stated, his attitude becoming negative.

"The law states that certain questions must form part of any statement. Just answer the question."

Taking a deep breath, Karl tried to stay calm. Several minutes later, his patience was again tried when Billings asked about whether he and Ann had vacationed with the Conklin family. Annoyed, Karl had to quell his first reaction that had been to point out that the question had nothing to do with Brett's death. Sensing that this was just the type of reaction Billings expected, he answered evenly, "Yes. On more than one occasion, my wife and I traveled with the Conklins."

"Were you involved with Patricia Conklin at that time?"

"Excuse me?"

"Were you involved with Mrs. Conklin when you went on vacation?" repeated Billings.

"I don't like your innuendo. If you mean were we all friends at the time we vacationed together, then yes, we were involved." As the sheriff continued to glare at him, Gunther decided that cooperation would be the fastest way to end the ordeal of the interview. "In fact, as you know, Brett and I were extremely close and discussed almost everything. At one point when I was disturbed about the situation at the clinic, I mentioned that perhaps the best solution would be to leave town. Brett stated that leaving town would be an act of cowardice. In fact, that was one of the topics that we discussed that afternoon. We also discussed the rumors that were going around that I was involved with Holly."

"So you admit that you and Mrs. Conklin were having an affair?"

His jaw clenched, Karl answered, "That's not what I said."

Aggravated by the young doctor's unflappable composure, Billings continued to look at him to gauge his reactions. Tapping his pen on the pad, he asked, "Are you sure that the issue being discussed wasn't that of your affair with Conklin's wife?"

Gunther's face turned red as anger surged. Afraid that he would end up punching Billings, he got up and walked to the window. When that failed to still his rage, he left the room, terminating the interview.

After Gunther's retreat, Billings sat for several minutes mentally reconstructing the interview. Before, he had questioned the doctor's statements as to the way the accident had occurred. Now he was sure that Gunther had been involved in Brett's death. The problem was how could he prove it? He would have to convince others that the doctor had been more than just an observer before he would receive support in further investigating Gunther.

Hesitant, Ellen decided to go. "Sheriff Billings?"

"Is there any particular way you want this interview transcribed?"

"Actually, I'd like it done up the same way that you would a court transcription, if it's possible. That way there's no question of who said what. By the way, I'll need six copies as soon as possible."

Gary Passmore was surprised to see that his friend was upset as he left the interview. "Is everything all right?"

"I really don't know," Karl answered morosely. "I don't know why Billings is determined to challenge my account of the accident, but that's what he's doing. I really think he'd arrest me if he could."

Shocked, Gary said, "You can't be serious. Everyone knows how close you and Brett were. That's ridiculous."

Not wanting to go into Billings's questions regarding Holly, Karl just shook his head. "It may be ridiculous, but that didn't make it any less annoying."

"So what are you going to do?"

"Nothing. We were the only ones in the woods and regardless of what he might think, the mighty sheriff can't change that."

The Viewing and the Funeral

The soft, gentle breeze brought the sweet smell of lilac as it caressed him. Kevin stood on the patio alone, questioning once again how life could continue to be beautiful as his son lay in a casket and he and his wife suffered. The private viewing had been difficult for all of them. Linda was now upstairs with Darlene. He heard Tim open the door and turned to accept the scotch offered by his friend. They had shared a drink on the patio many times over the years, but today the normally calming sensation was absent.

"I have a feeling that you need to talk things out, Kevin. Whatever it is that's bothering you won't go away until you confront it. I know you well enough to know that you haven't. I saw that same haunted look on your face when they told you to forget the pickup in North Korea. That look only disappeared once we were in the air against orders." Smiling wryly, Tim continued, "I couldn't say much because we were in the air and you'd made the decision on your own. Just as I was there for you then, you know I'm here for you now, whatever the problem may be."

Kevin's eyes filled with tears once again. "I just can't understand how I can be so blessed and cursed at the same time. This afternoon we stood around my son's coffin, Tim—his coffin!" His face twisted with anguish and his voice wavered as he tried to control it. "We were surrounded by the people we care about most and who knew and loved Brett. Where do I find an explanation? How do I accept it?"

"I'd be lying if I said that I knew. But I do know you well enough to know that something else is on your mind. I've always been able to read you like a book, and whatever it is, you'd feel better if you got it out in the open."

His shoulders slumping with the weight of his pain, Kevin shook his head. "Not tonight, Tim. You're right, something about the whole situation is nagging at me, but, honestly, I don't think I can deal with it at the moment." Looking at his friend with his heart in his eyes, Kevin asked for understanding. "What would I ever have done without you and Dar? I know she's upstairs with Linda right now and I only hope that Linda will finally let go. I thought she was going to collapse when we approached the casket today. Fortunately, Brett appeared peaceful so she managed to control herself. She's so strong for everyone. She always puts herself last."

"Dar and Linda are really close so if Linda needs to let go, Dar will know how to deal with it. Both of you have been putting on an amazing show consoling everyone else."

The light had begun to fade as the two men sat talking quietly, and now as the sky began to darken, Kevin's gaze was drawn to the ghostly splendor of the dogwood. "You know, I've tended each of the shrubs and trees in this yard with insect repellent, fertilizer, and even stakes to ensure straight growth and wire cages for protection. And they've thrived." Pausing, he thought about how to make his point. "We did the same thing with Brett and he thrived too."

"Nobody could ever doubt that. You, Linda, and Brett were always extremely close because of the way you raised him. You set an example and showed him how to follow it while giving him leeway to be his own person. Because of that you never had a harsh moment with him, unlike so many others I know. You can't possibly be feeling guilty about how you raised Brett." Tim's brow furrowed in concern.

"No, I guess I was just musing out loud. It's been a hell of a day and we need to find something to eat before we go to bed because tomorrow is going to be even more difficult."

Nodding his agreement, Tim finished the last of his whiskey and stood, stretching. "I'm even going to offer to cook, believe it or not."

His mood lightening, Kevin said, "Since all you have to do is open the refrigerator and choose one of the many dishes that everyone has been bringing, I guess it's safe. Come on, I'll set the table and then we'll see if our wives want to join us." Turning toward the door, Kevin looked over his shoulder, "Thanks."

The children had gone to bed right after supper, tired out by the day spent with Holly's mother who had tried to keep them continually occupied so that they would not ask for either their father or mother. Now that the house was finally quiet, Holly stood looking out the kitchen window, lost in thought. The big yellow lab lay at her feet, afraid to let her out of its sight. Even the dog was feeling the changes.

She was glad that she had been firm about not having the children see the body of their father at the private family viewing that afternoon. They were too young to understand the meaning of death and would only be more confused. When Tommy had asked where his daddy was, Holly had answered that God had needed him in heaven. Since he had been to church and Sunday school, Tommy had been accepting, though she was sure he still expected Brett to come home.

She didn't have to try hard to picture the anguish-filled faces of her in-laws and knew that next to their very visible grief she had seemed cold and detached. But then, that was how she felt. Though both Kevin and Linda had been effusive in their offering of support, Holly had been unwilling to get closer to them emotionally. As far as she was concerned, the only part of the Conklin family that interested her was her children.

The public viewing was not until Saturday, but the floral offerings from the many people who knew the Conklin family already surrounded the coffin and filled the two visitation rooms. Worried, Holly had approached the coffin hesitantly. While she was sorry that Brett was dead, her grief was more like that of an admired acquaintance than anything else. When she finally stopped to think about why she was uneasy, she was surprised to realize that anger was the predominant emotion that she was feeling.

If Kevin hadn't seen her with Karl, things wouldn't have become so complicated. If Brett had been willing to accept her leaving him, the accident wouldn't have happened. But Kevin had seen her and Brett was dead. Instead of things having been simplified, they were more complicated. Now when she needed his reassurance and support most, Karl was keeping his distance because Darnell Harrison had given him an ultimatum.

It was all so unfair. Keeping up the pretense of grief that everyone expected had been nerve-racking and she was exhausted. Tomorrow would be worse. People she had known all her life would surround her, trying to ease the pain that she wasn't feeling. How would she manage to get through the day? Sighing, she turned restlessly. She was too wound up to go to bed but couldn't concentrate on anything either.

The phone rang and, approaching quickly, she lifted the receiver, praying that it would be Karl. "Hello?"

Karl's concern was obvious as he spoke rapidly. "I only have a minute while Ann is in the shower, but I had to know that you were all right."

"I would have been better if you had called earlier." Her sarcastic tone of voice left no doubt as to Holly's mood. "Suddenly it seems as if instead of coming first, I come last."

"You know that's not true. It's just that things are so complicated at the moment that I have to take everything I do and every move I make into consideration."

Not satisfied with Karl's answer, Holly was silent. Didn't he realize how scared she was and how much she needed him at the moment?

As he listened to the silence, Karl shook his head in frustration. Now was not the time for Holly to act like a petulant child. All their plans for the future had become much more difficult with Brett's death. Softly, he said her name. "Holly? Sweetheart, you have to try to understand. Things will get better, but right now the last thing I want is for anyone to think that Brett's death did not happen the way I said it did. If there is any reason for them to renew the rumors about you and me, everything will only be more impossible." Listening for the shower, he continued, "I would give more than you know to be with you right now, but we have to be careful. The sooner all the commotion dies down, the sooner we'll be able to get on with our lives the way we planned. I love you."

"I'm so frightened and I feel so alone. I can't even sleep."

"Take one of the pills that Harrison left you and some warm milk." Hearing Ann's voice he said, "I have to go. I'll see you tomorrow. I love you."

Not satisfied but powerless to do anything, Holly hung up the phone.

In order to make sure that no one connected either Paul or himself with the area, they had moved on to the next town to stay for the night. Though the town of Great Bend was no bigger than the town of New Milford, at least the motel was in clear sight of the highway and that allowed both of them to rest easier. Walking out to the parking lot to wait for Paul, Rossi looked over toward the bridge that crossed the slow-moving Susquehanna River. Shaking his head, he mused at the slower pace of everything in the area, so unlike the bigger cities he was used to. Small wonder the death of Conklin and the upcoming trial of the three local boys was causing such a commotion.

The Captain had covered all bases and felt that things were under control, which was what he would tell the counselor after breakfast. Talking with Harrison the day before, he had been sure that there was no question of any connection between the family operation in the area and Conklin's death. Harrison possessed tunnel vision and could see no further than how anything would affect his plans for the hospital. His greatest concern had been to make sure that the hospital not be connected with Gunther and to feel Rossi out about possible funding.

His thoughts turning to Tony Russell, he was satisfied. Though Russell had been hesitant to get involved, he had said that he would make low-skey inquiries at the Bendix plant and in town to see if there appeared to be undue interest or speculation that they weren't aware of.

Paul had laid out the situation at the jail clearly and concisely. The potential problem was Meeks and that would also be taken care of. Approaching Rossi, Paul said, "I can't wait to get out of this hellhole."

Nodding his agreement, Rossi started walking toward the diner on the other side of the parking lot. "It's too small. Everyone knows everyone else and that makes it dangerous for us." Motioning toward the diner, "I'd take odds that someone will be discussing the Conklin 'accident.' So little happens here that it's big news when the neighbor's cat has kittens."

Grinning at his boss' description, Paul asked, "Are we clear to go back yet?"

"No. I decided to wait until after breakfast to call. When I speak with the counselor, we'll know what to do." Opening the door to the diner, he turned and looked at Paul over his shoulder as an unidentified voice said, "I don't understand how Conklin could have been so careless."

Later, wanting to be alone when he called, Rossi sent Paul to get gas. He dialed from memory and the phone was picked up on the second ring. "Don Anthony, this is Joseph," Rossi identified himself as "family" protocol dictated. "I wanted to let you know what was happening before we headed back."

"Is everything taken care of?"

"Yes. The situation at the jail is under control and I'll make sure that there isn't any liability left. Then we're heading south, unless you think otherwise."

"Have you heard anything about the Bonano family's operation in that area?"

Surprised, Rossi frowned as he answered. "I wasn't aware that they were operating here."

"Well, they are. It seems some of their clients got nervous with the death of the kid and decided to look for another source. They've been down in the city nosing around and that's how we know what's happening. It looks like they have the college in Binghamton pretty well sewn up." The man known as the power behind the throne continued, "That's not necessarily bad for us because it leaves us with someone to take the heat. What we don't want is for them to try to muscle in on the operation you've set up. Losing face wouldn't be good."

The counselor wanted reassurance. Rossi said, "I'll stick around and make sure that they're not nosing into our area, now that I know what to look for." Hanging up, Rossi stared up at the wall, only moving when Paul knocked. As Paul entered, the Captain gave his orders. "I want you to take care of Meeks." At the other's nod, he continued, "It seems Bonano's group is working close by. That's not necessarily bad, but it means we have to be sure of what's happening. While you go back to the jail, I'm going to make some calls. Tomorrow, just to be sure, we'll go to the funeral to make sure none of his crew is on hand. Then we head for home."

Taylorville was the county seat and also the site of the courthouse and jail, so after being Sherriff of Taylor County for fifteen years, Will Billings was acquainted with the majority of the leading families and business people. A caring human being, he often attended viewings and funerals as a matter of paying respect, but today was different. Nothing he had tried to accomplish since hearing about Conklin's death had been "normal." Gunther had been unavailable for questioning, the autopsy hadn't been performed until the next day, the coroner wasn't making any comment about the situation, Kevin and Linda weren't spending time with Holly, and the trooper's report lacked clarity and detail. Something was definitely wrong. He didn't know what, but he was certainly going to find out.

This was why his presence at the funeral home was twofold. He lamented the loss of Brett Conklin, whom he considered to be a fine individual, and wanted to show Kevin and Linda his support. But he also wanted to observe the actions of the supposed lovers.

As he stood listening to Jim Walsh, Will was very much aware of the actions and attitude of both Holly and Karl. It had been fleeting, but he had seen the caressing action of Gunther's hand when he had hugged her in the pose of paying his condolences. That had been with Ann by his side. Taking advantage of the opportunity to see if Ann Gunther mentioned anything about Deer Run, Will moved next to her and said, "I hope you're feeling better. I really didn't expect to see you here today."

"Oh, I'm all right and I wanted to pay my respects to Kevin and Linda." Glancing around, Ann found no escape from the sheriff's scrutiny and hoped he would accept her explanation. "I'm feeling much better than I was. I guess the toxins are all out of my system by now."

"It must have been a shock for your husband to find you in the hospital so soon after seeing his best friend die."

Stiffening at Billings's words and afraid of the direction in which his questions and comments were leading, Ann decided to terminate the conversation. "Excuse me?"

Will watched as Ann crossed the room to stand by her husband. Gunther had not lingered long with either Kevin or Linda, in itself surprising, for Kevin was often involved in whatever Brett was doing and had spent much time with the doctor. Moving back to where Jim Walsh was still standing, Will nodded toward Holly. "Guess Holly was pretty distraught over Brett's death, considering the fact that it was so sudden."

Shaking his head, Jim was pensive as he responded. "I don't really know how she felt because we all react differently. But, truthfully, my Susan seemed more upset than Holly did. Maybe Holly just couldn't accept it."

Will debated the wisdom of further trying to draw Walsh out on the subject. "I'm sure more than one of the locals will be all too eager to try and read more into the accident than what really happened."

"No doubt you're right. Not even death seems to deter the old biddies." Looking around slowly, he said, "So many of the people in this room have lived long and well. It's not that I wish any of them ill, but it just doesn't seem fair."

As Jim turned, a sudden rush of movement caught his attention at the same time as everyone suddenly stopped talking. Acting as if he was afraid to slow down, Austin Greene strode over to Holly and without excusing himself began to speak. "I want you to know that I'm sorry that things worked out the way they did. Your husband was a straight-up kind of guy and always willing to help, but we just wouldn't let him." Pausing only long enough to inhale, the overwrought young man continued, "None of us knew what would happen when we got involved. I really am sorry."

Puzzled as much by the appearance of Brett's partner's son as by what he said, Holly nodded, searching for something to say that would make sense. Her own emotions frazzled by the viewing and dealing with the people there, she imagined that the youth was having trouble dealing with the idea of death. "Yes, Brett always tried to treat everyone fairly and find equitable solutions for everything. None of us were prepared for the accident, but then, an accident is something which happens unexpectedly."

Looking at Holly, Austin wondered if she had understood what he had been referring to. It was one thing to justify the use and sale of drugs which he did admirably on a daily basis, but he had never anticipated anyone getting hurt as a result of his actions. While he really didn't know whether the Captain and Paul had anything to do with Conklin's death, it seemed too much of a coincidence. And that scared him. Nodding at Holly, he murmured the appropriate words as she thanked him for the lovely floral wreath and continued moving toward the door. He needed to get outside where his bag of white powder would give him peace and reassurance.

"Thank you. I can't believe it either." Shaking hands with Walter Stern, Kevin hoped he would be able to survive the next hour. Glancing toward the other side of the room, over the heads of the people who were filing quietly by the casket, he saw Linda speaking with yet another couple. She was white around the mouth and this was apparent to him in spite of the pallor that had replaced her normal rosy-cheeked look. But then, what did he expect?

Moving toward the door with his friend, Tim was quick to agree that Kevin needed a few minutes of fresh air. He had never been one to lie, and now, thinking that Kevin needed to begin to face what had happened so that he could go on with his life, spoke with a conviction born of experience. "When a life is lost in its prime, especially as the result of violence, it always seems senseless." His pain echoed in his voice, Tim continued, "How do you make sense of the death of seven three-year-olds who will never even see maturity? Their parents thought they were doing their best to keep them safe and happy by enrolling them in one of the most exclusive nursery schools in Boulder. Yet, they all died the same day because the jealous boyfriend of one of the teachers torched the building." His brow furrowed as he relived the horrifying day in his mind. "Each one of the parents wanted to know why. I had no more of an answer for them than I do for you."

Hands in his pockets, he turned to face Kevin. "I suppose every death is hard to accept for someone. When a person is very old or has been very ill, we are better able to digest the fact that they will no longer be around because we can say that they lived a full life or are no longer suffering. But regardless of the where or how, death is never easy to accept."

In spite of the warm sun heating the parking lot where they stood, a chill traveled down Kevin's back as he stood listening to his friend. He could empathize with what Tim had said, but it did little to ease his grief.

Walking out of the building, Jim Walsh was immediately drawn to the expression on Kevin's face. Anguish and pain were etched deeply, as if chiseled in stone. He wondered if he would ever see the other man smile readily as he had in the past. "The sun feels good. But then I never did like being indoors for long."

"You'll always be an old farmer at heart," Tim said with a smile. "No matter where you go or what you do, your first love will always be the land."

Nodding his agreement, Jim spoke pensively. "Life seemed to be much simpler when we lived on the farm. I never considered myself uninformed, but I have to admit that when we read about what was happening, like the drug problem in the suburbs and cities, Susan and I never thought that it would end up in this area." Continuing in order to draw Kevin's attention away from Brett, Jim asked, "Kevin, did you see the Greene boy just now?" At Kevin's negative response, he said, "He rushed in as if pursued by demons, spoke to Holly, and left again so quickly that no one could have stopped him if they wanted to. I wonder if he's on some kind of drug to make him act that strange."

His interest piqued by Jim's story, Tim asked, "Have you been having a lot of trouble with drugs in this area? I don't remember anyone ever mentioning it before. This area has always seemed to be the last bastion of true Americana, so I find it hard to equate drugs with Taylor County."

Finding a neutral topic easier to talk about, Kevin responded. "For the last few months we've been seeing a lot of drug-related incidents amongst the high school crowd. At one time, if there was unruly or unacceptable behavior we usually found drinking to be at the bottom of it. But lately that isn't the case. Just last month three young men were charged with the death of a fourth. The shooting was said to be drug-related because a deal went wrong. They're at the county jail because the body was in Pennsylvania when they found it. But the three are from Taylorville. In fact, Brett was defending them."

Nodding his head, Jim added, "Family doesn't seem to make a difference either. Some of the ones we're concerned about come from the town's best families. Like I said, the Greene boy was sure acting strange."

Sunday morning dawned clear and bright. As Kevin sat at the table with Tim watching Darlene make toast, he once again felt lost. A beautiful summer day was supposed to be filled with hope and promise. But what hope and promise could there be when you were getting ready to bury your child?

Taking his coffee cup, Kevin walked out onto the patio. Looking at the dogwood, he noticed that the tree was already beginning to lose its sparkle as the flowers wilted, their short lifespan having reached an end. His pain was visible in his posture, as his shoulders slumped under his unbearable burden.

His eyes following his friend as he left the room, Tim spoke softly, "I wish there was something I could do to take some of his pain away."

Answering over her shoulder as she buttered the toast, Darlene said, "I don't think that there is anything that could possibly make either Linda or Kevin feel better. That's the trouble with an accident or senseless violence. Some unwitting bystander is in the way and becomes an unplanned casualty while all those who surround him are hit with the fallout."

Going over to his wife, Tim kissed the nape of her neck. "I'm lucky that you understand. I'll check on Kevin while you look after Linda. Today isn't going to be easy."

Walking out to join his friend in the yard, Tim was silent, hoping that his presence would provide a measure of comfort.

Kevin began to speak softly. "I don't think that anyone is ever prepared for a death unless there had been a long-lasting sickness beforehand. But to have death enter your life in the form it has ours leaves you totally in the air. I can go through the motions of doing what needs to be done or saying what needs to be said, but it's like I'm watching someone else do it. I don't know how to deal with the feelings of anger and frustration I have because I have no outlet for them. So how can I possibly help Linda?"

His voice hoarse with his despair, Kevin turned to Tim, tears running down his cheeks. Putting his arm around his friend, Tim replied sadly, "I guess the best way to help her is to be honest with her and let her know how helpless, angry, and frustrated you feel, because she's feeling the same things. What neither of you needs to think is that you're letting the other down, because you're not." Hugging Kevin once again, Tim cleared his throat. "I think we'd better get going. Unfair as it seems, time does not stand still for anyone."

The protestant church on Grow Avenue was packed to overflowing. Those who had known Brett and the family had joined those who normally attended the church. The altar was full of flowers and people were standing in the aisles. As he looked out at the packed church with the people standing, Reverend Matthews made the decision to change his sermon and take advantage of the brotherhood in evidence.

Sitting in the front with Linda, Kevin was relieved that Matthews did not speak of God's goodness and the need to accept without question. The senseless death of his son had shaken his beliefs to their foundation.

Applauding the congregation for their compassion and care in the face of the tragedy, the reverend noted that the lending of a hand to another was something that should not be reserved for tragedies or bad moments. He reinforced the idea that support for others should be incorporated as part of each person's daily life.

Linda listened with her head bowed as Reverend Matthews invoked his congregation to try to be more giving in the future. Days before, she would have been the first to applaud his initiative as she had always lived that way, but now the effort seemed too much.

The procession from the church to the cemetery was a solid mass of moving humanity as almost everyone in town followed the family and the coffin on foot. The cemetery was four blocks from the funeral home, but the pallbearers had insisted that they wanted to carry the coffin rather than have it taken to the graveyard by the hearse.

Looking at Linda, Kevin squeezed her hand as they walked though. He could not say anything past the lump that now seemed to be lodged permanently in his throat. Returning his gaze to the tree-lined street, he was surprised to see the same white car with the Carolina plates that he had seen the morning when he had confronted Austin Greene. Someone had parked it slightly beyond the entrance to the cemetery. Glancing at it, Kevin wondered what it was doing there.

The look of those walking toward him told their own story. Tear stained and blotchy, they provided a vivid testimonial as to the important part Brett had played in so many lives and how much he would be missed. As people spread out along the gravesite, Will Billings was able to identify most of them. The family, immediate and distant, was gathered closest to the gravesite. Forming a circle around them were the friends and business associates. Further back, as if reluctant to get any closer was still a third group. It was in this group that seemed to hang back, that he spotted Darnell Harrison approaching with Ann and Karl Gunther.

As Harrison walked into the area, Will was surprised to see him raise his hand in recognition. Following the direction of Harrison's hand, Will saw a man standing almost hidden behind one of the last trees before the knoll. His brow furrowed in thought. Will wondered why the man appeared to be so reticent to be seen or take part in the funeral ritual.

He didn't recognize him and his interest was further heightened when he saw Tim watching the man with a frown.

Reverend Matthews called for testimonials and Will found his attention drawn to the people who were paying homage to Brett. Later, when he looked down toward the trees, the man was gone.

Rossi hadn't gone to the church. Spotting Tim Reeves walking down the street with Conklin, he had decided to maintain as low a profile as possible as the risk of being seen was too great. He chose the place where he stood for its proximity to the road as well as a clear view of the gravesite. The raw, hideous hole was tempered by the artificial carpet of grass that had been laid over the mound of dirt. The day was so beautiful that it seemed somehow obscene to be at a funeral. Choosing an unobtrusive spot where he could remain behind the trees, Rossi watched closely as the friends and family began to arrive.

Seeing Reeves added a new urgency to making sure that there was no possibility of the Rossi family being linked in any way to the Conklin death. A frown appeared on his face as his thoughts stayed with Reeves. The astute district attorney from Colorado had already begun to make inquiries into the players behind the drug scene in Colorado. While there had been no proof to date of any involvement by the Rossi family, the Captain knew that inquiries in both New Jersey and New Mexico had been made. Thus it was even more essential to avoid any tie to the distribution that was taking place in Broome and Taylor Counties. While no one else might realize the scope of the family involvement, there would be no doubt in Reeves's mind that it was all connected.

Paul had used his opportunity to perfection in casting the blame on the widow and the doctor. From what he had said, the young widow was not about to mention anything about what had happened in the woods because she believed that she was responsible for her husband's death. But Rossi had to be sure. He had found that the more simple the plan the better. In this case, counting Greene's son and the trio in the jail, there were too many players involved. Removing the threat represented by Brett Conklin would not have been a problem in any city, but it had become extremely complicated in this rural backwater.

Watching Holly walk up the slight incline to where the hole in the ground waited to swallow up the earthly remains of the unfortunate lawyer, Rossi was quick to see her tension. She was dry eyed and appeared irritated rather than grief stricken. As she reached the graveside, she turned to observe who was coming behind her as if looking for someone. Noticing her expression turn to one of disgust, the Captain followed her gaze to where the doctor was approaching with his wife.

He smiled to himself as he turned to walk away. He would be able to call and give a positive update on the situation. Now they could go home to South Carolina. Paul had been right. If the young widow and the doctor continued to act the way they were, no one would connect the family to what had taken place. During his second visit to the jail, Paul had made sure that Meeks would no longer be a problem.

At the door of Legion Post 1010, Linda stood next to Kevin, pale and drawn, shaking hands and kissing cheeks as people came to pay their respects to the family. She understood their lack of words. What could they say? It was only human nature that while they expressed their sorrow, deep down they were relieved that this time fate had seen fit to leave their loved ones alone.

Holly had not taken the children to either the service or the funeral but had them brought over to the Legion for the luncheon, knowing that they would not distinguish one gathering from another. Seeing her granddaughter eagerly talking to her brother as she spooned Jell-O into her flower-bud mouth, Linda's eyes lost their dazed look for a moment, and a small genuine smile touched her lips. For the little ones, the gathering was simply another party. They did not question the reason for a party but simply enjoyed it. She envied their innocence while hoping at the same time that it would continue.

"Sweetheart, you really need to keep up your strength. Can't you try to eat something?"

Her husband's concern breaking into her reverie, Linda placed her hand over his. "I'm all right. I was just watching the kids thinking how beautiful they are, how innocent."

Following his wife's gaze, Kevin focused on the children. Tommy would never know what it was to fish or walk the woods with his father. Janie would never again hear Brett tell her that she was the apple of his eye as he nuzzled her neck threatening to eat her. Turning his hand over to hold Linda's, Kevin spoke softly so that only his wife would hear. "It's them that we have to think of now. Regardless of how we feel about Holly and what happened, we have to look toward the future. We need to maintain contact with the children to make sure that they never forget their father. They are both a part of him and we don't want to risk losing them too."

Too Many Questions

Later, Linda found herself seated in the living area of the kitchen. Those closest to her hovered nearby to lend support, but all she wanted was to isolate herself in her bedroom. Hearing her name, Linda turned to look at Susan Walsh.

Concern evident, Susan said softly, "Sweetheart, I won't tell you to cheer up, because you can't be expected to do so. You have a right to hurt and need to feel the pain before the healing starts. But I do need you to know that the pain will change and become more tolerable."

Her attention on her old friend, Linda's eyes were bright with unshed tears. Susan continued, "You'll never stop missing Brett, none of us will. But memories will fill the empty place that seems so large now. Your memories and the love you give and receive will help to give you back your will to face the future. Time will help. You need to go forward to be there for your grandchildren. Only you and Kevin can help Holly make Brett a continuing part of their lives."

Sitting on Linda's other side, Darlene Reeves nodded. Picking up where Susan had left off, she said, "Your family has always been your first priority. Kevin will need you more than ever. He's feeling just as lost and confused as you are." As tears began to run down Linda's cheeks, Darlene took her hand. "Whenever you helped someone out of a situation like this you always reminded me that you could afford to be generous because 'There but for the grace of God go I.' Remember that like you've been there for others, we're here for you. I might be in Colorado, but I'm only a phone call away any time of the day or night."

Nodding their agreement, Linda's sister, Janet, and Susan answered in unison, "Me too."

For the first time since she had heard of her son's death, Linda felt relief as she cried with her friends. This time the tears seemed to ease her pain as she shared her sorrow with them. They sat with her, letting her cry, knowing that the heartrending sobs were the first step toward healing.

Kevin was standing a few feet from where Tim stood with Jim Walsh and Will Billings. Though he appeared to be staring at the dogwood, Tim doubted very much that Kevin was aware of his actions. Tim couldn't explain why he felt something wasn't right, but his gut feeling was that there was more to Brett's death than any of them knew. That was why he had asked Billings to return to Kevin's house with them.

Will had not been surprised by Tim's invitation. He had watched the man listen to and digest all the information people had volunteered throughout the weekend and knew that Reeves didn't buy Gunther's story any more than he did. Turning to face Billings, Jim stated, "I don't mean to be rude, Will, but I don't understand why Tim asked you to come back to the house. So do me a favor and tell me what that hell you two were talking about. I don't want to see Kevin any more upset."

"I have to go back to Colorado tomorrow." Sighing, Tim went on, "If I'm right, we need to map out a plan and there is no other time to do it." Looking at Billings, he continued, "Besides, time is not on our side."

As Billings nodded, Tim began to outline the reasons he was uncomfortable with the verdict of accidental death. "There are a few reasons why I find Brett's death hard to accept as 'accidental.' But right now I don't think Kevin is able to process the information that I want to share with you. After I tell you my thoughts and hear what you think, we'll ask for his input." Accepting the other men's silence as consent, Tim began to list his thoughts.

"First of all, Brett was just too good a sportsman to run through the woods with a loaded gun. Both of you know Kevin, and you know that from the time he was old enough to shoot a BB gun, Brett was taught how to handle a gun safely. Why, after all these years, would he suddenly run with a loaded gun? Next, I don't know if you knew, Will, but I'm sure that Jim knew that Brett had been having quite a bit of trouble with his back again."

At Tim's words, Jim nodded while Billings's brow furrowed in a frown. "Brett had to give up active hunting several years ago due to herniated disks and the pain they caused. He wasn't able to carry a gun for any distance nor could he walk for long distances without his back causing him tremendous pain. This being the case, how do you explain that he would suddenly take off after a porcupine, an animal he never even bothered hunting before?"

"Nor does Brett shooting himself with Gunther's gun make sense. He had his own, so why would he pick up Gunther's gun just before he started running? Doesn't it seem odd that Gunther smashed the gun against the tree once Russell was there to witness his actions? Maybe you can accept all this at face value, but I'm having a difficult time trying to see the logic."

"I agree. There are just too many coincidences," said Billings. "I wonder if that's where it ends." Pausing, he looked at the other two to gauge their reactions. "Did either of you read this morning's paper?" At the negative response, he continued, "It seems that one of the young men that Brett was representing in that drug-connected shooting was found dead in his cell last night."

Not overly surprised by Billings's news, Tim spoke pensively. "So that's why the Captain is this far north. I wondered when I saw the car with the South Carolina plates."

Perplexed and annoyed at his own confusion, Jim spoke peevishly. "What are you two talking about?"

"We've been working for over seventeen months trying to find a solid connection between the drug distribution in Boulder and the Rossi family." At the other's puzzled expression, he continued. "The Rossi family is one of the oldest crime families on the east coast. Over the last fifteen years they expanded what was a lucrative operation from the center city to the outlying areas of New Jersey and Pennsylvania. As soon as they began to spread the operation outward, they began looking for more direct means of obtaining the drugs. That's what led to their incursion into the western states. Being there let them operate with the direct sources over the Mexican border. It became easy for them to procure drugs, especially from Mexico by flying them into the remote little traveled areas of the state. We've developed quite a file on their operation and the principal players."

"How does that have anything to do with us here in Taylorville?" asked Jim, distress obvious in his tone of voice.

"One of the people we know to be involved with the Rossi family is Captain Joseph Rossi," continued Tim. "He was in Korea at the same time as Kevin and I. We saw him there on various occasions. Darnell Harrison was also there at the time we were. To my knowledge, Kevin hasn't had anything to do with Rossi at any time, but nonetheless, I recognized him standing on the knoll at the cemetery. Coincidence? Here he is, in Taylorville, just at the time that one of the accused being defended by Brett is killed in jail. Did he have anything to do with the death of Meeks? Maybe not, but my bet would be yes."

"The whole issue of drugs has become a growing problem throughout the country," interjected Billings. "But it seems to be much greater in the areas next to the Pennsylvania border. Both Taylorville as well as Little Meadows have had their share of incidents lately. What Tim says goes a long way toward explaining the strange white car with the South Carolina plates that's been around town lately."

Thinking out loud, Jim picked up the thread of Tim's idea. "Rossi is known to be involved with the drug trade and Meeks was arrested on a drug-related murder charge, so it makes sense that the two incidents are related. Rossi could feasibly be behind the influx of drugs into this area. But I don't see how this makes you leery of accepting Brett's death as an accident. You can't possibly think that Brett was involved with these people. Frankly, I can't picture Gunther being involved either."

Nodding, Tim spoke confidently. "I see that you can follow my line of reasoning. If I hadn't had all the experience that I have with how the most unlikely people end up involved in the strangest situations, I'd be inclined to agree with you. I don't have any proof, but something isn't right with this picture." Looking over to where Brett was still lost in thought, Tim shook his head. "We really need Kevin to focus on what we're discussing if we plan on making any headway. I know that he has his own ideas as to what happened and the events leading up to it. But I don't think that he's in any shape to deal with it just yet."

Suddenly feeling as if the chair had shifted underneath him, Jim shook his head in negation. "I can't believe that Gunther would kill Brett. They were best buddies." Suddenly directing himself to Tim, he said. "You don't think that Gunther has any connection to the drug group, do you?"

"It doesn't seem likely, but as I said, this kind of situation makes for strange bedfellows." Sighing, Reeves turned to the other two men once again. "Is it worth trying to get Kevin to listen to me? Right now I know he's not functioning the way he should be, but I'd like to get things set up before I leave. What do you think?"

"I agree with you," Billings raised his shoulders in apology to Jim. "Something's not right about Gunther's story. I don't know if he actually shot Brett or if he's covering up for some other reason. When you factor in the death of the kid that Brett was defending with the Rossi family, the whole situation becomes much more complicated." Pausing, he looked over at Kevin. "If Conklin isn't able to pursue this himself right now, I think that we owe it to him as his friends not to let it go."

Coming out of his reverie, Kevin turned and approached the other three. "You didn't wait for me before you started solving the world's problems?" Sitting down, his sad smile made his attempt at humor fall flat.

Smiling back, Tim replied in the same vein. "Hardly, far be it from me to try and undermine the mayor's authority." Becoming serious, he drew Kevin into the conversation. "Actually, we were just talking about the drug problem here in Taylorville. Believe it or not, there are certain similarities with what's happening here and what we've been experiencing in Boulder."

Knowing that he had Kevin's interest, Tim rapidly repeated what he had told Billings and Walsh about the information that they had been gathering on the operation of the Rossi family.

As Tim finished his narrative, Kevin turned to him with a puzzled look on his face. "I'm not sure why, but the name Rossi sounds familiar to me." Catching the glance that passed amongst the other three men, Kevin wondered out loud, "Or did I?"

Not sure of how to break the news, Tim decided on a forthright approach. "You've heard the name before. While we were in Korea, one of the officers in charge of supplying the troops was Captain Joseph Rossi. We met him one night when we ran into Darnell Harrison and then saw him several times later." His feelings about Rossi obvious in his tone, Reeves hesitated. "If you remember, no one was ever able to prove anything but Rossi was always able to get hold of surplus cigarettes, linens, and whatever else any of the MASH units needed. In fact, because of Rossi, Harrison's unit never lacked anything in the way of medical supplies."

Distracted from his own problems for the moment, Kevin leaned forward to pick up his glass. "Wasn't there some murmuring about missing drug supplies?"

Tim nodded. "Yes, but they never could prove anything."

"That's why the name sounded familiar to me."

"Right, but you may recently have read something about the Rossi family. Though they try to keep a low profile and avoid any mention of the family in the news, there have been articles over the last year. The Justice Department mentioned them in their profile on organized crime, though I don't know if you would have seen it."

Seeing that the other two were watching Kevin, Tim decided to take advantage of Kevin's interest. Trying to be casual, he broached the subject of the Captain. "Have you seen Captain Rossi at all since we returned from Korea?"

His brow raised in question, Kevin answered immediately, "No, why do you ask?"

"I thought I saw him standing by the tree at the cemetery this afternoon just before the service."

Wanting to add credibility to Tim's statement, Billings spoke rapidly. "That's why Tim asked me to come back to the house with you. He knew about the problems we've had with drugs in the area lately and wanted to make us aware of what he knew."

"Are you sure it was Rossi?" asked Kevin. "It's been a few years."

Smiling wryly, Tim answered, "He hasn't changed much. You know how finicky he always was about his appearance, how his uniform or clothes had to be just so. He's stayed in shape and his "style" makes him stand out here just as he did all those years ago. It was him."

Pausing, he looked around at the others before he spoke again. "We were talking about how the drug problem has augmented recently in this and neighboring counties. Seeing the Captain in the area made me wonder if the Rossi family wasn't involved in the distribution of product in this area. Also, Will told us that there was a story in today's paper about how one of the men that Brett was defending had been found hanging in his cell. A guy named Meeks."

At this piece of news, Kevin's head jerked up. "You think that Rossi may be involved with Meeks's death?"

"I really have no reason to link the two, other than that Brett was defending Meeks who was involved with drugs, and we know that the Rossi family is too. This might just be coincidence, but you know how I feel about that. It's been my experience that where there is smoke there is usually fire." Wanting to convince Kevin that there was reason to pursue a further investigation, Tim spoke persuasively.

"Nothing about Brett's death has been easy for me to accept. I know how hard this has been for you, but I think you're burying your head. I can understand you not wanting to accept that what happened wasn't an accident because the alternative is even worse. But there are too many things that just don't click. You and I both know what was going on with Holly and that makes Gunther's explanation even less credible. It's just too easy."

He sat mulling over what his friends had said and as they waited for his input, Kevin sighed. The anguish of what he was thinking was visible on his face, though the others had yet to hear what was causing his distress. If he made any more overt moves to question what Gunther had said, Kevin knew deep in his heart that action would cause a total alienation from Holly. He had promised Linda that they would stay on good terms with Holly for the sake of maintaining contact with the children. Could he go forward with any investigation without losing the children and breaking his promise to his wife?

His face a mirror of his concern and uncertainty, Kevin finally spoke. "I know you mean well. If I thought that there was even a remote possibility that Brett's death was linked to the Rossi drug distribution, I'd give you my blessing and even lead the investigation. But at the moment, the only explanation of what happened in the woods is that of Karl Gunther. Like it or not, I'm going to have to accept it."

Dumbstruck by Conklin's words, Billings asked, "Why, for God's sake? I'm here because I believe that an investigation should be conducted. How is it that you feel that you have to accept it?"

Tim knew immediately that Kevin was referring to Holly. Turning to Billings who was totally confused, he tried to explain.

"The rumors you've been hearing about Gunther and Holly are based on fact." Turning to apologize to Kevin who had winced visibly, Tim continued, "The problem is that now that Brett is dead, Holly will in all likelihood try to establish a more permanent relationship with Karl Gunther. If she does, Kevin and Linda's attitude toward him will undoubtedly play a part in how often they see the children."

Jim had been listening silently to the others. His heart went out to Kevin who seemed to have more burdens thrust upon him each minute. They needed to pursue the search for information without placing Kevin in an untenable position with Holly. "What if we do it without Kevin?"

"What do you mean, Jim?" asked Tim, not sure of where the other man was leading.

"Well, what would happen if Will continued to raise the question of doubt using his legal channels? After all, the sheriff would only be doing his duty."

"You're a wily old fox, aren't you?" smiled Tim. "I think you just might have thought of a viable compromise. And I'll help Will with all the information and resources I can from my end. You won't be breaking your promise to Jo, and maybe we can find out what really happened."

Gratitude and dread battled for first place as Kevin looked at his friends. He was lucky to have them and know that they cared so much. But could he live with what they might find out?

Kevin lay staring up at the ceiling thinking that he had never felt so tired, or drained in his life. Though he felt as if he didn't have anything left to give, knowing his wife lay next to him suffering silently, he forced himself to roll over and pull her against him, hoping that the warmth of their contact might help both of them.

Sighing deeply, Linda knew how painful it was to speak about a future, but they both needed to start the healing process and continue with their lives. Her voice was a shadow of itself as she finally spoke. "I feel so lost, I have no idea how to continue. How can we go back to living our normal lives when nothing will ever be normal again?"

His anguish intensified by his wife's hopeless tone, Kevin summoned every ounce of his remaining strength to answer her in a way she would find acceptable. "We've lost an important part of our life and nothing will ever take the place of our son. And I can't tell you that we'll ever stop missing him because I don't really believe we will. But what we have to do is concentrate on what we still have: each other and the children. We owe it to Brett to make sure that we spend as much time with them as possible."

Her voice mirroring her concern, Linda asked, "Are we going to be able to do that? You know how strangely Holly has been acting toward us over the last few months."

Not wanting to further worry his wife, Kevin decided that it was better that she know where they stood. "The reason that she's been acting so strangely is that she doesn't know how to act with us. If the relationship between Karl and Holly continues, we are going to have to accept the fact that Karl will play a large part in the lives of Janie and Tommy. We are going to have to deal with that, as painful as it may be, if we want to continue seeing the children."

Linda felt dizzy as the importance of what Kevin was saying hit her. "You mean that I have to prepare to see Karl filling the place that was Brett's."

"I don't like it any better than you do, but that is exactly what I'm saying. We have to go on with our lives and that will be one of the conditions that we will have to deal with." Holding her tighter, Kevin sighed. "It won't be easy, honey, but if we make the effort, I'm sure that Holly will respond positively."

Relaxing against Kevin's strong body, Linda didn't answer. She only hoped he was right.

"I'll be fine, Mom. I need to be alone and try to organize my thoughts." Leading her parents to the door, Holly continued, "I'll have to get used to being on my own at some point, so it might as well be now." Kissing her parents on the cheek, she ushered them the rest of the way out the door and, spent from the tension of the day, leaned against the frame as she watched them drive off. Thank God! Finally peace and quiet!

The past five days had taken their toll. Even her hair showed the strain to her nervous system, hanging limp and lifeless. Everyone just assumed that she was grieving and trying to cope with her husband's death. No one but Karl knew what she was really upset about, and she couldn't even talk to him! The irony of the situation suddenly became apparent. Brett was an even greater obstacle in death than he had been in life. Not even a week ago, Karl had agreed to speak to Brett about her divorce. They had been sure that by the weekend they would no longer be in a limbo. And now they were farther away from being together than they had ever been! The phone rang. Holly looked at the instrument, as if afraid of what she might hear when she picked up the receiver. "Hello?"

Alerted by Holly's dull, hesitant tone, Karl was quick to identify himself. "Sweetheart, it's me. I wanted to wait until you were alone before I called you. Can you talk?"

As she closed her eyes and hugged the receiver closer to her, emotion threatened to overwhelm her. "Yes Mom and Dad left about ten minutes ago. They meant well by offering, but I didn't want anyone to stay to help with the kids. I needed to be alone."

"You don't sound right. Do you have something to help you sleep?"

Her irritation showing, Holly answered, "No, I didn't take anything to sleep. How do you expect me to sound when things continue to get more and more confusing by the minute? Brett's death certainly didn't get me any closer to being with you, did it?"

"Calm down. I'd be there with you if I could, but it isn't prudent right now. We're going to have to take it slow."

"Why? Because Harrison says so?"

"Partly. I am a partner in the clinic so whatever I do reflects on the clinic as well. Besides, I don't plan on making you change how you live. You wouldn't want that and neither would I." Not getting an answer, he continued softly, "And the other reason is that I don't want anyone to talk about Brett being out of the way when we get together. If we move too quickly, there's sure to be talk."

Reluctant, but recognizing the logic of Karl's argument, Holly was silent as she tried to come to terms with what he had said. "I can't go on like this. I need you to be there for me. I'm scared and alone and I don't like either feeling."

"I know, I know. And I want nothing more than to be with you, but we have to be cautious. See if your mother will watch the children for a while tomorrow afternoon. We'll meet where we usually do and at least be able to talk." Hearing Ann call, he said, "I have to go. I'll see you tomorrow."

Staring at the phone, which had gone silent in her hand, Holly vowed that shortly no one would be able to tell her what to do or how to do it. She had let herself be guided first by her parents and then by Brett, and where had it gotten her? No one was going to keep her from being with Karl. Feeling better now that she had something concrete to focus on, she hung up the phone.

Why had the Captain been at the cemetery? To his knowledge he hadn't had contact at all with Kevin after he left the service, so what was he doing there? The question had been plaguing him since he had seen Rossi several hours before, and he was no closer to knowing the answer now than he had been then. His brow furrowed with concern, Darnell Harrison walked over to the sideboard and poured some scotch into a glass. The last thing he needed was an additional complication.

No one knew that he had acquired the necessary funding from the Rossi family when the original clinic had gone up. He remembered it so clearly that it seemed as if it were yesterday and not almost twenty-five years before. He had tried to work within the framework of the town and what the committee members thought should be done, but the truth was that Darnell considered the hospital project his and his alone and wasn't about to let them dictate his actions. Discussions had dragged on endlessly, first about the site and then later about how the hospital would be run. Fed up with the failure to get started, he had decided to find other sources to back his project.

It had been so simple. While agonizing over how he was going to acquire the monies he needed, he had suddenly remembered Joseph Rossi and how interested he had been in all of Darnell's plans. He had also thought about the knack that Rossi had for making things happen even in the godforsaken hellholes they had seen overseas. When Darnell contacted him, Rossi didn't let him down. He had arranged a loan at a ridiculously low rate of interest. It was only later that Darnell realized what a high price he had actually paid.

For the first five years there had only been sporadic contact between the two men. Rossi called once a month or every six weeks to see how things were going and to ask whether Harrison needed anything. Only later did the demands begin. First it was a request to buy linens and towels from a supplier who Rossi favored. Next it was pharmaceutical supplies, and finally the demand to issue checks in lieu of the cash which Rossi would give Darnell.

The first time the quantity had only been five thousand dollars and none of Darnell's suppliers had questioned the use of cash to pay the bills. Many of the rural families still avoided banking. But when Rossi's request was repeated over and over again, it finally dawned on Darnell that he was in all probability involved with something illegal. By then he was in too deep to get out.

Through prudent planning and adding Karl as a partner, Darnell had been able to refrain from going back to the Rossi family with any of his plans for the hospital, though he had no doubt that they would be more than happy to help him. He didn't want to be any more involved than he was.

Because of his monthly contact, the Captain knew the financial state of the hospital and was privy to the information that Darnell was seeking funding and where. Rossi figured that with Gunther being involved in the accidental death of Brett Conklin, Darnell would be caught short of funds if the investigation continued for any period of time. And unfortunately, Harrison realized that Rossi was right. Recognizing that Rossi would inevitably be involved in future negotiations; Darnell suddenly felt his whole body relax. As he felt the calm descend, he laughed sardonically. It was ironic that the solution to his dilemma lay in accepting help from the one source he was trying to avoid.

Cops and Crooks

As he left the Conklin house, Will felt better knowing that the men agreed with him. He understood Kevin's motives in not pushing to continue the investigation, but he was relieved that the others were not about to let it go. It had been decided that Reeves would continue to gather information on possible connections with the Rossi family through his extended network from Denver while Billings would try to get a handle on what had really happened at the site of the accident.

His relief was short-lived as he thought about how little cooperation he had gotten thus far. He wondered how hard he would have to fight to get support for what he wanted to do, which was interview Gunther.

For the remainder of the evening he continued to replay all that had happened and the various responses Conklin's death had elicited. Obviously, he wasn't alone in thinking that the scenario as described by Gunther was odd. Both of the game wardens, DA Tim Reeves and Jim Walsh, found the actions ascribed to Brett too far out of character to be feasible. There were too many details that just didn't click. Why was he still holding the clay pigeons? And why had Gunther bashed the gun against the tree?

Monday was June 7th. Having thought about the situation during the weekend, Billings decided to make a trip out to the state police barracks. He entered the building and sought out Lieutenant John Drann in hopes of using him as a sounding board. Their friendship included having worked together on various occasions, and each had a healthy respect for the other.

Taking a seat before John Drann's desk, Will sat back and took a deep breath before explaining the situation. Though Drann had not known Conklin personally, he had also heard rumors that had left him uneasy with the situation. Rocking back on his chair, Drann nodded solemnly. "Gunther was the only one out there other than Conklin, and being dead Conklin can't tell us anything. No one else seems to question Gunther's statement. What did you have in mind?"

"I think Gunther should take a lie detector test. He came in voluntarily to be questioned a couple of days ago. There shouldn't be a problem with his cooperating with us in taking the test. In fact, it would probably work best if a couple of the troopers were present when he did it to give the whole proceeding more of an everyday appearance. What do you think?"

"It sounds like it might work." Pausing as he thought about the legality, Drann was serious as he continued, "There has been no talk so far as to charging anyone with anything, so you'd be on shaky ground if he were to object. Because he hasn't been formally charged or booked for suspicion, you realize that you can't force him into taking the polygraph. It has to be voluntary. You don't have a leg to stand on if he refuses."

Rubbing his hand across his brow, Will answered, "I know, but I don't have anything else to go on either. This way I'll at least be able to judge his reaction to taking the test."

As he agreed that the sheriff should move as quickly as possible, Drann said, "I'll have Salinkas and Fekette assist you. Both of them know Gunther, and the request might seem more feasible to him if Gunther doesn't feel threatened or uncomfortable.

Upon being informed, the two troopers left to get the testing materials, arranging to leave with Billings so that they would all arrive together. Once in the hallway, Salinkas was grim as he walked next to Fekette. "I don't like this at all. They must think something's wrong with Gunther's account of the accident or we wouldn't be doing this."

"I know what you mean. I only know Conklin by reference so I couldn't really say whether the questions about what happened are logical or not. But the alternative is even worse. I don't want to believe that Gunther could have intentionally shot him."

God! His parents were stupid! No matter how ridiculous the story, they always believed him. It was beyond him how they could command respect from the people in this town, but then again, maybe it was understandable. When you lived in a pimple of a town at the end of the earth, even idiots became power mongers. Austin couldn't think of a better word to describe them. Because they believed themselves to be perfect, they had to believe that he was too. After all, he was their son.

As long as he told her that he had been sick, his mother would stand up to his father and argue for him. She never even asked what it was that made him sick. The last thing she would think of was drugs or alcohol. Not her Austin! Thinking about his father, his anger flared. Why the hell should he have to go to college just because the old man had gone? His father had lots of money, so why did he have to worry about making any of his own?

Having heard his father's car leave the driveway, Austin Greene decided that it was safe to go talk his mother or the maid into making him breakfast. Rapidly donning slacks and a polo shirt, he went down to the kitchen. Hearing his mother talking to one of the people of one of her never-ending committees, he served himself some juice and sat down at the table. Grabbing the Sunday paper, he began to idly skim the headlines. When he scanned the stories on the front page, a small two-column story at the bottom of the page captured his attention.

Murder Suspect Found Dead in Cell

Juice sloshed out of the glass as Austin's hand began to shake uncontrollably.

As she walked in checking a list she held in her hand, his mother said, "Good morning, Austin. How are you?" Not getting an answer, she glanced at him and was startled by his pallor. As the juice continued to spill out of the glass, she asked, "Austin, are you all right?"

Scared by what he had read, Austin dropped the glass.

"What's the matter? You look like death!" she said, placing her hand on his head to check for fever.

Pushing her hand away irritably, Austin rushed out of the house. His hand trembled as he tried to place the key in the ignition. Finally getting the car started, he pulled out and headed for Salt Springs. Reaching the refuge of the deserted parking lot, he laid his head back and tried to make sense of all that was happening. He certainly had not expected things to develop in this manner.

He had not intended to bring drugs to the high school and get so many kids into using them. But he had needed the money to support his own ever-growing habit and before he knew it, what had started as a means of simply supplying his own habit had turned into a full-fledged business. Only he was no longer in control.

He thought he had been so very smart, finding a new market for the people that Coombs had put him onto in South Carolina. And it was so easy! He was the son of a respected lawyer and one of the oldest families in the county. Who was going to think twice about his coming and going in this little hick town? No one would ever know that he was involved with drugs because he wasn't the one doing the selling, others took care of that.

His thoughts brought him back to what he had seen in the paper. Meeks was dead. He had known Tim since they were in grade school and if there was one thing he was sure of, it was that Tim was too much of a coward to kill anyone, let alone himself.

He was sure that Coombs was responsible for the death of the man that had landed the three of them in jail.

The timing of their arrest had been terrible. Captain Rossi had made his thoughts crystal clear when he spoke to Austin, and what he had implied had left the young Greene shaking. The people behind him didn't want any more trouble with their investment and, as Austin had suggested the venture, they considered it his responsibility to make sure that nothing else went wrong.

While Brett Conklin was handling the case for the three in the Broome County Jail, Austin had felt confident that everything was under control. He had heard Conklin talking one day and knew that he had planned to plea bargain for the three men. But that had been before Conklin had gone up to Elmira. When Brett had returned, he had been excited about having additional information. But Austin hadn't been able to find out what that information was.

Now both Meeks and Conklin were dead. Who was responsible? Why had they decided that it was important to get rid of Meeks? Who was to say that whoever had decided that Meeks presented a liability might not have similar plans for him?

Austin was suddenly afraid. The Captain and the people he represented would listen, but only if they were about to hear something that would interest them. They weren't stupid.

Terrified at what might happen if they should come after him and with nothing to offer them, Austin decided to go to his father's office and find out what Brett had been so interested in. If needed, he would also go to the jail to talk to Coombs. But one thing was sure—he couldn't just sit there and wait for them to come after him.

Glad that he had refrained from smoking a joint, one less thing to worry about his father knowing, he ran his hand through his hair and headed back to town. Reaching the office, he entered and gave the secretary a big smile. Motioning toward his father's office, he said, "Is he in?"

Smiling back at Austin, the secretary answered, "Yes, he's reviewing the briefs that he needs for court this afternoon. I don't think he'd mind being interrupted."

Tapping the door, Austin opened it. Seeing his son, John smiled and waved him in. "Looking for money?"

"No, not this time." Austin grinned. "I actually need some advice."

Lifting his eyebrows, Greene sat back in his chair. "Shoot."

"I read in the paper that Tim Meeks was found dead in his cell." Trying not to appear worried, he continued, "You know that we went to school together and that we hung out once in a while."

Listening, John Greene simply nodded.

"I got to thinking about how Tim died. He wouldn't have taken his own life. But why would anyone else want him dead? What's going to happen to Charlie Coombs, since Brett's dead?"

"Don't worry about Meeks. Jail has a strange effect on some people, and some do commit suicide, though they haven't said that Meeks did. As far as Coombs goes, someone has retained a lawyer from out of state to represent him and Charlie, so they're taken care of. Quite honestly, I'm glad. With Brett's death, the backlog here is going to take a while to straighten out. I'm just as happy someone else is taking over. My office will turn over all pertinent records this week and that will be the end of it for us."

John Greene never realized that Austin's hand had started shaking with the mention of out-of-state lawyers.

Leaving his father's office, Austin only hoped that the end of the problem for the firm wouldn't be the beginning of a bigger problem for him.

Wanting to avoid attention, Billings spoke quietly to the hospital receptionist. "I'd like to speak to Dr. Gunther. Can we wait in his office until he's available?"

Uneasy at the sight of the troopers and attention they were receiving, she ushered them into the office. "I'll see that the doctor comes in as soon as he's finished with the patient he's seeing."

Knowing that he would be incensed if he weren't notified, after informing Gunther, she immediately buzzed Dr. Harrison. "Doctor, the sheriff is here with two troopers to see Dr. Gunther. They're waiting in his office."

As he replaced the receiver, Harrison seethed. Just what he needed, visits from the police. This was really going to look good for acquiring funding. "Hold all my calls." Opening the door to Gunther's office, Harrison nodded at the three law-enforcement officials. "Gentlemen. What can we do for you?"

Salinkas and Fekette were silent, letting Billings direct the operation. "We wanted to speak to Karl Gunther, Dr. Harrison."

"Is there something I can help you with?"

"No, actually it's just a few details I need clarified."

Not happy but having no legitimate reason to linger, Harrison said, "I'll have Dr. Gunther come in as soon as possible." Leaving the room, he saw Gunther approaching down the hall and signaled him into his office. "What are they doing here? I thought you told me that you answered all of Billings's questions the other day."

The working of his jaw muscle belied his calm appearance as Gunther answered, "I did."

"I don't like this."

Finding it harder by the moment to maintain his composure, Gunther replied sarcastically, "And you suppose that I do."

"I don't want the hospital compromised. Why didn't you arrange to meet them at the police station?"

"Because I didn't know they were coming!" Furious at Harrison's intervention, Karl continued, "Now if you're finished with your questions, I'll go see what they want."

"Be careful what you say. If you have any doubts, refuse to answer on the advice of your attorney."

Nodding tersely, Karl left Harrison's office and walked to his own. Opening the door, he was surprised to see the troopers with Billings. "Salinkas, Fekette, Billings. To what do I owe the pleasure?"

Billings took control of the conversation, acting as if Gunther's cooperation was a foregone conclusion. "Dr. Gunther, due to the fact that several questions remain regarding the death of Brett Conklin, we brought the equipment with us so that it wouldn't inconvenience you to take the test."

Looking from the sheriff to the troopers and back again, Gunther replied, "What questions would those be? I thought that I had answered all you needed the other day."

"I'd like you to describe once more what happened so that we're sure about the details."

"You know what, sheriff? This reeks of coercion. I've never heard of a polygraph being given to verify minor details. I have no intention of speaking to you any further, at least not voluntarily. Anything I do from here on will be with my attorney present." Pausing to make sure that he had the others' attention, Gunther continued, "I don't like the feeling I'm getting from this. Now if you have nothing else to say, I have work to do." Closing the door behind him, Gunther was glad that there was no one near enough to see how tightly his hand gripped the knob.

Darnell Harrison sat glowering at the door that Karl had closed behind him. If he had had any inkling of the problems that Gunther would bring with him, he would never have taken him on for a partner. Damn! How could things be so difficult? He would never understand why people let themselves be dominated by their emotions.

Darnell was uneasy and he knew that his intervention would only complicate matters. He had to depend on Gunther to handle the troopers and their request for a polygraph. Whether the sheriff had the authority to question Gunther's innocence or guilt was moot as far as he was concerned. What did bother him was the fact that the law-enforcement officials had invaded his domain. Someone might question what they were doing there and that would not be good, as the funding for renovations was still not locked into place. How could Gunther continue negotiations if he was being questioned at random by the sheriff and the troopers?

His locked jaw indicating his annoyance at having to intervene, Harrison picked up his phone. "See if you can locate DA Smalls for me." Waiting, Harrison thought about how Smalls might react. A capable politician, Ed Smalls was usually jocose, satisfied because he maneuvered things to his liking. Harrison hoped that he would not have to remind him about the financial backing he and the hospital had given him during the last campaign. He didn't particularly like the man but felt he was the best man to have in the position. Picking up the phone to find Smalls's secretary on the line, Harrison was not pleased at the obvious power play. Forgetting the amenities, he said tersely, "Please put DA Smalls on."

"Darnell? How are you? It's been a while," said Smalls.

His irritation apparent, Harrison answered, "Fine, Ed. You're aware that we've been busy with the funding for the hospital over the last few months."

Taking advantage, Smalls protested, "Well, Darnell, that's really your fault, isn't it?"

"What the hell are you talking about?"

"If you had gone along with the recommendations of the board when the hospital was originally being built, it would now be a public entity instead of a private one and the state would be paying for the renovations."

Furious at Smalls's condescending tone, Darnell worked hard to keep calm. "Ed, that happened over twenty years ago. Whether certain people like it or not, the hospital as a private institution has given the county just as much if not more than any public entity." Taking a deep breath, he continued, "But that's not what

I called about. I need you to find out what's going on with the sudden investigation into Brett Conklin's death."

"What do you mean?"

"As we speak, there are two troopers and Sheriff Billings with Dr. Gunther in his office, and frankly, I don't like it. Gunther has been trying to carry on as normally as possible though he's been hit tremendously hard by Brett's death. He doesn't need the harassment any more than I need law officers all over the hospital.

Listening to the silence at the other end, Harrison was sure that the DA had known nothing about the visit to Gunther.

His voice sincere, Smalls spoke quickly. "Darnell, I don't know what you're talking about. To my knowledge, and I would be the one to know, Gunther hasn't been charged with anything or even brought in under suspicion, so why would they be doing a polygraph test?"

"If I knew, I wouldn't have called you, would I?" His voice now sarcastic at the other man's lack of information, Darnell pursued his advantage. "I think that it would be wise for you to call off the dogs. All of this is only complicating things more for the hospital, and that might not be good for your next campaign. I'd hate to have people think that the district attorney's office didn't support our hospital."

Disturbed by Harrison's veiled threat, Smalls hastened to assure him. "I'll take care of it. Gunther won't be bothered anymore."

Will Billings was unused to the feeling of frustration that grew stronger at every effort to shed more light on Brett Conklin's death. Following the aborted attempt to have Gunther take a lie detector test, he had decided to be more careful in letting his intentions be known. He was unsure how Smalls found out about the visit to the hospital, but when he returned to his office, a message to call the district attorney was waiting. Smalls let him know that he did not take kindly to harassing an upstanding member of the community without justifiable reason. The irritated sheriff had received an undeserved harangue without being able to say a word.

That had given Will the idea of writing a letter. If he put down in writing all the reasons he felt that Gunther's story should be further investigated, then Smalls's ass would be covered and the DA might be willing to let him continue his investigation. Sitting at his desk, long after his wife had gone to bed, Will first wrote a note to Tim Reeves telling him about the incident with the polygraph. Next, he began to list all the information which he planned to include in the letter that would be mailed to DA Smalls the next day.

In the last paragraph, Will reiterated the request to continue the investigation, reminding the DA that he had been successful in the past. Satisfied with the way he had presented his arguments, Will was finally able to relax. Sure that his letter would bring the desired results, he shut off the light and went to bed.

The backlog waiting when Tim got back to his Boulder office after five days in Taylorville was enormous. Bracing himself with yet another cup of coffee, he began to work through the messages that seemed most urgent. Six hours later, having eaten a sandwich at his desk, he decided that he was caught up enough to take a break. Reaching for the phone and dialing the number himself, he waited for his counterpart in Raleigh, South Carolina, to pick up.

"Robinson."

Smiling at the gruff tone of voice on the other end of the phone, Tim's pleasure was obvious. "Hey, Brian, it's been too long!"

"Tim! How the hell are you? Are you here in Raleigh? What are you up to?"

"Slow down! No, I'm not in Raleigh, but hearing you makes me realize that it's been way too long since we've seen each other."

Knowing his friend, Brian waited for Tim to tell him why he had called.

"You remember me talking about my friend Kevin Conklin, the one who was in Korea with me?" At his friend's affirmative reply, Tim continued, "Unfortunately, his son, Brett, was killed last week."

"Sorry to hear that."

"There are too many loose ends for my liking, even though the death was called an accident." Pausing, Tim's doubt echoed in his voice when he picked up the narrative. "I'm not sure whether there is a connection with Brett's death or not, but what I definitely found strange was seeing Joseph Rossi at the funeral."

"You mean Rossi as in the Rossi family that we've been investigating for the past two years?"

"Yup! Imagine my surprise at seeing the Captain at a funeral in a small town in Ohio. Not exactly his usual venue. Then I heard that the town has an expanding drug problem so it is possible…"

"Let me guess. This is Rossi's home turf so if it has to do with him, we should be able to uncover any information that may tie him into Taylorville, right? Especially if I put someone on to monitor his movements."

"I knew I could count on you. I owe you, Brian. Get back to me if you find anything interesting." Replacing the receiver, Tim turned to look out the window. For the moment he had done all he could, but he wasn't finished yet.

Ed Smalls was comfortable in his job. Looking around the small, shabby office, he sighed. Though many wondered why he hadn't tried to move further up in the political arena, he was content to stay where he was. As a big fish in a little pond, he managed to make things happen and commanded an amount of respect that he wouldn't have had in a large city.

That was why Harrison's call about the Gunther polygraph had upset him more than he cared to admit. He should have been aware of what was happening with the Conklin accident, but he wasn't. *It is all too easy to fall into a complacent, slow-moving mold in this county,* he thought to himself. Not much ever happened, but when it did, one of the movers and shakers were always willing to tell you how to do your job. Many times their way was just as viable as any other, if you discounted their vested interests.

Harrison wasn't the only one who wanted the hospital to look good. With an election coming up next year, it was going to be important to get as much backing and goodwill in his corner as possible. He couldn't imagine why Harrison was so concerned about Gunther influencing the disposition of funds, but that wasn't his problem.

Ed had called Billings after the sheriff had tried to get the polygraph test from Gunther. Billings had been adamant and he was determined to continue ferreting out information regardless of whose toes he stepped on.

This morning a multiple-page letter from Billings about his concerns was on Ed's desk and some points did appear to be valid. Not wanting to think of what an investigation by Billings would signify, Smalls was sure that if he told Billings not to continue, the sheriff would only ask more questions. There was too much at stake to have him digging around. Picking up his pen, Smalls began to write, directing his letter to the state police barrack in Gibson.

There is no need to continue the investigation into the death of Brett T. Conklin.

Late June, 1976

As he finished his stretching exercises before his morning run, Kevin gave silent thanks once again for his friend Tim Reeves. Though he had originally looked at Tim in horror when he had suggested running the morning after Brett's death, Kevin knew his friend had been right in insisting that he try to do as much as possible to maintain the normalcy in his life. Now, two weeks later, Kevin was sure that if it hadn't been for discharging his frustration through his daily run, he would have suffered even more.

Turning the corner, he frowned at what he saw. At the bottom of the hill near a popular artisan spring, John Greene's Mercedes was again parked next to the older white Chevy with Carolina plates.

Jim Walsh, Tim, and Sheriff Billings had tried to convince him that there was reason to carry on a further investigation of Brett's death. Now he remembered the concerns centering on the Rossi family. Deciding to find out if there was any truth to the conjectures, he changed his course slightly to go closer to the two vehicles. As he approached the cars, he recognized Austin Greene at the wheel of his father's car. Glancing toward the Chevy, he forced himself to maintain his normal stride as shock hit him.

He didn't know the younger blond man on the driver's side, but there was no doubt in his mind that the man in the passenger's seat was the Captain. When they had talked following Brett's death, Tim had mentioned how little Rossi had changed. Seeing him now meant that Tim and Sheriff Billings had been right in their concern.

Always alert, Paul heard the thudding of footsteps before the runner came into view. Flicking his eyes over the man, he failed to recognize Conklin. Deciding that what he saw was no more than what it appeared, Paul turned once again to the drama unfolding on the other side of the car where the Captain was talking to Austin Greene.

Shocked by the Captain's suggestion, Austin was momentarily speechless. Each nerve ending seemed to be transmitting a distress signal as he tried to regain his composure. Swallowing hard, he tried to reason with the other man. "But I can't sell directly to anyone here in town," he cried. "That's why I had gotten Coombs and Meeks to work for us. They were the ones who dealt directly with the merchandise."

Unmoved, Rossi looked calmly at the nervous boy in the other car. He had no doubt that all his life someone else had been smoothing over the rough spots for the Greene kid, making sure that he could continue to do just what he pleased without thinking much about it. Well, that was about to change.

"Coombs is in jail and Meeks is dead. Unless you have some other solution, I don't think you have any choice but to handle the distribution yourself." Watching Austin's reaction, Rossi was reminded of the young troops suddenly confronted with death on the battlefield. When the situation was life and death, suddenly the glamour of fighting disappeared.

To explain why Greene had to take charge, the Captain began to speak slowly. "When you approached us with the idea of establishing a distribution network in this area, you were sure that there was a market for our product. You were right, and everyone in Carolina is impressed with the quantity of merchandise that has been moving recently. Unfortunately, there are now others who have realized that this area could be lucrative for them as well. They want to horn in on our territory." Pausing for emphasis, he queried, "Do you know who the Bonano family is?"

At Austin's silent nod, Rossi continued, "They seem to have developed quite a market in the Cincinnati and western Pennsylvania area. If we can't keep our clients supplied and happy, they will. So you don't have a choice. I don't want to know the details of what you plan to do, but just remember the problems that arose with the other goons you had working. If I were you, for the moment at least, I'd do the work myself."

Sensing the implied threat and seeing no immediate escape, Austin pleaded, "But the 4th is less than two weeks away. How am I supposed to get things together?"

Bored with the kid who obviously didn't understand what he was dealing with, Paul turned to Rossi, speaking loud enough for Austin to hear, "Maybe he should set up a booth on the square."

Amused, Rossi turned. "Whatever you decide to do, remember that the family isn't happy with what happened, so be careful." At his nod to Paul, the Chevy started up the hill.

Closing his eyes as he tried to control the shaking that had taken control of his body, Austin knew that this time he was on his own. He had known Meeks, and while Tim was now dead, he knew it wasn't suicide.

Deciding to keep his concerns about the drug conspiracy from Linda, Kevin waited until he got to the office to try and speak to Tim and Sheriff Billings. Unable to reach them, he shelved the call for later and turned to the work that was piled up on his desk. Checking his watch later, he decided to see if his wife wanted to accompany him to the town meeting. Ten days after the funeral, both he and Linda had resumed their normal activities, for as the adage stated, life did go on.

"Is that file so confusing? You're almost scowling," he joked.

Looking up, Linda said with a smile, "Not really. Some of these complaints and demands seem so petty." Wistfully she continued, "I guess the importance of everything depends on your point of view."

Moving to the desk, Kevin put his hands on Linda's shoulders and squeezed gently, his touch conveying his understanding. "Do you feel like going to the meeting with me this afternoon? With only two weeks to go, everyone could use some of your calming influence."

Smiling, Linda shook her head. "No, I'll pass. I planned on stopping at the church after I get done, then maybe I'll stop and see the children if Holly's home."

"Speaking of Holly, I spoke to her last week and arranged to help with the notification to social security about the children's entitlement to survivor's benefits. She's also entitled to widow's benefits, so between what they receive from social security and Brett's insurance, they should be financially secure." At Linda's frown, Kevin spoke again. "Sweetheart, you know that I've offered to help if Holly needs it, but she's adamantly refused on all counts. I think she feels she needs to take care of herself and the children. Give her time to acclimate, she'll come around."

Seated at the Inn, Walter Stern's discomfort was obvious as he spoke to Karl. "I wish I could give you the news you were waiting for. I know that Darnell won't be happy, but right now the board feels that because the clinic is a private entity, they won't be able to link the loan to a possible bond issue as planned."

The clenching of his jaw was the only outward sign belying Gunther's calm acceptance of Stern's news. "You don't think they'll back the issue?" The banker shook his head. "They could, but because the clinic belongs to Harrison, Kerr, and you instead of being public domain, they don't feel that it would be wise." His voice sincere, he continued, "Karl, I'm sorry, but there's nothing more I can do."

Realizing the futility in pursuing the issue, Karl called for the check. Harrison had been right. Because of his association with Brett's death, the clinic was now being penalized. As he walked back to the clinic in the afternoon sunshine, Karl dreaded the forthcoming confrontation. He had no doubt that Harrison would be expecting a full account of his meeting with Stern and the news wasn't good. Knowing that there was no benefit to be gained in putting Harrison off until later, he walked to Darnell's office and knocked.

Opening the door, Karl was deluged with questions. "What did he say? What are the terms? Interest rate?"

Karl knew that his monetary contribution added to his medical expertise had been the key to becoming a partner. But now that he forced himself to look closely, Karl knew that Darnell Harrison had always treated him as if he were of lesser importance than himself or Kerr. While Karl had noticed before, this was the first time that he had consciously recognized Harrison's action for what it was—a demonstration of power. And at this particular point, Karl had to admit he had nothing to offer that could defuse the other man's contention about how Brett's death would bring consequences for the hospital. "Damn it! I knew that your involvement in Conklin's death would present a problem for us," said Harrison, his frown deepening.

"Stern said that the issue wasn't Conklin's death so much as it was the fact that the clinic is privately owned, which makes it impossible to float a bond issue for the public benefit."

Derision dripping in his tone, Darnell replied as a sneer marred his expression. "And you believed him? I guess you haven't been here long enough to realize that they can do anything they damn well please." His volume little more than a whisper, Harrison spoke as if the weight of the world had suddenly been placed on his shoulders. "If Stern gave you a definitive no, then I suppose I'll have to fall back on my contingency plan."

"Then the bank's decision isn't going to hold up the renovations after all, is it?" queried Gunther, his relief obvious.

Looking contemptuously at the younger man, Harrison was silent as he weighed what he would say. "Everything has a cost, and you of all people should be cognizant of how high some alternatives can be."

Still unsure of what the older man expected of him, Karl was quiet. Knowing Harrison's dedication to the hospital, he had no doubt that Harrison would pull strings to make sure that the funding would appear from somewhere.

Still sitting at his desk after Gunther had gone, Darnell wondered how he was going to manage contacting Rossi without appearing to be subservient or weak. He still bought from many of the suppliers that the Captain had suggested, but he hadn't been asked to give any checks lately. He wanted to keep it that way.

Gerald Weir, the pharmacist, had been concerned about the changes in formula for some of the medications supplied by the laboratory Rossi had recommended. The Captain had explained it as a way of using less costly components to prepare medications with the same effect.

Harrison's frown made his eyes even darker as he glanced at the pictures that lined the top shelf of his bookcase. How had it happened that he had allowed himself to be blinded to the truth of how the young captain was able to obtain anything and everything that he had asked for? When had he made the conscious decision to accept what Rossi offered without thinking about how it was obtained? Lost in thought, the ringing of the phone startled Darnell. "Hello."

"And how is the good doctor today?" queried a voice known and simultaneously feared.

I had just been thinking about calling you and the phone rang. But, I'm being rude, it's your call. What can I do for you?"

Listening to Harrison, Rossi smiled. The gruff doctor was so transparent. He had obviously decided that he needed help. In order to ensure Rossi's cooperation, he was being almost too helpful, which was totally out of character.

"I was just calling to see if you had any more news as to the death of that lawyer at the beginning of the month. You know that the people I work with are concerned about the possibility of an inquiry."

"I don't think you have anything to worry about. As far as I know, and I assume that I would have heard if it were any different, the death has been labeled an accident."

Wanting to be sure that there was no change or confusion, Rossi again queried, "You're sure?"

Annoyed by the other man doubting his word, Darnell's voice dripped with displeasure as he replied, "I know for a fact that the idea of an inquiry into Conklin's death had been tabled because I spoke to the DA."

Not liking what he was hearing, Rossi was silent as he wondered why the district attorney had been involved in the first place. Preferring to make sure, he decided to ask. "Why was the DA involved if it was an accidental death?"

"We have an overzealous sheriff who wouldn't accept Dr. Gunther's description of how the accident happened. He had asked DA Smalls to allow him to investigate. In fact, he had actually started an investigation on his own." Wanting to make sure that Rossi recognized his importance, Harrison's tone was self-righteous as he continued. "I told Smalls that Billings's investigation was a waste of time and didn't help matters within the community, so he told the sheriff to let it go."

Listening to Harrison, Rossi processed what he had just been told against what Paul had reported. It was obvious that Gunther had not told anyone that Patricia Conklin had been present when her husband died. Nor had he mentioned Paul's presence to anyone. It was clear that Harrison had his own agenda and wanted the whole thing forgotten.

Unable to control his curiosity, Darnell suddenly asked, "Why are you so interested in the death of Brett Conklin? I thought you hadn't seen Kevin Conklin since we were all in Korea."

Having sensed Harrison's relief at his call and preferring to keep him on the defensive, the Captain's tone when he answered made clear that he would be the only one asking any questions. "The board I work with has been looking into new capital ventures. It's my job to do the background check into any area that they might be considering for investment and make sure that there are no hidden problems."

Taken aback, Darnell was quick to make sure that Rossi realized that he was in agreement with whatever the board thought correct. "That sounds logical."

"You had said that you were going to call me. Is there anything I need to know now that we're speaking?"

Wanting to regain control of the conversation yet leery of angering the other man, Harrison was careful with his reply. "I'm not sure. I had mentioned to you that we were on the verge of renovating the clinic and bringing our equipment up-to-date during one of the last conversations we had." Uneasy in the position of the postulant, Harrison continued, "In light of the successful repayment of the loan I had from your principals, I was in hope that I would be able to secure the necessary funding from them."

"The local banks won't fund you?"

"There seems to be some reluctance at the moment due to the private ownership of the clinic and I'd rather not wait."

Realizing he now had the answer as to why Harrison was so eager to have the investigation into Conklin's death dropped, Rossi smiled as he said, "I'll get back to you shortly."

After testifying in court, Will had tried again to speak with Lieutenant Drann at the Gibson Barracks. Once again, Drann had been busy and couldn't take his call. He hadn't received a return call and, as he drove toward Gibson, Will was irate. Something was going on and he planned on finding out exactly what it was. He had been friends with Drann too long to believe that the lieutenant would avoid speaking to him.

Billings kept asking himself the same question: who wanted the investigation stopped and why? Pulling into the parking lot, Will barely noticed the dark clouds that were forming in the east. Entering the barracks, he asked to see Drann, half expecting to be told that the lieutenant was busy. He was surprised when he was ushered immediately into Drann's office. Entering, Billings said sarcastically, "Well, it's good to know that you're in one piece. I was beginning to wonder."

Understanding his friend's ire, Drann diffused the situation by saying as he stood, "I imagine you did. Come on, let's go grab a cup of coffee."

As Will began to speak, Drann signaled his friend not to. Only when they were seated in the front seat of Will's truck did he nod at Will to talk.

Concerned by the cloak-and-dagger maneuvers that his friend seemed to think necessary, Will exploded. "What the hell is going on? First you don't return my calls and now you don't want anyone to see me talking to you?"

"Put this box of bolts in gear," ordered Drann, wondering what would happen when he told his friend what was going on. Only when they were on the approach ramp going north on Route 81 did Drann begin to speak. "You're right. I didn't answer your calls and I didn't want to speak to you in my office." Pausing, he looked at his friend and saw that, though the frown still dominated his face, he was listening attentively.

"You know I was in complete agreement with you as to continuing the investigation of Conklin's death. I wouldn't have helped you out with the lie detector equipment if I wasn't." At Will's nod, he continued. "I also know that you wrote a letter to DA Smalls because you told me you were going to, but after he received it, I received one as well."

Glancing at Drann, Will queried, "A letter? Who from?"

"From Smalls. In it he said he saw no need to continue with the investigation of Conklin's death. The certificate stated the cause as an accidental gunshot wound and that the eyewitness testimony of Gunther corroborated it."

"Gunther is the one I had doubts about."

"I know that. Someone high up has decided that it is not in the town's best interest to continue looking into the case. I was told in no uncertain terms that the state police were not to expend any more man hours tracking down minutia in an accidental death; there were other unsolved cases that needed our attention.

Absorbing what Drann had told him, Will said, "And Smalls warned you off?"

"You got it. Now, why might he be so concerned with you continuing the investigation?"

Will was silent as he pulled off the New Milford exit and headed in the other direction. "I don't have a clue. If they've ordered you not to help, you can't. But I have no intention of letting this go, not now. This stinks to high heaven and I plan on finding out why."

As a measure of extra insurance, the Rossi family had decided to remove Coombs's defense from Greene's law firm. Finding an attorney among their ranks suited for the job had been more complicated than Rossi had expected. The man had to be sharp but also tolerant. In dealing with the people of the Broome and Taylor County area, the Captain often felt that he had entered a time warp. The regular family retainers would find it quite different if not difficult, defending people like those in the Broome

County Jail. Not one of the three could be said to have "street smarts." That would complicate understanding and relating to any streetwise lawyer who had to defend them.

Rossi looked out at the sluggish river running behind the Ramada Inn on Court Street in Binghamton. Nothing special, at least this hotel had a bar and the usual services available at all the national chains. It might take him longer to reach Taylorville, but he had a feeling it would be worth it, if only to placate Scalzo.

The lawyer, with his oversized pinky ring and gaudy cufflinks, often handled family problems. An additional plus was that he had worked in upstate Ohio when he was getting started. He had balked at leaving his family and office to run and defend a couple of hicks in Broome. Rossi had sweetened the pot by suggesting that it would provide a mini vacation for him and his girlfriend. So Scalzo and his "assistant" were down the hall in a suite.

Paul was supposed to take Scalzo to the jail later that afternoon. Having spoken with the Greene kid early in the morning, Rossi decided that he would visit Russo and find out what he could about what had happened with Harrison's funding for the hospital. If any money was available, it was always preferable to know. At the knock on his door, Rossi turned, hoping it was Paul. "Come in."

As he entered, Paul shook his head, smiling. "You should have heard the complaints. Scalzo asked me if we had intentionally looked to find the worst place possible."

Smiling, Rossi replied, "He should have seen the place in Centerville."

"I managed to get him to calm down by saying that I'd find out the best restaurants and if there were any clubs."

"Good. I'm going to leave him with you this afternoon while I do some errands in Taylorville. Call Scalzo and have him come here."

Several minutes later, Scalzo entered the Captain's room. "Some vacation, Captain. You owe me."

"Get this over with and then we'll talk about compensation. Did you go over the notes and the file that Greene's office forwarded?"

Serious, Scalzo answered pensively, "I did, and I'm not so sure that this is going to be as easy as we thought."

"Why's that?"

"I've dealt with the legal system in upstate New York before. There is much less volume of drug-related crime than there is in the city or even where we are in the southern cities. The district attorneys and the judges are more apt to try to set a precedent in hopes that it will deter further crime of this sort. With Bonano operating in this area and making a big splash of his involvement, they'll do all they can to warn off others."

Nodding his head, Rossi's tone was grim. "I have no doubt that you're right in what you're saying. The problem with Bonano will have to be taken care of, but right now we have to focus on what we do with Coombs and Radner. What can you get them off with?"

"With any luck, I'll be able to get the date delayed until October, because of the change in counsel. If that's possible, I want to have both Coombs and Radner placed in a drug rehab program until then. As an accessory, Coombs should get off with time served through October. With Radner, I plan on a plea of involuntary manslaughter due to the effect of the drugs."

"Sounds good. Let's see how it flies."

Independence Day

On the morning of the Fourth of July, Linda opened her eyes and seeing the sunshine slanting into the room, smiled. The day had dawned crystal clear with the blue skies and popcorn clouds that one hopes for but sees only rarely. The weatherman had been cheery, and, fortunately for the town, he had been right.

Yesterday's storm had dispelled the humidity and pressure and had left in its wake a gorgeous summer day. Stretching languidly, Linda realized that for the first time since Brett's death, she felt good about getting out of bed and getting on with the program of the day. Feeling more like herself, she hoped that this was the first step to retaking her life from the malaise and anguish that had dominated it for the past few weeks.

Wanting to enjoy the moment, Kevin stood watching quietly as Linda, unaware, continued working between the counter and the table, taking time to fold the napkins as she placed them where they belonged.

Becoming aware of Kevin's eyes on her, Linda smiled mischievously. "I decided to make muffins to sustain us through the parade. Think it will be enough added to the hug and kiss you're about to give me?"

Crossing the distance in two strides, Kevin hugged Linda to him. "I'm glad to see that you're looking forward to the day."

Her voice serious, Linda replied, "So am I. This is the first morning since Brett's death that I've actually felt happy to wake up." Pausing, she looked into Kevin's eyes, noting how they had darkened with emotion. "I don't think we'll ever get over his loss, but maybe we will be able to live with it."

Not trusting himself to speak, Kevin nodded against her hair. Pulling back against her husband's arms, Linda said, "If we don't get busy we're going to be late, so let's have breakfast."

Pouring Kevin's coffee and refreshing her own, she told him what plans she had. "You know I'm going to pick up the children at Holly's. I'll bring them over to you so they can ride on the float with us. After the parade, we can meet up with Jim and Susan and go over for the chicken barbecue at the fire hall."

"Sounds good to me. I just hope they don't get restless with the speeches. You know how long-winded some of these people can be."

"I'm sure they'll be fine. Especially when you give them the candy to toss out to the crowd."

"Remember last year?" asked Kevin, smiling. "Instead of throwing the candy to the crowd, Janie sat down and shoved as many as she could fit into her little mouth."

"And Tommy got so upset when she did that he threw the whole bag instead of a handful. This year should be better because I'm sure Tommy has been telling Janie just what to do."

Thinking of his grandchildren, Kevin frowned as he wondered how to protect them and all the other children from the vermin who had decided to make Taylorville their base. Looking at his wife, he replied, "I get so frustrated thinking that, even as we speak, somewhere there is someone who is plotting the downfall of our children, and I don't know how to stop them."

"What are you talking about?" asked Linda, puzzled by Kevin's comment.

"I hadn't mentioned it before because you had enough on your shoulders, but a few weeks ago Jim Walsh told me that there had been an increase in the number of kids using drugs." Refraining from telling her that the discussion had originated during the talk about continuing the investigation into Brett's death, Kevin explained how he had discussed the matter with Tim, Jim, and Will Billings after the funeral. "At the time, I didn't think much of it when Tim said he had seen Captain Rossi at the cemetery, but this morning I saw him while I was out running."

"Rossi? The name doesn't sound familiar to me," said Linda.

"There's no reason why it should. He was in Korea at the same time I was, but while Dr. Harrison seemed to be chummy with him, he wasn't someone I was comfortable with."

"But why should seeing him concern you? He might have been here visiting the Harrison family. What does that have to do with what you said about the drug problem?"

Remembering that Linda didn't know what had been said, Kevin continued, "Tim and I always thought that there was something strange about the way Rossi was always able to obtain supplies that no one else could get. Tim explained to me that our Captain Rossi was directly connected to the Rossi Family, one of the largest crime families in the country."

Now as serious as Kevin, Linda asked, "And you think that he's involved with the distribution here in Taylorville?"

Nodding his head, Kevin said, "It looks like it."

"So what can we do to stop him? I know that the problem has been escalating because of what I've heard at the church. Can't he be arrested?"

"That's just it. He hasn't broken any laws. Until he does, or can be connected with the breaking of a law, there's nothing we can do."

"No wonder you're frustrated. Does Darnell Harrison know that he's around?"

"I don't know." Suddenly silent, Kevin seemed to lose himself in his thoughts. Deciding it was better not to hide anything from his wife, he continued pensively, "You know, the day before the accident, Brett went to Elmira to speak to the district attorney. Though he didn't get into details on the phone, he mentioned that he had gotten quite a bit of information. Since he was working on the defense of those three kids from here who were in jail on the drug-related murder charges, I wonder if what he found out wouldn't help us deal with the problem."

Knowing that Kevin would not rest until he had done all he could to curtail the spread of the drugs, Linda was supportive. "It can't hurt to take a look at the files. Why don't you ask Holly for the notes? She still has Brett's things."

Nodding in agreement, Kevin looked at the clock, surprised. They had less than an hour to be at the float. "If we don't get going, the kids aren't going to get to throw candy and the mayor is going to be late! Go ahead and get dressed, I'll clean up." Stopping to give Kevin a peck on the cheek, Linda went to get dressed.

Her good spirits stayed with her as she drove to pick up the children and only flagged when Brett's dog came running out to greet her. Shaking off the sad feeling, she hurried to the door where two small bodies hurtled into her.

"Grandma! Let's go!" squeaked Janie, who at age three already had her mother's perky attitude.

"Slow down, sweetheart," laughed Linda. "Give me a minute to talk to Mommy." Giving Tommy who was trying to act less excited a hug, she smiled at Holly, "Quite a bit of excitement for this early in the morning."

"I'm glad you're the one who has to try and calm these two! Tommy remembers from last year, but I think Janie thinks it's something in *Sesame Street*." Grinning, Holly continued, "Of course, you could equate the grand master to Big Bird."

"Don't let him hear you say that!" Linda laughed, pretending to be shocked. Glad to share the moment, Linda asked, "Why don't you come over and have lunch with us?"

Holly shook her head. "No, I don't want to be with a crowd. But thanks for asking." Turning to the children, who had each grabbed Linda by the hand, she gave them each a kiss.

Watching Linda drive away, Holly breathed a sigh of relief. She wasn't going to spend time with Kevin and Linda unless absolutely necessary. It wasn't their fault. Though they tried to help, it was becoming more and more difficult to see them. She had to force herself to count to ten before speaking, especially when Kevin was around. Almost as if it had taken on a voice of its own, her conscience kicked in. What did she expect? He had found her in bed with Karl and, when he tried to talk to her, she had told him to butt out and that she hated him.

To be fair, it was amazing that he still maintained the same attitude toward her after what she had done. She didn't think he had told Linda because Linda still acted the same. Holly was the one who had changed.

She shook her head in exasperation. It was all so unfair. She had never meant to hurt anyone. All she wanted was to divorce Brett and be with Karl but that's where the problem had begun. She unconsciously began to straighten the living room, her eyes shiny with ire. If Brett hadn't refused to give her the divorce, none of this would have happened. They could have had an amicable separation and she would never have lost her temper in the woods.

Feeling slightly sick, her anger turned to dismay as her mind replayed what had happened. Holly sank onto the sofa. It wasn't her fault! She hadn't wanted Brett to die! Now things were no better than they had been before Brett's death—they were worse. She was no closer to being with Karl than before.

The ringing phone jolted her out of her thoughts. Her voice reflecting what she was feeling, Holly reached over and picked up the instrument.

Hearing Holly's listless hello, Karl was concerned. "Sweetheart? Are you all right? The kids are okay, aren't they?"

Karl's tender concern following her intense, emotional, introspective thoughts was the catalyst for her tears. Sobbing, she cried, "I can't take it anymore! You have to do something! I need you!"

Though Holly's distress upset him, Karl stayed calm and tried to reassure her. "Shhh, baby. You know there's nothing I want more than to be with you. We'll work it out, but right now we have to be careful. We'll see each other in less than two hours and spend the night together, so please calm down." His sigh audible to Holly, he continued, "I wish I could be there to hold you right now."

Hiccupping, as her sobs lessened, Holly's tears continued to fall as she clutched the receiver. "Me too."

As he drove toward town, Kevin pondered the day ahead of him. Depending on your point of view, the job of mayor had certain advantages. If you liked dealing with people and didn't mind being the focus of everyone's attention, one of these could be considered the high visibility at all town functions and celebrations.

The organizers had designated the lumberyard on the outskirts of town as the point of departure for the floats, and he planned to wait there for Linda and the children. He parked and after rounding the corner, he stood watching the people hustling, making final additions to the floats, or giving last-minute instructions. It never ceased to amaze him that when push came to shove, no matter how confusing or chaotic all the activity seemed to be, suddenly it all came together. Smiling, once again, he reminded himself to give credit to Laura and Mary.

"Grandpa! Grandpa!" The shouts reached him simultaneously with the children. As both of them held up their arms to be lifted for a hug, his eyes met Linda's and they shared a tender smile over the children's heads.

The pleasure of holding his grandchildren translating into a huge grin, he forced himself to be serious as he addressed the two. "All ready to throw the candy to the crowds?"

Tommy adored Kevin and wanted to please him. Looking at his grandfather, he solemnly nodded his head. The five-year-old had begun to lose the baby fat, so evident in three-year-old Janie, and suddenly appeared to have acquired the wisdom of the ages. "Yes, I am. I've been practicing throwing the ball so the candy will go farther."

"That's very good. I'm sure that will help get candy to all parts of the crowd."

Unwilling to be left out, Janie placed her chubby hands on either side of Kevin's face trying to force him to look at her. "Grandpa, look at me! I'm ready too!"

"Really?" said Kevin, laughing. "And what have you been doing to prepare for today?"

Very smugly, the three–year-old said, "I can take the papers off the candy faster than before and not get sticky!"

Linda watched the interplay between the children and their grandfather. As Kevin burst out laughing in response to Janie's statement, she laughed too. And it felt wonderful!

"Is it an inside joke or can you share it?" asked Jim, delighted to see his friends happy. As Kevin repeated Janie's preparations, Jim chuckled. Looking at the little girl in her grandfather's arms, he said seriously, "It is important not to get sticky. Now, all set to get on the float?"

Reaching out to Jim, Janie squealed, "Let's go!" Tommy pulled his grandfather by the hand and the group started for the float.

The VFW, Veterans of Foreign Wars, had prepared the float Kevin and his family were riding on. The float had four flags at each of the corners, and red-and-white bunting had been placed in stripes all the way around. A red, white, and blue four-foot floral wreath on a tripod dominated the center of the float. The banner read "In memory of all those fallen." The patriotic theme was reinforced by the men wearing their uniforms. Wilbur Wakely, age ninety-three, was seated on the chair in the center front of the float where he would reign as grand marshal. Wakely had lived in Post Hall, a historic Taylorville residence and part of the infamous Underground Railroad, since 1944. A veteran of

World War I, he had participated in many of the projects sponsored by the VFW, including the yearly drive for gifts for those in Veterans' Administration hospitals.

The parade would wind through the town and was the centerpiece of the day's activities. The seventeen floats included most organizations in the community and ranged from the American Legion to the Dairy Princess. The seven musical groups were from local high schools, plus the Shriners marching band, a local country western group, and a barbershop quartet. Added to the antique cars and antique farm equipment, the parade was almost half a mile long from start to finish, offering something for everyone.

Scheduled for ten o'clock, the parade wasn't the first activity of the day. Festivities had started at eight o'clock with the one-mile "Run for Fun." Many people were just arriving and others were already ensconced in their lawn chairs along the parade route. Still another group was busy going from one booth to the next at the village square. Each year the arts-and-crafts fair drew more exhibitors. More than one hundred booths were set up. Traffic had been rerouted in order to accommodate the overflow of vendors by using the street as well as the green. The normally quiet booth run by the Daughters of the American Revolution, affectionately known as Darlings, was doing a brisk business. Though their flags and patriotic buttons were echoed in many other booths, a lot of younger people seemed to be drawn to their booth.

Linda smiled at Kevin and squeezed his hand, gesturing toward Tommy and Janie as they got up on the float. Kevin needn't have worried about the children being bored. Tommy and Janie stood entranced watching all the color and movement. When their float finally began to move, Janie jumped up and down. Sitting next to Linda behind the grand marshal, Kevin was glad to see his family happy.

Each year more people from the surrounding communities attended the festivities and this year was no different. The lawn chairs and folding stools were set up all along the route.

As the band began to play one of the popular show tunes, a cheer could be heard. The smell of barbecuing chicken added to the sensual experience of the day. The firemen had started cooking at 6:30 that morning to get the coals just right, and the delicious aroma attested to their success.

The town was a riot of color. Floral displays and flags adorning most homes and area business, and balloons in all colors abounded. The crowd added to the colorful collage, presenting a never-ending variety of tones and colors.

Austin was pleased with himself. When he had offered to help his mother at the DAR booth, her eyes filled with tears of joy. He had dutifully sat next to her at the committee meetings these past two weeks, as well as working on the float and helping put up the booth last night.

As he drove to Salt Springs early that morning, for the first time he felt confident that the Captain would not be able to find fault with him. And he hadn't. In fact, Rossi had actually laughed and then congratulated him on his creativity. No one would know. As he was in charge of stocking the booth and keeping the counters filled, he had the ideal opportunity to talk with the people who came as well as take the money right out in the open.

Turning to Paul with a grin, the Captain said, "Looks like the kid decided to get his act together and get down to business."

Watching as Greene drove away, Paul shook his head. "I don't know. It would be better if he'd stay away from the horse himself. Everyone thinks they can ride it without getting thrown and then find they can't, like the ones in the county jail."

Nodding, Rossi was thoughtful. Vice had been around since the beginning of civilization. Someone was always waiting to take advantage of another's weakness. He wished that the family had left the drug business alone.

Jake Westcott got out of the car and wandered around to the rear of the house to see if his friend was home. During the three weeks since school had been out, the basketball hoop was the center of activity. Matt and two other boys were shooting hoops.

Seeing his friend, Matt yelled out, "Weren't you taking Amy to the parade?"

Dragging his feet as he walked toward the other, Jake replied derisively, "Yeah, I was, until Scott Randall got home from college last night. She thinks that it's more important to be seen with a college man, so the plans changed."

Rubbing it in, Matt laughed. "So, you decided to take pity on your buddies?"

Controlling his ire, Jake nodded. "Yeah, if you guys aren't doing anything, I thought that we could drive to town."

"Sounds good to me," Pete said rapidly. "You got the wheels, I've got the time. Besides, there are bound to be lots of chicks hanging around."

Jake grinned at Pete's antics and with a sweep of his arm indicated the way to the car. A few minutes later, the boys left the car in the Agway lot and wandered to the center of town. Seeing his uncle, Pete walked over.

"Hey! Uncle Tom! Have you seen my mom and dad?"

"Hey yourself! What are you doing here? I didn't think you'd come to a small town celebration!" Grinning at the look on his nephew's face, Tom asked, "You guys hungry? If you are, I can fix you up."

Looking at his friends' nods, Pete answered, "Yeah! Bring on the chicken!"

His hunger satisfied, Matt looked at this pals. "So what do we do now? The bands don't start playing music for dancing for another couple of hours."

Wanting to catch a glimpse of Amy and let her know that he was thinking about her, Jake said, "Let's go over to the square. There are over a hundred booths. Maybe there's something worth seeing."

Pete said, "Some of the girls are running the booth for the cheerleader squad. Let's go!"

❋

The firehouse was packed when Linda and Kevin arrived, but Jim and Susan had saved them seats. Going up to get the food while the women stayed with the children and visited with the people seated around them, Kevin and Jim had a moment to talk.

"So far so good," said Jim. "The guys have been checking for alcoholic beverages. So far, a warning was all that's been necessary. Most people are being cooperative and leaving the beer at home."

Nodding, Kevin replied seriously, "This certainly isn't the place for it. Did you notice how many more people were lined up along the parade route this year? I used to know most of them, but today I have seen more groups that I don't recognize than ever before."

Jim laughed. "Well, Mr. Mayor, it was your idea to take out the ads in the surrounding counties. It should be a great day for the local economy with all the additional people here," Jim pointed with his chin. "See that lady with the short brown hair sitting with Ida May Johnson?"

"Yes. Should I know her?"

"Probably not, but you will. That's Ann Clark, a reporter for the press doing a feature article on our bicentennial celebration. So with that additional coverage, next year's event will be even better attended."

Smiling at Jim's self-satisfied attitude, Kevin replied, "Then I guess you'd better start worrying about where everyone is going to park because it's already crazy this year."

"You're right, but I think I'll wait until tomorrow to start worrying about it." Saying hello to the lady in line next to him, Jim looked around at the crowded fire hall and the people passing by outside. As he and Kevin made their way back to their wives, he commented, "Do you notice how the kids seem to go around in groups of four or five now? It used to be that no more than three wandered around together."

"Maybe there's safety in numbers," quipped Kevin. "At any rate, I'm too happy to have Linda back to herself to worry about much of anything at the moment. So, if you don't mind, I'm going to enjoy my lunch."

Sitting down, Kevin basked in the glow of goodwill that seemed to surround him and his family. When empty plates were finally collected and discarded, the kids wanted to see what the booths had. With Tommy and Janie on either side, they started toward the village green, drawn by the color and movement.

The group's movement was slow as Kevin and Linda stopped to say hello. "I'll be glad when people stop acting like they're walking on eggshells around us," stated Linda as she smiled at yet another matron from the church. "They look at Tommy, start to say something about his resemblance to Brett, and suddenly change course, afraid that they'll upset me. Don't they realize that I'll never forget my son?"

"I know what you mean, sweetheart, but they mean well. Tommy looks more like his father every day so it isn't likely that they'll feel comfortable comparing them anytime soon." Pulling her against his side, he continued, "Your feeling somewhat better doesn't mean that everyone else has stopped seeing you as a grieving mother."

Suddenly serious at Kevin's words, Linda met his eyes. "A day won't pass without me mourning his loss, but life does go on."

Coming up behind them, Ben Granger was loud enough to be heard all over the green. "Why, Mr. Mayor and family! How are you all?"

Hiding his displeasure, Kevin turned to face the man he disliked. Whenever Ben was around, he had the feeling that there was something on the man's agenda. Now he had that awkward feeling again. "Fine, Ben, just fine. We ate at the firehouse and we're about to see what crafts people have come up with this year."

"Must be something. This place has been wall-to-wall people all day long." Looking toward the booths selling breads and pies, he commented, "The Legion Auxiliary and the 4-H booths are both about to run out of merchandise. Beats me where all these people come from."

Noticing Kevin's quandary, Jim stepped in, saying, "Well, Ben, regardless of where they're from, just be glad that they're here because each and every dollar they spend helps our town's economy."

Scowling at Jim Walsh, Granger broached the matter that really concerned him—the contract for the cement work on the updating of the hospital. He was just as anxious to know if there had been anything mentioned about the key club but had no way of asking. "Have you heard anything about the hospital renovations recently?"

"What makes you think that I'd have anything to do with the Taylorville Hospital?" asked Kevin.

Not diplomatic on the best of day, Granger realized that he had blundered and would now end up saying something that might upset Linda. Waiting until she had moved out of earshot, he said apologetically, "I just thought that they might be holding off with their plans because of Gunther's involvement with Brett's death."

His manner suddenly frosty, Kevin's tone was icy as he clarified his position. "There is no reason for anyone to hold up any plans so far as I'm concerned." Turning to Jim, he said, "Let's go give the girls a hand with the children."

Walking toward where Susan and Linda stood watching the children try out one after another of the many wooden toys, Jim shook his head. "How that man got himself elected commissioner is beyond me. He's about as subtle as a skunk in heat!"

Smiling at Jim's outburst, Kevin nodded. "You know, Jim, there's more to the man than he'd like us to believe. He may be a loud mouth and have no tact, but he's far from stupid." Looking back at Granger, Kevin mused, *I'd like to know what he was thinking about.*

"Grandpa, look at this carriage!" Janie cried, pulling him by the hand and effectively focusing his attention back to her. "It's almost big enough for us to sit in!"

The next hour was filled with exclamations of awe and, as he paused to look around, Kevin thought once again how amazing it was that all the chaos and confusion had fallen into an orderly pattern. Suddenly he stood staring at the booth sponsored by the Daughters of the American Revolution. What was Austin Greene doing at the booth? Kevin couldn't imagine any young man willingly working at a historical booth while all his friends were wandering around in groups. Uneasy, Kevin nodded toward Austin as he said to Jim, "Doesn't that strike you as odd?"

Following his friend's gaze, Jim raised his brow. "Susan told me that Austin had offered to help his mother with the booth, and from what she said, he's been great. He even came up with the idea of the inexpensive stick pin as a means of drawing attention to the booth."

"I guess you and Tim have me seeing ghosts where there are none."

Hugging Linda, Susan steered her toward another booth. "Give her time, she'll come around. Let's go over and see what they have at the DAR booth, it seems awfully busy."

As they made their way to the booth, Austin was moving stock around. His mother had been so pleased to have his help that she had been waiting on his every whim all day. Smiling to himself, Austin thought that it was a good thing that she attributed his interest as wanting to help rather than the real reason. Now at almost two o'clock, he was just as busy as he had been all day. The tiny piece of tricolor ribbon on a stickpin had been a great idea for an inexpensive patriotic gesture. They had been going like hotcakes—especially among his clients.

Shaking his head, Austin continued to straighten out the statues and boxes of pins behind the white crepe paper, making sure that they covered his stash. If everyone who was wearing one of the stickpins had bought from his stand, he would have had no stock left to sell by ten o'clock! Rossi was in for a surprise. As it was, he didn't have enough reds to make it through the rest of the day and the blacks were just about gone too. Today had been a great day!

He liked the feeling of being the one the people turned to for it gave him power over them. If they sought him out to buy, so be it. He could find an explanation to justify his sudden popularity.

Many kids started by raiding the medicine cabinet for Seconal or Tuinal, originally prescribed for Mommy or Daddy. But what parent counted pills? Not his mother. She didn't even check the liquor cabinet.

"Hey, man, what are you doing behind the counter?" Pete asked, bringing Austin out of his reverie. "I haven't seen you in a while, but I didn't think that it was because you'd turned patriotic! Give me five!"

Seeing that Pete was in the mood to chat with Austin, Matt and Jake moved on to where several underclassmen were admiring T-shirts. "Catch up with us when you're done," said Matt.

Smiling, Austin slapped hands with his former schoolmate. "My mother needed help. What can I get for you?" Joking around, he continued, "We have these handsome tricolor pins or these eagle-head bookmarks, and here we have a short history of the Daughters of the American Revolution and their part in the history of Taylorville."

Laughing, Pete replied, "Man, if that's all you have, you don't have what I want." Getting serious, he went on, "You know, it's almost impossible to score around here since Meeks and Coombs got locked up."

"Really?" Feigning surprise, Austin asked, "There isn't anyone dealing around here?"

"You know how it is. I could probably get what I need in Binghamton, but you want someone you can trust. You know all the talk about the bad trips from contaminated PCP."

"Hang on a second," Austin said, turning to help one of the town matrons. Coming back, he continued, "So it's getting tough to score?"

"You know it. You have to watch what you take from home, and without Meeks and Coombs, there isn't anyone local."

Nodding his agreement, Austin worked up to his pitch. "I wouldn't do this for everyone, but I've replenished my stash, so if you want, I could let you have something to tide you over." Pausing as if deep in thought, he continued, "I wouldn't want anyone to get the idea that I was pushing this shit."

"Hey, man, I know better than that." Thinking for a moment, Pete said, "It would be great if you could let me have a few blacks and ten or twelve reds. Might be just what the doctor ordered to help my friend get over his girlfriend."

"The guys you're with are cool, aren't they? I don't need any hassle coming back on me for trying to help out a friend."

"Don't sweat it," replied Pete, getting his wallet and taking out a bill. "Will this cover it?"

"That's good. If you need anything else, let me know. Maybe I can help you out until you get someone permanent. I hope the rest of your day goes off with a bang."

Placing the packet with the pills in his pocket, Pete grinned. "Thanks to you, it just may."

As they walked across the green looking at the booths, Matt stopped to stare in the direction of the courthouse.

"Now what are you looking at?" asked Jake peevishly. "I thought that we were going to walk over to the cheerleaders' booth."

Grinning at his friend, Matt couldn't help but rub in Jake's discomfort. "I guess we should. With Scott's arm around her, I guess that you're no more than a memory to Amy."

Following his friend's nod, Jake looked and scowled even more. Seeing how upset Jake was, Matt was quick to try and rectify matters. "Hey, I was only teasing. You don't need her if she's too dense to realize how great a guy you are."

Jake shrugged and started walking again. "Yeah, it's easy for you to say, but it hurts anyway."

As the cheerleaders' booth was surrounded by football players, the boys moved on. Seeing three of the girls from school standing off by themselves, Matt said, "Hey, let's hit on them. It'll take your mind off Amy if nothing else."

"So what are you pretty ladies planning on doing to liven up this celebration?" Matt asked as he approached the girls.

Striking what she felt was a sophisticated pose, Pam was quick to answer. "We don't have anything much planned except to see the band play later. But we're open to suggestions."

Listening to Pam, Darla felt uncomfortable. She kept to herself in school and knew that the boys thought of her as a "little mouse." That was all right as long as they left her alone. It wasn't that she didn't like the other kids or didn't want to be with them, but it was hard to talk to them. Her father frowned at the mere idea of his daughter doing anything that might look wrong in the eyes of the church. Her father would be very upset if he could see her now. Sighing, she waited, hoping that the boys would move away. Any hope of that died as Darla saw the boys' interest at her cousin's perky answer. Suddenly she had a premonition that they shouldn't hang out with them.

Pam Matiss, the leader of the group, was a sophomore. Second cousin to Austin Greene, she had always resented not being born in his place. Surly, with a biting tongue and a chip on her shoulder, she had the unearned reputation of being wild. Shelby Dibble was Pam's best friend. The perky blond was friendly and a nice girl who was liked by her peers. She knew that many of Pam's actions were the result of her feelings of inadequacy and tried to help her friend cope the best she could. Today hadn't been easy. Not wanting to see her niece, Darla, left out of the celebration, Pam's mother had insisted that the girls take the shy, reticent freshman with them. Pam had been stewing all day. But Darla was blushing as Pam flirted with Matt, and Shelby felt sorry for her.

Darla thought that she should say something, but didn't want to draw attention to herself. Since trying to get her cousin's attention seemed hopeless, she tugged at the cuff of Pam's shorts, only to have Pam give her a dirty look. Darla waited until she could speak to Shelby, hoping she could reason with Pam.

Jogging to catch up to Jake and Matt, Pete was eager to share his news. He thought about Austin's admonition not to say anything and hesitated. Matt would want to get high, but he didn't know how Jake would react. As he walked up to his friends, he heard Matt trying to impress the girls. Assessing the situation, he decided that they could all end up having a good time, though the quiet girl with Pam and Shelby acted nervous. Breaking into the conversation, Pete said, "What did I miss? Have you decided on anything yet?"

Answering Pete with a smile and a raised eyebrow, Matt replied, "No, we haven't decided anything yet. Pam was about to tell us what the ladies planned to do for the rest of the afternoon."

As the boys turned to her, Pam felt a rush of pleasure. This was how things should be, people wanting to know what she wanted to do instead of assuming that she would just go along with them. Temporarily being the center of attention, Pam replied coyly, "Like I said, we were going to listen to the band later, but if you have a better idea, I'm listening."

Her mouth dry with anxiety, Darla whispered to Shelby, "My father doesn't like me hanging around with boys. He'll have a fit if he finds out."

Happy to see Pam in a better mood, Shelby reassured the other girl. "Darla, your aunt said that you were to stay with us and have a good time. Why don't you forget about everything else and try to just do that?"

Unable to find an argument and knowing that she would get Pam in trouble if she returned to her aunt's house without her, Darla tried to convince herself that Shelby was right. Besides, how did she really know? She had always been such a loner that maybe if she did what Shelby said, she would have fun.

Still miffed at seeing Amy with Scott, Jake decided that he too would go along with Matt's idea. Amy certainly wasn't worrying about whether he was having a good time, so why not? Looking at Matt for approval, he stated, "The competition of the bands doesn't start for another couple of hours. If you guys have seen enough, we can stop at the Pump and Pantry for something to drink and go up to Salt Springs and hang out."

"Sounds good to me," said Pete. "We can walk the springs or hang out by the car and listen to music."

Worried, Darla addressed Pam. "Don't you think we ought to let your mother know where we're going and who we're with?"

Disdainfully, Pam explained. "Darla is my cousin, and my mother said that she should come with us today." Turning to Darla, she continued, "No, I don't see any need to call my mother. She doesn't expect us home until somewhere around 8:30, so there isn't any problem."

Shelby was quick to second Pam; this was her opportunity to spend time with Matt. Placing her hand on the younger girl's shoulder, she said, "You're with us, so what can possibly happen?" Smiling at the boys, she said, "Let's go."

Tired out by all the activity and pacified by having gotten balloons and lollipops, Tommy was asleep in Jim's arms while Janie nestled peacefully against her grandfather. As they walked toward the parking area, Kevin looked at the people still packing the streets and listened to the happy noise and laughter. "So far so good," Kevin commented, thinking how last year at this time the festivities had already been marred by two incidents of kids drinking and acting out. "It looks like the additional planning for the patrols and the extra coverage by the state police has had some impact. Even with more people, things have been calm. You know that we would have heard if anything bad had happened."

"I, for one, am certainly glad that the legal drinking age in this state is still twenty-one. It doesn't prevent the kids from crossing the state line to go drinking, but it sure makes it easier to control here. In fact, they could close down the Ahwaga Inn and Red's Tavern without a protest from me," said Jim.

Smiling his agreement, Kevin added, "The fact that the only places selling beer and liquor are state stores doesn't hurt either. If you want to keep your liquor cabinet full you have to plan in advance and that serves as a deterrent too. But people find a way around it if they are determined."

"Another couple of hours and we'll be home free," replied Jim thankfully. "I have to admit that the drug situation has me very uneasy."

Pausing as he wondered if he should tell Jim his plans, Kevin shrugged. "Me too...I told Linda this morning that I'm going to do some scouting around into the case that Brett was working on. You know the one, the defense of those three that got tied up with the murder charge. There just might be something in Brett's notes that might help Sheriff Billings or Tim with their investigations."

Appalled at the thought that had crossed his mind, Jim paled. It was so ludicrous that it didn't even bear consideration, yet he was reticent to share the idea with Kevin.

Noticing his friend's lack of comment, Kevin looked at Jim. Startled by the other's sudden pallor, he asked, "You don't think it's a good idea?"

"No, of course I do. It's just that it suddenly struck me that if Brett stumbled on to anything, could it have been related to his death?"

As the group walked toward Jake's car, Pete waved at Austin. Watching Pete and his friends walk away with the three girls, Austin smiled. Being able to give people a little pleasure made him understand exactly what had motivated the song "Candy Man." It was a potent feeling.

Stopping at the convenience store known as the Pump and Dump to the locals, the group went in and picked out what they wanted to snack on. Doritos being the munchies of choice, the boys added two bags to the two six packs of soda sitting on the counter. Waiting for the clerk to take care of them, Matt turned to Jake and said in an undertone, "I hope you didn't forget to pack a cooler. These chicks aren't exactly super stimulating."

"No sweat. In fact, my mother teases me about the cooler having welded itself fast to my trunk because I'm always using it. Besides"—he continued, laughing—"Genny beer never lets me down even when Amy does."

Clapping his friend on the back, Matt raised his voice to get the other's attention. "Let's go."

Having heard about the springs but never having been there, Darla loved them at first sight. The cleared picnic area where they left the car was peaceful, sunlit; surrounded by maples and oaks that threw their cool shadows. As they got out of the car, she could hear the spring gurgling to the right and her apprehension disappeared. How could anything bad possibly happen in such a beautiful place?

Pete had been talking to Pam, and turning to the others, laid out his plan. "Why don't we walk up to the top of the springs to the swimming hole? It's really nice up there and it's a great place for a picnic."

Reaching over to grab the other handle of the cooler while handing the radio to Shelby, Jake said, "Lead on."

Walking up the sun-dappled incline, Darla was surprised to find that she actually felt good. She was part of a group, and even her father couldn't object to a walk in this beautiful glen.

Seeing Darla's smile, Shelby said happily, "Aren't you glad you came?"

Nodding, Darla let the sunlight warm her. When they reached the flat rocks surrounding the swimming hole, she relaxed against a stone and dangled her legs in the water.

"I don't know about anyone else," said Pete, "but I'm going swimming." Stripping down to his Jockeys, he jumped in yelling "Geronimo!"

Laughing with the others, Darla's eyes widened as she saw Pam taking off her top. Before she had a chance to say anything, her cousin was in the water splashing with Pete. Shelby, Matt, and Jake followed suit, and though she had never done anything like this in her life, Darla found herself yearning to join in.

"Come on in!" yelled Jake, his hair slicked back by the water. "We won't splash you if you don't want."

Hoping she wouldn't regret her decision, Darla threw caution to the wind and joined the others in the water. Later, lying on the rocks with the sun drying them, she smiled, feeling good just to be alive.

"You know, you should smile like that more often," Jake said, lying next to her. "It lights up your whole face."

Surprised, Darla was suddenly tongue-tied. Jake continued to speak. "I really like the peaceful feeling you get up here. Just watching the shadows change can keep me occupied for hours." Turning as he moved to get up, he asked, "Want a Coke?"

Nodding, Darla looked at Shelby, who put her thumb up together in a sign of approval. As the sun shone down, the group lazed around. Reaching into the cooler, Pete handed out cans of beer as he said, "Let's toast to the summer of '76. Sunshine, friendship, and fun!" He touched his can to everyone else's and then drank deeply.

Accepted for the first time in her life, Darla also drank. Relaxed and happy to begin with, it didn't take more than a few swallows before she began to feel a slight buzz. After finishing the can, she found that she could talk and laugh without feeling shy.

Lulled by the sun and feeling good, Pam was happy for her cousin. Nudging Shelby, she said, "Look at Darla. She's finally acting human."

With a lot of laughter, the sun-dried teens got back into their clothes. Reaching into his pocket with a knowing look at Matt, Pete took out the bag of pills and swallowed a red one.

Pam asked, "What are you taking?"

Smiling, he answered, "Just something to make the day even better. Want one?"

Before Pam could answer, Matt held out his hand, and following Pete's example downed one of the red pills.

"I don't know," said Pam. "I never did drugs. What does it make you feel like?"

"Mellow, really mellow," replied Matt, stretching. "It makes you more aware of what's going on around you but makes you feel good at the same time. Try one."

Hesitating briefly, Pam took the pill. Her own inhibitions already forgotten, Darla stuck her hand out, saying, "You weren't thinking of leaving me out, were you?"

Smiling at her, Pete shook his head and handed her a pill. Putting the bag back in his pocket, he pulled Pam up, saying, "They're playing our song."

Thoroughly enjoying dancing for the first time and feeling good as part of the group, Darla thirstily downed another beer.

"Hey, you'd better go easy," Jake said, seeing how high the younger girl was.

Her canned confidence speaking, Darla smiled and shook her head. "Don't worry, I feel fine." Suddenly she looked strangely at Jake and stopped moving, swaying as a dazed expression filled her eyes. Sitting down heavily, she leaned back against a rock.

Seeing what had happened, Pete yelled, "Not to worry. She'll sleep it off and won't even feel bad when she wakes up; I've had it happen before."

Taking his friend's word at face value, Jake shrugged and lost himself watching the shadows playing over the springs. He jolted out of his reverie as Darla's hand slapped against him and her body convulsed, trying to rid itself of the poison she had ingested. Looking at her, Jake felt ill as he saw her body twitching. "Pete! Something's wrong! What should I do?"

Unsure, Pete said, "I don't know if it's better to move her or not. Maybe it will pass."

Suddenly sober, the five youths formed a circle around Darla, wanting to help yet not knowing what to do. As Pete had said, suddenly the fit seemed to pass and Darla lay still again. Trying to shake her awake, Shelby smelled the sour smell of vomit as a line of spittle dribbled from the corner of Darla's mouth. "I can't wake her! Someone go for help!"

Each of the five would later remember the day in their own way, feeling responsible for what had happened. The extreme price paid by one shy, unassuming girl for an afternoon of happiness would haunt them for the rest of their lives.

The Holidays

The cold, gray light of the November day seemed fit illumination for his thoughts as Kevin stood at the window. The summer of the bicentennial had not been kind to the sleepy county seat. He was only the first to suffer the loss of a child. Within a month, three children had died. The holidays would be difficult for the Meeks and Dibble families, as well as for him and Linda. It would mark the first time that their children wouldn't be with them at Thanksgiving and Christmas.

Each of the deaths had been senseless. There was still doubt as to whether Brett's death might ultimately have some connection to illegal drug dealing. There was no question that the loss of Tim Meeks and Darla Dibble was directly attributable to the drug use which had invaded their community.

Kevin felt, for the hundredth time, the frustration that accompanied any thought of how the influx of drugs had disrupted his community. As far back as the history of the town went, there had always been a town drunk. Alcohol abuse had always been recognized as undesirable and had been the cause of more than one death over the years. Death was never easy, but the death of Darla Dibble had been a bitter shock. It was the first but not the last time he would have to see the cold, sneaking, relentless finality that was the result of unwitting drug abuse.

Returning to the evening of the 4th, Kevin shuddered as he again felt the horrible juxtaposition of the warm, happy celebration and the cold, harsh death that had been its conclusion. Five shocked teens had been witnesses to Darla's death, a death that could have been prevented had they known to turn her over so she would not choke. Though they had all been warned about the dangers of any drugs, let alone mixing them, the lure of the illusive "high" had been too great. They had not known that mixing barbiturates and alcohol would ultimately kill Darla by relaxing her gag reflex.

Kevin was sure that each of the five remaining kids and their families would be giving thanks this year that they had been given another chance. He knew that he would be joined by many others in the community who were thankful that no other drug-related death had taken place since then.

Kevin watched Mrs. Meeks leave the bank across the street, another casualty of the drug problem. She had admitted that Tim had been running with a bad crowd, but she had not recovered from his death. She refused to accept the explanation of suicide, and from what he had uncovered, Kevin was inclined to agree. He hoped someone would offer her some form of comfort when the holidays rolled around and she would again face the reality of Tim's death.

Kevin hadn't gotten Brett's file or the notes for the murder defense of Meeks, Coombs, and Radner from Holly until late August. What he had found had been disturbing. There was a drug cartel at work in the area, and Brett had been convinced that they were the suppliers of his clients among others. In his notes, Brett outlined how he and the county's district attorney thought that the supplies were coming into the area from the south. The Bonano family was supplying Tioga and Stuben counties. But Tim Reeves had gotten information that the Rossi family was distributing the drugs in Taylor County, coming from South Carolina.

Suddenly Coombs and Radner were represented by a high-priced lawyer. Slick bargaining allowed Coombs to make a deal. In return for testifying against Radner and casting blame for supplies on the Bonano family, the prosecution had counted the time Coombs had served in rehab as sufficient. He was now out on parole.

Kevin was convinced, as were Billings and Reeves, that this was a form of red herring to effectively move the investigation away from the Rossi family. There was nothing concrete on which to base their suspicions. In spite of Brett's notes and the fact that the car with South Carolina plates kept showing up in town, no hard proof existed to substantiate their theory. But without proof, nothing could be done.

His jaw clenched in anger, Karl placed his hands on Darnell's desk and leaned closer, speaking through his teeth. "I bought into this clinic as a partner, an equal partner. The last six months you have been telling me what to do and how to run my life as if I was a first-year resident, and I don't like it."

"Someone has to monitor what you're doing because you certainly don't act like you know." Calmly scrutinizing the irate man in front of him, Harrison drove his point home. "If it hadn't been for my having a source of alternative funding, we would still be at square one so far as the renovations and updating of the clinic are concerned. You know that I'm right—we lost the bank support because of your involvement with Conklin's death."

Struggling to control himself, Karl glared at the older man. "As much as you think my actions have been detrimental for the hospital, let me remind you that because of my pediatric specialty, we now have a backlog of patients who prefer to come here rather than go to Barnes-Kasson. So my input has been positive, leading to the need to expand." Forcing himself to relax, he watched the older man, waiting for his reply.

"You can't deny that I was correct in my assessment of your situation with Holly Conklin, can you? So if I hadn't insisted on your backing off, you would have made your relationship public and made matters worse."

Fighting to retain his composure but unwilling to take any more abuse, Karl said, "If you are so concerned about how my actions are affecting the clinic, then buy me out. I'm sure I can find somewhere else to practice."

Unwilling to leave the discussion on such a negative note, Harrison tried to reason with Gunther. "Will you please stop pacing and sit down? No one is disputing your expertise as a physician, but you can't deny that what's happening with Holly is affecting your work. It's no secret that you've moved out of your house and are renting the Kerr's garage apartment. That is only going to lead to additional speculation by the gossipmongers. We need to get this straightened out for everyone's sake—yours and Holly's included."

"So what are you suggesting?"

"What I propose is the following." Narrowing his eyes, Darnell looked at Gunther, wondering if the other man would buy his proposal. "I want you to continue with the hospital until the conjecture about Conklin's death, as well as the infamy about the key club, dies down. You and Holly will have to put your plans on hold."

Knowing that Harrison had a definite agenda, Karl said, "I'm listening."

"At the end of next year, I'll buy you out or have my financial backers do it. I'll make it a stipulation of the deal to help you establish a new practice. You might want to return to New Mexico, or choose somewhere else. At any rate, what I'm offering is an overall solution where everyone comes out ahead."

Leaving Harrison's office half an hour later, Gunther had to admire the man's ingenuity, if not his methods. Now the only problem was getting Holly to go along with what Harrison had proposed.

Though the late fall day had started out sunny, gray clouds had chased the sun away and the day was overcast and glum. *The way I feel,* thought Linda. Kevin had suggested that they drive to the cemetery and tell Brett yet again how much they missed him. It had become a habit over the past few months to visit their son's grave and voice what they felt and what they were doing to fill the empty spaces left by his death.

Afterward, they had both felt better. They had promised their son, as well as each other, to maintain the family closeness that had existed during his lifetime. It might be hard, but they had every intention of keeping that promise. Eager to share their feelings with Holly, they had decided to drive by the house.

Seeing the car in the driveway, they had gone to the door where they saw her sitting at the table with Janie, who was talking her usual mile a minute. Holly had actually seemed glad to see them.

"Come on in, the coffee is fresh" Holly greeted them as she stepped out of Janie's way. Smiling at her daughter's antics, she had poured coffee as they entered the kitchen with Janie chattering as she hung around Kevin's neck.

Even though the conversation had centered on Tommy's success in kindergarten and Janie's upcoming role in the preschool Christmas show, all the adults had been relaxed. The neutral topic of what was happening around town had been fine. However, when Linda had mentioned that she would like them to be together for Thanksgiving, Holly had put the barrier back in place.

Hurt by Holly's failure to respond but not wanting to argue in front of Janie, Linda had remained silent. Unfortunately, the glum mood that had then settled over her had stayed with her.

As the phone rang, Linda tried to shake herself out of her slump. Forcing herself to be calm, she pushed her worried thoughts to the back of her mind. "Good afternoon. This is Kevin Conklin's office, how may we help you?"

Hearing Linda's cheerful salutation, Ann hesitated, ready to hang up the phone. Now that Brett was no longer here to help her, maybe his father would. "This is Ann Gunther. I'd like to make an appointment to see Attorney Conklin."

Masking her surprise, Linda replied, "May I ask in reference to what matter?"

"It's rather personal. Would there be any possibility of seeing Mr. Conklin either today or tomorrow?" Ann asked, afraid that she would lose her nerve.

"One moment while I check his calendar." *This is strange,* Linda thought, checking Kevin's agenda. Ann obviously didn't want to talk to her. Shaking her head, Linda picked up the phone.

"He has a 10:30 slot available a day after tomorrow, but if it's urgent, he has a 5:30 this afternoon. Will either of those work?"

"Could you schedule me in for this afternoon? I'd prefer to see him as soon as possible."

"Certainly. He'll be waiting for you."

Hanging up, Linda sighed. Ann and Karl Gunther had frequently been included in family celebrations and Ann's standoffish attitude was difficult to accept. But many things had changed with Brett's death, and accepting them was difficult.

At the sound of the door, Linda smiled. Kevin had been at the courthouse and usually shared what news he picked up.

"Lots of people waiting for their turn at justice?" asked Linda.

Stopping and grinning at his wife, Kevin shook his head. "Sometimes I wonder if counsel has a bigger ax to grind than the plaintiff. You should have seen Kelley grandstanding as to the benefits of subdivision. If things continue in this manner, there won't be a single farm left in the county by the year 2000. I wish everyone would work as hard to get new industry into the area."

Moving around her desk to hug her, Kevin glanced down at Linda's notes as he asked, "Anything new I should know about?"

"Actually there is," replied Linda. "I got a call from Ann Gunther a little while ago. She asked to see you and said it was urgent, so I set her up for 5:30."

"Why do I get the impression that's not the whole story?" asked Kevin, turning to look at Linda.

Ruefully, Linda looked back at him, saying, "You know me too well. She acted so distant and standoffish on the phone that she might have picked your name from a phone book instead of knowing us. So many things have changed."

Leaning against the counter, Holly listened with relief to the sound of her in-laws driving away. A frown marred her face as she thought again how unfair it was that everything was so difficult.

She was the same person she had always been. When she had married Brett, she had believed in her vows. They had been together all of the time and he had lavished her with the affection and attention that she needed to feel wanted. During the last year and a half he had become so obsessed with his work that the cases he was working on had become a rival for her attention. But it hadn't only been Holly. Brett had been so involved with the murder case he was pursuing that the children had lacked his attention too.

Both of them had seen the dinner club as a way to spend more quality time together. It might have been, had they spent the time alone. But in the long run, the weekly outings had proven to be the death knell of their relationship.

"Mommy, Mommy! I want a drink," said Tommy, breaking into Holly's reverie. "And Janie's thirsty too."

Smiling as she gave the children some Kool-Aid, Holly felt her heart swell with her love for them. Gulping, they rushed back to their building project, leaving Holly to her thoughts once again.

The attraction that blazed between them had taken her by surprise. She and Karl had known each other for years and neither one thought of the other in any context than that of a friend. But love wasn't always predictable. When they realized that their feelings were different and reciprocal they had seized the moment, and once found neither was willing to let it go.

Troubled, she busied herself making a cup of tea. She wasn't handling things well and she knew it. Until the affair with Karl, she had always been very straightforward and open about her thoughts and actions. Now the very essence of who she was seemed to have changed. She couldn't talk to anyone other than Karl about Brett's death and her concerns, but she didn't. She was afraid of being made to face an unpleasant truth. It was bad enough that Brett was dead and she would have to live with the horror of his death for the rest of her life.

Kevin and Linda had been supportive and loving throughout the whole ordeal, but that only made everything worse. Her guilty feelings became even greater by her in-laws' caring attitude. She had returned to work both to retain focus in her life and to see more of Karl, but even that was a problem. Dr. Harrison was adamantly against their publicizing their relationship. That meant that they had to watch how they acted in front of everyone and had to tiptoe around if they were to spend any time together.

Sighing as she filled her cup, Holly knew that things had to change fast. She had been alone long enough to realize that she didn't do well on her own. She belonged with Karl and wanted to get on with their life together.

As if summoned by her thoughts, the phone rang. Picking it up, she smiled as she heard his voice.

"I've missed you so much the last two days. I can't get you off my mind," he said, wonder evident in his voice.

"That's good, because I feel the same way. I was fixing a cup of tea and thinking how I can't go on like this much longer. We see as little of each other as we did when Brett was alive and we still have to hide our relationship," she replied, her displeasure obvious.

Exasperated, Karl spoke softly. "Baby, you know that there is nothing that I want more than to be with you on a daily basis. But right now, things are still complicated and I have to humor Harrison."

"Then leave the hospital," she answered angrily. "I don't care what Darnell Harrison says. He has no right to tell us when and where we can be together."

"Sweetheart, be reasonable. I have my money tied up in the hospital. I don't want to start off a life with you and the kids without being able to support you."

"Right now I don't care. I don't want to wait on anyone else's whims to be together." Her distress obvious, she continued, "Don't you understand? You're the only one I can talk to without being careful of what I say. I'm not used to the complications that seem to be taking over my life."

Trying to mask his own concern, he spoke quietly. "Take a deep breath and try to calm down. You're getting yourself all worked up and that won't help either of us. I can see that we're going to have to rework our timetable. I don't want you worried or upset any more than necessary. The only thing that matters to me is having you and the children happy."

Surprised at Karl's sudden acquiescence, Holly was momentarily at a loss for words. Taking advantage, Karl continued with his train of thought. "I think that what we need to do is decide where it is you want to live. I don't think either of us really wants to stay in Taylorville, but if I leave the hospital that means that we are going to face relocating to another area." Pausing to let her digest what he had just said, he asked, "Are you all right?"

Still shocked but feeling better at Karl's show of concern, Holly spoke breathlessly, "I'm okay, just a little surprised. I feel as if the boulder I've been trying to shove out of the way suddenly started moving on its own. I guess I wasn't expecting you to agree with me."

Glancing at the clock on his bookcase, Karl said quickly, "You know I love you and I want to be with you too. Look, I have to go. We'll talk more later."

Entering his office, Kevin looked at his agenda. Seeing the meeting with Granger and Harrison scheduled for 1:30, he sighed, wishing that he could avoid it. As mayor he was expected to participate in town planning, and Christmas was one of the busiest times. The idea of serving on the committee itself didn't bother him. What he didn't relish was the idea of spending any time whatsoever in the company of Ben Granger. More and more he found it difficult to mask his dislike.

It wasn't unusual for the commissioner to serve as liaison between the hospital and the community service groups, especially during the holiday season. But the man was not concerned about what benefit could be gained for anyone other than himself.

Deciding on how to use the time prior to the meeting, he began to jot down notes for a brief he was preparing. His attention wandered as his thoughts continued to ping-pong between Granger and Harrison. Making no progress with his brief, he decided to try and pin down what had him on edge. Clearing his desk and leaning back in his chair, he let his thoughts come as they would.

Tim Reeves had always questioned Harrison's actions, even when they were in Korea. While other MASH units fought tooth and nail for the barest essentials, it had been easy for Harrison to get what he needed. Kevin hadn't given it much thought at the time, but he realized that Reeves had been right when he pointed to Rossi as Harrison's connection. Now it was obvious that the connection between Harrison and Rossi had continued even after Korea.

While funding for his hospital had presented problems after his return from the war, it had been Rossi's group that had provided Harrison with the needed backing. At the time, Kevin, as well as most others in the town, had not thought beyond the benefits of enhanced medical facilities for the community. No one had been overly concerned about how Harrison had acquired his financing. Now, knowing what he did about Rossi's connection to the drug problem in the community, Kevin couldn't seem to shake the feeling that any alliance between Rossi and Harrison could not be healthy.

A frown crossing his brow, Kevin unhappily followed his thoughts down a complicated and ugly road. If Rossi was responsible for bringing drugs into the county, was Harrison aware of it? Could he actually be participating in the trafficking? Appalled at this line of thought, Kevin shook his head as if to clear it away. It wasn't possible! Harrison was a doctor, committed to helping others and saving lives. He wouldn't ignore the illegal use of drugs, would he?

If he felt ambivalent about Harrison, Kevin had no doubt whatsoever as to his feelings for Granger. The mere thought of the man was distasteful. Granger had been firmly entrenched in the political arena of county for decades. Both behind the scenes in the beginning and later from center stage, he had manipulated contracts and construction projects both on a local and state level. Regardless, the result had ultimately been the same, more money in Granger's pocket.

Brett had shared his feelings about Granger. Knowing this, Kevin was further puzzled by his son's involvement in any club where the commissioner was a member. To Kevin's knowledge, prior to their involvement in the key club, Brett had never socialized with Granger willingly, not liking the man any more than his father did.

So what was Granger's connection with Harrison? Darnell Harrison had never even made a pretense of disguising his disdain for the loud, bull-like Granger. That being the case, why had he given Granger the contract for all the renovations of the hospital? There were certainly other contractors who were just as reputable and economically viable if not more so.

With the intention of stopping by the church, Linda left the office around five. Days always seemed so short at this time of year because it became dark so early. Sighing, she turned onto the street. Her movements were automatic. Her mind was elsewhere.

Since the time Brett and Holly had started going out, Thanksgiving had become a tradition for the Conklin's. Wanting to avoid the pressure of having Brett have to choose where to go, they prepared Thanksgiving dinner while Holly's parents had the kids over for Christmas dinner. Anyone who had nowhere else to go always seemed to end up with Kevin and Linda for the holiday.

Her brow furrowed, Linda felt the sense of desperation welling up in her throat again. It had taken months for her to accept the fact that Brett would no longer be a part of her life. The children were all that she had left of her son. Could Holly really expect her to stop being a part of their lives? Pulling into the parking lot of the church, Linda said a prayer. Though it was said that the Lord didn't give you more than you were capable of handling, she wondered how she was supposed to get over this latest hurdle.

Year's End

Driving back from his cement plant, the last thing on Commissioner Granger's mind was the obvious conflict of interest in using his firm for county projects. He had been doing so for so long, it had become the norm. Besides, if needed, he could show prior work completed as a justification for the present contractual award. No, he wasn't worried his business interests would present any problem as to his reelection. But the key club might present a problem, if he didn't manage to kill the rumors.

Things had been calm lately. A call to DA Ed Smalls had ensured that Billings had been told to drop the investigation into Conklin's death. Ben had been surprised when Smalls had laughed, saying that Darnell Harrison had already taken care of the request. He did not know why Harrison didn't want Billings snooping around, but he was glad that Billings had been stopped. There were things that Ben wanted left buried.

One thing these small-town hypocrites insisted on was that their elected officials be paragons of virtue. In spite of the fact that they themselves applauded everyone who got away with any kind of wrongdoing, a blemished moral record would not be tolerated of anyone in authority. Should the truth come out about the key club, he could forget all about being reelected, and he liked being commissioner.

Checking his watch, he saw he had a half hour before his meeting. Just enough time to stop and see if he could catch Walter Stern. He was sure the banker wouldn't be any more anxious than he was to see their escapades made public.

Seated with Granger at their preferred corner table at the Inn, Stern waited for Cathy to leave their drinks before asking, "What's so urgent? Nothing's been said by anyone as far as I know."

Wrapping his large hand around the gin and tonic in front of him, Ben drank before answering. "You're right. Nothing has been said yet, but that's no guarantee." His brow furrowing, he asked, "Did you know that Ann Gunther went to see Kevin Conklin about handling her divorce?"

"No, I hadn't heard, but I'm not surprised. It's no secret that Karl wants his life to include Holly Conklin."

"But don't you think that Ann is likely to bring up the key club when she files for divorce?"

Stern silently contemplated the man in front of him before answering. He had heard rumors on the grapevine of Granger's animal-like behavior. Calmly, Stern replied, "Maybe. But I still don't see why you're worried. The whole thing can be explained as a dinner club and all of the members were consenting adults, so why should she use it as an argument? She has enough grounds with alienation of affection and adultery." Stopping to think, Stern continued, "We haven't met frequently since Conklin's death. I think we've only had dinner once on a Friday since then and that was by accident. I really don't think that anyone believes the club still exists."

Nodding his agreement, Ben let the matter drop. He wasn't about to explain his anxiety over what Ann Gunther might say. If his actions ever became known, he could kiss reelection goodbye. While his business was lucrative enough to maintain the lifestyle he now enjoyed, it was not able to give him the power that he exerted as one of the three county commissioners—and he had no intention of relinquishing it.

He had kept a close watch on Coombs's activities since his release from the Broome County Jail the month before, and Will Billings had to admit that he seemed to be keeping his nose out of trouble. The people he had keeping an eye on Coombs in town had nothing to say either. Maybe the scare and the possibility of doing prison time had straightened the kid out. His uncle had arranged a job with Ben Granger and it seemed as if he had every intention of staying straight.

But Will was still uneasy. Sighing, he picked up the notes that Kevin had handed him several weeks before. As he reviewed the information, he once again felt that somewhere in Brett's files was the key to the county drug problem. So there might be a more plausible explanation for Brett's death and hell would freeze over before he accepted the idea of it being accidental.

Repeatedly he had argued with Smalls and Cummings. They were beginning to think that he was delusional. Why continue to look for culprits and explanations when Gunther's testimony as to accidental death had been accepted as record? Even his wife thought that he was acting obsessively when it came to the Conklin death.

Maybe they were right. There had been no evidence that Conklin's death had occurred in any other manner than what Gunther had said. Though he continued to question what had happened, he was operating on his gut feeling and instinct, but you couldn't take either one to court.

Looking out the window, Will wondered if it was going to storm. The weather hadn't really been cold enough for there to be snow, but right now the gray clouds announced that rain was a possibility. Yet the weather wasn't his major concern.

Since the death of Darla Dibble, there had been no other deaths directly attributed to drug use. That didn't mean that the problem had disappeared, quite the opposite. Last month several kids had been taken to the hospital and had their stomachs pumped. And what about the one who had broken his leg jumping from Devil's Elbow because he was under the influence and thought he could fly?

He had hoped that the kids had been thoroughly scared by Darla's death. He also prayed that parents were paying more attention to the access of both the medicine and liquor cabinets at home. In this community, the consensus was that "my kid wouldn't do that." The high school had cooperated by having a series of assemblies where the dangers of drug use had been discussed and the kids were given a chance to ask questions. He had participated along with several of the local troopers in one panel discussion.

Since District Attorney Smalls had written the letter to the Captain of the state police barracks at Gibson indicating that no one was to help Billings with his investigation of Conklin's death, John Drann had been leery of speaking with Billings. But Will couldn't blame him. His friend had too many years invested in building his sterling reputation to risk jeopardizing his pension and retirement. The only thing that John did was alert him to a situation that he felt was problematic.

Salvatore Romano had moved into the area, buying a house in Fleetville. Since then, the local lodge of the Fraternal Order of Police had been the recipients of a satellite dish antenna, as well as a big screen television.

Romano had a plane that he flew himself and landed in a field he had cleared close to his house. It was rumored that he worked for the Rossi family, but there was no proof. Supposedly, Romano landed his plane loaded with illegal substances destined for New York City on the strip near his house, a few miles from the Gibson Barracks. The drugs were then picked up by members of the distribution ring at Romano's house and moved to the city. Several neighbors had mentioned that Sal, as the locals knew him, was able to drive his car at excessive speeds along Route 81 without fear of being stopped by the police.

Route 81 was under the jurisdiction of the state police because it was an interstate highway and Drann had mentioned the situation to Billings in hopes that Will would be able to nail Romano on one of the local roads. But Will didn't have the manpower to set up a trap, so the knowledge had become only another source of frustration.

Tim Reeves had continued contacting his sources, passing on information that he received from both Kevin and Will. Surveillance had increased in both Boulder and Raleigh, but no operation had been mounted in the northeast. It was almost as if those in the position to do something were intentionally turning a blind eye to what was going on.

The only concrete facts that had come from Reeve's sources was that Captain Joseph Rossi and his underling made at least one trip a month into Taylor County and that the defense council for Meeks and Radner had been provided by the Rossi Family. Neither of these actions constituted a breaking of the law, so Will's hands were tied. All he could do was hope that when the need arose, he would find some way to rid himself of the shackles.

It had happened again. The invoice didn't match the shipment that they had received. As he checked the boxes in front of him to make sure that he hadn't made a mistake, Gerald Weir shook his head in dismay. Ever since the fiasco with Gunther, he had been even more careful to make sure that he was the one to receive the boxes and open them. According to this latest invoice, there was once again a difference between what had been shipped and what had been received.

For all the years he had worked at the hospital, there had never been any doubt that he knew exactly what new products were being developed in the market. In fact, Dr. Harrison had often conferred with him as to the wisdom in changing one or another of the medications that they used.

That was generally the extent of their infrequent communication. It had been years since he had consulted with Harrison about returning outdated stock or changing the ordering patterns, and he was proud that the doctor trusted him with so heavy a responsibility. In fact, there had never been a doubt as to Gerald's integrity or competence until the incident with Gunther. It had been the worst day of his life.

Though he couldn't say why, he had never liked the young doctor. Perhaps it had something to do with the fact that Gunther was handsome and confident and his negative feeling was nothing more than jealousy. Or it could have been Gunther's overconfident attitude that had turned Gerald off. Even now Gerald didn't really know, though he had often thought about it.

In any event, he had not had too much to do with the younger doctor until the fall of 1975 when Gunther had begun coming to the pharmacy for his own medications. At first Gerald hadn't thought much of it, but as the doctor's visits became more frequent, Gerald had begun to keep track of the medications that Gunther was using. When there was a difference between what his records said and what was actually on the shelf the logical conclusion was that it had to be Gunther. There had never before been a discrepancy in his stock versus his records, and he had been all too ready to place the blame on the young doctor. But Gunther hadn't been near the pharmacy in the last eight months and there were still discrepancies! So what was the explanation?

Accepting change had never been Gerald's strong suit, but it hadn't really presented a problem until Dr. Harrison had insisted that they start using Alpha Drugs, the suppliers recommended by the Rossi group. Other than keeping up on the new drugs, Gerald hadn't had to worry about his routine being varied until the change in drug suppliers.

Weir had started with the hospital when it first opened and had made it a habit to inventory the stock on a weekly basis. He also made unscheduled stock checks in the emergency room and nurses' station when he saw an increase in the number of admissions during the week. Lately, things had been calm and it had been months since he had to increase the quantities of medication ordered. He hadn't changed his order but the invoice indicated a fifteen percent increase in both Tuinal and Seconal. Even worse, the additional medication hadn't arrived with the order. So what was going on?

The invoice had been fine and everything had checked out fine last month. But the month before, the invoice had also shown an increase in the quantity of Seconal ordered. Then, as now, the actual merchandise had been missing from the delivery. Not wanting to bother Dr. Harrison, Gerald had called the company about the discrepancy.

Mr. Roman, the accounts manager for the company, had been quick to tell him that he would take care of correcting the error on the bill. He had urged Gerald to let accounts payable know that they should pay the lesser amount, and Gerald had done just that. *Having already made this mistake once, you would think that they would be more careful,* thought Gerald.

Frowning, he again rubbed his temples as he thought back to Harrison's reaction. Weir had simply done as Mr. Roman had suggested, but someone in the business office had said something to Darnell Harrison and he had come to see Gerald.

Turning to reach for another bottle, Weir saw Harrison standing in the doorway. His hand on the bottle, Gerald spoke calmly as he asked, "Do you need anything, Dr. Harrison?"

Smiling, Harrison answered, "Nothing urgent. I just came by to ask you to stop by my office after meds so that we can talk, and I was admiring how you know exactly where everything is."

Pleased, Gerald said, "Well, I should know where everything is. I've been here since you opened the doors in 1958. Don't you remember? You stipulated when you hired me that I would have to help set up the pharmacy."

"True, but in spite of how easy you may find doing this, I, for one, don't minimize the importance of what you do. It's no secret that some of these lifesavers are deadly if abused. With you in charge, I don't have to worry about that happening; you always know exactly what's going on." Noticing the other man's pleasure in his comments, Darnell continued, "When you finish, stop by my office."

Nodding, Gerald had turned confidently back to his work. He hadn't wanted to continue studying beyond his pharmacology degree; his disappointed mother had always referred to him as being simply a cog in a big wheel. But he was happy with his lot in life. He knew that even the best doctors and the greatest hospitals didn't succeed if all the little wheels didn't function well. He had the satisfaction of knowing that Harrison recognized that he did his job well.

Later, entering the office to find Harrison on the phone, Weir glanced around the room. As he caught a glimpse of the familiar invoice on Harrison's desk, he suddenly began to feel uneasy. What was the invoice form Alpha Drugs doing on Darnell's desk? He had done as Roman suggested and had notified the billing department, so why was the invoice on the desk? Had there been another problem?

Sitting down at Harrison's signal, Weir's discomfort had increased with the length of the phone call. Something was wrong. Never a very confident man, Gerald wondered what Harrison was going to say.

"Sorry about that," said Darnell as he hung up the phone. "It seems that there just aren't enough hours in the day. So now I make the calls whenever I get a minute."

Nodding, Gerald had found it difficult to keep his gaze from dropping to the papers on the desk. Though he had worked for Harrison for almost two decades, he still felt uncomfortable when he talked to him. Clearing his throat, he replied, "It must be hard to keep on top of it all."

"Sometimes," admitted Harrison. "But thankfully, I have a great backup staff." Looking intently at Weir as if weighing what he was about to say, Harrison continued. "The running of this place gets complicated sometimes. Especially with all the new technology we need to keep up with and the renovations to the building during the last six months."

"I can imagine. I'm glad that I don't have to deal with that end of things. At least things don't change constantly in the pharmacy."

Nodding, Harrison continued, "I'm glad you understand how difficult my job can be." Turning the pen that he held end for end, Darnell chose his words carefully. "In fact, sometimes I feel like a juggler trying to keep all the balls in the air at the same time."

"I guess it can't be easy to keep things going on an even keel," replied Weir.

"No, it isn't. Sometimes, much as I'd prefer not to, I end up having to weigh the alternatives between compromising to get things done or not having them done at all."

Looking at Weir to make sure he followed his argument, Darnell continued. "There are very few people who understand how difficult it is to make sure we are able to provide the high quality healthcare that we do. With new advances, it isn't enough simply to be aware of new medications and new research. One has to make sure we have the capacity to deal with any kind of emergency that may come up. That means having the proper equipment."

"But we do have it, don't we?" questioned Weir, confused. "Surgery isn't my area, but I thought that the majority of the renovations we underwent were to ensure that we were able to provide all the latest techniques."

Nodding again, Darnell asked, "And how do you think we paid for them?"

Frowning, Gerald hadn't been able to answer. "I don't know. I suppose through bank loans or government grants?"

Laying the pen down on his desk, Harrison rubbed his brow. "Unfortunately, I wasn't able to get financing through either of those sources."

Confused and uneasy as to why Harrison was discussing the hospital finances with him, Weir waited.

"I ended up going to some friends for a more personalized loan." Seeing Gerald's nod of understanding, Darnell continued. "I got the money I needed, but I was asked to help out in return by using one of their companies as a supplier."

"That doesn't sound bad, but I don't know much about big business," Gerald admitted.

"That was the reason for changing to Alpha Drugs as our supplier. Like it or not, we're going to have to work with them."

Relieved that was all that Darnell had wanted to say, Gerald had shrugged the problem off as a one-time thing. Now, as he thought back to the meeting in Harrison's office, Weir realized that Harrison had been neither upset nor surprised at the mistake on the invoice. He had been resigned to having to deal with Alpha Drugs and Gerald hadn't thought about it any further—until now. The discrepancies couldn't be ignored because the quantities missing were too large to gloss over as mistakes. Barbiturates were under strict government control, not to be dispensed without a prescription, and they had to be accounted for in all pharmacies. Harrison couldn't have meant that he should turn a blind eye to the discrepancies, could he?

Putting down the phone, Joseph Rossi smiled in satisfaction. From the conversation he had just had with Darnell Harrison, he would have good news to give the (Don Rossi)don right after the New Year. As it was, it looked like the year would end on an even more positive note than he had anticipated.

The operation in the city was running like clockwork and had been since Salvatore Romano had suggested moving the drugs from South Carolina to Ohio, instead of directly into Cincinnati. Romano seemed to be doing an excellent job. Ingratiating himself with the state police had been an excellent move. He was able to move with impunity, and the police never bothered his house or the landing strip.

They had increased their position in relation to the Bonano family and their hold on the upstate market. Now much of the merchandise being moved into Tomas, as well as Hartford and Taylor Counties, originated with the Rossi family.

He knew this latest news would be even better received. The possibility presented by Harrison was almost too good to be true. Becoming full partners in the Taylorville Hospital would provide even greater benefits to facilitate their moving merchandise into the area. Even more important was the additional opportunity to legitimize the Rossi name.

Yes, the (Don)don would be happy. A frown crossing his face, the Captain picked up the latest report on Harrison. One of the reasons he had been so successful in extending his network was that he never left anything to chance. Just as he had monitored the lawyer's activities prior to staging the "accident" in June, he was constantly vigilant to what Harrison was doing. The most trustworthy, levelheaded person could get in over his head, and when that happened, he wanted to know. Knowledge was power and information could often provide leverage.

From what Russell had said, Conklin's death had been the catalyst for change in the community, especially in the "Key Club" group. He had known about the activity since they had first gotten together and had kept close tabs since then. Apart from the fact that Brett Conklin and his wife had been participants, the rest of the group was composed of the movers and shakers of the town, and it was always beneficial to know what they were planning.

Dr. Gunther and his wife were no longer living together and she was now seeking a divorce. Rumor was rife that the relationships of the other couples weren't faring much better. The Healys were said to be having problems. In fact, it was said that Healy had been spending time consoling Ann Gunther. The Sterns, a second marriage for the banker, also seemed to be on rocky turf. They hadn't been seen together in the past month, and she had been spending time with her parents in Carbondale. The only ones who seemed to be on an even keel were the smarmy commissioner and his wife. Thinking about Granger, Rossi shook his head. If the man had been Italian, he would have fit in beautifully within the organization as one of the bosses. But Granger didn't have the finesse to deal at a higher level: if he wasn't amoral, then he was close to it. In the year Rossi had been operating in the Taylorville area, he had unearthed quite a few questionable operations initiated or backed by Granger. That certainly didn't bother him because, if the time came, he would know exactly what to do to make sure that the local politician did what he wanted.

Harrison was also easy to manage. Helping Dr. Gunther relocate would not be a problem, though the irony of Harrison's request did not escape him. Had it not been for Rossi's intervention in the first place, Gunther's life wouldn't have taken the turn it had. Satisfied that the folder containing Harrison's information was current, Rossi smiled as he leaned back. The year was ending very well indeed.

Looking up from the brief to check his watch, Kevin saw that he had fifteen minutes before Ann Gunther was supposed to arrive. Stretching as he got up from his chair, he went to the small kitchen to put on the kettle for tea. At the doorway, he smiled. Anticipating his needs, Linda had laid out cups with saucers and tea was already in the teapot on a tray. As he lifted the kettle, he realized she had even filled it with water.

Turning on the flame, he leaned against the counter, letting his thoughts roam. He knew that he would have to speak with

Linda and try to find some way to make her accept Holly's decision not to spend Thanksgiving with them. He would miss the children too, but he understood Holly's need to start rebuilding her life independently of former ties.

The kettle whistled and his thoughts shifted to the upcoming meeting with Ann. Too much a realist to deceive himself, he was aware that Karl and Holly continued to see each other, though they were being discreet. Ann had accompanied Karl to various family gatherings, but Kevin realized he really knew little about Ann.

Hearing a car pulling into the parking area, he carried the tea tray back to his office and went to answer the door. Kevin remembered Ann as being thin, but now it seemed as if her bones were ready to break through the thin layer of skin covering them. Masking his concern, Kevin led the way into his office. Taking Ann's coat, he said, "I decided I needed a cup of tea. Care to join me?"

Ann forced herself to smile and said, "Yes, I think I will. Thank you."

He had placed the tea tray on the table in front of the couch and now, having dispensed with the initial talk of the weather, he leaned back with the cup in his hand. "What can I do for you?"

Ann's hand trembled slightly as she placed the cup and saucer back on the table and folded her hands in her lap. Her voice was low and almost introspective as she finally began to speak. "I really don't know if I should have come to you or not, but the more I thought about it, the more I felt that I needed to tell you how much I admired Brett and what a help he was to me."

Somewhat surprised at Ann's words, Kevin kept his silence. Skilled at listening and letting people explain their problems in their own way, he waited, sure that Ann would continue and provide clarification of what she meant.

"You know that we, Karl and I, were friendly with Brett and Holly," at Kevin's nod, Ann took a breath and continued,

"Actually, the friendship was much stronger between Brett and Karl. At any rate, we often did things together. Some of what I'm about to tell you may not make much sense, but I think you need to know in order to understand." Pausing, she took a sip of her tea, now more comfortable as she began to lay out her thoughts. "A year ago last February, the four of us went out to dinner at the Inn. When we walked in, we met Jack and Diane Healy along with Walter and June Stern at the bar. Ben and Lana Granger and John and Sally Greene were also there. I don't remember who suggested it, but somehow it was decided that we all eat together. The differences in the group were more than outweighed by the similarities of our positions in the community." Shrugging, she said, "We all ended up having a good time. Toward the end of the evening, I think it was John Greene who suggested that we do it again. So we started getting together every two weeks for dinner at the Inn."

Nodding, Kevin said, "Yes, I knew that a group of you had formed a supper club. In fact, Brett was quite happy because he felt that it gave the couples a reason to get out and socialize."

Nodding, Ann sighed sadly. "I felt the same way at first because I saw it as an opportunity to spend more time with Karl...but that wasn't what happened." Suddenly Ann fell silent. How could she explain what had evolved? The weekly get-together that had started out as a means of relieving boredom and fulfilling social obligations had with time taken on a different significance. For the women of the group, the weekly reunion had become a challenge to dress better and had added a new dimension to the shopping trips that were on their individual agendas. The men found that the information gleaned over a drink at the bar or later during dinner was often advantageous and in more cases than not, beneficial, as they often found out which contracts would be coming out ahead of public announcements.

On the surface, these dinner parties seemed a positive thing, but as with everything, there is always a negative to offset the positive. As the months passed and the members began to feel more comfortable as a group, a certain undertone began to appear at the meetings. Looking at Kevin, Ann continued, "Somewhere after the first two months, someone suggested that the couples not sit together. I really don't know why the suggestion was made, but that's what happened. By the following get-together, it had become unwritten law that you did not stay with your spouse exclusively."

Quietly waiting for Ann to continue, Kevin began to understand how the dinner outings had encouraged mutual attractions. He had seen it happen many times, inhibitions were often forgotten as cocktails and camaraderie put people at ease. Not sure what Ann was working up to, he didn't say anything.

"I think that those evenings were the highlights of the week for some of the group," she commented sadly. "To be honest, I think that's where the relationship between Karl and Holly changed from friendship to something else." Sighing, she went on. "Last February, we all had dinner and then some of us decided to go dancing afterward. When the weather got bad, it made more sense to stay at the Ramada than to risk the roads coming home, so that's what we did."

Giving Kevin a wry smile, she continued, "By that time, Karl and I were beginning to have problems. He seemed distant and involved with what was happening at the clinic. That was when he had the problem with Weir over the access to the drugs in the pharmacy. I thought that staying with Karl away from home would give me the chance to rekindle our relationship. Now, I think it was Karl's idea to switch keys, but in any event, the next thing I knew, Brett had come into the room." Her eyes filling with tears as she remembered, Ann's voice became choked, "Brett was such a good listener. I poured my heart out to him about how distant Karl had become and all the other things I felt were wrong. He just let me talk and cry."

"When I was finished, he explained things from his point of view, urging me to try and work things out with Karl." Sadly, she went on. "I really don't think that Karl and Holly were involved at that time. Brett was sure that our marriage was worth fighting for and offered to help me in any way he could, even if it meant only being there to listen. I felt better after we talked and decided he was right. I guess my attitude had something to do with how I was seeing things," she continued. "Anyway, things did seem to even out until the (Key Club) 'key club' became a group activity."

Her eyes taking on a faraway look, Ann continued. "It started one night when we decided to make a night of it and stay in Binghamton instead of driving home in various stages of intoxication. At first it seemed harmless, a kind of joke." She continued pensively, "I don't know who the first to suggest the key club was. Obviously, the men brainstormed one night, discussing the pros and cons, and finally came up with some kind of scheme they agreed on. The end result was more than slightly Machiavellian, but I didn't want to be a spoil sport, so I went along with it."

"Collectively, most of the group felt that one of things that had disappeared from their marriages was the allure of a relationship when you did not know the other person completely. Ergo, it would do all of them good to wonder exactly what their respective spouse had done during the time of the 'swap.'"

"Each room would always have two beds, thus, only the people in the room would know what had happened. And it was laid out that anything that did or did not happen had to be consensual. Also, no one partner was to question the other about what they had done during the time they were not with their spouse."

Not happy at what he was hearing, Kevin was quiet, knowing that this wasn't easy for Ann. "It's hard to believe that any of you agreed to this, but it's even harder to picture Brett agreeing."

Nodding, Ann replied with a sad smile, "I know...but peer pressure can be a huge motivator. Anyway, it was decided that we would all to meet for breakfast the following morning, to defuse the situation if anyone was seriously angry. I guess it was to be a form of safeguard of good behavior. Since the "macho" element of being ready and innovative had already come into play, none of the six men was likely to intentionally violate the rules for fear of being found wanting by their peers, a truly convoluted Machiavellian form of logic."

Shaking his head, Kevin said, "I can't understand why any of you would go along with it. Didn't anyone realize that you were playing with fire?"

Suddenly Ann was quiet, a distant look on her face as she relived the horrible night in March that had been the beginning of the end of her marriage. Kevin waited, knowing that as painful as reliving of a situation might be, healing would only begin once it was confronted. Watching the changing expressions on Ann's face, he wondered what hell she had gone through.

Though sitting in Kevin's office, Ann's thoughts were far away. The feelings of fear and disgust were as real and intense now as they had been the first time around. Only now she knew what was to come. Making an effort to bring herself under control, Ann told Kevin about the night at the Ramada and the incident with John Greene that subsequently led to her attempted suicide.

She looked totally drained as she finished her story. "I just wanted you to know how important and special a person Brett was. I hoped that if I explained how things were for all of us, it would be easier for you to understand what happened. I really don't believe that any of it was planned; it just happened." Her eyes brightening for the first time since she had entered the office, Ann's voice was stronger as she said, "What I would really like is for you to handle my divorce but I'll understand if you choose not to."

"I don't think I can represent you," Kevin said, looking at her apologetically. "I hope you understand because I realize the courage it took for you to come speak to me and try to help me understand. I know it wasn't easy."

Smiling wanly, Ann held out her hand. After shaking with Kevin, she turned and left the office without another word, leaving Kevin to digest all she had told him.

Pensive, Tim stared out the window toward the mountains without really seeing them.

He had talked to Will Billings and the news had been more than somewhat disturbing. Since Brett's death in June, Tim had spoken to Kevin and Linda at least twice a month. He and Darlene had tried to convince them to come out to Boulder for the holidays, but they had wanted to be close to Tommy and Janie.

Tim had continued to press for the investigation into Brett's death but Kevin had remained adamant. He was not going to do anything to further jeopardize the relationship with Holly. He would let sleeping dogs lie, if that would help Linda. While he respected his friend's decision, Tim wasn't sure that it was right.

Yet the sheriff's news seemed to point in that direction. Will had passed on the information that Lieutenant Drann had provided about Salvatore Romano. Tim had then followed through with his own investigation and the results had been eye opening. Romano had begun as a soldier in the organization and had risen rapidly after foiling a murder attempt against Don Rossi. A trusted lieutenant, he had worked closely with the Captain until he had taken over the supply route in Ohio. That didn't necessarily mean that he wasn't working with the Captain. If he was, it could explain how the influx of drugs into Taylor County was taking place. Until there was proof to back up the theory, the Drug Enforcement Agency could not act.

It didn't surprise Tim that Sheriff Billings had sounded disillusioned and bitter. DA Smalls had effectively fettered his movements in the Conklin investigation as well as the drug investigation by withdrawing state trooper support. There was not much that one man could accomplish working on his own after hours.

In both Colorado and South Carolina, information on the family had been scanty during the last two months. Yet the amount of drug-related crimes continued to rise. There had to be some way to penetrate the Rossi bastion, but so far they hadn't found it. If he could only find the key! Pushing the folder labeled "Taylorville" to the side,; Reeves picked up the phone and asked for the Rossi file.

1978

He felt awful. Hoping to calm the headache that threatened to overpower him, Gerald Weir removed his glasses to rub his eyes and temples. Having joined the ranks of those who suffered from headaches, he had a new respect for them. Now he understood how a headache could knock you out.

In Greek, "alpha" stood for "the beginning". As far as Weir was concerned, the supplier had been the start of all the problems for the hospital. If there was one thing he was determined not to do, it was to lose Harrison's trust. In a world more morally corrupt every day, Weir knew that he had Harrison's respect and he didn't want that to change. Since he started, he had been the sole pharmacist for the hospital and there had never been a question as to his honesty or his capacity to keep track of the medications.

This time the discrepancy was too big to ignore. According to the invoice in his hand, they should have received a five-hundred-count bottle of 5 mg Tuinal as well as a five-hundred-count bottle of Seconal, also 5 mg. He hadn't ordered them because they didn't need them—especially in those quantities. Worse than that was the fact that they were missing from the shipment. Trying to control the ever-increasing abuse, the FDA had made it mandatory to number the production runs in order to monitor their movement. If he didn't notify Alpha about the inconsistency, the hospital would be liable should there be any problem.

The pain had increased to the point where it felt as if someone were stabbing his eyeball with an ice pick. Sighing, Gerald knew that he had to take some kind of action. The headache caused by the tension and insecurity would continue to be a problem until he did. Praying that he would be able to take care of the situation without bothering Harrison, Weir picked up the phone on his desk and dialed the number Mr. Romano had given him.

Snowflakes continued to fall onto the heavily blanketed backyard. Linda sighed, wondering if she would ever again find pleasure in the things that had meant so much to her before. Snow carpeted the ground, giving everything a pristine, untouched look. The stately, noble pines appeared to enjoy being dressed in their winter cloak, while the oaks and poplars seemed to lift imploring branches to the sky. Though its branches dipped slightly with the weight of the snow, the dogwood tree was beautiful in its symmetry. Now after the losses and disruptions of the past year, she took little pleasure in what she had always thought of as her winter wonderland. Instead of seeing the blanket of snow as a protective covering for all the new growth, now she looked out and wondered what secrets might be hidden beneath it.

Feeling cheated, she turned to the stove and lit the burner for tea, not really wanting a cup but needing immediate activity. Last year if the snow had fallen, she would have immediately called to have the grandchildren come over to build a snowman together. Now she no longer felt confident calling Holly, and the unease seemed to grow each time they spoke.

So many things had changed since that fateful day in June eighteen months before. Perhaps it was the world which they lived in, but the violence and nastiness portrayed on television seemed to have filtered through the screen to contaminate the sleepy county. *Today you don't need to turn on the early afternoon soap operas to find deceit and anxiety. A few minutes at the Stables would convince you that the scriptwriters had come to Taylorville to get their ideas,* she thought wryly.

Darnell Harrison fought to steady himself. If Rossi were to sense his anxiety, he would realize just how weak Harrison's position was. Breathing deeply, he asked calmly, "So you'll be here next week?"

Derision obvious in his voice, Rossi answered, "That's what I told you. Have I ever let you down before?"

Darnell spoke emphatically, "No, no. It's just that we're entering into the final stage before Gunther leaves Taylorville. I'm hoping that meeting with you directly will allay his fears."

Sensing the other man's concern, the Captain probed to find out why Harrison was so uneasy. "Why? Haven't you gone over the proposal with him in depth? Everything was clearly laid out, if I remember correctly."

"Of course I have," replied Darnell, trying to hide his annoyance. "But these past eighteen months haven't been easy for him. He's ready to get on with his life and he's anxious to leave."

The reason for Harrison's anxiety was suddenly clear. "So you're not quite ready to have him pull out, are you?"

Knowing that there was no point in trying to deceive Rossi, Harrison closed his eyes, glad that they weren't face to face. "Just about, but it isn't simple trying to find a replacement. Gunther is a fine doctor and he won't be an easy act to follow."

Mentally replaying previous meetings leading up to the present conversation, Rossi realized that Harrison was only stating the truth. Looking to gain advantage by having a family member directly situated in the hospital, the Captain had offered the position of pediatrician in the rural area to one of the don's nephews. But any interest on the part of the young doctor had died as soon as he visited the area.

"All right, relax. I'll meet with him next week and impress upon him how important it is to stay until we say so." Taking advantage of having Harrison on the line, Rossi changed the subject of the conversation. "By the way, Mr. Romano called me earlier this week." Silence met his statement so the Captain continued, "He wondered if there was any problem with the way the invoices had been coming through."

His hand moving through his hair, a clear sign of his anxiety, Harrison fought to keep his composure. There was no doubt that Rossi was referring to the inquiries initiated by Weir. "What was Romano's question? Why didn't he come directly to me?" Harrison replied brusquely, hoping to regain lost ground.

"After all this time, he was wondering why he was still being questioned about the invoices. We all thought that the operation was understood."

"It is." Coming up with a feasible excuse, Harrison said, "There is a new person in billing, the inquiry must have come from him. I'll take care of it."

"Good, I'll see you next week." Smiling with satisfaction, Rossi hung up the phone. Controlling the operation of the hospital was going to be easy.

Replacing the receiver, Harrison wondered how he had placed in this last round with the Captain. His relief at the Gunther situation was clouded by his concern over the Romano incident. Once again, he wondered if he had made a mistake in asking the Captain to buy into the hospital.

Her head nestled against Karl's shoulder, Holly purred in satisfaction. "I can't wait. As soon as we leave Taylorville and arrive in New Mexico, we can be married and start living the way we want to."

Smiling at her impatience, he pulled her closer. "I was just thinking about how difficult the last year and a half has been and how happy I'll be to put it behind us. Just so you are aware, things may not be as simple as you think in the beginning."

"I know that," Holly said. "We'll be in a new area with the problems of settling into our home and a whole new life in front of us. I don't expect it to be easy. But at least we'll be away from here." Thoughtfully, she continued, "I always loved Taylorville and never thought that I would want to leave the area. Now I realize just how close-minded and clannish this town is. I'm so sick and tired of having people turn their heads or try to disguise their feelings when they deal with me at the hospital."

Nodding, Karl answered, "I know. We listened to Harrison and have been discreet in seeing each other, but it's as if you're always on display and have to watch what you say or how people react. That's one thing I'm certainly not going to miss."

Snuggling closer, Holly said dreamily, "We won't be totally alone. I'm so glad that Mom and Dad decided that if we were going to move they would go with us. It will make things so much easier to have them close by. The kids won't feel so much of a shock."

"I hope your parents will be happy in Las Cruces. They've been so actively involved in community efforts here that they might find it hard to start over." Thinking about Holly's brother, he continued, "I know Rob will like it out there, especially if his girlfriend goes too. Kowalsic's decision to throw some money in my new office will certainly make it easier on me."

Nodding, satisfaction was obvious in Holly's voice. "The kids are still young enough that a move won't hurt them where school is concerned. In fact, being a more suburban area, they'll probably have more opportunities." Turning toward him again, she continued, "With me in the nursing position, Ted Kowalsic doing the x-rays, and the others there for backup if we need them, we shouldn't have any problem getting the new office up and running. Mom can do the books until you get to the point where we need a full-time bookkeeper. You'll see. With the new equipment and the backing of Captain Rossi, we'll be fine."

Continuing to hold her, Karl was silent. He hoped that she was right. Now if he could get Harrison to release him.

The day that had started out with gray skies had suddenly brightened. Heading into Taylor, Will Billings shook his head. This was one area that needed a whole lot more than sunshine to make it look any better. Taylor had seen its glory days at the time the railroads were used as the main source of transportation. Built along the river, the town now appeared neglected and forsaken. As the mountain rose, so did the winding, narrow streets. The houses seemed to hang on to the steeply sloping terrain as if ready to slide off. Parking was nonexistent.

The town had been a beehive of activity when passenger trains stopped, but that hadn't been for over thirty years. Anyone who could leave did and now the longtime residents of the town had the same beaten, dull look as the buildings. Most of the problems in what was rapidly becoming a welfare town could be traced to the lack of work and low self-concept of the people. Years back when everyone hid their troubles behind closed doors, wife beating and child abuse had been almost unknown. Today beatings and abuse were the reason behind the majority of the calls Billings answered.

Checking in, he found a message to call Lt. Drann at the Gibson Barracks. Eager to hear what John had to tell him, he picked up the phone and dialed. "Sheriff Billings here, returning the Lieutenant's call. Is he available?"

Waiting to be connected, Will tried to calm himself. He was determined to pursue the matter of Brett Conklin's death, but since DA Smalls had ordered the state police to refrain from assisting him, he had gotten nowhere. The information that Drann had given him about Romano's movements in Harford was all he had to go on.

"Will? Glad you got back to me so quickly." Drann had been friends with Billings for years and resented having been told not to help him. But, with his pension in the balance, he couldn't afford to make waves.

"Were you able to get a line on the blood stains that were on the boots?" Billings asked.

Wishing he could say something different, Drann took a deep breath and said, "Will, I hate to admit it, but it looks as if there's someone in my office who's gunning for me. I put the request in my name, but someone cancelled it. I got my hand slapped on top of it."

"Man, I'm sorry! You know I wouldn't want you to do anything to jeopardize your position." He continued, "I just wanted to see if the bloodstains would prove my theory that Gunther was closer to Conklin than he said."

John listened to the deflated tone of Billings's voice. "Will, you know this Conklin investigation has become an obsession with you. Our wives happened to meet the other day and yours mentioned that you aren't even sleeping well at night. For the sake of your family, you're going to have to come to terms with the fact that you can't do any more on your own. Everyone knows how adamant you've been about continuing the investigation into Conklin's death. No one could ever fault you for not trying."

"I know you're right, John. But I can't let it go. The more I go over it, the less I like it. Tim Reeves and I discussed the possibility of there being some connection between Brett's death and the drug defense that he was working on. Somewhere there has to be an explanation."

"Well, friend, I wish you luck," said Drann. "If you get to where you can show probable cause, let me know and I'll try to give you a hand. But for now, I don't dare get involved."

Hanging up the phone, Will sat at his desk pondering his next step. If he could pinpoint what had really happened, he was sure that he could find the proof needed. Knowing his only support lay in Tim Reeves, he checked the clock and dialed the Colorado number.

Russell was in the garage preparing to fix the molding around a leaky window, but his thoughts were far from what he was doing. Tony had been grateful to the Rossi family for their support after the union problem. It had taken a while, but once he and Jan adjusted to small town life, he considered himself lucky to be out of the rat race.

Over the years, there was little contact with the family. They had asked for little other than general information regarding Bendix and the local community, and he had become complacent. That had been a mistake. The family took care of their own, but always at a price.

Tony wasn't stupid. It didn't take great powers of deduction to figure out that the Captain's frequent visits had coincided with the increased drug problem in the area. He frequently thought about what had happened to Brett and had never been able to shake the uneasy feeling that Conklin's death was somehow related to the Captain's visit to him the same day. Rossi hadn't said anything, and Tony wasn't about to ask. *If the family had ordered a hit, so be it,* thought Tony. Yet he didn't feel any better.

Historically little had happened in the sleepy rural community. But beginning with Conklin's death, things had begun to change for the very group that the Rossi family wanted to know about.

Dr. Harrison had tried to keep the matter under wraps, but Tony knew that the night of Conklin's death, Ann Gunther had tried to take her own life. Ironically, the troopers sent to question Gunther about Brett Conklin's death had saved her. If they hadn't arrived when they did, Ann Gunther would have died the same day as Brett Conklin.

Walter Stern, bank resident, had separated from his wife at the end of that summer, and Healy and his wife had filed for divorce just before the holidays. The rumors had led to Dr. Harrison losing his local support and seeking financial support for his renovations outside of the county. Tony guessed that the Rossi family had been instrumental in providing funding because the renovations had gone on pretty much as scheduled. At the same time Harrison had suddenly begun construction on Pine Park, an assisted-living community for senior citizens.

Ben Granger had obtained the contract in spite of the fact that both Kolba and Lane Construction had entered lower bids. There had been comments made as to the conflict of interest, but nothing had been done.

Granger's involvement had become source of black humor when, just before the actual election for commissioner, Old Clancy, the town drunk went around swearing that he had seen them stuffing a body into one of the cement forms in the foundation. Because Clancy had been known to tell stories, no one had given much credence to his ramblings, but Tony had wondered about what Clancy was saying when the Cincinnati press ran a story on the disappearance of one of the Bonano soldiers. It wouldn't have been the first time that someone decided to hide a body at a construction site. Years from now, if they ever needed to make repairs and found Clancy's tale to be true, it would be interesting to see how they explained the strange filler.

Dr. Gunther and his wife had divorced. It was common knowledge that the doctor and Holly Conklin were seeing each other in spite of their being discreet. Speculation had continued for months after Conklin's death as to whether the facts given by the doctor were accurate, but even that had died down. Now, rumor had it that Dr. Gunther and Holly Conklin would be leaving Taylorville and that Ann Gunther was seeing Healy now that both were divorced.

Strange in Tony's opinion was that Austin Greene had stayed in the area. If he had the money the Greenes had, he would focus on his children going to college. It struck him as odd that Greene didn't insist on his son going to school when Austin seemed to be doing nothing. Nonetheless, young Austin always seemed to have money.

Why the Captain wanted to know all this was beyond him. Shaking his head, Tony carried the window back to the house. Opening the door, he saw Jan preparing lunch with the television on. As he recognized the theme song from "The Young and the Restless," Tony thought to himself that what he told the Captain often seemed like a soap script. One didn't have to go far to find drama, deception, and deceit.

As he heard Harrison's voice on the intercom, Weir felt his legs turn to Jell-O. The doctor wanted to see him in his office when he finished preparing the morning meds. As if on cue, his head suddenly started to pound. He had been afraid that Harrison would find out about his call to Alpha and now it seemed that he had. Suddenly, the bright orange of the Darvocet capsules he was counting spilled onto the counter. Sitting down, Weir removed his glasses with shaking hands and tried to ease the pounding in his head by massaging his temples.

The ramifications of his thoughts were too ugly for Gerald Weir to contemplate. He finished his work and dragged his feet to Harrison's office.

"Gerald, Gerald..." Harrison said, looking down at Weir. "I'm not too thrilled. I thought we had gone over the problems surrounding Alpha months ago. But Mr. Romano just called to tell me that you'd called him again. I know I told you that we had to use them as suppliers to fulfill an obligation to a business associate, in spite of their sloppy shipping practices."

His hands gripping the chair arms as if they were lifesavers, Weir cleared his throat. "You did, Dr. Harrison. For a month or two we didn't have any differences between the invoices and what we received. But lately that hasn't been the case. There have been discrepancies again, even bigger than before." Weir's voice became stronger. "This time there was both bottles of Seconal and Tuinal on the invoice that were missing. The FDA regulates both of those and if there should be a problem, they can be traced back to us. That makes the hospital liable. The funny thing is that I never ordered either of them in the first place."

Frowning at the logic of what the pharmacist said, Harrison knew he had no alternative but to follow what he had agreed to with the Captain. Weir was just an unfortunate victim of circumstance. Though he had nothing to do with the situation, he was definitely affected. Harrison kept his tone calm as he explained. "I know that what you're saying is correct, Gerald. But right now I have no option but to go along with the invoices that Alpha sends us."

As Weir stared at him in shock, Harrison continued, "There will be inconsistencies from time to time, and as we do now we're going to accept them. I don't want to lose you after so many years of fine service, but if you can't handle this, I will write you a recommendation for any job where you think you might be happier."

Stuttering in his anxiety to reassure Harrison of his loyalty and protect his job, Gerald answered as he turned to leave, "No, Dr. Harrison, that's not necessary. I just wanted to make sure that you were aware of our liability."

Watching the door close slowly behind Weir, Harrison wondered if his liability hadn't just gotten greater.

Aware of Tony's discomfort, the Captain had prolonged the meeting intentionally, making sure he was there when Jan came home. He knew that those distanced geographically from the family found it hard to maintain ties, but he had no intention of letting Russell forget his debt. Rossi had given support when Tony needed it, allowing him to provide a good life for his family.

Rossi was more than satisfied with the information that Tony had given him. He had expected there to be fallout following Conklin's death. The breakup of the various couples didn't affect him one way or another, save for that of Dr. Gunther and his wife.

Gunther had been in the right place at the wrong time. Had he not been in the woods with Conklin, Paul would still have found a way to engineer Conklin's death. That he had been able to utilize the drama played out between Conklin, his wife, and Gunther had been a lucky fluke. Due to shock and how rapidly things had happened, neither Gunther nor Holly Conklin had questioned Paul's directions. They hadn't told the authorities at the time, and if they were to do so now, they would not be believed. Their relationship was common knowledge providing motive. Who would believe that there had been someone else in the woods?

Conklin was no longer a problem. If he could continue to complicate Sheriff Billings's investigation, Billings wouldn't be able to dig up anything dangerous by accident. Smiling, the Captain reached for Billings's file. The man was thorough and persistent, just the kind of man they wanted in the position of sergeant within the organization. The problem was that now Billings had recruited District Attorney Tim Reeves to help him, and Reeves had access to more information than Billings. In fact, if anyone were to make the connection between the family and the operation in the area, Rossi knew it would be Reeves.

It paid to get Gunther out of the area. Hopefully, out of sight would be out of mind. With the help he planned to offer the doctor, he had no doubt that Gunther would be eager to go along with him. If it meant waiting a few months in order to placate Harrison, so be it. Satisfied that all was in place for his meeting with Gunther, Captain Rossi knew it was time to see him.

Driving toward Cincinnati, Karl wondered why they were meeting there instead of Harrison's office in Taylorville. Harrison had said that it was to prevent speculation as to his leaving, but it seemed pretty cloak and dagger to meet the people who were going to help him in a hotel restaurant.

Frowning, he thought about Holly. She was isolated, except for her family, but he had to admit that the fault was partially hers. The town dowagers were quick to turn their backs after Brett died. As she was now a 'single' female for all intents and purposes, many of her so-called friends no longer felt comfortable including her in their plans.

Holly could not afford to be careless should she inadvertently let slip something about Brett's death and this had limited her from developing new friendships. In part, it was a mixture of guilt and fear that kept her from accepting overtures made by Kevin and Linda.

Parking, he entered the hotel and moved toward the restaurant at the end of the corridor. He made a conscious effort not to think about the many times that he and Ann had dined there with Holly and Brett. Folding his coat over his arm, he entered the dining room.

Seated at a corner table with Harrison, Rossi watched Gunther approach. The man was obviously confident and self-assured. For Paul to have manipulated him, he had to have been under severe duress at the time. As Harrison rose, Rossi remained seated. He had no intentions of revealing the family connection but wanted to establish who was in control from the beginning. Taking Gunther's proffered hand, he said, "John Rossi. Sorry to inconvenience you, but I won't be in town long."

Nodding, Karl introduced himself and sat down in the chair indicated by Harrison. "Darnell said that with your help, I might be able to leave the area by the end of the year."

"As soon as the transfer of the hospital stock and the negotiations are completed, I see no problem in your moving." Staring at Gunther, he continued, "You understand that the group funding Taylorville Hospital is the same one that is going to help you establish your new practice in Las Cruces." At Karl's nod, he went on. "The only concern at this end is finding someone who can replace you. Dr. Harrison has been interviewing rigorously, but to date there have been no outstanding applicants. I hear that you won't be an easy act to follow."

Reading between the lines, Karl asked, "So you want me to wait until you've found a replacement?"

"I think it's only fair." Rossi signaled to the waitress before continuing. Looking at Gunther, he said, "We waited to order." As soon as the waitress left with their orders, he went on. "We're willing to help in any way we can because Dr. Harrison made it a stipulation in our buying your shares."

Unaware of Darnell's request, Karl glanced at him. In spite of the many arguments he had had with Harrison, he knew the doctor to be fair. "That's good to know. As you're working on both ends, maybe things can be tied up more rapidly."

"My group has already found office space according to your description in Las Cruces. Physically, the building is in good shape and all that needs doing prior to opening your office would be to paint and outfit the consulting rooms the way you want them. We've had our real estate contacts look into a number of suitable houses which are available for you to look at next week. We considered the school system, so I think you'll be happy when you see the area. If you like, you can fly out next weekend and see, and then we'll go from there."

Speechless at having all the burdens he had been carting around for months so effortlessly removed, Karl looked back at Rossi. Here was a man willing to help him find what he wanted and needed. But Gunther wasn't naive. No one gave without benefiting in some way. Careful not to show too much enthusiasm, Karl replied, "It sounds like you have everything covered. I can plan to visit Las Cruces next weekend. Thank you for organizing everything so thoroughly."

As the waitress returned with their food, Rossi smiled in satisfaction. Gunther may be leery, but he needed Rossi's help. And that put Gunther just where Rossi wanted him.

The Lull Before the Storm, 1988

As he ran down the street, Kevin automatically checked his pace to allow a car to pass him. Naturally observant, had anyone asked him, he could not have said who was driving or the color of the car. He paced himself instinctively. His thoughts occupied by how to handle what had become a bone of contention between Tim Reeves and himself.

Still firm and fit, the last ten years had taken their toll. Gray wings had replaced his dark sideburns and there was no disguising the lines that now furrowed his forehead. Unlike then, now when he left to run, a myriad of unresolved conflicts went with him.

After Holly left the area, Kevin had tried to put the past behind him, refusing to dwell on what he couldn't change. It was bad enough to lose the children, but to speculate on the possibility that the man raising his grandchildren was actually a murderer was just too painful.

There had been heated discussions regarding his reluctance to pursue the investigation with both Jim Walsh and Tim Reeves. Both men refused to accept the story given to the police by Gunther. Sheriff Billings had brought forth arguments that proved that Gunther wasn't telling the truth. Despite repeated entreaties to find out why everyone seemed so anxious to cover up and forget about Brett's death, Kevin was adamant in his refusal.

While Holly and the children were in Taylorville, his friends had accepted his refusal to look into Brett's death, agreeing that he didn't want to alienate her. Lately, Tim had become more and more insistent that the case be reactivated.

Had he not known Tim so thoroughly, it would be easy to think that his friend was obsessing. Yet Reeves hadn't achieved the position of district attorney for the state of Colorado based on a record of unfounded suppositions.

Checking his watch, Kevin was lost in thought. The lack of information and answers surrounding his son's death was strange. When Sheriff Billings told him that he planned to examine the clothing and pictures taken at the scene, Kevin had reluctantly agreed, insisting that the queries be low key, not general knowledge.

He had been surprised when Billings was denied access to the evidence. Looking back, he realized that there had been other oddities. Tim had been outraged that a law officer would be denied support in an investigation. At each opportunity during the last twelve years, Tim had insisted that there was more to Brett's death than Kevin thought. If he agreed to review the information on Brett's death, at least he would get Tim off his back.

Running up the driveway, he hoped that he could live with the results when he began to dig.

At the sound of his intercom, Tim Reeves glanced up. He had come in early to catch up before he left on his long overdue vacation. He was surprised to see that he had been working for over an hour. By now the rest of his staff would have arrived. He said, "Good morning, Cindy," as he activated the intercom. "I came in early to get caught up and didn't realize how late it had gotten."

"No problem. You said you'd do that and I decided that I'd try to keep things quiet, but Kevin Conklin is on the phone. I knew you'd want to take the call."

"Thanks, you're right." Picking up the phone, Tim hoped that everything was all right. "Hey, guy. Decided that if you didn't get me early you wouldn't find me?"

Chuckling, Kevin replied wryly, "No, I know your habits. You'll be locked in there for the rest of the day. You always do that prior to a vacation."

"So what can I do for you?" Tim asked. "God willing, we'll see each other at the airport day after tomorrow."

Not allowing his resolve to weaken, Kevin quipped, "You'll be glad you're sitting when I tell you why I called." Taking a deep breath, he said, "I've decided to try and reactivate the investigation into Brett's death. Why don't you bring the folder with all that material you and Billings kept trying to shove at me? We'll find some time to go over it while the girls are shopping."

"I hope you're going to tell me what prompted your change of heart," Tim said. "I want to know who or what changed your mind when I couldn't."

"I'm not really sure myself. But now that I made the decision to do it, I hope you'll help."

"You're damned straight I will, anyway I can," replied Tim. Until now, Kevin had refused to budge. He had been adamant about leaving things alone. Now, twelve years later, he had suddenly decided to go forward. Suddenly saddened, he thought that it was a shame that Will Billings would not know. Tim had admired Billings from the moment they first spoke. As district attorney, Tim had ample opportunity to work with all kinds of law officers: the dedicated ones, ones who were only putting in their time, ones who were lazy, those who had burned out, and all others who fell somewhere in between.

He was adept at sizing up those he came in contact with and there had been no doubt in his mind that the county sheriff was truly dedicated to his job. Will Billings had wanted the county to be a place where people felt safe, knowing that their children could play on the streets without fear. But, much as Billings tried to make that possible, Tim knew that his job had become ever more difficult—and not only because of the increase in crime nationwide.

In spite of his repeated efforts, Billings hadn't been able to find anything conclusive about Brett Conklin's death, stymied everywhere by the refusal of help from the state police and the county district attorney.

Nothing done during the investigation made any sense. The autopsy had been based on information given by Gunther. The coroner, accepting without question the information given by the doctor, had signed the death certificate. In fact, the coroner's report had been written as if he had been speaking to Gunther though Cummings hadn't even seen him. Pictures of the accident scene taken by the game commissioners showed inconsistencies in Gunther's statement. Conklin visibly held clay pigeons as he lay on his back. Yet no one had pursued that line of questioning, and the list of inconsistencies went on and on.

When he and Darlene had gone back to Taylorville at the end of that summer to stay with Kevin and Linda for ten days, he had managed to talk extensively with Billings and Jim Walsh. Neither of them felt that enough had been done. One evening they had talked about what motive there was to want the investigation stopped.

They had tossed around various different theories, ranging from getting the hospital renovations done on time, to quelling the rumors that were flying around about Holly Conklin and Karl Gunther. One of the theories that Tim personally found all too logical had coincided with the possibility that Brett had discovered something related to the drug problem while putting together the defense for the murder case he had been working on.

He thought again that it was a shame Billings would never know that Kevin had finally come around. Billings had died trying to subdue a prisoner at the county jail in 1985. To Tim's knowledge, no one else had thought about continuing the investigation.

Tim forced himself to get back to work. Now he was looking forward to his vacation even more than before. Whatever Kevin had to say would be extremely interesting.

Clearing his desk earlier than expected, Darnell Harrison decided to check on Weir. Joe Cosmello had said something seemed to be bothering the pharmacist. Harrison preferred to take care of whatever it was before Cosmello said anything to Rossi.

Darnell had never questioned Rossi's offer of financial help, assuming that it was just another aspect of his family's business interests. Only years later, when he had been asked for checks in return for cash, had doubts crossed his mind. But they had been fleeting, and Joseph Rossi had been sly. Rossi had never stressed his requests to the point where Darnell would balk until Harrison was so fully ensnared in the situation that he had no hope of extricating himself. When he had finally woken up to the reality of what the 'family' was, it was too late to change what was happening. It was then that the kid gloves came off and the demands became greater.

Sitting down with a sigh, his proposed check on Weir forgotten, he thought about just how heavily entwined he had gotten. When Rossi had requested his support in buying from Alpha Drugs he had found the request reasonable. It was only when Gerald Weir had voiced his concerns about the discrepancies in the invoicing that Harrison had taken a good look at what he had unwittingly become involved in. What he found had been disturbing.

He was a doctor, bound by the Hippocratic Oath that began with "first do no harm." Yet he was now indirectly responsible for the spread of drug use, more than likely affecting his own community. Though he had finally accepted his involvement as part of the price he had to pay for fulfilling his dream of providing better medical care for his community, he now wondered if the cost had been too high.

When Weir had voiced his concerns, Darnell had contacted Alpha Drugs himself. To his surprise, he was contacted in turn by the Captain. The threat had been veiled but the implication was clear. If Harrison wasn't the one in control of his operation, the family would certainly question the logic of backing him. So it would be to the doctor's benefit to make sure the nosy pharmacist refrained from asking questions or it would be necessary to find a replacement for Weir.

Frowning, Darnell stared unseeing at the door of his office. He had only seen what he wanted to see, almost as if he had worn blinders, certainly not thinking of any of the collateral effects to getting his dream completed. Worse, he had deluded himself into thinking that Rossi and his family were backing the hospital because of their concern for providing adequate health resources. He should have realized how they had manipulated him. All it had taken was a casual mention of the need of a senior citizen home and the next thing Harrison knew, Rossi was suggesting that he flesh out a plan for where he wanted the facility to be and how he wanted it set up. They had been sitting at the Inn finalizing the details of the loan for the renovations when Rossi set his trap. It had been so easy!

Relieved at having found a solution for the financial portion of his project, Darnell had been uncommonly loquacious. "I really want to thank you for having interceded again on my behalf. I'll make sure that as in the past, the payments are on time and your family has no reason to regret having backed your suggestion."

Lifting his hand dismissively, Rossi replied, "If they hadn't already had proof your word was good, they wouldn't have gone along with it. You were never late on a payment, so they know it's a good investment. Besides, I know they like your attitude of looking out for your community." They also liked the idea of having the doctor in their debt should his help ever become necessary, but the Captain was too smart to let Darnell know.

"When I went to medical school, I vowed that I would do whatever I needed to change that situation. Fortunately, with your help, I was able to make my dream a reality."

Shrewdly utilizing the other's need to talk, Rossi had simply nodded.

"Now with this loan, I'll be able to assure that we can continue to provide the best medical care available. The new machinery will mean that we no longer have to send people to Cincinnati or Taylor for testing or x-rays."

Taking his time as he spoke, Rossi baited the hook. "Your attitude is admirable." Smiling, he continued, "Though I've heard some say that you lack a well-defined bedside manner, no one could doubt that you have your patient's best interest at heart."

Nodding, Harrison kept talking. "I guess when I came back after seeing the death and destruction in Korea, I lost all patience with hypochondriacs as well as anyone else who made more out of their illness than what it was. When you see men who continue to milk their herds in spite of having walking pneumonia, you lose patience with those who complain of 'vapors.' The only problem I have at the moment is keeping space open for those in the community who are no longer able to be on their own and have no family to care for them."

"So why not build a senior facility?" asked the Captain.

Darnell had been hooked. Looking back twelve years later, he shook his head, wondering how he could have been so naive. Rossi had known exactly what he was doing and had led Harrison like a lamb to the slaughter. He had known that Harrison had been hurt financially by his divorce and had dangled the idea of an additional source of income like a carrot. He had made it easy for both Harrison and Kerr to agree, setting up the same kind of partnership that they had for the hospital while retaining only a small percentage for the family.

Once verbalized, things had rapidly fallen into place and Pine Manor had been born. Again, the fact that Rossi had asked that they use specific suppliers hadn't seemed problematic. Granger had been more than happy to handle the contracting by utilizing the subcontractors that Rossi specified. It was only in retrospect that Darnell was able to see how terribly he had been hooked. Over the years, it simply became that more obvious.

Rousing himself, Harrison headed to the pharmacy.

Shaking, Gerald Weir sat down to catch his breath. The antacids hadn't afforded any relief which was really no surprise. The pain escalated proportionately with his dismay at what was happening around him. Grasping his stomach, he waited for the pain to lessen, thinking about his garden to distract himself from the ulcer.

Dr. Harrison had told him not to concern himself with the discrepancies in the invoices. But it was his nature to take his job seriously and he hadn't been able to let things slide. More than once, he had found himself wondering if he hadn't been hasty in accusing Gunther of taking illegal medications in light of what continued to happen.

His malaise coincided with the hiring of Joe Cosmello as a pharmaceutical assistant. Though Cosmello was hired primarily to deal with the paperwork, Gerald hadn't been able to close his eyes to what was happening. How could he?

Gerald no longer made out purchase orders or was responsible for receiving. But he knew that there continued to be discrepancies in what was needed and what supposedly arrived. The whole situation had become a living nightmare for him. He lived on tenterhooks because of it and had nowhere to turn. Dr. Harrison had made it clear that if he couldn't accept how he ran his hospital, Weir was free to leave. But where would he go? Worse yet, he had to carry the burden himself for he didn't dare say anything—though he had a fairly good idea of where the drugs were coming from.

He had no clue how to justify his continued inaction. How could he ignore what was being said or what was happening? Cosmello had a very friendly relationship with Roman at Alpha, and after Harrison's warning, Gerald had been careful not to say anything. Knowing that Cosmello was watching him was one reason for his tension. Worse than that was his feeling of deception. How could Dr. Harrison, the life-saving man he had admired for so long, allow such things to happen? Straightening up slowly, Gerald found himself facing the subject of his thoughts. Hopefully Harrison would see his distress as having a purely physical explanation.

Having watched Weir clutch his midsection, Harrison knew without being told that the pharmacist was suffering either a severe gastritis or an ulcer. "How long have you been having these attacks?"

Blanching further at Harrison's question, Gerald answered guiltily, "For a while. I have an antacid to take, but I forgot it." Smiling weakly, he continued, "So now I'm paying the price."

Harrison said, "You're not doing yourself any favor by not taking the medication. The medication prescribed for gastritis or an ulcer is not dangerous or habit forming, as you are well aware. If what you're using doesn't do the trick, let me know."

"Thanks, I will," assured Weir, breathing a sigh of relief as Harrison turned to leave.

With the years came changes in the organization of the family. Initially reluctant, the consigliere had finally realized that they could not afford to be considered old-fashioned. The drug trade was too lucrative to refuse to participate.Sitting behind his well-polished walnut desk, Rossi stared out the window at the building going up across the road. Business was business. Whether bookmaking, prostitution, construction, or drugs, the bottom line was that they did what they had to do to make money and exert control.

Prior to the purchase of Alpha Drugs, only Don Rossi had seen the logic in involving themselves in the pharmaceutical industry. Absorbed in their own growing bank accounts, most of the older mustache Pete's had felt that there was no need for change. Why risk getting involved in something that was so complicated? Better to leave well enough alone. When Rossi had presented his proposal to back Darnell Harrison in the hospital venture, only the (all Don should be capitalized) don had seen the connection with Alpha Drugs. The others had ultimately agreed to back Harrison as it could be translated to giving a loan. Only Rossi and the don had known the true reason for backing the hospital. The hospital would become one of the primary venues for their drug distribution in northeastern Ohio as well as Pennsylvania and upstate New York—and it had.

After taking measures to remedy the rocky start of their enterprise in Taylor County caused by the careless and untrained recruits, they had found that it had been a propitious move. They not only expanded their own circle of influence but had been able to take over a significant portion of the Bonano family's territory. This had been a relatively calm takeover. Having the private airport outside of Hallstead in Ohio available to them had made distribution easier than expected.

The Bonano clan had been the first to lay claim to Broome and Tioga counties. But that family was even further locked in the past than the Rossi family. The continual infighting amongst the Bonano themselves had made their area ripe for the taking. The Captain easily infiltrated their territory. Hours from the city and having little communication with each other, by the time the rest of the Bonano council realized what was happening, the takeover was a fait accompli.

Expansion into the upstate area had also proven beneficial for other reasons. Through financing the building of the hospital, they had been able to obtain a handle on an untouched area of the construction business. His mouth curving into a slight smile, the Captain thought back to the first discussion he had with Granger. The first encounter with the arrogant town leader had been in Harrison's office when they had met to go over the construction plans for the original hospital building. He and Harrison had been reviewing the plans and organizing the construction needs when Granger arrived half an hour late.

Nodding dismissively at Rossi, Granger had immediately tried to take control of the meeting. Stretching out his hand to Harrison for the plans, he had said superciliously, "I need to see what the basics are so I can tell you what the schedule will be."

Although used to the brusque manner of the contractor, Harrison had been annoyed at his attitude. "Don't you think you're putting the cart before the horse? You haven't even been introduced to my financial broker, Joseph Rossi. Have a seat." Turning to Rossi, Harrison tried to cover for Granger's offensive attitude. "As you guessed, this is Ben Granger of Granger Concrete. Fortunately his knowledge of construction is greater than his people skills."

At the Captain's nod, Harrison continued, "In spite of his rough manners, he does know what he's doing. He's worked extensively with all the construction companies from Cincinnati to Wilkes-Barre."

Once involved in a conversation centering on the building, Granger had proven himself knowledgeable and eager to direct the project. It would be a coup for him, and Rossi had been quick to use Granger's desire to his advantage. Later, Rossi spent quite a bit of time on the job site, visiting contractors with Granger, giving the other ample opportunity to satisfy his curiosity about Rossi's connections. Careful never to refer to the organization as other than a family business, the Captain had made sure that Granger knew that their areas of interest were varied and that they rewarded loyal collaborators.

By way of Granger, the family had been able to obtain an entrance into local construction unions. This had proved beneficial in providing work for those no longer able to work in the city, as well as obtaining information as to what was happening in the area. Rossi had been delighted when Granger decided to run for, and later retained his position as, county commissioner. It was helpful knowing what was happening in the political arena and Granger, a braggart, was eager to share all the information that came his way.

Just prior to his second term as Taylor County commissioner, the Captain made sure that they would never have to worry about Granger again. Granger was well aware of who the Rossi family was but had never been asked to do anything for them. Reminding Granger of the family's help in covering up a particularly ugly personal situation created by Granger's odd appetites, Rossi had insisted that he pour an additional two feet of concrete in the footers for the new senior citizens center. The concrete had been poured at night and one of the Bonano soldiers had become part of the foundation.

Through Granger, Rossi had managed to meet and later take advantage of the district attorneys in Taylor County over the years. Everyone had something they preferred to leave hidden. If they didn't, Rossi was quick to orchestrate a situation leaving them in his debt. Shaking his head, Rossi reflected that, just like sheep, most people were frighteningly easy to control.

Tapping a pencil, Rossi continued to mull over the latest information he had received from both Tony Russell and Paul, who now ran the upstate operation. Noting that an hour had passed in thought, he rang his secretary and asked her to bring coffee. Standing, he arched his back to stretch his spine. His thoughts turned toward the subject that most concerned him. Even if the Conklin case was reopened and went to trial, there was nothing to connect the family to the lawyer's death. But other things might come to light if they started to investigate using now-common methods—and that couldn't be allowed to happen.

Stirring sugar into his coffee, he picked up the folder with Granger's name on it. Though no longer commissioner, Granger still controlled much of what happened in the sleepy county seat from behind the scenes. He had not needed Rossi to tell him that it was advantageous to maintain control. With money not a problem, Granger thrived on power.

The current commissioner was one of Granger's puppets and had the ear of the current DA, John Smallcomb, whom he had helped to elect. It was common knowledge that Granger did not like Smallcomb, but no one questioned his continued interest in the county. Smallcomb had been grateful for Granger's support. Now it appeared that the current district attorney had pretensions of running for governor. According to Paul, rumor had it that Smallcomb was entertaining Conklin's request to reactivate the investigation into his son's death. What better way to garner attention statewide than to solve a twelve-year-old case?

Through the years Rossi had kept track of Gunther and occasionally contacted him. Gunther had no idea of the extent of Harrison's involvement with the Rossi family, and the Captain had kept it that way. Four years before, Gunther had contacted Rossi when he decided to move to North Carolina. Rossi had obliged and helped the doctor open his allergy center, asking Gunther to use Alpha Drugs as a supplier. Fortunately, nothing had been done to make Gunther question the invoices.

The question was just how far the DA was willing to push on the one side, and how determined Kevin Conklin was to pursue the investigation on the other. Turning to the file cabinet to which he had the only key, he returned Granger's file and removed another. Once he reviewed the material he had filed regarding the investigation into the 'accident,' he would be able to determine the best course of action.

Pouring the water over the tea bag, Linda picked up her to-do list. Unconsciously sighing, her forehead wrinkled as her thoughts turned to Kevin. Though he tried to downplay his growing restlessness, she had known that one day he would have to find out what had really happened the day Brett died.

Taking a sip from the cup, she continued to stand, thinking about how their lives had been put on hold the day their son died. Watching the shadow of a blackbird cross the yard, her thoughts were also shadowed. She had lost her grandchildren as well as her son. The hope that Holly would relent and they would be allowed to be a part of the lives of her grandchildren lives had also died. In support, Kevin had known her hopes were tied up with letting the investigation slide, so he had.

Sadly she remembered how many birthdays and holidays she had spent counting the minutes until the time difference allowed them to call and hear their grandchildren's voices. Each call was more bittersweet as Tommy and Janie grew more distant with the passing of time. It wasn't the children's fault, for she and Kevin had ultimately become strangers to them. They had been young enough when they left Taylorville to forget their life prior to Holly having been with Karl Gunther.

Kevin had managed to move on more rapidly than she had. Both had continued to participate in the community, though when asked to run for a third term as mayor, Kevin had refused. Their extended families and friends had become even more important through the years, and they had become particularly close to their nieces and nephews.

The first three years had been the hardest. After losing Brett it had been difficult to see less of the children. But that hadn't been the only change. Right before deer season of the year that Brett died, she and Kevin had spent a long weekend at Deer Run. Surrounded by memories, they had wanted to see if they could be there without feeling extreme anguish or melancholy. Deer Run had been the site of so many happy occasions with family and friends that they were grateful to find they felt better being there. At Deer Run, as at Brett's grave, they were able to feel his presence and think about the good times.

During the past year, as retirement loomed on the horizon and their involvement with the community began to lessen, she had realized that it was time to let go of her broken dreams. Tommy was now a senior in high school and Janie was a sophomore and neither had made any effort to communicate with their grandparents. It was time to let Kevin find out what had really happened that day in the woods.

She was aware that theirs weren't the only lives affected by Brett's death. A domino effect seemed to take place with his death, one unhappy incident after another. All the members of the infamous "key club" became fodder for the gossip mill. The Healy, the Gunther, and the Stern marriage had all fallen apart and the couples divorced as a result. Only the long-married Granger and Greenes had managed to remain intact despite the innuendos and rumors.

Shaking her head, Linda wondered how many other people would be affected by the information that would come to light. She was sure that neither Kevin nor Tim would stop until they knew the truth about what had happened. What she worried about was finding out that the death of her son had not been accidental.

Clouds Begin to Gather as Questions Multiply

At his office window, Kevin noticed that the lawns were beginning to show the first hint of new growth. It had been a long, hard winter and the balm of the new green was welcome. The lack of clarity and suspicion of cover-ups during the last few years had severely shaken his beliefs. The moral underpinning that had been the foundation of his life had been fissured.

Today, with the frustration he was feeling, he knew that it was time to begin to let go and make plans to retire. Financially, he and Linda had been wise and they had no worries about how they would manage. Besides, who was there to inherit?

His thoughts had gone full circle as they always did, beginning and ending with the pain of Brett's absence. Sighing, he picked up the copy of the motion that his lawyer had most recently submitted to Judge Seaman.

As he sat down, his thoughts wandered to all that had taken place since he and Linda decided to pursue what had really happened the day that Brett died. There was much to think about.

Having nothing pressing to take care of, Kevin let his mind bring forth the images of what had been said that day four years before on a day when he and Linda had visited Deer Run. They had been sitting outside watching the antics of several jays that were competing with the squirrels for nuts. They had always talked openly about everything and the only area that had remained out of bounds for discussion had been the investigation of Brett's death. As they sat warmed by the late afternoon sun, Linda had taken his hand. "I know that you've waited patiently," she said in a soft tone, "and I thank you for that." Responding with a soft smile as he brushed his lips across her forehead, she had continued, "But it's time to move on. I know that I've been selfish in refusing to recognize that the children have long been lost to us."

As he thought about what to say, Kevin studied the face he woke up to each morning and his heart swelled with love. He wasn't surprised by Linda's statement, for he had known that she would let him know when she finally accepted the loss of the kids. "You're sure? You know that we may find some things that won't be pretty and others that might be quite painful."

"I know, but I also know that it's time to lay the doubts to rest. We won't be able to do so until you find the truth."

Once the words had been spoken, calm had settled over them. Kevin had long since realized that the doubts surrounding Brett's death continued to cloud their days. Relief flooded through him as he digested the fact that he could now pursue the investigation.

The discussion at Deer Run had taken place several weeks prior to a vacation they planned to take with Tim and Darlene Reeves. Knowing that his friend had wanted to pursue the investigation from the beginning, Kevin had decided to review what materials he had. Then he had called Tim and told him that he wanted to discuss the case while they were together. Kevin remembered how relieved Tim had been to be able to speak his mind about the case. They had sent Linda and Darlene shopping and met poolside, bringing the files with them.

Kevin explained, "What I want to do now is find out why it seemed so difficult to obtain answers at the time of Brett's death." Thoughtfully, he went on. "If we find that there is reason to believe that Gunther lied and Brett's death was not an accident, we'll take it from there."

Nodding his consent, Tim had opened the folder he had placed on the table. Let's start by going over what you have and then we'll add what I know."

With that, Kevin rapidly summarized what was general knowledge about Brett's death which was little more than what Karl Gunther had reported. Looking at his friend thoughtfully as he finished going over the scant information he had as to the day in question, Tim wondered if Kevin had any idea as to the abnormalities surrounding the investigation from the very beginning. Wanting to spare his friend additional hurt and upset, his experience told him that the only way to make sure they accomplished a thorough investigation was to leave no stone unturned, no matter how ugly the slime they uncovered.

Taking a deep breath, Tim began to speak, "You know that Jim Walsh, Will Billings, and I had several discussions in the days immediately following Brett's death." At Kevin's nod, he continued, "From the beginning none of us accepted Gunther's story for a variety of reasons. First, Brett was too experienced in the woods to ever run with a loaded gun. If that hadn't raised suspicion, Brett's back pain would have deterred him from running."

"Secondly, the load in the gun didn't coincide with what would normally be used for shooting clay pigeons. In fact, there were two different loads in the chamber. When Jerry Thorne unloaded the gun at the trooper's request, they found that the discharged shell was for large game."

"Thirdly, that raises the question as to Gunther's action with the gun. Knowing that Brett was dead, he drove to the Russell home for help. While there, he called Bob Wood to see if he would pick up the body. Why call Woods rather than any of the other emergency services?"

"Also, Dr. Grace performed the autopsy. Why not Cummings? As coroner, it would have been assumed that since he was at the funeral home and had access to the body, he would have substantiated the information given to him by Gunther."

"But then you have all the other inconsistencies such as what the pictures taken by Thorne show as opposed to what Gunther is saying. Something just doesn't add up. If Brett was chasing a porcupine the way Gunther said he was, why did he hold onto the clay pigeons? He would have needed both hands on the gun for balance. Though his shoelace was untied, the shoe wasn't loose enough to make him trip and the lace itself had no dirt on it from being stepped on." Pausing in his recital, Tim waited for Kevin to respond.

As he listened to Tim, Kevin's concern continued to mount. Sure, he had questioned how Brett could have been so careless. But what he was hearing now put a totally different slant on what had happened that day at Deer Run. The more he heard, the more uneasy he became. "Are you saying that Gunther intentionally lied about what happened?"

Giving Kevin a chance to think about what he had said, Tim continued laying out his arguments. "Passion can be a tremendous motivator. The fact that Karl and Holly married dispels any doubt that they had a motive for wanting Brett out of the way."

Shaking his head, Kevin said, "I can't believe they plotted his death. Brett was the father of her children!"

Overwhelmed by dual feelings of anguish and anger as they washed over him, Kevin stared at the sunlit pool. How could he be discussing death and murder on such a beautiful day in such a peaceful place?

"Are you all right?"

Coming back to himself, Kevin looked at his friend sadly. "I feel as if I'm in the middle of a surrealist plot. How could things be so terrible and cruel in such a lovely, tranquil place? Death and doubt don't belong here, do they?" Looking around to make his point, Kevin continued, "Yet that's life. While things for one person may be happy and bright, right next door lives are falling apart."

Tim knew that there were many stones to move. What they would find would not be pretty. He hoped that Kevin and Linda would be strong enough to withstand the results of the investigation.

Neither he nor Kevin ever considered their ages when they were together. The reality was that they were both over sixty. Outwardly, there appeared to be little change from the man Tim had served with in Korea. Fortunately, all of them had remained physically fit. But what about that part of his friend that wasn't outwardly visible? Had the sorrow and anguish weakened the core of the person in front of him? Would Kevin be able to face all that he might find?

Tim searched his friend's eyes as he continued, "You're going to wonder why you didn't know about much of what I'm going to tell you. Just remember that once you decided that you weren't going to push to find out what happened, we decided not to bother you with the information we gathered. We didn't tell you because you didn't want to know, not to keep you from knowing."

"Who is the 'we' you're talking about?"

"Basically, it was Jim Walsh, Will Billings, and I. Even after you told us that you didn't want to pursue the investigation, we continued to try and find out as much as we could."

"I may not have wanted to look into Brett's death at the time, but I do now. Let's have it."

So Tim had done just that. For the next hour and a half he had recounted what he and the others had done to find out the truth. There had been many things that Kevin wasn't aware of.

As he listened, Kevin found it hard to accept that Billings's repeated appeals for help had fallen on deaf ears and that the authorities had refused to either corroborate or refute his suspicions, nor given Will the reports he had asked for. Even worse was the attitude of District Attorney Smalls who had written the letter directing the troopers to deny assistance to Billings. He had obviously wanted to see the case dropped.

But that was just the beginning. Listening to Tim, it had become obvious that the whole town seemed eager to label Brett's death an unfortunate accident and move forward. Becoming more disturbed and confused as his friend outlined what he had found, Kevin was sure that his decision to get to the bottom of what had happened would take place with or without the help of the justice system.

Thinking about that day four years before, Kevin remembered how incongruous their actions had seemed at the time. In the bright sunlight, next to the tropical pool, nothing could have been more out of place than the dark, underhanded dealings that had finally seen the light of day.

His heart pounding, Gerald Weir checked to make sure that the door to the pharmacy was closed. Holding a vial in his hand in case he needed an excuse, he moved between the shelving toward Cosmello's desk. For weeks he had been trying to gather his courage to find out just how bad the discrepancies were between the drug orders and the deliveries.

The chance to find out had come when Cosmello's wife had called earlier. Hysterical because young Joey had fallen and knocked out a tooth, she had insisted that Cosmello come home. In his rush to leave, Cosmello had forgotten to lock the drawers, giving Gerald his long-awaited opportunity.

Taking a deep breath, Gerald reminded himself to be careful not to move anything. It wouldn't be a good idea for Cosmello to realize that he had gone through the paperwork, and as he was anally compulsive about his filing, anything out of place would be a giveaway. By the same token, Gerald was glad because it would make what he wanted easier to find. Glancing over his shoulder, he approached the heavy metal desk with the built-in file drawers. Gently sliding the top one open, Weir was happy to see that the filing system remained much as it had been when he was responsible for it. Folders handling individual items were placed under one of three categories. The first, general supplies, contained orders for bandages, surgical, and emergency room supplies. A second section was labeled non-narcotic drugs, while the third was labeled narcotics.

Moving directly to the third sector, Weir took out the four folders he was most curious about: folders labeled Seconal, Tuinal, Valium, and Librium. Opening the folder for Seconal, he saw that there had been little change in the quantities utilized by the hospital. Already sure of what he would find, he did the same for the other three medications. In each case his suspicions were confirmed: usage continued at a normal level.

Being careful to replace the folders exactly as he had found them, Gerald moved back to check the door. As he approached his workstation, the door suddenly swung open as one of the nurses strode in.

Noticing Weir's nervous reaction, she said, "Sorry to startle you. I just came down to see if you'd give me some aspirin."

Taking a deep breath, Gerald hoped he appeared normal. "No problem, I just didn't expect the door to open. Would you prefer Tylenol?"

"Whatever will take care of this headache more quickly. I still have four hours to go and I won't make it at this rate."

Nodding his agreement, Gerald breathed a sigh of relief as the door closed behind the nurse carrying two Tylenol in her hand. Sinking onto his stool, he tried to quell the shaking sensation inside. Taking several breaths, he moved back toward Cosmello's desk. With any luck, lunch would keep everyone else busy until time for afternoon meds. Quickly reaching for the next drawer, he found the folders marked for invoices and orders. Hoping to be wrong, he placed them on the desk.

Scanning the last three months was all he needed to confirm his worst suspicions. While extra quantities of Seconal, Tuinal, and Valium had been ordered on a regular basis, he knew that they had never been entered into stock, in spite of the invoices that said they had been delivered.

The shock of finding proof of his suspicions hit Gerald hard. He felt weak and his muscles suddenly turned to water. How could it have happened? Harrison was a man of healing, how could he possible condone what was being done through his hospital? Why had Harrison told Gerald not to do anything when he first discovered the discrepancies around the time of Brett Conklin's death?

As his thoughts chased round and round Gerald became even more depressed. If he were to say anything about his suspicions, he would be out of a job. Where would he go? He had lived here more than half of his life. He had made Taylorville his home and was a respected member of the community. What would be left if he disclosed the drug abuse taking place? What would people say and who would they believe?

The sick feeling persisting, he returned the folders to the drawer, not realizing as he did so that he inverted the order of the one containing information on Tuinal with the one containing data on Seconal.

She had known that things would change if they began to investigate Brett's death again, and they had. She had put off giving Kevin her blessing longer than intended, afraid of what the rehashing of past events would do to their lives. Even after she knew there would be no relationship with Holly and the children, she had been reluctant to encourage Kevin to search for the truth. She was still afraid that they would rip off the shallow veneer of normalcy that covered their existence.

Kevin had waited, containing his frustration because of his love for her. She had known that eventually he would have to find out the truth behind their son's death. Sighing, she thought of the many times since Brett's death that she had seen Kevin get a faraway look in his eyes. He had been left to deal with his questions and frustration on his own. He hadn't even encouraged Tim

Reeves and Jim Walsh to pursue the investigation, not wanting to risk hurting her.

His relief had been no surprise to her four years before when she told him that she thought they should reopen the investigation. Once committed to a course of action, she knew that nothing but the truth would satisfy Kevin. After Kevin and Tim had discussed the case while they were on vacation, Kevin had begun to move on the plan they had mapped out.

He had spent hours filling pages with questions and queries. Working with him at the office, Linda knew exactly where he was directing his efforts, even making some of the phone calls and obtaining documents from the court house herself. With each misguided query and each elusive answer, she had wondered again just what they would find and if they would be able to live with the results.

Of the many difficult facts that she had had to review and finally accept, the machinations of the district attorney's office had been the worst. As Kevin's right hand, she had over the years become very familiar with the law. She had always had a healthy respect for the legal system, knowing that it was the one factor that helped society retain a semblance of order. Only the legal system provided an equalizing set of checks and balances over those who decided to violate it and the victims.

Shaking her head, she still had a hard time accepting it. How was it possible that the men who had worked with Kevin and interacted with them on social occasions would have participated in such an aberration of justice? What had they stood to gain that would make them jeopardize their ideals and bury the evidence of foul play in Brett's death? How often had the questions been asked?

Once Kevin had decided to move forward, he had unearthed the fact that all of the DAs who had held office in Taylor County from the time of Brett's death to now had all served as prosecutors for the attorney general in Brunswick at the same time. Starting with Smalls, all of the men had begun their careers as aides to the man who was now state senator, and they had all ended up in Taylor County. So what was the connection to Brett's death?

A chill ran down her spine as she digested the thought. Thanks to the advances in telecommunications over the last years and the desire of the public to know the truth beginning with Watergate, there had been more and more disclosures about wrongdoing in public office. But could it possibly happen in Taylorville? What was there to gain?

Though Kevin and Tim had not been able to pinpoint any reason for a cover-up of the evidence in Brett's death by the district attorneys, they had definitely found reason to believe that there had been a conspiracy to avoid pursuing the investigation. Many things had come to light, including the spread of drugs within the area dating from just before Brett died. Today drugs were an underlying economic factor of the world they lived in, but in 1976 they had been a distant problem of others.

Once he and Tim had discussed the different aspects of Brett's death and the subsequent investigation, they had mapped out a plan to find the truth. Kevin had approached the district attorney's office to ask for the reports and information relating to Brett's death. Tim had tried to prepare him for a lack of cooperation, but nonetheless Kevin was dumbstruck by what he saw as the refusal of the district attorney to help him.

He had called and requested an appointment with the DA the same as any other constituent of the county. He knew who Kelly was, due to his continued involvement with the legal community, but he had never had any personal dealings with the man. When he asked for an appointment he was given one without a problem—six weeks away.

Kevin had prepared extensively for his meeting with the DA, wanting to utilize his time to the best of his advantage. Arriving fifteen minutes early, he had taken a seat in the familiar waiting room. Time passed quickly, filled with the greetings of those who stopped to talk to him as he adroitly brushed off their queries as to why he was there. Ushered into Kelly's office, he found that not much had changed from the way Smalls had kept it, though Kelly had replaced Smalls as DA in 1980.

A political animal by nature, Kelly's view of Conklin as potential voter was obvious in his greeting. "And what can I do for the former mayor of Taylorville?"

Shaking the proffered hand, Kevin had answered sincerely, "Hopefully help me find some answers."

Until that point, Kevin had tried to maintain an open mind, unwilling to believe that there had been such a blatant lack of support from the county prosecutor. The district attorney's office was supposed to maintain files of all pending cases and any information relevant to the case. Kelly had insisted that he had never come across the Conklin file nor had he looked for it. Listening to him, Kevin realized that he had run into the same wall that had stopped Billings.

Appearing annoyed at Kevin's questions as to the help that had been offered to Sheriff Will Billings, Kelly had insisted that Billings had never spoken to him about the case. He also maintained that he had never seen the letter from Billings to Smalls. He insisted that when he took office, the Conklin case had not been one of those mentioned as pending by the state police. Kelly wouldn't comment on the action of his predecessor either. When Kevin had tried to contact Smalls, the former DA, to see if he would give him any information, Smalls had stonewalled, delaying their meeting time and time again with one excuse after another.

It had been at this point that Kevin had spoken with Stewart Bentley, a forensic scientist. A resident of Taylorville all of his life, Bentley had applied for the job of coroner but hadn't managed to dethrone Cummings. Bentley had been intrigued since the beginning and had begun to store information on his computer. When asked by Billings, Bentley was eager to look at the findings—or lack of findings—that had been released in connection with Brett's death. He had kept track of all the information gathered by the state police and also listened to all that was said by anyone in town with hopes of learning something that might help his friend.

Forewarned that he shouldn't expect any cooperation, Bentley had approached the matter from a different perspective. Crime reconstruction from the examination of the wounds and body had come a long way over the intervening fifteen years, and Bentley knew how to utilize the information to his advantage. Knowing what to look for in establishing the details of a crime, he had decided to talk with Dr. Grace and the county coroner, John Cummings.

Disguising his interest, Bentley had made it a point to bump into the doctor. Once he was talking with Grace, he casually commented on Conklin's death. From what Grace had said, the appearance of the wound did not coincide with the version Gunther had given of how the accident happened. Had the gun gone off while leaning against Brett, there would have been evidence of powder burns, and Dr. Grace had made no mention of them.

Nor had Bentley received any help when he broached the matter of Conklin's death with John Cummings. Hoping to find out something, he had danced around the facts, but Cummings refused to talk. Not content with what he garnered by means of omission, Bentley had discussed the matter with the sheriff. Convinced that things were not right, he had begun a reconstruction of the accident.

Thus Kevin's job had been simplified. Bentley had actually been studying the accident and working on its reconstruction, so Kevin had no need to be persuasive. Bentley was more than willing to work with him in finding out the truth of what had happened in the woods when his son died.

When Kevin described the problem to his friend, Tim had suggested that they begin with the information from Bentley and proceed as if they were going to trial. Arming themselves with expert testimony would ultimately allow them to present a strong case before a judge. Once decided, the execution of their plan had been easy. For the first time in his career, Kevin applied his talents to his own benefit.

Working on what they felt had happened, they hoped that they would find the evidence they needed to validate their ideas. Because he was now listening to what people had been trying to tell him since the death of his son, Kevin found himself confronted by information that became more and more incriminating against Karl Gunther.

Nelly Jones, one of Gunther's former patients, came forward to tell him that prior to Brett's death Gunther had been asking her about the Catholic religion. He had wondered whether Holly would be able to join another church if they were to leave Taylorville. Then Holly's former babysitter had approached him to tell him that one time after they came home from a Friday evening outing, she heard Brett tell Holly that he wasn't going to let Gunther destroy their family.

Recalling Ann Gunther Healy's comments, when she had come to him soon after Brett's death, Kevin was able to find new meaning in what the doctor's former wife had said. Why had Ed Smalls, then DA for Taylor County, handled the divorce on behalf of Ann Gunther instead of sending her to another attorney?

The more information he looked at, the more reason Kevin had to assume that something was drastically wrong in the way his son's death had been investigated.

Finishing up his rounds, Darnell Harrison made his way back to his office. Aggravated and unsettled, he walked to the bookcase and fixed himself a scotch and water. With any luck, as late as it was, no one would come looking for him. He hoped not, for he needed the time to think.

Why had Rossi suddenly become adamant about what was happening in the pharmacy? Never before had the Rossi family interfered in anyway with the running of the hospital, not even when he had been erratic with the loan payments. So, why now? If anything, with the tie-in of Pine Manor, they had more control of what happened than Harrison would have liked. What was bothering them? Nothing had changed except the increased complaints against Weir.

Feeling deflated, Harrison rested his head in his hands. How had it gotten so far out of control? He was a doctor—a saver of lives—not a supplier of poisons. How could he have been so blind as to what they were actually doing?

The ringing of the phone bringing him back, Darnell picked up the receiver. "Dr. Harrison speaking."

On the other end, Joseph Rossi pictured the doctor sitting at his desk. The need for power could be a tremendous monkey on a person's back. Did the doctor have any idea as to how often his monkey had been calling the shots? His mouth pursing as he thought, Rossi kept his voice even. "A dedicated man, still at work at this time of night."

Tensing as he recognized Rossi's voice, Darnell fought to keep his annoyance from his voice. "A doctor doesn't normally punch a time clock. Most of the time the days are longer than anticipated."

"I have a reliable source informing me that the person in question is becoming more and more unstable. In fact, Weir questioned his colleague about the orders again." Pausing for emphasis, Rossi spoke tauntingly, "I'm surprised that you would allow this much input or questioning on the part of an employee."

Closing his eyes and swallowing hard, Darnell wondered what he could say that would protect Weir. If Rossi were directly involved, matters might have already gone beyond his control. "I don't, but I'll make sure to take care of it."

"Make sure that you do. If you don't, I will. You wouldn't want any question about your invoices to be made public. It just wouldn't look good, would it?"

Hanging up the phone, Harrison found his hand shaking with the implied threat. For the first time, he realized that along with his reputation, Weir's life was in danger. If they were not convinced that he could control Weir, the family would themselves take measures to remove the problem. Staring at the wet mark that continued to spread around the glass, Harrison realized that he was trapped in a cage of his own making.

As he drove toward his office, Karl Gunther was preoccupied. Rather than mentally reviewing his daily schedule, his mind was focused on what was happening far away in the town in Ohio that he had left over ten years before. What had happened to suddenly motivate Kevin Conklin to force a further investigation into Brett's death? Why now? Unaware that his brow was furrowed, Gunther continued to try to find a reason for the sudden interest in a case that had remained untouched for almost a dozen years.

Following their marriage, Karl had encouraged Holly to remain in contact with Kevin and Linda for the children's sake. For three years they had faithfully done so, but gradually all contact had ceased. The situation was too emotional for Holly to handle and, rather than continue to have her upset, Karl had agreed that if the children did not want to keep in touch with their grandparents, they shouldn't be forced to do so. Tommy and Janie were young and had adapted to their new environment, rapidly leaving the past behind. As he had always been in their lives, their acceptance of Karl was wholehearted. Holly was happy and so were they.

Though he personally did not make the calls, he had kept in touch with what was going on in Taylorville and the Conklin family through his new sister-in-law. Clarissa called her friends on a monthly basis, so it was fairly easy to keep track of what was happening. With that and the availability of the Internet, Karl had kept track of what was going on with the hospital and Harrison. Though Holly wondered at Karl's interest in the news, she never pursued the matter. As there was little contact with the past other than the phone calls, what was happening in Ohio was of minimal interest.

Suddenly, in the fall of 1988, the phone calls had taken on a new significance. The Internet had become a vital link to knowing what happened in the county seat. Things had taken a new twist when Kevin Conklin began to explore what had happened the day his son died. Though Kevin didn't make a fuss or tell anyone in particular what he was doing, as soon as he called for an appointment with District Attorney Kelly the news was all over the grapevine.

But that was only the beginning. Kevin Conklin has hired Stewart Bentley to help reconstruct what had happened. Lost in thoughts of the past, the only thing that kept Karl from a serious accident was the blaring of the horn by the driver he had run off the road.

Taking a deep breath, he tried to concentrate on his driving. He had become complacent and that had been a mistake. For the eight years they had spent in New Mexico and since moving to Lincoln, everything had worked smoothly. With the help of the Rossi family contacts, Karl had been able to establish his practice. His new family had prospered.

All of his worries about being able to leave Taylorville and support Holly and the children disappeared with the appearance of Captain Rossi. With Rossi willing to buy Gunther's share of the Taylorville Hospital, a great weight had lifted off his shoulders.

With the additional help offered by Rossi regarding the move to New Mexico, Karl came to view Rossi and his "family" as his guardian angels. Though he had maintained only sporadic contact with the Captain throughout the years, he still felt as if he could call the man should he ever have a problem. Did he have a problem?

Gerald Weir could feel Joe Cosmello studying him. Had Cosmello realized that someone had gone through his files? Breaking into a sweat though it was cool in the pharmacy, Gerald tried to steady his hands. It wouldn't do to have Cosmello see him so nervous. Though the discrepancies had started long before his arrival in Taylorville, Weir had no doubt that Cosmello was a part of what had been happening at the hospital.

Jumping as the phone rang, Gerald watched Joe pick up the receiver. "Pharmacy, Cosmello."

"Are things any less tense at the moment?" asked a gravelly voice.

"Not particularly." Shooting a sidelong glance at Weir, Cosmello continued, "It's been a strange day. Nothing out of the ordinary, but the vibe is strange."

"Is Weir still as jumpy as before?"

"I'd say so. I don't know what to do to rectify the situation," replied Cosmello, glancing at Weir. Turning to keep Gerald from hearing him, he continued, "Harrison says the behavior is due to an ulcer, but I don't know."

"You know that we can't take any chances. You won't have to do anything, but it's been decided. The boys will pay him a visit later this evening. Make sure you have an alibi."

"If you say so. I'll talk to you later on."

Listening to the one-sided conversation, Gerald couldn't explain why he was so nervous. Maybe because Joe kept looking at him out of the corner of his eye, he had the feeling that they were talking about him. But why would Sam talk to anyone about him?

Glancing at the clock mounted over the door, he was glad to see that it was 3:45. Fifteen more minutes and he could leave the problems behind, at least for the day.

His spirits lifting at the thought, Gerald finished preparing the medications for the night shift and put away the bottles he had been using. In a much better mood he was able to answer truthfully when Sam asked what he planned to do that night.

"My wife is out of town so I think I'll take advantage and putter in the garden. Then I'll watch the ball game, it'll be a quiet night." Lifting his hand in a wave, Gerald went out the door, not realizing that Sam quickly picked up the phone.

Stopping at the Acme to pick up some milk, he noticed the car parked across the street. Feeling better at being away from the pharmacy, he shrugged off his apprehension. Why should he know every vehicle that came to town?

Later, content with the job he had done on the garden and having talked to his wife, Gerald settled in front of the television with a glass of iced tea. For the first time that day, he was truly relaxed and even hopeful. Maybe he was just imagining things. Wrapped in his familiar armchair, the idea of Harrison being involved in underhanded drug dealings seemed ludicrous.

A sudden noise in the basement diverted his attention from the screen. Damn! Just when he was comfortable, that old raccoon was scavenging again! Deciding that he had better check it out, on his way past the console he shut off the TV, hoping to hear more. Turning on the light at the head of the stairs, he made his way down to the basement. With any luck he would be able to take care of the problem in time to see the final play. As he turned to grab a 2 × 4 leaning against the wall, the man who had been hidden in the recess under the stairs made his move.

Dropping the large black plastic sheet over Gerald's upper torso, he effectively immobilized his arms. Not bothering to answer the terrified questions, as Weir's breath began to come in gasps, he tightened the plastic even more and waited until Weir stopped moving.

Finally they were making progress. It had taken more than a little persuasion and quite a bit of political muscle to obtain the records that had been denied to them for so long. *Now we are getting somewhere,* thought Tim Reeves with a sense of satisfaction. It hadn't been easy, and the continuing inquiries into Brett's death were certainly ruffling feathers in different areas, but they were not going to give up—not now.

Only after Jeff Snyder won the 1988 election for district attorney had they been able to get some answers. When Kevin had approached him, Snyder began to think about the intentional mismanagement that the case implied. His conclusions had led to ordering a search for the elusive information.

Well versed in political maneuverings, Tim was sure that the young DA was not acting out of selflessness, but that didn't bother him. More than one ambitious DA had seen their career take off after resolving some long-forgotten case. The public loved to see justice served. Undoubtedly, if the case went to trial, Snyder would benefit from the publicity and get a push up the political ladder.

Intrigued by the possibilities offered by the Conklin case, Snyder had tracked down Kelly's former secretary, now a detective in the police department. She had been able to pinpoint the location of the Conklin file in the courthouse. That had been the first step. After reviewing the file and agreeing that there were inconsistencies that should have been further investigated, Snyder met with Kevin, Linda, and Reeves who had flown in from Colorado specifically for the meeting. The outcome was that Snyder agreed to review and assess the state police investigation.

From that point on, things had moved quickly. Snyder rapidly arranged a meeting between the state police and the Conklin family. Following that gathering, Snyder met with troopers Salinkas and Fekette several times in order to review the evidence, files, and reports pertinent to the case. Snyder had visited Deer Run to see for himself the scene of the purported accident. By 1989, Snyder was convinced that at the least there had been a mismanagement of the evidence from Brett Conklin's death. Accompanied by state troopers, Snyder took the file to the University of Ohio for presentation before a group of forensic specialists who reviewed the physical evidence again using the methodology that had not been available at the time of Brett's death.

Thinking back, Tim remembered how the news had affected Kevin. Out of twenty-nine forensic specialists present, twelve had indicated that there was basis to believe a homicide had been committed, while the other seventeen maintained that the death could have been either, accidental or intentional, refusing to commit to the death being a murder.

Snyder made sure that all of these reports reached the state police, at which point it became apparent that the local police sergeant wanted the case to remain closed and refused to help. When Salinkas and Fekette were asked to give an opinion as to the cause of Conklin's death, both had stated that they were undecided. Having insufficient evidence to prosecute in 1989 at the time of his inquiries, DA Snyder had said that he would see that the case was filed as a "suspicious death."

Far from being upset or disillusioned by Snyder's decision, Tim and Kevin had begun to plan a campaign that would allow them to bring the case to trial. His years in the legal system serving as precedent, Tim knew that the burden of proving a reasonable suspicion of homicide was up to them. The only way that he saw that happening was to find sufficient data from expert witnesses to allow them to ask for an exhumation of Brett's body. To this end, Stewart Bentley had continued with his quest to reconstruct what had happened as he searched for evidence. After a prolonged investigation, he had met with Kevin and Tim to discuss the findings. At that point the three decided that it was time for Bentley to approach the state police.

On January 30, 1990, representing himself as consulting forensic scientist of the group Forensic Reconstruction Consultants and Resource Services, Stewart Bentley had written to Major Darnell Jordan of the Ohio State Police. In the letter Bentley had described in detail the methods he had utilized to duplicate the size and shape of the wound in Brett Conklin's chest. Mentioning his examination of the clothing worn by Conklin the day of his death, Bentley pointed out that the bloodstains could now be used to determine the position of the body at the time of discharge of the gun. Also discussed in this letter was Bentley's request to access the evidence held by the state police in order to conduct an in-depth study of the same that would include a photomicrography if approved by DA Snyder.

The prior consultation with Dr. Eric Mitchell, chief medical examiner for Onondaga County, was referenced. Mitchell had indicated that "the chances were good" that sufficient evidence would be found in a second autopsy of Conklin's body to indicate that the death had been a homicide. Consultations with other specialists concerning powder burns and blood spatter had increased Tim's confidence that they would soon have sufficient evidence to take before a judge and ask for an exhumation of the body.

The file that he had started at the time of Brett's death now took up the space of three accordion folders, the last two having been collected within the past five years. As bits and pieces of information continued to appear, Tim had been skeptical as to their chances of convincing a judge that the case should be reopened and the body exhumed. In spite of the snail's pace at which things were going, Tim was convinced that they were moving toward a resolution.

Exhilarated that he would be able to talk to Kevin and give him the good news, Tim dialed his friend's number. As he listened to the ringing on the other end of the line, he smiled thinking about Kevin's reaction.

"Conklin speaking."

Kevin's tone warned him that something was wrong. "What's bothering you? I was all prepared to be the bearer of good tidings and you sound like you're at the bottom of a pit."His sigh indicating his mental anguish, Kevin answered tiredly, "You know that I'm always glad to hear from you. It's just that I got some unexpected bad news and can't seem to digest it."

"Nothing wrong with Linda is there?"

"No, thank God. But last night they found Gerald Weir, the pharmacist at the hospital, dead in his basement. It doesn't make any sense."

"Why's that?"

"Gerald has always been a staunch, upright member of the community. He and his wife were at church every Sunday, Bible study, Boy Scouts, and helping out with fundraisers whenever asked to do so. He and his wife have been married almost thirty years and seemed to have a good relationship. She was visiting her sister, so she wasn't home last night."

"So what was so strange about his death? Did his heart give out?" Tim asked.

"They found him in the basement, wrapped in a large plastic sheet."

Pausing to think about what Kevin had just told him, Tim asked, "Any possibility of auto erotica?"

His doubt obvious, Kevin answered his friend, "Anything is possible, but I find it extremely hard to believe. You and I both know that auto erotica was more common than any police department would have liked about ten years ago, but in this case it just doesn't seem a likely explanation." His voice dropping, Kevin continued, "But neither does suicide. Anyway, the funeral is tomorrow. Weir's death seems just one more of the inexplicable things that have happened in town lately. I guess the thought of another questionable death in light of what we've learned about Brett is what has me upset."

Nodding, Tim spoke his agreement. "That's understandable. Getting back to why I called, I think now is the time to push for a petition of exhumation. We've gathered all the information we can and from here on it's a matter of getting a judge to agree."

Kevin listened intently as Tim outlined what he thought they should do.

The Petition, 1994

Why was Kevin Conklin so set on stirring up what had happened at the time of Brett's death? How could it possibly make a difference to him to find out after all these years? Sure, he had been aware that Conklin had been gathering information for the last six years, but petitioning to exhume? Unable to find an answer though he had tried to look at the question from all angles, Darnell Harrison rubbed his hands over his face. The tired feeling had become his almost constant companion. It wasn't as if he didn't know what was causing him to feel like this, for he did. But knowing the reason behind how he felt and being able to remedy what was causing it were two different things.

Sitting down again, he looked at the picture of himself in his military uniform. Had things been different, he would have been the first one in trying to help Kevin find out how his son had died. But as it was, he couldn't afford to be involved. In fact, for reasons of his own, he really didn't want further scrutiny of Brett's death.

He had fought having to admit the truth for a long time. Not wanting to believe it, he had finally acknowledged that the people who had backed the renovations of the hospital, as well as the residence for seniors, were part of the Rossi crime family. Recognizing who they were did nothing toward finding a solution for what was occurring now, or preventing the Rossis from getting an even stronger hold on the area. Their tentacles were so far reaching that they could insinuate themselves into anything and everything imaginable. Once he admitted that he had been manipulated, it was a small jump to recognize that these people were capable of making things happen how and when they wanted.

District Attorney Smalls had refused to assist Sheriff Billings in his investigation of Brett's death and so had the state police. At one time, Darnell would have questioned whether he was being paranoid in his attitude. Today, he had no doubt that when the Rossis wanted an obstacle removed, it would suddenly disappear, regardless of whether it were a stone or a human life.

Harrison's line of thinking about the family methods of problem solving led his thoughts to Gerald Weir. Nothing pointed at the Rossi family as being responsible, but he had no doubt that they had been scrutinizing the pharmacist's actions prior to his death. Had they decided he was a liability and done something about it?

He didn't know. But what he did know was that he would rather not find out. It had been almost two years and, while people still mentioned the strange way Weir had died, the speculation had calmed down. Would Kevin's investigation of his son's death lead to further inquiries into events that happened at the same time? He wasn't sure, but if they did, Darnell knew that neither he nor the hospital would come out unscathed.

As the July sun beat down on the garden, the mid-afternoon heat bathed everything in a soft haze. At the base of the dogwood, the annuals that they had planted were thriving, their colors set off by the jewel green of the lawn that served as their backdrop. The petals had lost their fresh pristine look, but the well-tended tree still looked lovely.

Suddenly, feeling cold in spite of the warm summer day, Linda rubbed her arms and moved away from the window, stopping to pick up the mug of tea left steeping on the counter.

Moving into the family area, now brightly lit by the afternoon sun, she paused to look at the picture that had graced her end table for over fifteen years. It was the last family portrait of Brett, Holly, and the children, done the Christmas prior to his death. They looked so happy and content that it had rapidly become her and Kevin's favorite picture.

Once Kevin had made up his mind to look further into Brett's death six years before, finding out the truth had become an ever-present preoccupation. Money had not been a problem. Their economic situation was always good and had only become better through the years. With no family close by to spend on, Linda had seen no reason to deny Kevin her support, financial as well as moral.

Tim Reeves, their closest friend, had been of inestimable help. Throughout the years he and Darlene had served as a support system for both of them. When they had finally decided to pursue the investigation, both Tim and Darlene had insisted on helping in any way possible. It hadn't been easy to gather the necessary data. In 1992, DA Snyder had met with them to discuss the possibilities of once again focusing on the case. Though he had been willing to work with them, he had eventually said that there was not sufficient doubt to petition the courts.

Fortunately, Tim's long tenure with the DA's office in Boulder had made him privy to many areas of information. He had kept current of new methods in evidence analysis even after leaving office, and he continued to put all his knowledge and expertise at Kevin's disposal, calling in markers where necessary. But it hadn't been easy. Even after he had begun to gather data on the blood spatter and the bullet trajectory, they still didn't have enough grounds to ask for an exhumation of the body.

Working as Kevin's right hand in the office made Linda the logical one to coordinate the information they received. Fortunately, the development of the personal computer and the possibility of utilizing one at home had simplified the job significantly. She found that the hardest part of helping prepare for the case was trying to make sure that Kevin did not become aware of the anguish she often experienced when reading the reports and collating the data. Working with Stewart Bentley had been fortunate for them. Stew was following the case and had been trying to get permission to look at the evidence because of his own doubts even before Kevin placed him on retainer. As a forensic pathologist, his professional interest had been the motivation for following the case from the onset.

The financial aspect of pursuing the investigation had been manageable as the only large expense incurred had been in retaining an attorney to represent them. The issue had not been the money. Instead the problem had been to hire someone who would accept both Kevin and Tim being on top of every move the attorney made. She knew firsthand that it wasn't easy working with attorneys.

Now they were finally ready and had gotten all the information they could. The data had been analyzed and the structure of the case, including the arguments, had been prepared. A date was set for next week. One way or another, things had been put into motion and hopefully, they would soon know the truth.

His hands in his pockets, Karl looked out the window of his office. A sigh escaped him and his confident aspect suddenly seemed to disintegrate. The day had been busy, but that was normal, a sign that the business was thriving. If only being busy was the problem! It had taken time to establish the family the way he and Holly had planned once they left Taylorville.

While it had taken the people of Lincolnton a long time to accept him as their doctor of preference, he now had patients booked months in advance. More so, he again felt that he was making a difference. He liked the challenge of working with allergies, an area of medicine glossed over all too often.

Life would be wonderful if it weren't for Conklin's sudden push to reexamine Brett's death. After living peacefully for so long, the strain of thinking that their whole world could come tumbling down around them was beginning to show on both of them. Holly wasn't sleeping well and was more irritable and angry with the passing of each day. For him, going home was no longer the pleasure it had been. Now when he crossed the threshold he wondered what he would find. Thinking back to when he had first heard of Conklin's decision to pursue an investigation four years before in 1988, Karl remembered Holly's outrage.

"You must be joking! How can they possibly think that anything they find now can help establish what happened when Brett has been dead for over twelve years? Why are they doing this? They haven't even spoken to the children in the past two years!"

Unable to give a logical answer, Karl had tried unsuccessfully to calm her. "I don't know. The only thing that worries me is that if their petition to the court goes forward, we will undoubtedly be involved."

"Why? What can you possibly tell them that you didn't tell them at the time? Nobody questioned what you said then, why should they now?"

"Sheriff Billings never believed me and he tried various times to have me questioned again. I was just lucky that Ed Smalls, then district attorney, was a good friend of Darnell Harrison's and pushed to leave the statement as it stood for the hospital's sake."

Quivering with anger, Holly had been sarcastic. "You almost sound as if you think that it's a good idea. I don't want this dragged up now. How will it look if the local news finds out? 'Allergist Questioned in Old Death' isn't exactly positive publicity."

Doing his utmost to remain calm, Karl had tried to reason with her. "I don't want this any more than you do, but if we don't keep on top of it, we may be in for a nasty surprise. Forensic science is much more advanced now. Much as I don't like it, I'd rather know what's going on."

"Well, I don't want to know. This whole thing could be a tempest in a teapot, so why get any more involved than we are now?"

At that time it had taken hours to calm Holly down and even more time to convince her that they had to know what Conklin was doing. Though he had not told Holly the extent of his interest in the inquiries that were being made, he had kept a close watch through his local contacts in Taylorville. When Kevin retained Stew Bentley to reconstruct the accident he knew that they could not avoid involvement.

They had been granted a reprieve when DA Snyder had found insufficient grounds to ask for a petition of exhumation—but Conklin hadn't stopped. He had continued to gather testimony from expert witnesses and had finally put together a case strong enough to present to the court.

Karl had been afraid from the beginning that if Kevin and Linda lost contact with the children, they would eventually try to obtain further details to explain Brett's death. Now his fears had become a reality. Once he realized that Kevin and Linda planned to ask for an exhumation of the body in order to have a second autopsy performed, he had no alternative but to involve Holly. As Brett's wife at the time of his death, Holly was the only one who could petition to have the exhumation stopped.

Accepting that the future of her family depended on what she was able to achieve, Holly had ultimately redirected her anger into working toward arguments that would serve to block Linda and Kevin. She had willingly lied about her relationship with Karl prior to Brett's death and now was afraid she would be accused of perjury. Now she was as concerned as Karl in keeping abreast of what was happening in Taylorville.

They had retained a Brunswick attorney, Peter T. O'Malley, to appear in court in July on their behalf. Hopefully, he would be successful in managing to block the exhumation request. Even though Karl and Holly were not going to be present, the strain of knowing that the date was fast approaching had made their life a parody of what it had been. Going through the motions of presenting an unconcerned, confident front was taking its toll on both them and the children. Worse yet, the newspapers had tried to contact them and this had heightened their anxiety.

Not happy, but having no choice, Tony Russell continued to serve as the Captain's eyes and ears in Taylorville. Through regular communication, Rossi had been able to keep his finger on the pulse of what was happening in the Taylor county seat, and was now glad that he had.

When Kevin Conklin had begun making inquiries in 1988, Rossi had known immediately. From that time on he had insisted on regular reports as to what Conklin had uncovered. In spite of the fact that measures had been taken to ensure that the Rossi family was never connected to Brett Conklin's death, the Captain still wanted to know what was happening.

As the summer of 1994 began, Rossi knew that Conklin was ready to file a petition to exhume his son's body. Diligent work by family retainers let him know that Conklin had compiled convincing arguments. Sufficient evidence could be produced to warrant doubt, and that was a problem. Never one to leave anything to chance, Joseph Rossi picked up the phone and dialed the number of Paul's private line.

The man who picked up the phone could never have been taken for the soldier who had carried out the Captain's orders in the summer of 1976. Along with his elevated position, Paul had achieved a studied polish and refinement. The only remnant of that time was his continued skill and expertise in resolving the problems sent his way. His confidence echoing in his voice, he reassured Rossi, "There isn't any way that we can be connected. Not one scrap of evidence at the scene, and only you and I know what actually took place. That place is so far behind the times that the coroner still keeps the records in his garage and charges rent for doing it! To be on the safe side, I helped myself to them years ago. If he can locate them in the chaos that he uses as a filing system, I'll be surprised."

"What about the information the sheriff had been so persistent in trying to track down?"

"I really don't see a problem," Paul said. "But if you think it prudent, I'll make sure that the information held by the DA's office conveniently disappears."

Satisfied, Rossi hung up the phone, mentally making a note to check on the outcome of the hearing. It never hurt to be careful.

As closely attuned as he was to Linda's body language, Kevin didn't need the bruised shadows under her eyes to know that Linda was worried. Usually a time when they relaxed after dinner, at several points he had glanced up to find her scrutinizing him. She was doing it again and Kevin pushed her to tell him what was on her mind.

Leaning so he would put his arm around her, Linda sighed as she tried to find the right words. How could she explain her fear when most of the time it seemed irrational even to her. They were justified in trying to find out what had happened the day of Brett's death so there was nothing to be afraid of. But she was.

Intuitively, she sensed that before they were finished, they would have opened more than one door to find an unpleasant surprise. Were they ready for that? How could she explain her feelings to Kevin? During the six years since they had decided to pursue their quest for information, things had begun to change. But she wasn't sure that the changes were for the better. Could she tell Kevin that she had seen him become distracted and sad after a meeting with Stewart Bentley or a phone call with Tim Reeves? She was supposed to be as eager as he was to find out the truth.

Her calm, caring husband began changing the day they decided to begin examining the information about Brett's death.

Originally she had thought that it was a good idea. The children were lost to them. So why not let Kevin put his doubts to rest? Initially he was animated and upbeat about the investigation and she had felt justified in supporting his decision. But as the data began to come in and the discussions began to have more scope and depth, she wondered. How could he not be upset when told that his son might have suffered prior to dying? She certainly was—and that was part of the problem.

She often felt sad and anguished after incorporating the new data and reports into the computer bank but tried not to let it show. She had decided to support Kevin in his quest for the truth, but now she faced a dilemma. Wouldn't she be letting him down if she made him feel bad by showing him how she was being adversely affected by what they were learning? As close as they had always been, the fact that they were both trying to disguise their feelings seemed a big price to pay. Sighing, Linda looked at Kevin and lowered her eyes.

Finally, her voice a whisper, Linda began to speak. "I feel so torn. I realize that you need to find out the truth about what happened, and I've been doing my best to help you, but that doesn't stop me from worrying."

"Do you think that I don't know you've been hurting and trying to hide it? What I don't understand is why you haven't talked to me and let me know what it is that's bothering you," Kevin answered sadly.

Sighing deeply, Linda said, "I'm so torn. I know that you have a need to find out exactly what happened that day." She looked into his eyes, beseeching him to understand. "It took a long time for me to give up, but once I knew that the children were no longer a part of our lives, I gave you my support. I hoped that by finding out the truth we would finally be able to move on without the past weighing down our future." Sighing, she continued, "Instead of finding any relief in knowing that we were getting closer with all the data that came in from Stew Bentley and Tim,

I began to see that looking into Brett's death was not only opening up old wounds but might even cause new ones. I don't know how either one of us will be able to live knowing that there was and possibly continues to be such deep-seated collusion around us. This community has been part of our lives forever. We have always been honest and open with everyone we know. Now I feel as if our digging into the past will rip the scab off the infection surrounding us." Shaking her head, Linda continued, "I'm afraid that we're going to find out much more than what really happened to Brett."

Kevin remained silent, squeezing her arm to let her know that he understood how hard it was to share what she was feeling.

"You were as reluctant as I was to face the possibility that our son's murderer was raising our grandchildren," Linda continued softly. "But the possibility exists, and Tommy and Janie will side with Karl Gunther if this goes to trial. He's been their father figure for over fifteen years."

His eyes mirroring her anguish, Kevin allowed Linda to see that he agreed with her. Pressing her against his side, he said, "I know, I kept hoping they would eventually come around. Unrealistic, wasn't it?"

"You've missed them every bit as much as I have. But that's only part of the problem." Turning to look into his eyes, she continued, "What's been happening to us during the last six years is what really has me concerned."

Linda's words were totally unexpected and Kevin felt suddenly chilled, as if by a premonition of evil. Had he committed the ultimate sin? In his fervor to find out the information he considered necessary to put closure to Brett's death, had he taken his wife for granted? Unsettled, he waited for her to continue.

"We have to be thankful. We had two years longer than we might have had and we made every possible effort to stay in touch"—pausing, Linda seemed to mull something over—"which brings me back to six years ago. I was convinced that finding out what had happened would be cathartic for you, regardless of the outcome. I noticed that you were inventing things to do around the house once you cut back on your caseload. Our dogwood tree has to be the happiest specimen in Taylorville with all the attention it gets."

"Why didn't you say anything?" Kevin asked, smiling, "Weren't you afraid I was losing it?"

"The thought never entered my mind. I didn't say anything for the simple reason that I had nothing else to offer you. I've always been involved with one group or another, so my situation didn't change with your cutting back. The one afternoon we took together, we always spent together either shopping or going to a movie. That part of our routine continued."

"So you saw my interest as a way to keep me out of your hair," Kevin teased.

"Maybe, but not long after we got back from our vacation, I began to wonder if we weren't making a big mistake."

"Now I'm really curious. Mistake in regard to what?" Kevin demanded.

"In spite of the fact that we followed the logical steps to get the data you wanted, suddenly things didn't feel right. You'd worked in the legal community of the county for over forty years and suddenly the doors that should have opened readily slammed in your face."

His jaw tensing, Kevin braced himself for what was coming. He had been surprised at the reactions he had encountered but had not said anything to Linda. Now, as his wife gave voice to her thoughts, he found himself deeply disturbed.

Getting up and moving restlessly to get a glass of water, Linda turned and asked, "Do you want coffee?" At Kevin's nod, she busied herself filling the carafe, continuing her monologue from the kitchen as she worked. "You never really got into how you felt, but it was clear that you were disturbed and so was I. Working with you for so many years, how could I help but think that something wasn't right?"

Coming back, Linda placed the coffee mugs on the table and sat down sideways so she could see Kevin's face. "The new television shows and the reports in the paper didn't help either. Suddenly I found myself wondering why the public officials would collectively try to cover up the real details of Brett's death."

"At the time we lost Brett, the power structure in the community didn't seem affected either. Granger, Stern, and the rest of the crew who controlled the town continued much the same as always. The only link that I could find between Brett and the rest of that group was the fact that all of them were part of the key club." Raising her eyebrows in question, Linda continued, "Who would have thought that white-fenced Taylorville in the heart of farmland would have been the site of a sex club? But I can't imagine any of them worrying about being tied to the group as it was pretty much common knowledge. So that brought me back to what Brett might have been doing."

"Sweetheart, you're assuming that there was something happening that someone did not want made public. But you don't have the remotest idea of what it could be and there is absolutely no proof that there was any wrongdoing taking place at the time."

"Then why did everyone refuse to give you the information you asked for? And before that, why didn't they help Will Billings with his investigation?"

A frown darkening his forehead, Kevin replied cautiously, "I really don't know. I have to admit that I've wondered about that myself. After all the times I worked on cases that involved the state police, it surprised me when they seemed so reluctant to help out with what we were asking for. I was shocked when I heard that they refused to collaborate with Will Billings." Kevin went on, "But it's a big jump from failing to help us to covering up an investigation. Who stood to gain?"

"I don't know," said Linda. "All I know is that once we began to put the case together, everyone seemed to back off. That's when I started to wonder about what the motive was. Unfortunately, I still haven't come up with any theory that makes sense." Sighing, she fell back against the cushions and snuggled against her husband as she said, "It's so confusing. I'm almost afraid to think about what will come out at the hearing next week. So many questions remain to be answered."

Staring at the constantly changing shadows outside the window, Kevin wondered if Linda was right. Had he distanced himself from her as he became more involved with finding out the truth? It hadn't been intentional. Thinking about what she had said, he wondered if Linda had intuitively come much closer to recognizing the problem than he had. What would the new trial uncover? Was she correct? Was there reason to worry about their life changing as a result of what might come to light?

Distressing as his thoughts were, Kevin knew that he was committed. He would know what had happened and whether Gunther was responsible. If any of the facades so carefully hidden within the community crumbled as a result of bringing the truth to light, so be it.

Each Had His Reason

Watching her husband as he stood in front of the mirror running the electric razor over his beard, Maria Campolongo wondered if he realized how the pressure of his office had affected him. She had watched him change from an idealistic believer to a cynic, as Joe found that the theories that were taught in law school existed only in textbooks.

As his disenchantment with the legal system grew, his focus on what he believed to be right had also changed. Lately, since the Conklin debate over the exhumation of their son had taken on national importance, he had become more animated, but she wondered if it was healthy.

Seeing his wife's solemn reflection in the mirror, Joe rubbed his hand over his chin. "Look close enough or did I miss a spot?"

Her attention drawn to the man she knew since childhood, Maria smiled, "You look fine. I was just wondering why you were so interested in the Conklin case. It's been almost eighteen years since Brett Conklin died. If no one's wanted to pursue the issue until now, why do you want to?"

Splashing on aftershave, Robert looked at his wife in the mirror. "Maria, we've been through this before. You know that I plan on being more than an assistant DA. One of the most logical and quickest ways to make sure that I move up is to be involved with a high-profile case that is drawing public attention."

"Do you really think that Gunther is guilty?"

"I don't know, and frankly I don't really care. What interests me is the fact that so much was covered up during the investigation. Someone, for some reason, did not want the death investigated.

And it wasn't Gunther. Working on his own, he wouldn't have had sufficient clout to ensure that the investigation be dropped. Whoever contacted the district attorney either had heavy weight backing or had an ulterior motive for covering up the investigation. I can't be sure, but right after Conklin died we started to see a lot more drugs in the area. Whichever the reason, I'm going to know why the death wasn't investigated thoroughly." Exchanging his towel for underwear, he continued, "Taylorville may be very picturesque and quaint, but I'll bet that there are a lot of skeletons hidden behind those pristine white doors. I plan on finding out where they are."

The dogwood had bloomed and was now covered with fragile white blossoms. Looking at the tree, so beautiful in its white cloak, Linda thought about the legend she had been told as a child. To her eyes, the dogwood leaves had appeared torn and stained and she had wondered why a flower would look that way. When she had asked, her grandmother finished arranging the dogwood branches in the vase on the table and had settled Linda on her knee to tell her the story of the dogwood tree.

Long ago, the dogwood had been a much larger tree, much like an oak. As such, it was chosen to be the wood used for the cross on which Jesus was put to death. Sensing the tree's distress at being used in such a fashion, Jesus had promised that never again would a dogwood grow big enough to be chosen for use as a cross. Instead, the trunk would become slender and twisted. From then on the tree would also have beautiful white flowers in the shape of a cross that would be symbolic of what Jesus had suffered. The petals would have holes at the ends representing the holes of the nails that held him to the cross and their rusty red color would represent the blood that had been shed. Unlike other flowers, the inside would resemble a crown of thorns in order to make sure that no one forgot what had taken place.

Linda had always been drawn to the dogwood tree as a child. Perhaps because of the legend, as an adult she had always thought that part of the tree's beauty was that it represented the suffering that Jesus had endured to let man live as he did. Now, as she looked at the strong, beautiful tree, a frown creased her forehead. Had man learned nothing in the years since Christ had died on the cross? There were new machines and life-saving techniques developed every day to better the quality of life. In spite of that, did man suffer any less?

With a sigh, she realized that her frustration and anger were not directed toward mankind in general, but toward the situation she was living in particular. But how could she feel anything other than angry and frustrated? Two years had passed since the petition for exhumation had been presented in front of Judge Seamans in July of 1994, yet again they had again been blocked from taking the petition to court.

Holly Conklin Gunther had blocked the order of exhumation for Brett Conklin's remains. Months had dragged by as the lawyers representing Holly had answered each of the demands presented by Kevin and his lawyer. After many months of legal give and take, Brett's body had finally been exhumed on April 29, 1995, almost nineteen years after his death. As Kevin and Tim had anticipated, new evidence using the updated technology had countered the original finding of accidental death.

Vindicated in their belief that the investigation had been incorrect at the time of Brett's death, Kevin and Tim finally felt that they were making progress. Knowing the legal profession inside out, neither of them was overly concerned at the amount of time it had taken to get this far.

Perhaps because they are men—Linda thought, turning from the window and moving to the familiar comfort of the couch as she continued to muse—*they seem not to feel the strain and tension that surrounded them living with the investigation ever present in the background. Nor do they seem to worry about the fact that it contin-*

ues to drag on. But she did. The investigation had been hovering on the fringes of their every waking hour for the past two years. If asked, she would have said that it had taken on a form and substance of its own, coming to dominate many other areas of her life.

How much longer could they continue to live with the stress? And what were they ultimately going to gain by having done this? Tommy and Janie wouldn't speak to them at all. While she knew that Kevin made a conscious effort to share what was happening, Linda still felt that they had lost much of the tranquility of their lives prior to the petition. Would the viable presence that shadowed their every day disappear once this whole nightmare was over?

Looking at Paul Simon sitting across from him in his office, Captain Joseph Rossi smiled. Who would have thought that the tough, blond thug who had done much of the dirty work required by the family as they began their operation in upstate New York and the polished, demure gentleman who spoke on the phone in front of him could be one and the same?

Many times over the past twenty years Joseph Rossi had found himself thinking his intuition had been correct. When he had first seen the tough young man in his early twenties, he had recognized in Paul a barely disguised hunger to achieve—as well as little knowledge of how to do so. Having the soldier transferred to his operation had been the first step leading to the metamorphosis that had transpired.

Paul had rapidly proven himself not only loyal, but shrewd and intelligent. This had also helped Rossi's rapid rise within the family. In Paul, he had acquired a lieutenant who would oversee the carrying out of his orders to the dotting of every last "i" and the crossing of the last "t." It had soon become known within the family that dealing with Paul was the same as dealing with the Captain.

Quick to seize the opportunity afforded him, Paul had followed the advice of his mentor and had begun to refine himself. He had lost the slouch and tough-guy walk and had modeled his speech on the more refined members of the family. He adopted the vocabulary used by the lawyers. As business had expanded into upstate New York, Paul had become indispensable to Rossi. Relying on his young lieutenant to manage the daily routine and oversee the brunt of the street operations, the Captain had managed to maximize his time, avoiding the many irritating interviews with lower-ranking members of the distribution operation.

Rossi's efficiency and success in dealing with the myriad operations had not gone unnoticed by the head of the family. Over the years, the don had accorded him the leadership in operations of greater complexity and import. Rossi didn't need anyone to tell him that he would not have had the latitude to devote himself to so many areas had it not been for Paul.

When Kevin Conklin had reopened the investigation into his son's death in spite of all they had done to discourage him and make it difficult for him to obtain information, Paul's role had become vital. Though Rossi himself retained the contact with Tony Russell, Paul had been the one who had ensured the disappearance of Smalls's letter to the state police. He was also instrumental in ensuring that anyone who tried to find information in the coroner's files would be met with confusion.

Listening to Paul quietly and concisely summarize his instructions for the person on the line, the Captain knew that he had nothing to worry about. If anything, he was sure that the man in front of him would have anticipated any possible problems and acted accordingly.

As he hung up, Paul thought out loud, "I wonder if it has always been this difficult to make certain people understand instructions."

Smiling at the younger man, Rossi shook his head in affirmation. "Some things never change and communicating down the line of command is one of them. Regardless of how clearly you explain how or what you want done, someone will always try to second guess you by coming up with a different method of accomplishing the same thing." Looking shrewdly at the man he trusted with his life, Rossi continued, "Perhaps its human nature, but most people will try to impress you with what they know or how competent they are. This includes showing you that they are just as capable as you at resolving problems. Believe it or not, that's one of the reasons why I immediately saw that I could count on you."

His brow furrowing, Paul's was puzzled as he said, "But I don't recall ever trying to convince you that there was another way to do something unless you asked for a suggestion."

"That's exactly my point. More specifically, it's the reason why I decided you and I were going to do well together. Whenever I asked your opinion, you thought about what you would suggest and invariably were correct in what you said." Smiling, the Captain continued, "Now that you're finished on the phone and your secretary is holding your calls, let's have a drink and discuss the Conklin problem."

His answering smile genuine, Paul said, "Good idea," as he walked over to the built-in liquor cabinet. Having a good idea of what was on Rossi's mind, he was unconcerned. Knowing that he would be able to reassure his mentor that everything was taken care of made him eager for the coming discussion. Placing the crystal glass of scotch in Rossi's hand, he said, "Salute."

Lowering his glass to savor the amber liquid that bathed the ice cubes, Rossi toasted the other man. As the business expanded, he had less personal contact with the man in front of him, though they frequently spoke on the phone. He had looked forward to seeing Paul. Having listened to him handle a problem on the phone as he waited, the Captain was convinced that this would be a good meeting.

Taking advantage of the relaxed atmosphere, Rossi asked about Paul's family, thus removing urgency from the meeting. The amenities dealt with, he finally turned the conversation to what was bothering him. "You're aware that Conklin has refused to let the exhumation issue drop?"

At the other's nod, Rossi smiled. "Actually, I was sure that you were, but I prefer being safe than sorry. Not many of the old guard who were in power when Conklin died are left, but I wanted to know if you felt that there was any reason to be concerned."

"You don't have to worry. They found nothing at the time because I picked the casings up. While I was further away than Gunther or Conklin's wife, the blast from their gun made sure that no one would ever question whether any other gun had played a part in Conklin's death. Why would they? Gunther said it was an accident and no one questioned that at the time." Sipping his drink, Paul said, "If any question was to arise regarding the cases that Conklin was working on at the time, there again we're covered. The weak link of the trio was removed at the time of Conklin's death and the other two continue to be at our mercy." Smiling at Rossi's raised eyebrow, Paul went on to explain the measures taken to keep the two under tight control while making sure that the area expanded to benefit the Rossi family, in spite of the displeasure of other New York and New Jersey families.

Satisfaction visible in his eyes, Rossi nodded as he said, "I needed to ask. You know that I've always preferred being safe to sorry and I wanted to check to make sure we wouldn't be connected regardless of what they might find if they go ahead with the exhumation."

Nodding, Paul said, "I know. But there is nothing to worry about. Things have been running like clockwork in that area since the Bonano family decided that it was not to their advantage to try to retain control. While several members of their family still live there, none of them have been even remotely involved in what goes on for the last ten years or more. We did them a favor by moving them out."

To illustrate his point, Paul reached for the latest distribution charts and statistics. Watching his protégé, Rossi once again congratulated himself on his lieutenant.

His success had been frozen for posterity. The visual record in their varied frames graced the bookcase against the wall. Normally a source of satisfaction, today there was no reaction at all. Sitting at his desk, Darnell Harrison stared in the direction of the shrine to his achievement.

His motive in making life better for those in the area had been pure. He had the satisfaction of knowing that more than one life in the county had been saved due to his vision and impetus. But he was only human. For some reason, individual success stories had become routine and lost luster. Looking back, it was easy to identify where he had lost control. It had been at the height of the expansion and the controversy over Gunther. He had let himself be wooed into accepting help from the Captain and that had ultimately led to his present situation. Becoming angry, Darnell hit the desk with his fist.

Blinded by his ambition to make the hospital the best it could be, he had never bothered to wonder what kind of payback would be required. Before he knew it, the organization had been utilizing the hospital as a means of distributing drugs through creative billing. The hospital had also been the perfect front for laundering their money. He had no proof, but Weir, an excellent pharmacist, had suddenly died when he questioned the invoices. Harrison had no doubt that Weir's death was a result of the Rossi family's operation. At this point, he had no way of changing anything without incriminating himself.

In for a dime, in for a dollar, Harrison thought with a sigh. Much as he didn't like the idea, the only solution he could come up with was making sure that the Captain knew that the distribution operation would be put in jeopardy if any questionable information surfaced when they began to question Gunther. Not allowing himself time to back out, Harrison reached for the phone and dialed the number that would connect him to Rossi.

At the other end, when the phone rang, Rossi wondered who would contact him this late on a Friday afternoon. Shrugging, he picked up the phone, drawing a notepad toward him and said, "Rossi."

"Captain, Darnell Harrison. Normally I wouldn't call this late on a Friday, but I thought it important."

Rossi wasn't surprised to hear Harrison. He had been expecting the call. What surprised him was that Harrison had waited so long. Harrison's arrogant, cocky attitude had dissipated little by little, seeming to coincide with the rate at which he found himself indebted to the family. Rossi took note that Harrison sounded anxious. "Darnell! It's been a long time. How are things in Taylorville?"

As if you didn't know, thought Darnell. Gritting his teeth to keep from saying something snide, he counted to ten prior to answering. "Everything here is much the same as always. A rash of the flu went through the town ten days ago but everything is back to normal now."

"Good, good. Always glad to hear that things are all right." Refusing to help, Rossi allowed the silence to grow heavy. Reassured by Paul, Rossi was content to wait for the doctor to state his concerns.

Annoyed at having to relinquish his pride and ask for reassurance, Harrison finally said, "I imagine that you're aware that the Conklin exhumation is a given at this point."

"I had heard that Judge Seamans was inclined to let Kevin Conklin have the body exhumed."

Making an effort to keep his voice level and controlled, Harrison continued to fish for information. "There has been some discussion of looking at the cases Conklin was handling when he died for evidence that his death wasn't accidental."

Amused, Rossi answered slowly, "I hadn't really heard anything about that, but it doesn't surprise me. What baffled me is that they waited this long to take action if they didn't believe Gunther's story from the beginning."

"I've wondered about that myself," said Harrison, his voice reflecting concern. "I need to know that you've taken care of any damage control should there be a backlash related to Gunther. You know that there has been too much family involvement in the hospital to risk making the connection public knowledge."

"It has always been our policy to remain in the background," answered Rossi, his voice dropping contemptuously. "Your real worry is how you will look if any of this comes to light and the connection is established, isn't it?"

Furious, Harrison fought to remain calm. "Of course I don't want to be involved. The only way that I would be held accountable is if the whole operation became known, and that would be equally bad for the family."

Rossi said soothingly, "You've never had to worry about anything before and you don't have to worry now. Everything is under control."

Reassured but no happier, Harrison stood and grabbed the decanter angrily, pouring himself a large drink. Swallowing without tasting, he forced himself to analyze the conversation. He rubbed the tension points on his forehead, striving to hold off the headache that threatened. He had the reassurance he wanted but, in spite of Rossi's reassurance, Harrison knew that if the exhumation brought new evidence to light, he would be the loser.

Holly had felt the tension building all day. Now, as she lay next to Karl, she began to relax. As always, the feel of his body cradling hers as they nestled together made her feel protected as well as loved. Though she inevitably moved out from under the weight of his arm during the night, that weight represented her security.

Sighing as she lay against him, Holly wondered how much more she would be able to take. By unspoken agreement, they had never discussed what had really taken place in the woods the day Brett died. Once in a while, Holly would be brought to a standstill by the vision of Brett falling to the ground. But the visions had become less frequent as time passed and she had almost managed to convince herself that she had no part in what had happened. She didn't want to think about it now, but her subconscious refused to allow her to forget.

If only she could shut down the constant turmoil of her mind. How was it that now after so many years, everything she had worked for was in jeopardy?They had truly become a family in all senses of the word. Karl could not have loved the children any more if they had been his own blood. He had made it a point to be at all the plays, recitals, and ball games that he could possibly attend. No weekend went by without some kind of family event taking place.

If she had loved him before, through the years Holly had come to love Karl even more. The passion that had ignited their relationship continued in spite of the fact that they had now been together twenty years. Even more important was the deep-seated sharing and caring love that had developed over time. As well as being her lover, Karl was her best friend and confidant as she was his. There was nothing that they didn't share, and now the fear and uncertainty of their situation made their lives unbearable. A miasma of doubt hovered over every waking moment.

But it wasn't only the uncertainty that made things so difficult to bear. Because no one in Lincolnton knew of the cloud that had descended on them in Taylorville so many years previously, they could not speak of what was happening to anyone. Afraid of censure and negative reactions, both she and Karl had distanced themselves from their normal community activities. Other than going to church on Sunday, it had been months since they had accepted all but the most pressing social invitations.

Added to the anxiety created by not knowing what might come to surface in a trial was that caused by the reaction of Tommy and Janie. They had never lacked a father, thanks to Karl. Now both were suffering because they felt her stress and weren't able to help her. Now adults, how would they react to people saying they had been raised by a murderer? Karl's love and nurturing had led to their being as well adjusted as anyone who lived through the volatile 1980s. Bill now twenty-five, was still studying, and Janie was settled in her life. Could they be spared if the case was reopened? Holly knew that the answer was no.

Of the two, Janie was hurt the most by the resurgence of interest in her biological father's death. Janie had actually contacted her grandparents trying to dissuade them from proceeding with the investigation. But Kevin and Linda were determined to find out the truth about how their son had died. Now they no longer seemed to care how their actions affected their grandchildren.

Finally getting drowsy from the warmth of Karl's body, Holly nestled down under the comforter. What would she do without him? It was a question she hoped that she would never have to answer. Living a nightmare on a daily basis, she closed her eyes and hoped that her sleep would be dreamless.

The first step had been taken. Brett's body had been exhumed and forensic pathologist, Dr. Isadora Mihalakis, had performed a second autopsy. The findings were what he and Tim had expected all along. Brett had not tripped and accidentally discharged the shotgun. In response to the findings, the lawyers retained by Karl and Holly Gunther were still disputing the findings and demanding a third autopsy to be conducted by experts of their choosing. Regardless of what would come, it was obvious that Gunther had lied.

Kevin looked out toward the town square as he had thousands of times in the past. Could he really have been blind to all that had gone on behind the scenes and beneath the surface of the town for so many years? Or had he conveniently overlooked all the irregularities? Had he refused to pick up on what was happening in hopes of retaining his code of ethics and living peacefully? Looking at the serene scene in front of him, Kevin couldn't find a simple answer.

The feelings that he had suddenly been forced to face were even worse. Any possibility of reestablishing contact with Tommy and Janie would die with the trial. The awareness of betrayal and confusion now plagued Kevin and both were the result of information indirectly obtained while looking for evidence to support his request of the exhumation. He wasn't naive. A realist, he had not reached his late seventies without having heard all kinds of excuses and motivations for many different behaviors. In fact when they had started investigating Brett's death, he had expected to find certain allusions to misconduct or abuse of office. To find out that there had been collusion on all levels of the town and county governments had been a terrible blow.

Why? Kevin could come up with no logical reason for why District Attorney Ed Smalls had written a letter telling the state police that they should not cooperate with Billings. What had Smalls stood to gain? Kevin had worked with the man on numerous occasions and, though he would not call the man a friend, he had considered him a competent colleague worthy of respect. The last thing he had expected to find was that Smalls had impeded the investigation of Brett's death. If Smalls had not been acting on his own, who had he been answering to? What could have made the respected DA subjugate the workings of the law?

Reactions to Gunther's Arrest

Taylorville, June 20, 1996

Only an act of God would have been able to quell the good spirits of Attorney Robert Campolongo. After much grumbling, Judge Seamans had come to the only logical conclusion: Gunther had to be arrested for the murder of Brett Conklin.

Thanks to Conklin and Reeves, Campolongo's job had been made easier. Both Kevin Conklin and Tim Reeves had done their homework in finding the proper experts to give testimony as to what had really happened when Brett Conklin died. They had been so meticulous with their expert witnesses that Gunther's lawyers hadn't stood a chance of discrediting them.

The moment that Kevin Conklin's lawyers began presenting their petition for exhumation, the evidence that Gunther had lied about Conklin's death had been overwhelming. But why the local officials had accepted the ruling at the time remained a mystery. Sheriff Will Billings had adamantly refused to accept the ruling of accidental death, issued by then coroner John Cummings. This and other facts raised doubt.

Stewart Bentley, the forensic reconstruction consultant later hired by Conklin, had stated that Conklin's death was a homicide. Using technology recently accepted by the courts to support his finding, he proved that the shotgun barrel had to have been between three and five feet from Conklin in order to have produced an injury consistent with the shape and size of the death wound. And that meant murder.

Dr. Eric Mitchell, examiner for Onondaga County, New York, lent weight to Bentley's findings with his own information. Mitchell's analysis of the clothing stated that Conklin had been in a sitting or stooping position when he received the fatal shot. Both of these testimonies were in direct opposition to Gunther's statement that Conklin had been running and tripped which proved he had perjured himself when he first testified.

For the eight months prior to Seamans's ruling to allow the exhumation, Patricia Gunther had done everything in her power to prevent it. She went so far as to try to show Conklin's death as the result of a successful suicide attempt. To that end, she had brought forth the fact that Conklin had changed his will only three weeks prior to his dying.

Holly's efforts were in vain. For reasons understood only by him, after maintaining silence for many years, in spite of having full knowledge of Kevin Conklin's quest for the truth, the county coroner, Robert Burton had added his weight to the request for exhumation by filing his own criminal action petition. Finally, following the hearing held on April 28, 1995, Seamans issued a decree granting permission to County Coroner Robert Barton to re-autopsy the body of Brett Conklin.

Now, almost nineteen years after his death had been listed as an accident, the body of Brett Conklin was exhumed from the Holy Nave of Mary Cemetery. Later the body was transported to the Lehigh Valley Medical Center on Saturday, April 29, 1995 where a second autopsy was performed, lasting six hours.

Thinking about the exhumation, Campolongo shook his head. Investigating the death of Brett Conklin had become a veritable Pandora's box. Each time someone went near it, something else came jumping out.

Amongst all the other issues brought up at the disinterment hearing, former DA Snyder was accused by Dr. Isadore Mihalakis of having lied when he presented the findings of a group of forensic pathologists who had been convened in Philadelphia in May of 1989. According to Mihalakis, one of the pathologists at the convention presented evidence and photographs of Brett Conklin's death. The findings were not of accidental death as stated by Snyder; in fact, the consensus was that there were obvious indications of homicide.

After the second autopsy, the irregularities continued to mount. Mihalakis conducted the examination on Saturday, April 29th, while the findings had not been made public until Monday, June 26, 1995. Almost anticlimactic, the evidence showed that the specific manner of death of Attorney Brett Conklin was homicide.

Instead of having Gunther arrested, DA Snyder refused to prosecute the case himself and also sidestepped the request for a special prosecutor. Following the release of the finding of homicide being made public on Monday, Gunther had held a press conference in Clark Summit, Ohio, at the home of his attorney, Peter T. O'Malley, on Tuesday, June 27th.

Campolongo had not been present but he had to admit that he would have loved to see what must have amounted to a three-ring circus. O'Malley had put on quite a show. During the conference, O'Malley had told the police to "put up or shut up." He told the state police to either arrest and charge his client or leave. The lawyer also accused Mihalakis of being dishonest and, in the next breath, said that he had every intention of going after anyone who went after Gunther. All in all, O'Malley had done a good job of defending his client by trying to sully the reputation of anyone who did not support him. Later, a colleague who had been there told Campolongo that he had missed a great show. But that was only the beginning.

After fighting tooth and nail to prevent the exhumation of her former husband's body and decrying the action as desecration, Patricia Gunther had suddenly filed a petition to once again have the body exhumed and reexamined by her own experts. Was the timing for the petition a coincidence? Robert Campolongo didn't think so. It occurred right after Taylor DA Snyder requested that the attorney general's office of Ohio appoint a special prosecutor to handle the new investigation and possible prosecution.

The filing also coincided with the hiring of the Philadelphia law firm of Sprague and Sprague to assist O'Malley. Patricia Gunther had done everything in her power to complicate and delay the inquiry. She claimed that she had been denied due process in having her experts examine Brett Conklin's remains when Barton exhumed the body. Another argument she used was that of the damage which had been done to her and her family. Adverse publicity created by the investigation was responsible for both the mental and the physical anguish they suffered. She also claimed that the investigation was jeopardizing her future income as Karl Gunther was the breadwinner for the family. Shaking his head, Campolongo was once again struck by her zeal in protecting her husband.

In August 1995, Tommy and Janie Conklin? had joined their mother in a request to once again exhume the body of their biological father for reexamination, but their petition was denied.

Simultaneously, the courtroom had become a battlefield of legal wills. Instead of moving forward, the attorneys continued to lock horns. Giangreco, representing Coroner Robert Burton, was determined to prevent his client from being subpoenaed. The prosecution was arguing with the defense and O'Malley piqued by the addition of Sprague and Sprague to the Gunther representation, continued to argue for a forensic examination by the Gunther experts.

Everyone wanted to be involved with the proceedings on one level or another. At the end of August 1995, the county commissioners began asking for a special prosecutor so that the county could be relieved of any further expense. Their argument was that expenditures related to the investigation were in excess of $34,000 and had already caused the Taylor County financial hardship.

When Campolongo thought about it, he had to agree that the numerous delays during the investigation of the case had been costly. While unfortunate, they all had a logical explanation. Just prior to pathologist Mihalakis releasing the finding of homicide, the attorney general at that time, Preate, had been forced to resign as a result of a federal plea bargain, though the reason behind his action remained unclear. He was replaced by Attorney General Tom Corbett.

If there was any substance to the various allegations or not, the truth of the matter was that a special prosecutor was not assigned. Information was gathered at a very slow pace and it was not until October 1995 that Robert Campolongo and Joseph McGettigan were assigned to the case.

After the case was assigned, more delays prevented moving forward with the inquiries. At one point an appeal hearing for January 9th was set back by an early blizzard that month. That had led to joking in the office that there were superior forces at work to prevent Gunther from coming to trial. Though the hearing was rescheduled and conducted ten days later, the reality was that the ruling was not handed down until the end of March when three more months had passed.

More than once, the attorney general's office looked foolish if not incompetent. The local county newspaper continued to follow the investigation and interview the locals involved. The transcript had gone so far as to publish a report from the FBI crime laboratory supporting evidence that Gunther had lied. Though these documents were legally correct, their publication raised doubt as to whether proper procedure had been followed by the state in investigating Conklin's complaint.

He himself had questions he would like answered, thought Robert. What had been going on to allow for such a blatant foot-dragging by multiple county DAs? He knew that the probability of getting his questions answered was next to nothing. The truth was that for whatever reason, the investigation had been mishandled and sidetracked twenty years before. And it didn't look much better now.

It was no surprise at the end of February 1996 when the three-judge panel of the Commonwealth Superior Court reversed the ruling of Judge Kenneth Seamans. This in turn allowed Patricia Gunther to have the body re-autopsied by her own experts. In spite of the prior injunction and stay issued by Judge Seamans to prevent another exhumation, on May 11, 1996, a third autopsy had been performed on the remains of Brett Conklin.

Gunther's experts, Dr. Darnell Baden, Dr. Cyril Wecht, and Dr. John Shane argued admirably on points that had a degree of validity. However, the bulk of the evidence against Gunther remained overwhelming. No matter how hard they tried to divert the attention from the fact that Gunther had pulled the trigger, Sprague and his team had been unable to have the case dismissed. Not even bringing in expert testimony to swear to the fact that the particular shotgun had been recalled for a malfunction had helped. The evidence was irrefutable. Karl Gunther was to be arrested for the murder of Brett Conklin.

With any luck, today would be the day that Judge Seamans issued the warrant for Gunther's arrest. Smiling to himself, Campolongo fought to keep his ebullient feelings under control. The Gunthers had fought long and hard, with every means at their disposal and then some. Nonetheless, the findings presented by Mihalakis had ensured that a trial would occur.

Brett Conklin had died twenty years ago, but the interest created by the news reports was steadily increasing along with fact-based movies and Internet awareness. Those now away from Taylorville kept up with the news through e-mails as it became public immediately as it occurred. Abductions, assaults, and murder by John Doe became the subject of movies, television, articles, and books, feeding the morbid fascination of the public.

The components of the Gunther case: sexual liaisons, betrayed friendship, and murder, guaranteed that the interest would escalate. The courtroom was packed on a daily basis and media exposure in this high-interest case was just what Campolongo needed to launch his career and achieve the recognition he wanted. The only problem might be avoiding contamination of the skeletons buried in the county archives. But who was to say? Perhaps what he uncovered would also be beneficial in the long run.

Officially retired, Darnell Harrison still spent much of his time at the hospital. His original goal—to provide good health care for his community—had somehow dwarfed everything else in his life. After three failed marriages, he had accepted the reality that the hospital would always be his mistress.

Harrison walked through the waiting room toward his office, returning the multitude of greetings that followed him. Secretly, he looked forward to the people trying to get his attention as he passed by. It validated his being there, almost like the movie stars who thrived upon public recognition.

Though an unproven theory, Darnell was sure that the family had been instrumental in making the currently popular drugs readily available to the youth of the county. Rather than risk butting heads with Rossi, he had turned his back on the issue and he wasn't proud of having done so. He justified his actions by constantly reminding himself that without the support of the family, he might not have been able to accomplish his goal. It was a fact that the health care of the county had improved.

But people were quick to forget the good. If his connection to the Rossi family became linked to the possible drug distribution, the ostracism would be so great that he would never again be able to hold his head up.

He would have liked to talk to Rossi if only to reassure him that the family had taken steps to ensure that there would be no repercussions from anything that might be said when Gunther went to trial. After all, the family would be as averse to publicity as he was—and neither wanted to be connected with Gunther. Thinking about it, the Rossi family had done much to help Gunther too. They had allowed the young doctor to relocate when he first left Taylorville and had provided Harrison with the necessary financing to make his pet project—the senior housing complex named Pine Park—possible.

Darnell knew that he would do whatever necessary to keep his connection to the Rossi family a secret. He had hoped that it was merely idle talk when Kevin Conklin started talking about reopening the investigation. It had been many years since Brett Conklin's death, but deep down Harrison knew that Kevin wouldn't let go. Since the VCR and cable had made all kinds of media news more available, the public had developed an insatiable hunger for fact-based, made-for-TV movies about crimes committed by people like those they knew. The morbid fascination had provided the entertainment industry with a whole new source of material. You had only to think about the OJ Simpson trial and the public's fascination to know that this phenomenon was true. The two leading competitors for the public's attention were anything having to do with the havoc wreaked by the drug situation in all sectors of society and any kind of information divulged about wrongdoing by any public official.

Having decided that contacting Rossi would not be wise, Darnell Harrison straightened out the papers on his desk. Glancing at his watch, he decided to go over to the Taylorville Inn to see what news was being discussed. As he stood to leave his office, the phone rang. His voice calm, in spite of his mental state, he picked up the receiver saying, "Dr. Harrison, how can I help you?"

"Darnell, this is Ben Granger. Tell me what you know about how the situation is going at the courthouse."

Afraid about what might come to light during the trial, Harrison refused to get annoyed at Granger's demand. He had known the former county commissioner and businessman for many years. And he had learned that for all the money he might have, common courtesy was not Granger's strong point. His voice dripping with sarcasm that he was sure would escape Ben, Darnell replied, "Good afternoon to you too. What was the information you needed?"

Well aware that Granger did not want any connection with the Rossi family to come to light because bodies actually were buried in various construction sites, Darnell played dumb. He wasn't about to let Granger know just how concerned he was or why.

"You know as well as I do that any connection with the Rossi family would not do us any good. There has been a lot in the news about organized crime. Just look at how much has come out about the Gambino family in the last three months."

Wanting to hang up, Darnell replied coldly, "Listen, Ben, we both made use of what the Captain had to offer when it was beneficial to us. But that was years ago, so as far as I know, there's no reason to believe that anyone will ever tie either of us in with the Rossi family. Even more basic than that, there's nothing to tie the Rossi family to the death of Brett Conklin." Pausing to let his words sink in, he continued, "If I were you, I wouldn't waste any more time worrying about it." Hanging up the phone, Darnell hoped that he would be able to follow his own advice.

New Jersey, June 20, 1996

Unlike Darnell Harrison, Paul had no questions as to what was happening at the courthouse. He had made sure that he would know what reaction Judge Seamans was having to the evidence being presented on a daily or, if necessary, hourly basis by making sure one of his people was always present.

Thinking about the trial, he shook his head. It was too bad that after all this time Gunther would take the fall for something that he hadn't done, but it couldn't be helped. There was no way that the defense could be allowed to prove that there was any relationship between Conklin's death and the men Conklin was defending in the drug/murder trial at the time. Even if the question were raised, all the information on the three men Conklin had been defending twenty years before had been disposed of. Other than the record placing all three men in the Broome County Jail at the time of Conklin's death, nothing else existed.

His thoughts wandering back to what had actually happened in the woods that afternoon, Paul wondered if Conklin's wife had ever realized or admitted to herself that she had pulled the trigger of the shotgun. Paul knew without a doubt that his shell had been responsible for Conklin's death, but no one other than Rossi was aware of that. Gunther would undoubtedly be found to blame, unless Holly Gunther admitted being in the woods. And from what he knew about Holly, he doubted that would happen.

Pensive, Paul let his mind wander back to the beginning of the drug distribution in Taylor County. Who knew that small towns in rural America would be the gold mine they had become? Mentally reviewing what had happened, he still was surprised at how lucrative the sleepy towns in Ohio and upper Pennsylvania had proven to be. If anything, the growth curve was even steeper than in the cities! As Rossi's disciple, he had learned that it was always beneficial to double check what he already knew even after this much time had passed. It was no surprise that Dr. Harrison was worried. With the drugs being siphoned into the community through the hospital, Harrison had reason to be concerned. The doctor had turned a blind eye to the discrepancies in the pharmacy and even the sudden death of Gerald Weir. What the doctor didn't know was that the arrangement had become much too lucrative to allow anything to disturb the operation. If there was any question in the future, Darnell Harrison would be the sacrificial lamb.

Knowing that he could easily let Harrison know that his reputation was not in danger of being muddied, Paul smiled derisively.

Harrison's mental health was no more his concern than Gunther going to prison, so why bother? Having decided to let Harrison continue to worry, he turned back to the stack of reports in front of him.

Lincolnton, North Carolina, June 20, 1996

The day was already beginning to show signs of fulfilling the weatherman's promise of sunshine and balmy temperatures at 8:30 in the morning. In contrast to the peaceful freshness of the woods beyond the house, the tension in the Gunthers's(Gunther's is correct) kitchen was palpable.

"I don't know how you can be so calm!" Holly hissed through grated teeth. "I'm ready to scream! I can't remember ever feeling so helpless and out of control. It's like we're being persecuted regardless of what we do. The one home that is really ours might have to be sold. If we have to go to trial, because of all the lawyer's fees, we'll have almost nothing left to show for eighteen years of working and saving!" Her anguish evident, she continued, "Janie and Tommy can't believe what's happening, and since the show on channel Xjb where they mentioned you being questioned in regard to Brett's death, I can't go anywhere without people looking at me askance. But you just continue to be calm!"

Fighting to keep his emotions tightly under control, Karl walked over to where Holly stood with her head bowed, gripping the counter, and placed his arms around her. As she began to relax against the familiar warmth of his chest, the color began to return to her hands as she relaxed her grip. Letting her head be pillowed by his shoulder, she placed her hands on Karl's arm, looking back at him as her eyes filled with tears.

As always, Karl found himself feeling his wife's suffering more deeply than his own. Silently he gave thanks for having Holly by his side during the last twenty years. Needing to reassure her, he spoke quietly and calmly. "Everything will be all right, sweetheart, I promise you. You know that nothing moves rapidly in the law. I only hope that Sprague is right about Seamans's response to the charges Campolongo is planning on filing. I'm still not sure that bringing in his firm from Philadelphia was necessary, but what's done is done." Hoping he was right, Karl said, "Regardless, you know that I have nothing to fear."

Turning in his arms to face him, Holly leaned back so she could look in his eyes. Fear and anguish, now constant companions, darkened her eyes working to extinguish their characteristic sparkle. "I couldn't live without you, Karl. I don't know how I'd survive; you really are a part of me."

"As you are of me, my love. The best part of me," he whispered, cradling the back of her head in his hand. As he felt her relax, he lightened his tone, saying, "Don't worry, everything will work out, but right now I have to go to work. I don't want any more kinks thrown into our routine than are necessary, and following a routine helps. What are you doing to fill your day?"

"Anything and everything I can in order not to think about what's happening. Milly Southworth wanted to go to lunch and discuss the upcoming church bazaar, so I'll meet her around one, but I'll be home by the time you're through at the office."

Hugging her to him as he kissed her gently, Karl picked up his jacket and turned to go. "Try to stay calm, love. Letting fear and worry dominate our lives won't help."

By 11 a.m. the beautiful summer day had become a reality. The temperature was in the 90s in Raleigh, North Carolina. As he walked toward the chief's office, Gayford Siekes shook his head as he continued to read the warrant in his hand. "Chief, I can't quite believe this. We have a warrant to pick up Dr. Karl Gunther of Lincolnton on a murder charge that's twenty years old."

Glancing up from the warrant Siekes had handed him, Bureau Chief James Trent asked, "Why can't you believe it?"

Looking at his boss, Siekes replied, "You know I live in Beauville." At the chief's nod, he continued, "Well, last year my nephew seemed to be coming down with one virus or flu after another. No one seemed to know what was wrong until one day, while he was passing through the emergency room, Dr. Gunther stopped and, just by looking at Jamie, was able to tell that there were underlying allergies complicating his recovery. We did what he said and Jamie hasn't had a problem since. My sister-in-law says that it's been like that for a lot of the people he's treated."

"You never really know a person, do you?" said Trent. "If we have received the news that Seamans's issued the warrant, you can bet that, if he is any good at all, Gunther's lawyer has been burning up the wires to talk to him. That means that the man may already know that he's about to be arrested. And who knows? He could be desperate. I don't want to take any chance in spite of the fact that you know he's a good doctor. Send Burns into me, will you? He's down in the file room."

Mentally organizing the detention, Trent was ready when Burns entered his office. "To avoid any possibility of a high-speed chase through Lincolnton, I want three cars with three men each. In no way do I want any kind of action that will place the bureau under criticism. There's been too much adverse publicity lately, so I don't want any action that can be considered questionable. That means no rough stuff, unless it can't be avoided. If Gunther is clean as he says, he'll probably be at his office. If he has run, I want the teams to be ready to split up to begin questioning neighbors to make sure we don't lose any time in covering as much ground as possible."

Listening to the orders, Siekes shook his head. You never knew. Could a man who spent his life working to help people and better their lives actually have committed murder? Hoping that Gunther would give up peacefully, he left Trent's office and watched as Burns went to take care of grouping his men.

The morning of June 20th had been more busy than usual at the building that housed the Lincolnton Allergy Clinic and Karl Gunther's office. Due to the frequent absences occasioned by the Conklin problem during the previous spring, many of the patients had been rescheduled, but things were still not back to normal. Now at noon, the last patient for the morning hours still hadn't been seen.

Janet Withers, his nurse, constantly complained about the hubbub and activity, but it really didn't bother Gunther. Though others might have found the constant traffic in and out of his office disconcerting, he found himself reassured by the movement. The noise and activity indicated that he had managed to achieve his goal of making his practice a success and it also meant that he was helping his community. It had taken time to build his patient roster to the point where he had no more gaps between appointments and he was proud of reaching that goal.

Looking at the stack of charts on his desk waiting for the notations that would bring them up-to-date before being filed by Janet, Karl sighed. Normally he didn't mind the paperwork, but after seeing Holly so upset this morning, he would have preferred running home to see her. Checking his watch, he reached over and dialed his home number, hoping to catch her before she left for her luncheon. At the sound of his wife's voice, he said, "Hi, love. I just wanted to call and let you know I was thinking about you."

Happy to hear from Karl, Holly's pleasure was obvious as she returned his greeting. She rapidly filled him in on what her morning had been, ending with a question as to what he wanted for dinner.

"Anything you feel like making," Karl answered. "Are the kids going to be home or will it be just the two of us?"

"Probably not, so if you want to stop and pick up a video, go ahead. I've got to run or I'll be late for my meeting. See you later."

Relieved that Holly sounded much calmer, Karl looked at the pile of papers that waited on his desk. She had no idea of how worried he really was, and he would try his best not to let her find out. From the first day, he had encouraged her not to think about that day at Deer Run. For his part, he had refused to let down his guard and allow himself to relax. He feared that if he stopped thinking about what had happened in the woods, he would be vulnerable. It had not happened in all these years, but the appearance of the unknown man who had witnessed the shooting remained a possibility.

Only after the move to Lincolnton from Las Cruces, New Mexico, had he slowly begun to relax his vigil, relegating all thoughts of what had happened to the nether regions of his mind. Now, as the threat of a trial hung over his head, he was once again plagued with the uncertainty as to whether the unknown man would appear or not. Only time would tell, so meanwhile he would deal with reality and not conjecture. As soon as he finished with updating the files he would force himself to go over that day and make notes of anything he could remember. Pushing the thoughts of the past from his mind, he opened the first folder.

In spite of constantly complaining about how busy the office was, Janet wouldn't have traded her job for the world. She truly liked running the office and had the utmost respect for Karl as a doctor. She was conscious that more than one of his patients, including her nephew, would have been worse off if he had not come to Lincolnton.

Standing outside his office, she was worried by his pale appearance. He put on a good face for all he was going through, but she could see that the accusations and constant upset of his routine were taking their toll. Knocking on the doorframe so as not to startle him, she entered the office. "I had a feeling you were going to try and catch up on paperwork," she said, placing a sandwich in front of him. "I'll get you a fresh cup of coffee to wash it down."

Glancing at his watch, Karl was surprised to see that over an hour had passed since he had begun to work on the files. Leaning back in his chair with a smile, he stretched, saying, "I don't know what I'd do without you, Janet."

"Probably starve to death. Now put down your pen and take a few minutes to eat. Your first appointment is at 1:45, so you have almost fifteen minutes." Leaving the office with a smile, Janet moved back to the reception area, her thoughts focused on checking the charts and getting ready for the afternoon appointment.

Having unlocked the doors in preparation for the afternoon hours, Janet wasn't surprised to hear the front door open a few minutes later. Often the patients would show up early, spending the time they waited socializing. Glancing up from her appointment register, she smiled at the older Mrs. Abbott, saying, "You're so punctual, anyone would think that you like coming here! Or maybe you have a crush on my boss?"

Enjoying the banter, Mrs. Abbott replied, "Now you know he's young enough to be my son." Slowly moving to sit down, she said, "I swear these bones get stiffer by the day."

Before Janet could reply, the door flew open, the force causing it to bang against the wall as Agent Burns burst into the room with his service revolver in hand, shocking both women.

Startled, the file slipped from Janet's hand as she blanched at the sight of the gun, wondering if they were being held up. Seeing a second agent entering from the back, also with a gun drawn, Mrs. Abbott shrieked. Recovering herself with an astounding rapidity at the other woman's cry, Janet asked brusquely, "What's going on?"

"I have a warrant for the arrest of Dr. Karl Gunther," stated Burns coldly. "Is he here?"

She had experienced many things in her years in the nursing profession, but nothing had prepared Janet for the feelings that flooded her consciousness as she absorbed the words. Shock, anger, and disbelief vied for dominance as she fought for composure. "There is no need for the guns. Dr. Gunther will talk to you without them."

Refusing to heed Janet's suggestion, Burns walked rapidly down the hall, checking the rooms as he passed them. Nothing could have prepared the people in the clinic as the next fifteen minutes turned into a living nightmare. Reaching Gunther's office at the end of the hall, Burn's walked into the office to find Gunther looking up from his desk, alerted by the noise. "Dr. Gunther?" asked Burns.

"Yes, what can I do for you?"

Without further thought, Burns said, "You are under arrest for the murder of Brett Conklin."

Realizing the futility of saying anything else, Karl listened as he was read his rights. As the agent approached him with the handcuffs extended, Gunther said, "I don't think those are necessary. I'll go with you peacefully."

Refusing to listen to the man in front of him, Burns attached the cuffs. Still brandishing their guns, the seven agents took Karl out to the squad car. The waiting room was now full with patients staring in horror as the doctor was led away.

Karl placed one foot in front of the other and looked straight ahead as if in a trance, but his thoughts were churning. He had hoped it would never come to this. The possibility of keeping the truth under wraps had seemed attainable once the Rossi family had stepped in to help. Now that he was under arrest, his only hope was that he would be able to brave it out.

There were only two options. Either he would be acquitted of the charges or be forced to admit to having committed the murder. Whichever the result, he knew he would find the strength as long as he managed to keep Holly in the clear. The last twenty years of his life had been the best years by far, in spite of all the relocation and career changes. Had it not been for finding Holly, he would never have known what it was to truly love and be loved. As is so often the case with those that truly love, Karl would sacrifice his life and freedom to protect the woman who was his world.

Lincolnton, North Carolina, June 21, 1996

In spite of the many people doubting Gunther's ability to raise Janie and Tommy Conklin when he married Holly, Karl had been an excellent father. In the beginning Karl had seen them as extensions of his friends and had easily come to love them. After Brett's death, once Karl was living with them, he had learned to love the children for the individuals they were.

And they loved him reciprocally. Holly had insisted that they try to put Brett's death behind them and they had. While no one ever tried to make them forget their natural father, the children were young enough when Brett died to automatically accept Karl in his place when he became a permanent part of their lives. On his part, perhaps as an unspoken form of atonement, Karl had been the best parent he could and had succeeded admirably.

These were the thoughts and feelings that colored the conversation as Tommy and Janie sat in the kitchen at 4:00 a.m., the day after Karl's arrest. Now adults, this promised to be one of the most difficult of their lives. Sitting with her legs drawn up and her chin resting on her knees, the strain Janie had been undergoing was visible. Shadows under her large eyes gave testimony to the sleepless nights she had been having. When she learned that her grandparents planned to petition the courts to exhume the body of her father, she had been shocked. But that was nothing compared to how the news of Karl's arrest had affected her.

Standing at the counter where he was filling the coffeemaker to make yet another pot of coffee, Tommy said softly, "I'm glad that they finally gave Mom a shot to calm her down. I just don't know how she is going to handle the stress this trial will bring." Sighing, he continued, "There is no way that Karl killed our father, regardless of what our grandparents believe."

Turning from the window to look at her brother, Janie could see that Tommy had been deeply affected by what had been going on, in spite of his calm analysis. Though both she and her brother had retained Conklin as their surname, they both thought of Karl as the only father they had ever had. How could they be expected to feel differently? At the time of Brett Conklin's death, both of them had been less than six years old, and Karl had been a part of their lives since they could remember.

With a sad smile, Tommy went on, "Remember when Karl took us to the Indian Reservation in Las Cruces for the first time? You wanted to know why they didn't have leather clothing like Daniel Boone. It took him a while to convince us that they were really Indians even though they rode around in pickups instead of on horses."

Returning her brother's smile, Janie shook her head. "It just isn't possible. Karl was never anything but gentle and patient with us and everyone else for as far back as I can remember. How can they possibly think that our father's death was anything but the accident that Karl said it was?"

"I don't know," Tommy replied. "What I can tell you is that this whole situation is destroying our family, both emotionally and financially. I don't think they wanted us to worry unnecessarily, but I have no doubt that they'll have to put the house up for sale to get the money for bail. Right now they've gone through what they had put aside for retirement and the few investments that remained intact after setting up the new office."

"We fought so hard to get that other autopsy performed," Janie sighed. In spite of the fact that they were each paid $3,500 a day, neither of the pathologists were able to come up with anything substantial enough to counter the findings of that Mihalakis. I wish he had never gotten involved."

"Well, sis, I can't think of a time when wishes were readily answered, and I doubt that this would be one of them no matter how hard we wanted to change things."

Taylorville, Ohio, June 21, 1996

Coming into the kitchen from his early morning run, he knew immediately that something had happened. All too often he had seen the same look of concern on Linda's face. But unless he broachedthe subject, Linda wouldn't say anything about what had upset her, and that had begun to concern him lately. After being so closely attuned for almost fifty years, it was as if their life together was becoming distorted, out of synch, like a VCR that needed tracking.

It was strange. His own reaction to the inquiry was diametrically opposed to Linda's. It wasn't that he no longer felt the pain of having lost his son, because he would never stop missing him. But, while all of the activity related to finding out the truth about Brett's death had been so upsetting to Linda, it had had a healing effect on him.

Knowing he was relentlessly looking for the answers to what had happened that day at Deer Run had helped to soothe the feeling of guilt and inadequacy he had carried with him since his decision to let things be at the time of Brett's death. Each new piece of evidence and every minute spent in the courthouse acted as a balm to the wound that had remained unhealed for so long.

While he knew that Linda was as interested in all the information that had come to light as he was, for her, each new disclosure seemed to tear off another scab and make the pain of the wound all the more intense. She had suffered each time they found new evidence that Brett's death may not have been an accident.

Throughout his investigation, she had unstintingly helped him correlate the information, encouraging him to spend however much time and money necessary to realize his goal without ever complaining. But Kevin knew that the investigation did not serve the same purpose for Linda as it did for him. Kevin really couldn't understand her concern at the time any more than he could now.

Putting a smile on his face, he took his cup and walked over to kiss his wife, saying, "The coffee sure smells good, almost like a reward for getting out and moving these creaky bones."

Shaking off her feeling of distress, Linda said wryly, "Right, you're the envy of everyone we know. In fact, more than one of our friends feels it's wrong of us not to share the secret of how you look fifty at seventy. Anyone who didn't know us would probably wonder what you see in an old lady like me."

"Fishing for compliments, are we? Is that what it's going to take to get my breakfast today?" Kevin joked as he reached for the paper that lay on the counter.

Watching him, her pleasure was overshadowed by sadness. As wonderful as he was, Kevin had no idea how badly the investigation into Brett's death had separated them. They had shared everything, including what they were feeling, since the day they had met. Anyone who knew them would say that they were two halves of a whole—the better half of each other—until the investigation was reopened.

Brett's death had made their unity even stronger, but somehow the current project had found them on opposite sides of the fence. Where Kevin was exhilarated and found new challenge and purpose in uncovering the truth, she had long ago admitted to herself that she was afraid.

Linda had tried to analyze why she felt as she did and had come to the realization that there were two basic reasons. Part of the problem was that she wondered if Kevin would blame her for waiting so long before finding out the truth. More so than that, the biggest problem was that she really didn't care—and that made her feel disloyal.

Regardless of whether Gunther had told the truth or not, nothing they found out would bring Brett back. Nor was there anything they could do that would repair the ties with Tommy and Janie. Worst of all, she had relived her son's death daily since they had filed the first petition. With a sigh, she moved over to warm Kevin's coffee, grown cold in his involvement with the newspaper. As he looked up with a jubilant smile, she tried to match his expression of happy satisfaction with one of her own. But it never reached her eyes. Lost in his thoughts, Kevin didn't notice.

Seeing Linda leave the kitchen, he got up and went outside. Not even a breeze stirred the warm summer air, and the constantly groomed backyard seemed frozen in the early morning stillness. As he stood looking out, the tranquility seemed at odds with the churning emotions that coursed through his body and mind.

They had done it. All the work he and Tim had done to bring the investigation back to life had finally paid off. Though Tim had never understood his refusal to pursue the inquiry at the time of Brett's death, Kevin knew that he had been right to wait. Nothing could bring his son back to him, and allowing Linda time to heal had been a priority.

The healing had taken a long time and he knew that it still wasn't complete, nor would it ever be. As he looked out into the sunlit yard, his eyes were drawn to the dogwood tree. He had planted the tree just before Brett's death and had been kneeling at its base when he learned of the accident. He had tended to it lovingly throughout the years, many times thinking back to the legend of the dogwood flower—and in thinking of that universally known suffering, he had taken strength.

Now the agonizing was over. He had done what he felt was necessary and the truth about Brett's death would be known. Karl Gunther had been arrested.

Epilogue

Taylorville, April 1998

Linda stood at the kitchen window looking out at the garden where the grass was already a lush green. It had been a very mild winter, bringing with it an early spring, the time of year she liked best. Many vibrant colors of green could be seen on the trees as the buds began to open. As always, she paused in her perusal to study the dogwood in the center of the yard.

This year she felt a new kinship with the loyal sentinel witness to so many changes in her life. The tree had once again weathered the torment and cold of the winter as she too had come through the storm. Though damaged, she had survived.

Turning to light the flame under the kettle, Linda paused, her thoughts going back to that June morning almost two years before when she had picked up the paper to find that Karl Gunther had been arrested for Brett's death. So much had transpired that it seemed as if each day had been overloaded, not the least by the continual emotional upheaval.

Just prior to his arrest, after seemingly endless arguments by the defense, Kevin and Tim had won their petition to examine Brett's body. This had been followed by a second exhumation, after which Holly refused to tell them where Brett's remains would repose, preventing them from the solace of visiting his remains.

Once he was in custody, Karl and Holly had changed lawyers yet a third time. While it may not have helped in the long run, the defense attorney had managed to convince the judge that

Karl should be allowed out on a reduced bail of seven hundred fifty thousand dollars. Instead of being hurt by the months of speculation and media attention, his increased notoriety seemed to increase Karl's appeal for his practice grew from fifty five hundred to almost eight thousand patients. All remained loyal, even after his conviction.

The trial had finally taken place in September 1997, after much haggling about the jury and technicalities. Karl continued to maintain his innocence in spite of the ever-growing body of evidence and expert testimony that were presented. It was only after the prosecution began calling witnesses to testify to his relationship with Holly prior to Brett's death that he had admitted 'accidentally' shooting Brett. At that point many people, including Linda, believed that he had only admitted his guilt in order to protect Holly from further disclosures.

When Karl confessed, it became obvious that Holly had committed perjury and the prosecutor had subsequently gone after her. For some reason even now, the current district attorney seemed reticent to pursue a conviction. To date nothing had been resolved, with charges left pending.

Perhaps it is enough, thought Linda. With Karl's conviction, Holly had lost her primary income and had been left almost poverty stricken. Besides, had Holly even known the truth about what had happened in the woods? Perhaps not. But it was almost certain that having their mother as well as their stepfather in jail would only hurt Tommy and Janie—and they had been hurt enough.

Sighing, Linda realized that she had learned much about her grandchildren as a result of the trial. Though one part of her had been offended by their unconditional defense of the man who had killed their father, she had been impressed by their loyalty. Both had put up their savings and inheritances in order to help Karl meet bail, and Linda knew that Brett would be proud of the people they had become.

Kevin's insistence on reopening the inquiry had been vindicated and the truth was that Brett had not died in the way they had first believed. But she couldn't believe that Karl had shot Brett intentionally. Congratulations were effusive and continual as people applauded them for having stood their ground in spite of all the obstacles and opposition they had faced. For a few weeks the constant attention was sufficient to fill the void left by the end of the trial.

Few were aware of the pain and anguish that they had suffered after the end of the trial. Having been for so long totally absorbed with pursuing the truth, Kevin had suddenly found a tangible emptiness in his days once the trial was over, giving him too much time to think.

Along with what had happened when Brett died, other things had come to light. What he had found out had shaken the foundation of his beliefs. Kevin had come to the damaging realization that the life they had lived, in the town they thought they knew, and even the government in which he had placed his trust, was fictitious. The life he thought he had led was surrounded by misconceptions and deceit. As is often the case, his in-depth investigation in one area had raised questions as to the honesty and morality of various people he had lived and worked with all his life.

The very precepts of honesty and integrity that were part of the man Kevin was had been undermined, as had the foundation of faith in his fellowman. He had grieved long and painfully for the demise of his trust. But only after suffering the anguish and heartache had he finally understood what Linda had feared from the beginning—that they would not escape unscathed.

Yes, his pursuit of the truth had been vindicated: some of those who had lied would be punished, while Karl Gunther was in jail and Holly had been proven a liar.

But what he had not taken into account was how finding the answers to his questions would change him. What Kevin had learned while on his quest had tarnished many of the other areas of his life, making him bitter and disillusioned, though he fought not to show it.

He had found out the truth about Brett's death, but by doing so he had raised many other questions that would continue to plague him as they remained unanswered. Yet Linda wondered, not for the first time, if what had happened at Deer Run would have been better left buried.